ALASKA
dragon

Alaskan wilderness is loved for its lavish diversity and grandness of scale. Among those who know it well, it is also notorious for attracting people who resemble it: people of uncommon passions, odd perspectives, idiosyncratic ideas, with their hatreds and loves larger than ordinary life. The wild land and its weird people mirror one another authentically in Alaska Dragon.

An exhausted copper mine and its ghost town provide a stage where the players meet. There is a Catholic priest with a whiff of Zen about him who seeks spiritual transformation in the wilderness. A Berkeley professor labors to preserve the land from miners, and the miners work just as hard to convert it into money. A trumpet-playing artist is also the local handyman who can blend three dead snowmachines into one that works. The widow who owns the hotel endures them all, nurtures them all, and her young daughter sees into and through them all with a child's wisdom. Then there is the psychotic with a murderous scheme to save Alaska at the cost of the townsfolk. All of them very nearly get what they're after.

The Alaskan wilderness is the central character that creates and informs the others. There is a dragon deep in its soul that presides, as all dragons do, over adventure and mystery. It tests those who enter it, and they grow or die from its challenges. It speaks through its mountains, rivers, winds, temperatures, and most eloquently through its plants and animals. The encounter between the priest and a grizzly bear provides a spiritual climax to prove that wildness speaks not only with power, but with joy and laughter as well.

Benjamin Shaine orchestrates this grand story with grace, wit, and craftsmanship. His prose flows with the arctic seasons, creating a narrative rhythm to which the characters, and the reader, dance. Alaska Dragon *is at once a philosophical novel, a tale of adventure, and a subtle mystery.*

— *Joseph W. Meeker*

ALASKA
dragon

a novel by

BENJAMIN A. SHAINE

Fireweed Press
Fairbanks

95 94 93 92 91   5 4 3 2 1

Book design by Cindy Wacker and Sheila Moir, Cynthesis Graphic Design
Front Cover: "A Typical American Scene" by Loy Green
Back Cover: "Alaska Dragon" by Polly Thurston
Map, pages vi and vii, and drawing, page 60, by Ayse Gilbert

Excerpt from *Markings* by Dag Hammarskjold, translated by Leif Sjobert and W.H. Auden. Translation Copyright © 1964 by Alfred A. Knopf, Inc. and Faber & Faber Ltd. Reprinted by permission of the publisher.

Excerpt from *Little Flowers of St. Francis,* translated by Raphael Brown, published by Doubleday. Reprinted by permission of the publisher.

Excerpt from "Burnt Norton" in *Four Quartets*, Copyright © 1943 by T. S. Eliot and renewed 1971 by Esme Valerie Eliot, reprinted by permission of Harcourt Brace Jovanovich, Inc.

Excerpt from *Meister Eckhart,* translated by Raymond Blakney. Copyright © 1941 by Harper & Row, Publishers, Inc. Reprinted by permission of Harper-Collins Publishers, Inc.

Shaine, Benjamin A.
    Alaska Dragon

    I. Title

ISBN 0-914221-12-4
ISBN 0-914221-11-6 pbk.

Fireweed Press
P.O. Box 75418
Fairbanks, Alaska 99707

Alaska Dragon *was birthed with the encouragement and support of friends and family, especially Marci Thurston, Joe Meeker, Elizabeth Minnich, Father Andrew Dufner, Helena Meyer-Knapp, Charles Harbaugh, Richard Gillespie, Yaakov Garb, John Tallmadge, Russell Lockhart, Loy Green, Helen Neill, Andrew Thurston, Paul Thurston, Jane Thurston and Doris Bliss. I send this work into the world with the hope that it will help Gaia and Ardea Thurston-Shaine, and all the generation of our children, keep alive the spirit of Alaska.*

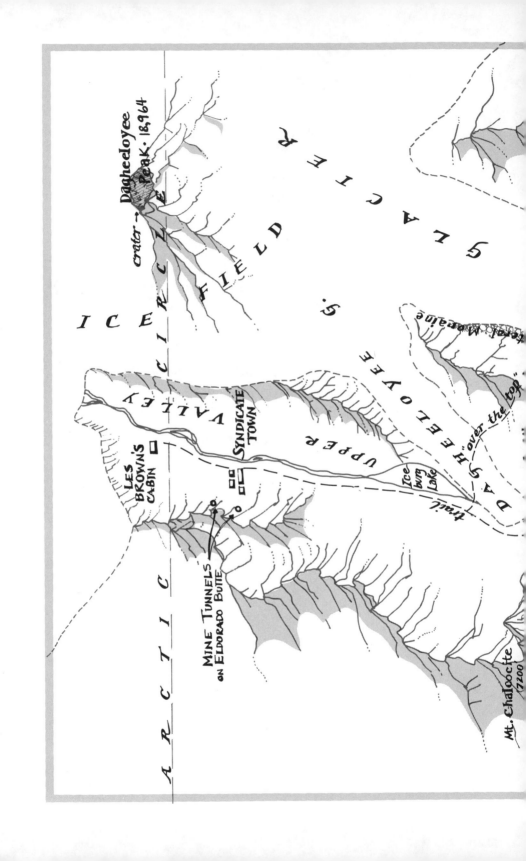

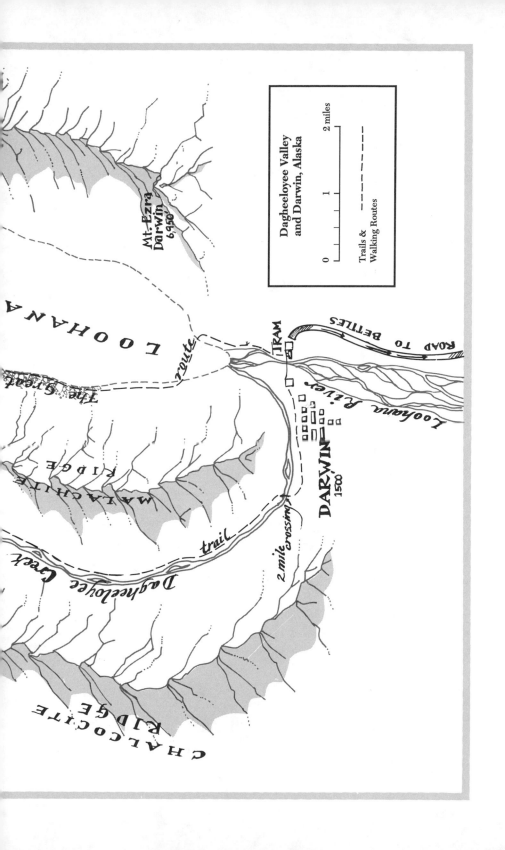

Dagheeloyee Valley
and Darwin, Alaska

Trails &
Walking Routes

0   1   2 miles

Mt. Ezra
Darwin
6,950'

L O O H A N A

The Great

route

MAIACHITE RIDGE

Dagheeloyee Creek

trail

2 mile crossing

DARWIN
1500'

Loohana River

TRAM

ROAD TO BETTLES

CHALCOCITE RIDGE

ELDORADO EXPLORATIONS UNLIMITED
Memorandum

July 2, 1981

TO: F. Carleton Manley, President
FROM: Ed Butler, Operations Manager

Things are not what they seemed. Like you said to do I rented a truck in Fairbanks & hauled in supplies for the helicopter and summer camp. When I stopped for gas they told me you cannot drive to Darwin. The road goes to the river about a mile before the town and quits. There was a bridge but it washed out. So I drove to the river and there is a cable strung over it. You have to put yourself or your stuff on a little cart hanging on the cable and pull the cart across the river by hand using a rope. With three tons of jet A in barrels and our other stuff I surely was not about to do that myself.

Darwin is a ghost town and there are hippies there. A couple of them were at this cable-cart thing when I got there so we loaded the stuff off the truck and got it across. Had to move the cart across a dozen times at least and it took half the day. The hippies worked pretty good so when it was over I offered them seven bucks an hour figuring to argue them down from what they demanded. They would not take money. Too much welfare I figure so they do not have initiative.

So I got over to the town and asked around for Russell to take me up to the mine in the 4x4. Town not much use except maybe the lodge where a guy can get a drink. Houses around here and there look not repaired or used since the Syndicate shut down in '36. So anyway I asked around for Russell at the lodge and it turns out he has not been here this year at all or last year even.

They told me his 4x4 was parked in the road so I tried to start it but it would not run.

Before I take it apart I see there was a greasy looking fellow working under another truck down the block so I asked him about it. This older guy named Les Brown says Russell's axle is broke and anyway you cannot get to the mine from here.

The Syndicate had a road. It is thirteen miles from Darwin to the mine but it washed out after they split. This fellow says Russell put it in again eleven bridges. Flood came along the next year and washed the whole thing out.

So the stuff is here in Darwin. Made a deal with the lodge to keep it for us. At least it is that far. We will have to fly it all up with the chopper from here. I will rather stay at the lodge than in that camp anyway.

What to do about the permanent camp & the road? We got to have a road all the way to the mine to get the camp in. I do not see how we can do it by September. I do not know how we can even get a cat in from the highway as far as Darwin. The river we crossed on the cable looks big and rough even for a cat to ford. It will take a big cat to open that trail from Darwin to the mine & a lot of work and stuff for the bridges. We got to start quick if you want me to have it set by September.

This place is primitive. No phones and mail comes once a week. So when I get word from you I will get started but I need to know what to do.

—Butler

ELDORADO EXPLORATIONS UNLIMITED
Memorandum

July 8, 1981

TO: F. Carleton Manley, President
FROM: Ed Butler, Operations Manager

Boss, mail goes out tomorrow so I want to get this out to you. Still have not heard from you about my last letter of course since I just got it out last week and there is no mail since.

You said no problems with the Park Service but I am not so sure. No Park Service has showed up but there is this beanpole fellow calls himself Jotham B. Shechter flew in in a chartered plane from Bettles a couple days ago. Big discussions he makes at the lodge about saving the country from us miners. He flails his arms around a lot when he talks and says something about God's country and nobody supposed to do mining here etc. Nobody listens to him much except to be polite but he apparently has connections with that Park Service and something to do with the government.

He is camped out in a tent by the creek and he has not taken a bath yet. I have not yet either but I am staying at the lodge so I can. They have a shower even if they have outhouses only and no inside toilets.

I get the feeling he will be watching everything we do. Tell me again about how the Park Service has nothing on us. We are just minding our own business and the government should do the same. If he gets in the way I can take him out behind the lodge for a lesson or two but I do not know about those connections he's supposed to have. What do you think?

—Butler

p.s. I learned since I wrote this that this Jotham B. is a professor at some big time university. That explains why he talks so much. He goes on and on

3

and I do not think anybody here understands him. But they listen and listen as if they did. I do not know how they can sit so long while he talks. I wander in and out of the lodge but mostly I am getting very bored. You are paying me good money and I want the thirty grand for this summer but so far I do not know how to start and I am still waiting to hear from you so write quick. And he has these great heavy mountain climbing boots he walks around town in that are so big on his skinny legs I am surprised he does not trip over them more often than he does. He says he will be here all summer and going into the mountains & up the creek to the claims & etc.

p.p.s. Send bug dope. The mosquitos are terrible.

I am Jotham Shechter. I was that beanpole twenty-five years ago, when I first arrived at Darwin, in Alaska's Dagheeloyee Mountains. At the moment I am a Jew living in a Zen monastery in San Francisco. That is a straightforward consequence of having lived in the Dagheeloyees. Perhaps you will understand when you know the story.

Blue monkshood and yellow cinquefoil bloom now on the ash and mud erupted by the volcanic explosion, where I saw the heat of the inner earth sear glacier ice. After those first tumultuous years I had my time of solitude in the upper valley, a time of loneliness and of deep satisfactions, which in its turn came to an end. Now I am passing middle age. The children of friends lost in the events of that time are grown now, and have children of their own. Few are left who knew Dagheeloyee Peak, the glacier, the town of Darwin in those days. If the story will be told, I must tell it, and now.

The telling will help me make my choice. Shall I return to that place now, before I am too feeble to haul firewood, fix machinery, and meet the necessities of life in those mountains?

It is now my habit to take long walks in downtown San Francisco. I like the vertical faces of the tall buildings. I like the newspaper stands at the corners, the colors of all the magazines piled on one another, and the lamp poles plastered with layer upon layer of bright posters. I come to the park at Union Square during the noon hour to watch the flowers grow and see the people. One day on a park bench I met an Orthodox rabbi. Rabbi Jacob Garbats and I often sit together on the north side of the park, facing the sun, feeding the pigeons. We talk. Over the past few years he has heard my story of the Dagheeloyees, more than once. We debate the fine points of meaning.

Rabbi Garbats says the story reminds him of a passage in the Talmud, the authoritative Jewish commentary on God's biblical law.

The passage from Talmud is itself a story:

The Rabbis have said:

> *Four people entered an orchard, and these are they: Ben Azai is one, Ben Zoma is another, the third one is called Acher and the fourth is Rabbi Akiva. Rabbi Akiva told them, "When you find stones of pure marble, don't say that these are water, because it is said in the Torah, 'Those who lie will not be brought in front of My eyes.'" Ben Azai peeked at the orchard and died. About him the Torah says, "He who is dear in the eyes of the Lord, the Lord brings death to his faithful." Ben Zoma, the second one, looked and was injured, and about him it is said, "If you find honey, eat only as much as you need, so you don't get full and vomit." Acher cut down the plantings. Rabbi Akiva, the fourth one, went out in peace.*

The rabbi explained to me:

"What you experienced in Alaska was a reenactment of the Talmud story. Various people peeked at the orchard, and each responded in his own way to the experience. One died, one was injured, one became destructive, and one went out from the orchard in peace.

"When you look at the page of Talmud, the primary passage is in the center. Around it are arrayed commentaries. Rashi, one of the commentators, says that when they peeked, they looked on the face of the Lord, entered Heaven.

"An earlier commentator, Rabenu Hananell, calls the orchard a sort of Garden of Eden, which is preserved for the righteous, where worthy sages pray and purify themselves from everything sinful, fast, bathe and sanctify themselves. They speak the different names of the Lord. And they watch and see how the Angels do what they do.

"So what happened to each of the four? Rashi says that he who was 'injured' went out of his mind—literally, 'His brain was addled.' As to he who died, it is said in Exodus 33:20, 'A man shall not see Me and live.' There isn't much more in the commentaries included in the Talmud volumes. The story was obviously not very clear to them. They don't talk much about it.

"There is another book, a contemporary Kabbalistic commentary called Leschem Schvu Ba'Achlama. The title is the name of three of the jewels on the breastplate of the high priest of the ancient temple. He had all sorts of jewels on his breastplate, which somehow could be used for oracular purposes.

"It is written there that this Talmud passage is a parable of men who are trying to breach the material world, to reunite the profane material world with the sacred.

"You can't have good without evil. At some point in history good and evil were split apart; at least we perceive them as separated. Our four men set out to transform evil into good. They wanted to get to the inner holiness of the material world. They didn't want to just see it at a superficial, gross level, but instead to get to the inner, sacred core of physical reality. That was their quest: to achieve wholeness, to reunite the material and the divine, which in their deepest nature are one.

"Now, the Kabbalists explain that reality consists of a series of 'klipot': shells or appearances that all fit inside one another. 'Klipot,' the same word as the shell of a nut or a fruit.

"Like those Russian peasant dolls, all nested one in the other.

"The four men in the parable were peeling back the shells. The other ones at some stage took what they saw to be ultimate reality. But Rabbi Akiva kept going. He said not to mistake shiny marble for clear water: do not confuse worldly appearance, a particular shell, for reality. He kept on going, shell after shell.

"We can take all this and apply it to our understanding of the Alaska wilderness. The parable is about why people go into wilderness, to try to peel away the different shells that cover divinity, to try to reunite divinity *and the material world. To try to undo the primordial sin of Adam that caused the separation between the sacred and the profane.*

"And various things happen to these people. Some can't handle it, and some manage to integrate the experience, each according to their initial approach.

"Now the next portion of the Talmud, following this parable, goes, 'They asked Ben Zoma, what are the laws relating to castrating dogs?' And he tells them you aren't allowed to, and so on. The Kabbalistic text tell the integral connection between this question and our parable. It is very complicated..."

I first came to Darwin, Alaska, in 1981 to conduct a study of the new Dagheeloyee National Park. I was thirty-one then. I had many reasons for coming North that summer: The chance for another publication for my resumé, the government grant, input on park planning and management, a season in the woods ... seeking inner peace in the wilderness as an escape from the tensions of my job as an untenured assistant professor at the Berkeley law school.

I stayed the summer, went back to California, then came up again. When all the events of that period were over, I found myself heir to a pile of documents that describe them. I gathered the diaries, the letters, the computerized files, the untranscribed dictation tapes of the people who had lived with me through this time. Some of the documentation I just found at the site, appropriated without asking—sometimes no one to ask. And I give my deep appreciation to those who have given freely of their personal records and the records of members of their families who had lived at Darwin.

Now, two and a half decades after the events related here, I can bring these documents into print without embarrassment to those involved, or their families.

So far as possible I tell the tale simply by letting the participants speak in their own voices, through the documents they left behind. Where necessary, I annotate for clarity.

When does the story begin? Perhaps it begins in the Triassic, time of the dinosaurs, when basalt upwelled as hot liquid rock through a weakness in the earth's crust, containing ever so tiny a proportion of the metal copper. Or fifteen million years later, when the bodies of quadrillions of tiny shelled sea creatures accumulated on the basalt ocean floor, forming limestones: wackestone, packstone, and grainstone, containing ooids, oolites and fossil fragments, and mudstones with scattered bioclastic debris, layers thousands of feet thick. Limestone: the stuff of caves. Hot water, seeping through rock under pressure, collecting copper in solution from the metamorphosed greenstone basalt, welling upward into the limestone, dissolving limestone, forming tunnels and chambers, depositing copper in veins and pods within the limestone rock, concentrating copper, making ore. The layers of rock compressed and twisted by earth's forces into the Dagheeloyee Mountains, carved into cirques and steep cliffs by Pleistocene glaciers, penetrated by volcanoes, a catacomb of passages and galleries hidden within, beneath their icy arctic surface.

The first people came tens of thousands of years ago across the land bridge from Asia, walking into the mountain valleys during those centuries when they were free of ice, during glacial retreats, keeping to the low country when the glaciers advanced. They hunted moose, caribou, and white mountain sheep on the slopes; found copper nuggets in the creeks, eventually learned to make tools of metal, used it in trade with the Eskimos on the coast. The Koyukon People were aware of the distant time prior to the present order of existence. They told the stories of the beginnings: "Kk'adonts'idnee," "in Distant Time it is said": Animals had human form, spoke human language, and eventually were transformed in a dreamlike metamorphosis into the animal and plant beings who inhabit the landscape today. The Koyukon people knew, as they traveled the land, that they walked among spirit personages. They learned rules for proper conduct in nature, and knew the punishments given by the powerful spirits for irreverent, insulting or wasteful acts.

At the turn of the twentieth century U.S. Army explorers charted the rivers and mapped the peaks. The officers reported tales of green mountains, the color of copper ore, and nuggets of pure native copper. So the prospectors followed. A Wall Street syndicate bought up their claims. It hired engineers to punch through an extension of the Alaska railroad to the site at the headwaters of Dagheeloyee Creek, at the base of Dagheeloyee Peak itself, on the Arctic Circle.*

The nearby service town was named after Ezra Darwin, entrepreneur, pioneer, and outcast nephew of scientist Charles Darwin. Rejected by his English family for unpleasant personal habits, Ezra emigrated first to Dawson, Yukon Territory, in the gold rush of '98, where he started a bank, grubstaking sourdoughs with loans at exorbitant interest.

Then when the Syndicate surveyed the railroad route, Ezra staked a homestead claim not far from the mines, where he knew the locomotives would have to stop for water. He subdivided the property, established the town, and got rich financing its whorehouses and speakeasies. Darwin grew to a population of five hundred people during the brief period, 1924 to 1936, when the Syndicate extracted a quarter of a billion dollars in profits from Eldorado Butte on Dagheeloyee Creek.

Suddenly it was over. The company announced that the last train would leave tomorrow. The train pulled out of Darwin station, taking the last residents, leaving behind dishes on the tables and linens on the beds. The company said the ore bodies were exhausted. And, it is true, production had been diminishing those final years. There had been rumor of a new discovery, but the company had no comment. Contrary

---

* The miners pronounced Dagheeloyee as "Dag´-he-low´-ee." The word means "mountain range" in Koyukon Athabascan and is unpronounceable in English.

to residents' expectations, the mines remained closed. As years passed, fireweed flowers took root in the streets of Darwin, and poplar trees grew up through the roofs of decaying buildings.

New people came to the country, not many, but a few. One was Jasper Russell. By 1981, when I arrived at Darwin, Laurance Jasper Russell, age fifty-seven, had been prospecting around the area for nearly thirty years.

He was a black man, formerly elegant perhaps, with gold-rimmed spectacles and an Oxford accent, slurred in recent years by alcohol and drugs. (His father had been a minor functionary with the Kenyan colonial administration, brought to London and thence to America by the British foreign service.) These characteristics had led Jasper to an undistinguished and brief appointment as Director of the Division of Minerals in the Alaska state government.

Through the decades in Darwin, Jasper lived in the several abandoned houses he appropriated, getting by on canned beans and gathering firewood day-to-day with an old chainsaw and a dull axe. His diet improved during his two marriages, both to women who believed in his discovery of the great lost mother lode of mineral riches. And wanted their share of the profits. Each marriage ended when the lady realized the returns were not forthcoming.

In fact, LJR (as he was fond of being called) first had his vision of the lost lode while employed selling Bibles door to door in the poor black neighborhoods of Tampa, Florida, in 1951. It came into his head on a particularly bad day (he had been rejected on more than two dozen consecutive doorsteps), as he was clearing his head with a puff of marijuana in his car on a humid street corner.

Projected on the inside of his skull he saw spelled out the word "DAGHEELOYEE." As the word faded, it was replaced by a map of Alaska, with the location of the town of Darwin indicated by a blinking, illuminated copper-colored arrow. Followed by a vision in day-glow orange and blue of a full trainload of valuable mineral ore, steaming to an Alaska port, with himself in top hat and spats in the attached luxury executive car.

Six weeks later he was in Darwin. He knew that the Syndicate had withdrawn from the Dagheeloyees without exploiting the biggest ore pod of all, located just beyond their deepest tunnels in the great Eldorado mines. He knew it was his.

In those days a person could just occupy any of the abandoned buildings. He did. He found an old D-4 Caterpillar tractor. A middling-to-good mechanic, he fixed it. That took six years.

He kept his salesman's suit. In it he attended conventions of the American Mining Congress and the Alaska Miners Association and met with bankers in Anchorage and Seattle. He projected an open honesty, an integrity, that appealed to the avarice and greed in potential investors. For only twenty-five hundred dollars they too could have a part in the great mother lode. That kept him in diesel fuel, spare parts, beans, whiskey and dope.

He spent long winter nights swallowing LSD and mescaline with Les Brown by kerosene lamp in an icicle-bedecked, dilapidated log house way up Dagheeloyee Creek, in the canyon below the entrances to the mine tunnels.

To make ends meet he sold stock in the mine six times over. The stationery mounted on his desk: The Great Eldorado Mining Corporation. Loohana Valley Industrial Enterprises, Inc., Mineral Exploration and Development Division. The North America Copper and Silver Corporation. Northwest Alaska Mining, Milling and Foundry Company. Dagheeloyee Mountain Mining and Manufacturing Corporation.

He acquired a side-kick, Jimmy Lang. Together they raised a flourishing crop of marijuana in the headwaters of Dagheeloyee Creek, collecting the sparse soil in five-gallon Blazo gasoline cans, carefully planting the Panamanian and Indonesian seeds, tenderly carrying the cans to sunny spots, taking advantage of the light and warmth of the long arctic day.

In July, 1978, they finished the eleventh and final bridge across Dagheeloyee Creek. It had taken Jasper Russell twenty-seven years to complete the job. For the first time since the flood waters of 1936, vehicles could drive from the town of Darwin to the mines thirteen miles upstream.

In July, 1979, Jasper and Jimmy appeared in Darwin ranting about a new chamber they had discovered in the mine tunnels. Jimmy had gone blind. Jasper had gone mad.

In August, 1979, following four days of torrential rains, Dagheeloyee Creek flooded, sweeping before it all eleven bridges and washing out long sections of the road.

Later that month, Jasper and Jimmy tried to return to the mines. Their hired Cessna hit too short on the gravel-bar airstrip. They walked out, Jasper leading Jimmy through the brush. Ten days later they chartered another pilot. Trying to land around the wreckage of the first crash, he demolished his plane against the poplars. They walked out again.

Jasper Russell left Darwin then. No one knew where he went, and he was gone more than a year. In June, 1981, the summer of my arrival, he sold Dagheeloyee Mountain Mining and Manufacturing to Carl Manley.

—JBS

_____

Transcribed from a dictaphone tape I found afterward, behind a frozen can of creamed corn in one of Jasper's cabins: —JBS

Um. Take a letter. Letterhead. DAGHEELOYEE MOUNTAIN MINING AND MANUFACTURING CORPORATION, L. JASPER RUSSELL, PRESIDENT. Tally ho, that's me. L. JASPER RUSSELL, PRESIDENT. Darwin, Alaska, zip 99726. June 21, 1981. Bank references and all that printed at the bottom of the stationery. The FIRST NATIONAL BANK OF SEATTLE. Hea. The bank. Hey ho.

Letter to Mr. F. Carleton Manley, President, Eldorado Explorations Unlimited, 18001 East Third Avenue, Seattle, Washington 98352.

Dear Mr. Manley,

I am in receipt of the contract and bill of sale for the Dagheeloyee Mountain claims as prepared by your attorneys Hayley, Goldberg and Fleischer. As per our discussion in Anchorage on June 20 last with Mr. Hayley the terms for the sale of this property are acceptable to the Dagheeloyee Mountain Mining and Manufacturing Corporation. My notarized signature as President of said corporation is affixed to these documents, your copies of which are enclosed. I have appreciated the opportunity to do business with you. The final details can be attended to by our mutual attorneys.

Sincerely,

L. Jasper Russell

President

Most Sincerely, Mr. F. Carleton Manley it is all yours now. Yours now, hey. Mine now, ONE HUNDRED THOUSAND big missulas. Yours the business, Mr. F. Manelton Carly. My business first class grass and a con-dominium in Hawaii. Dear Mr. Panley-Manlcy, have a toke. Take a toke. Take a tunnel. Mr. Ganley, note the report of my consulting geologists: By 1936, the syndicate had exhausted reserves in the four large pods of exceptionally rich ore located at the one thousand two hundred foot level, the three-thousand foot level, the four-thousand five-hundred foot level, level headed, steady there Jimmy, we've got her now, one more shove, the rock's free. Free grass. One hundred thousand dollars worth mine now. Yours the mine, Carley Farley.

Oh Jimmy, my head hurts. Jimmy, another toke to clear the old head, ahh.

Note the geologists' report: although these primary reserves were depleted by company operations, there remains an eighty-seven percent probability of undiscovered economic reserves exceeding four hundred thousand tons of ore averaging fourteen and one-half percent chalcocite and twenty-six percent malachite, with silver values of seven ounces per ton.

Seven ouches per ton, Mr. Manley. Take that. Ha.

Ouch, Jimmy, careful, the rock's heavy. Slow there, slowly, slowly, very heavy. Heavy, Manley, heavy, all yours now. Oh God, Jimmy, move the rock, it's the last one, the tunnel's open Jimmy, it's open we did it. Four hundred thousand tons in the tunnel. We've got it now Jimmy boy. I bet no one's been in here since. JIMMY THE LIGHT

JIMMY THE LIGHT'S OUT. JIMMY IT'S SO DARK. JIMMY THERE IS LIGHT DOWN THERE. JIMMY A GREEN LIGHT. OH JIMMY IT COMES. OH JIMMY IT FLAMES.

Jimmy, a drink, a toke. Mine is yours, Mr. Manley, pending attendance of final details by our mutual attorneys. Let it not drag on, hey, no more dragon.

ROLL JIMMY ROLL THE ROCK BACK OH JIMMY ROLL BACK THE ROCK CLOSE THE TUNNEL OH GOD JIMMY LET'S GET OUT OF HERE.

Rock and roll, the kid's music. They don't have to sneak and hide the grass anymore, but they don't appreciate good dope.

Hide in the grass, the bear is coming this way! Oh no, it's after the cat! It ate the seat off the D-4 cat, Les. We gotta fix the cat, Les!

Creek's roaring now, Les! Too loud, can't stand it! Damage report: all bridges flooded out, Les! Damage report: No way up the creek. Mine's gone, minds gone, my mine's gone.

Report to stockholders, from L. Jasper Russell, President: On July fifth at four thirty a.m. nineteen seventy-eight yours truly completed eleven bridges connecting the Dagheeloyee mines with the town of Darwin, thus completing the vital prerequisite for restablishing the production for transporting the ore for essential prospecting and developing supplies request require immediately four thousand dollars deposited Seattle bank for necessary diesel fuel, cribbing, associated supplies, gotta rebuild, all bridges out. Damage report: four days rain, cribbing, no fibbing, so much flooding, send the bucks, buck the timbers, rebuild the bridges, fix the cat, up the creek we go again, Jimmy.

New finds, hey, new finds in the mines, in the minds, connections gone, gotta rebuild the bridges. Oh Jimmy, another toke, another drink, gotta think. Think in the clutch, that's now, you know, creek's in flood, we'll be swept away, cat's busted, fix the clutch. Les, you got the grease? Bear ate the seat, you know. Bear will travel thirty miles to eat a seat. They like yellow best you know. Can't bear it, ALL bridges out.

Bear seat. Bare bottomed bear. Hey, that's a thought. Darwin, that's a bare bottomed town alright. Cat's busted in Darwin. Darwin, cat town. Mining days cat house town. Nobody home in the cat house any more. I got the only cat in town and its busted! Big busted cat. Tee-hee.

Um. Take a letter. Letterhead. DAGHEELOYEE MOUNTAIN MINING AND MANUFACTURING CORPORATION, L. JASPER RUSSELL, PRESIDENT.

Dear Mr. Manley,

Chalcocite, malachite, contract and bill of sale. Terms acceptable, notarized signature affixed appreciate the opportunity a lifetime of grass I'm condominium bound. My regards to old green eyes hot lips.

Sincerely,
L. Jasper Russell,
President

I came across the files of the Explorers in the attic of Carl Manley's old house near Seattle. It is still owned by the family. My thanks to Viki Manley Hoffman for access to them.   *—JBS*

ELDORADO EXPLORATIONS UNLIMITED

18001 East Third Avenue

Seattle, Washington 98352

June 21, 1981

Mr. Edward Butler

8313 Cold Storage Road

Wenatchee, WA 98731

Dear Ed:

Hayley and I met with Russell yesterday. It was easier than I had expected. We got rid of the old gent for a hundred grand. Hayley had the right idea. We took him up to the Crows Nest Lounge at the top of the Captain Cook Hotel. He was so impressed with the place that he bent entirely to our will. After a couple of drinks he was incoherent and completely pliable. The property is ours.

Jones and Ritmore are ready to come through with $250,000 for this summer's operations. There is another half million lined up for '82 if we can get results fast enough. So the job now is to put on a good show out there between now and September. Decisions will be taken then.

I expect you as operations manager to complete construction of the seasonal camp at the site by July 15. We have reserved thirty days of chartered helicopter for you beginning July 15. Schultz will come in on the helicopter with the gravitometric radar instrumentation. He says he can get a good reading on the gravity anomalies at the mountain in three days of flight operations. That will leave you 27 days to reopen the tunnels and complete exploratory operations. You will proceed to the target areas as Schultz determines from his analysis and obtain the core samples from the ore formation using the portable drill.

Materials for the permanent camp will arrive at the Fairbanks railroad depot on August 20. I expect to show the investors' group through the camp on September 15.

The required National Park Service forms are available in Fairbanks. We are operating on private property and they can't touch us.

Your immediate task is to truck the temporary camp with supplies and helicopter fuel to the mine site. Russell has four-wheel drive and will deliver the goods from Darwin to the mine. This will be a considerable convenience. I advanced him $1000 for this.

Good going so far, Ed. This is already thirty grand in the bank for you. Remember that half million out there for '82. Get the job done.

Sincerely,
F. Carleton Manley
President

My involvement grew out of a discussion I had with the park superinten-
dent, Albert Cooke. When we met the previous fall at a Sierra Club wil-
derness conference, I broached the idea of a policy study of the Daghee-
loyee area. Following are excerpts from my successful project proposal:
—JBS

PROPOSAL FOR THE STUDY OF OPTIONS FOR THE
ESTABLISHMENT OF A FEDERAL REGULATORY REGIME
TO ENSURE WILDERNESS PRESERVATION IN
DAGHEELOYEE NATIONAL PARK AND PRESERVE, ALASKA

Submitted to the National Park Service, U.S. Department of the Interior
By Jotham B. Shechter
Assistant Professor of Environmental Law
University of California, Berkeley
February 1, 1981

Last December, Congress set aside ten million acres of the nation's
most spectacular arctic wilderness landscape, designated as Dagheeloyee
National Park and Preserve. This action was part of a comprehensive decision on the future of federal land management in the North....

...Essentially, then, it is the intent of Congress that Dagheeloyee be
maintained as a wilderness. This area is pure wilderness at its best: Here
the American public can enjoy the clean waters and soaring peaks of our
heritage, unimpaired....Here the Nation can retain a nearly complete ecosystem in its unaltered state, a seamless whole preserved for the contemplation of future generations....

Clearly, the primary management goal in the Dagheeloyee area is the
emplacement of a regulatory and control regime by the National Park
Service sufficient for the permanent and inviolable protection of wilder-

ness values. There are, however, a series of complications which compromise the efficiency of the agency in meeting its responsibilities:

1. The existence of established incompatible uses (including the presence of permanent residents within the boundaries);

2. The existence of extensive private lands in the center of the Park and Preserve, outside of Park Service control. These inholdings include mining claims which, if developed, could severely impact Park resources; and

3. Statutory limitations on federal authority written into the legislation which established the Park/Preserve, including explicit exceptions to normal National Park Service policy limiting the ability of the agency to deal with the above.

At present the Park Service has insufficient information about the specific situation in the Dagheeloyee Mountains to construct an adequate management plan. Additional data is needed on the location and effect of inholder activities, potential impacts on wilderness resources of increased development on private lands, and options for increased tourist visitation which minimize degradation of wildland characteristics and habitat quality....The planning process will be rendered more efficient by an immediate field reconnaissance which isolates key issues, synthesizes complex problems, and produces a framework for further agency studies and planning....

From my field notebook:

5 July 1981
Location: Moraine ridge approximately 500 meters S.W.
of ice at terminus of Loohana Glacier, 1½ kilometers from
Darwin townsite, Dagheeloyee National Preserve, Alaska.

I sit atop a ridge of broken rocks, rising about twenty meters above the gravel flats at the edge of the great glacier. I look toward the glacier. I see no life. I feel drizzle, cold on my face and hands, and the fist-sized rocks beneath me. I smell cold air, empty of scent, moving as the glacier moves, slowly down the valley. I hear the hush of a world sealed over by cloud, the only sound a whispered roar of meltwater streams cascading from the ice.

From my vantage point the glacier itself is chocolate brown, heaped conical piles of gravels, cobbles and boulders which rest, I presume, on the ice. The glacier emerges from the mists, the wet surfaces of its rock blanket brighter than the white, but poorly illuminated clouds out of which it descends. There is nothing against which to measure scale, not a person, nor house nor road, no tree or flower or bush, nothing made and nothing growing.

Over most of its edge, the glacier slumps to meet the outwash plain. But at its closest approach, the edge is a sheer, turquoise ice cliff. The face must have failed recently, for an immense pile of fractured ice lies below and icebergs float in the brown lake at its base.

I turn around, sit facing southwest. Away from the glacier, there is life. Below me, not far away, I see scattered willows (*Salix spp*), stems growing between the rocks. Here and there are clumps of purple flowers. And in some places (the more stable areas, less often disturbed by floods of glacial meltwater?) the gravel plain is patched with a spreading vegetation, small leaves hugging the ground. I shall investigate them. Further away, the moraines are covered with small trees, poplar and spruce, it appears. Further still, the moraines end and the flat terrain is a forested expanse vanishing into the distance beneath low clouds.

Location: Next to the lake shore, approximately
100 meters from the glacier face.

I am sitting on a piece of eruptive breccia the size of a small house, made of angular lava fragments, maroon, orange, green. The boulder lies on a beach of wet silt, which quivers when I walk on it. A great pile of ice lies in the water, collapsed from the face of the glacier, which forms the far edge of the lake. How high is the face? A hundred meters? Again, there is nothing against which to judge the scale.

Meltwater streams cascade over the face into the lake, carrying along a rain of gravel and mud from the glacier surface. Rocks of all sizes teeter at the top of the face. Periodically one is undercut by melt, skitters down and plunges into the pool. The outer world remains shut out by mists and fog.

I was wrong: there is life here. I see a shrub growing atop the ice, amidst the rocks: a willow, soon to fall with the other debris to the pool below. Spiders scurry among the rocks at my feet. What do they find to eat?

The presence of the glacier is a comfort to me. The landscape glows in this spectral light, revealing the inner peace intrinsic to wilderness in the absence of the defilements of man.

What an opportunity lies before me! My task: To protect this wilderness within the cradle of benevolent management, even as it in its turn nurtures me; to seek its vulnerabilities, assess its strengths, measure the parameters of this wilderness; to propose a plan for its inviolable preservation. I sigh with the reassurance of its permanence, feel my muscles and joints, aching with the tensions of the city, relax in the quiet of this wild place.

Today is my first day in the Dagheeloyee Mountains. Day before yesterday, I flew from San Francisco to Fairbanks, a sprawling, dirty, noisy city: a too-new, yet dingy blight on the precious boreal landscape. Yesterday morning I met with the superintendent of the National Park, then flew by chartered plane, just me and the pilot, northwest to the Darwin airstrip. We flew under the clouds, over endless uninhabited forests penetrated by meandering rivers—the Tatalina, the mighty Yukon, the Tozitna; between bald hills reminiscent of northern New England; over the marshy flats of the Koyukuk, home to millions of nesting ducks and geese; up the broad

gravel floodplain of the braided, silted Loohana amidst mountains disappearing into cloud; finally reaching its source at the Loohana Glacier.

There is something of a mess near the airstrip: mining junk and the
abandoned townsite. A hotel currently maintained in one of the old buildings runs a generator for electric power. It whacks away during much of the
day and evening, pounding noise into the wilderness.

I walked away from sight and sound of the activity, camping on a terrace
forested with young poplars and spruce, my tent perched a couple of meters
above the gravel flats surrounding Dagheeloyee Creek. This will be my
home for the summer, although I will have to enter the townsite to initiate
my measurements of the present extent of the disturbance (as a baseline for
assessing the environmental impact of future developments), and to conduct the evaluation of the prospective consequences of inholder activities.
Despite the remnants of early twentieth century industrialism, the setting
—my camp, the proximity to this great glacier—is deeply fulfilling.

...As I turn from the glacier, leave the stone hills and barren flats and
reenter the poplar, willow and spruce, I hear the flute-like tones of a
Swainson's thrush, then the raucous cries of a pair of grey jays. I walk amidst
the blue and white of lupine blooms and the emerging purple of fireweed.
A single dewdrop rests atop each lupine stem, cupped in a circle of curved
leaflets. As I move away from the glacier, into the shelter of the forest, the
hum of mosquitos replaces the roar of meltwater streams.

6 July 1981
9 p.m.
Location: Base camp along Dagheeloyee Creek,
near Loohana River confluence.

Rain today, rattling on the tent as I write. This morning I dug into the
ground with a trowel at several locations on the wooded terraces between
the creek and the rise of Chalcocite Ridge. Even where covered by a thin
layer of soil and supporting a forest, the rocks are but inches below the

surface. Life here has but a precarious purchase atop the droppings of glaciers!

...This afternoon I walked into the townsite to begin an inventory of structures on the private inholdings. From my initial examination of the townsite surroundings, development impacts also include roadbuilding and logging (recent stumps on upper forested terraces ~2 kilometers S.W. of townsite)....

[I omit various charts, tables and maps of "impacts" and "inholder activities" included in the journal at this point.   —JBS]

12 p.m. midnight

The rain continues to drop from overcast. The light is steady and featureless, about the same intensity now as at noon.

7 July 1981

1:30 a.m.

Location: Atop the moraine overlooking the Loohana Glacier.

After midnight the rain ceased. The first sign of clearing was a blue streak between clouds to the south. I have not adjusted to the endless day and was wide awake. So I walked out through town, down the jeep road toward the glacier. By the time I broke out of the forest, the clouds had descended again, even lower. Except for the rocks and the glacier, I could have been in Kansas. But as I wound my way between moraine hills, heading for the ice, the sky overhead became saturated with blue. Mountain walls appeared beneath the clouds along the edges of the glacier.

Now white billows obscure only the upper parts of the ridges. Wisps of mist hang above forested hollows on both sides of the broad, brown ice tongue. As I watch, they uncoil, shrink and vanish.

2:30 a.m.

I can see now that the debris-covered ice pours forth from a vast amphitheater to the North, still blanketed with clouds. Is this basin large enough to engulf a city? A roar, then a crash as sand and gravel melts loose from the glacier face and slides into the pool below. Icy air seeks the crack between my gloves and my jacket, flows behind my ears and down my neck.

Now fog hangs low over the glacier. The grey air in the amphitheater condenses into distinct layers, separated by white. (The white of snow-fields?) Above, the cloud tops glint white, backlit by the morning sun. No, the highest cloud is not a cloud. It is a mountain peak.

3:15 a.m.

To the North: fluted ice walls, gleaming spires and, sublime culmination, the perfect volcanic cone of Dagheeloyee Peak, chaste spotless white. A small steam plume escapes the peak's summit vent, glowing against a sky of pure deep blue. As I watch, blinding rays explode from the peak's eastern skyline. The sun bursts forth in a glorious northern dawn! Instantly, I feel warmth on my cheek. The glacier basin still rests in shadow. But the ridgetops catch the new day, soaring exultant in the freshness of the boundless sky!

I hear an airplane. The motor cuts like a table saw through the mountain silence. The plane whines out of the icefields, circling for a landing. I descend the moraine and return to camp. As I walk through Darwin, I set off the barking of dogs, slovenly domestic beasts chained to trees. Soon the whacking of the generator will signal the beginning of another day of in-holder activity. I am returning to camp and to bed.

5:00 p.m.

...Even with the sun beating on the tent and the hordes of mosquitos banging on the door netting, I slept solidly past noon. I had some breakfast, then set out. My goal is the closest summit of Mt. Ezra Darwin, from which I should get a view of the whole area....

I first made my way through Darwin along the dirt road to the Loohana River, a few hundred meters downstream from the terminus of the glacier. The river is not bridged, but instead is spanned by a cable. I pulled myself across, sitting on a wooden platform which hangs from the cable. On the other side is the end of the road from Bettles and Fairbanks.

I walked upstream, around the edge of the glacier. The foaming brown river raged between me and the rubble-covered ice. About three or four kilometers upstream, this channel issues from a giant cave set into the base of an ice wall a hundred meters high. I could see blue-green ice within.

There I saw my first Alaska grizzly bear, *Ursus arctos*, unpredictable denizen of the deepest wild, safely across the river from me. Fortunately, the creature did not see me. He did something inexplicable: He walked into the ice cave, where he disappeared. What could he be seeking there? I presume he will find no food amidst the ice, nor the sunny resting spots grizzlies prefer. And it is not denning season....

[I failed even to get to the base of Mt. Darwin, blocked by what seemed impenetrable alder and willow thickets and wet ground.   —JBS]

10:30 p.m.

On my return I went over to the cave entrance. I dared not venture too close, for fear of falling rocks and ice (there is evidence of a previous ceiling collapse) and of the bear. The mud flats along the creek there are covered with bear tracks. The creature (or creatures) must come and go from the cave frequently. How odd.

Terri Charles owned the lodge in Darwin. She wrote to her sister almost every week. —*JBS*

July 8

Dear Sister,

We have finally got some sunshine & it is welcome, too, after the rain. It greatly improves Sara's spirits, and mine as well. I think it is harder for both of us to be cooped up in the lodge all day. For the past couple of days she has gone out in the afternoon, swinging on the big rope swing in the yard. I think I even see a smile on her face then.

We had guests in the lodge over the fourth, and it was pretty busy for me without help. Les came by and fixed the generator so at least we had power. Bless him.

Now we have just one fellow staying with us and that is not really too much work. But he is rather a boor and always making passes at me, which is not what I need now. I'm not afraid of him, I don't think he is that sort. He got rather tiresome when we were confined together in the rain. He's working for some mining company that bought Jasper's claims up the creek. We have reservations for their helicopter pilot and some crew starting on the fifteenth. It will be busy, but I think I will enjoy being the hostess. It pays the bills, too. Geologists are usually decent folks. Perhaps the others will get this first fellow to tone down. I also got a note from the Catholic Church down in Fairbanks asking me to reserve a place for one person for a week starting on the twelfth, a priest. That's all I know about him. Should be interesting, and maybe a good influence.

I am counting on the help Irma arranged to be here by then. Her name is Kitty Chambers, from Wasilla near Anchorage. That's farming country, so hopefully she will be used to roughing it. Goodness knows, I can't afford to pay hardly anything. I can't be choosy. She's driving in the road. It will be especially good to have another woman around.

Things are pretty quiet in town. There is one new person moved in, George Johnston. He bought one of the little houses near the edge of town.

He keeps pretty much to himself. A man hired by the Park Service to do some studies is camped out down by the creek. He comes by the lodge once in awhile. He's a bit ill at ease and has gotten into some arguments with our mining guest. The two of them are quite the pair, sort of Mutt and Jeff in appearance, one so tall and the other short and thick.

At least it's company and it keeps my mind off Ted and the accident. Next week it's a year that he is gone. Sara is still taking it hard. She still has that distant look in her face. I wish she had other children around to play with. I think it would brighten her up....

Well, tomorrow is mail day and lots of correspondence to catch up on, so that's all from us for this week.

> Love,
> Terri

> Darwin, Alaska
> Wednesday, July 8, 1981

Dear Aunt Peggy,

I went out today to swing on the rope swing. Mother likes me to swing because she says it makes me happy. I prefer to go for walks and write in my diary. Mother is still sad mostly. I think she likes to work hard and she is so it helps. We have guests in the lodge, but they are not very nice. This morning I swatted 14 mosquitos in one blow.

> Love,
> Sara

July 15

Dear Sister,

... Kitty drove in a couple of days ago. I was disappointed when I first saw her. She wears high heels and a flouncy dress with décolletage, lots of makeup, perfume, rings and necklaces! Like someone out of Darwin's old days of ill repute, I thought. *Not* what I needed! I need someone to make beds and bake eight loaves of bread a day with a wood burning stove. But she has a kind spirit about her, and here she is. So we'll give it a try.

Yesterday was her first day on the job. I think maybe she's had a hard time, poor girl, and she certainly wants to work. She hadn't ever baked bread before, but she picked it up pretty fast. She got flour all over her petticoat, but it didn't seem to bother her. She brought the priest with her, the man who has reservations with us for a week. She belongs to the Catholic Church, so they asked her if she could give him a ride. He is from a monastery back East somewhere and is looking for a place to be a hermit. I've never known a hermit before, but doesn't fit what I imagine them to be. He is a hale and hearty fellow with a big smile, very comfortable to be with. Yesterday afternoon he played horseshoes with Sara for hours. After dinner I came out and found *her* pushing *him* on the rope swing. He doesn't wear that backwards collar or any special uniform, just faded blue workclothes. This morning when I got up I could hear him saying prayers in his room.

LJR showed up Saturday. We hadn't seen him since summer before last. He is drinking too much beer. I sell it to him but I don't know whether I should. I guess he is sleeping in the abandoned hardware store. I see smoke coming out of the stovepipe there, so at least he is keeping warm and I hope he's cooking for himself OK. The weather is still pretty good, and he sits outside most of the day.

That prospecting crew was due in today, but they haven't shown up yet. Ed Butler, the one who is already here, spends most of his time just hanging around the lodge. He can't seem to find anything useful to do. If he weren't a paying guest, I could surely put him to work. He certainly hasn't volunteered to help with anything. I think he is getting nervous with the waiting. His lewd remarks are inappropriate. I don't like him acting that way in front of Sara. Since Kitty came, though, his attentions are diverted her way.

With the good weather, Les went to his place up the creek for awhile. The heat is melting the glaciers, so the creek is high and he couldn't cross it—had to go up and over the ridge. I hope he gets back soon. For the moral support as much as anything.

Lots of love from Sara and me,

Terri

ELDORADO EXPLORATIONS UNLIMITED
Memorandum

July 16, 1981

TO: F. Carleton Manley, President
FROM: Ed Butler, Operations Manager

Mail plane is due in an hour so I am writing you. It is still just me here as the helicopter has not arrived yet. As you know it was due yesterday. I certainly expect I will get word from you in the mail today so I will know what is up. I got no letter from you last week either so have not heard anything since I got here. I am very bored & can make no progress in our projects until I have a way to get to the mines.

Presently I am thinking we cannot have everything done in time. I think about the money counted out on the table but here I am and the job is not hardly begun.

The beanpole is still around. Mostly he is out in the woods & mosquitos. I saw him yesterday down on his knees, looking at a stump. Maybe he was looking for gold in it. He doesn't seem to be doing anything serious at all. He is a spoiled brat but is not much in the way at this time.

Big news is Russell showed up. This you will not believe but he is colored. Of course you know this because you saw him. He is off his rocker. I told him he owed us that truck ride and he just mumbled nonsense. I think he is useless to us, but he says he has got a D-4 cat up at the mine which would be a big help. He wants more money but I will advance him not one penny since we paid for the truck and have not gotten a thing out of it. I am not prejudiced but we cannot trust him to do a job.

Boss, I need to hear from you quick. This whole place is nuts. There are too many mosquitos. There is the beanpole bent over some damn plant all the time with his butt stuck into the air. The truck is broke. The helicopter has not showed up. Here I am all alone and there is lots of money to be made but no way to do it and this is not good. Now there is this monk character staying at the lodge, too. He is a priest he says so I got to watch my language and act proper which is not now my inclination to do. He does not act so proper however himself. Yesterday I come out of the lodge and am smashed into by him swinging on a rope from a tree. So I am waiting to hear from you what to do.

—Butler

From Sara Charles's diary:

July 18, 1981

Dear Diary,

This morning I showed Kitty how to bake muffins. I think she is making progress because she spilled very little flour on her fancy dress. They came out really well. We put in raisins and honey. She wanted to put in white sugar. I explained to her that too much sugar is not good for us. We sold two muffins to some tourists. Then at lunch Ed Butler came in and ate just about all of them that were left. We had to save some for his dinner, too. Mother, Kitty and I had to go without at our dinner. Mother didn't even get to try one.

This afternoon I went down to the river to talk with Mrs. Henry. Her beautiful yellow flowers are just opening. So she is feeling very happy these days herself. The bee people visit her a lot. She says their feet tickle in a nice way when they walk on her. We sat together in the sunshine. It was really hot out there today. The sun felt good.

Mrs. Henry agrees that Ed Butler isn't a very nice man. Sometimes I am afraid of him, but she told me that he will not hurt me. Actually I am more worried about mother and Kitty. He follows them around and says things that are not very nice. If he does not get his way exactly his face gets all red and perspirey. He thinks that because he is a paying guest he is everybody's boss around here. He doesn't do anything except sit around.

The helicopter crew still hasn't come. Ed Butler is waiting for them. He paces up and down and reads the old magazines in the sitting room. By dinner time his neck is very pink and he is very sweaty. I wish he would take a shower. He knows that paying guests get to shower whenever they want for free. He knows because I told him so. He told me not to be sassy. Maybe I was just a little bit sassy but he is making our lodge smelly.

I didn't get to play at all today with Father Mike. He was in his room all morning doing his prayers. He does that every day. This afternoon he went for a walk by himself. He says he needs lots of alone time. I guess it is part of his work as a hermit.

Les got back from up the creek today. Just in time, because the water pump broke and we are just about out of water. I would have to haul it from Clearwater Brook. I don't like that job but I will do it gladly if Ed Butler will wash with it.

Les says he is tired of having to climb over the top of the ridge to get to his house up the creek. He has to do that when the water is high. When the creek is too deep to ford he can't use the regular trail. So he is going to put some ferry boats at the creek crossings. He is driving out to Fairbanks tomorrow to get them. I hope he comes back soon.

July 19, 1981

Dear Diary,

Today it rained. Kitty burned the hamburgers. The kitchen was full of smoke. She tried to cool the stove by closing the damper. She left the draft open so it smoked up of course. I showed her what to do. Mother was out fixing the water system. She came back soaked from head to foot. The pipe broke where Les had taped it together. Kitty laughed when she saw her. I was sad that mother had to do all that work by herself. I think she got happier when Kitty laughed at her.

It rained all day. I got tired of being at the lodge with M.O.E.B. (mean old Ed Butler). So before dinner I went out to see Mrs. Henry. I asked her if she thinks Jasper is crazy. She said he is but that is OK. She says they have Mutual Friends. She says she has seen Jot Shechter quite a bit lately. He has not noticed her. She says if he keeps his eyes open he can learn a lot. Well, I think he still has a lot to learn. Mostly he doesn't pay attention to anything around him. Yesterday he tripped over the flowerpots I left on the porch. He broke two of them. I wish he would watch where he is going.

From Father Mike's journal:

Fairbanks, Alaska
July 11, 1981

Zoomed up on the jet from Rochester, N.Y. Such ecstasy that Father Abbot finally gave his approval to the endeavor! I felt his blessing as I left the community of my brother monks, then the pure, unadorned power of the airplane as it roared free of its entanglements into the cleansing air. The wings themselves cried for joy as rivulets of rain sped off their surfaces in our leap skyward.

May this trip be my embarkation on the journey to the desert, oh God! Void my ego in the expansive and featureless emptiness of Your holy solitude and let me find peace at last.

...In Fairbanks, I am staying with Tom and Becky O'Leary. It was set up by the bishop's office. I admit it was comfortable to be surrounded by the warmth and love of a family again, despite the clutter of a house overstuffed with material possessions. Grossest was the television, an endless enticement to greed and a bombardment of the senses. Actually, *Sesame Street* was pretty good. It is a program for children I watched with Mary O'Leary, who is four. Several endearing monsters live on Sesame Street. My sort of monsters, and quite the Lord's type, fitting for the time when the lion shall lie down with the lamb, and so forth, after He comes again, in the time of His serene peace, which we anticipate with such longing.

I read Mary a bedtime story out of a book written by the same people who do the Sesame Street television show. This book is supposed to teach the kids about the letter "D", so the story is about Duke Dumdeedle of Dundee and his delightful daughter Dora and the dreadful dragon Donald. Donald lives in the dank, dark dungeon below the castle. When he threatens dear dimpled Dora, the duke dramatically dumps him into the duck pond. Donald is allowed to remain at the castle, but henceforth (on threat of redunking) he must be Donald the dog, wag his tail politely, do what is expected, and bark on command. Mary and I both had fun reading. I like the version about St. Francis and the wolf better, however. For it is the Saint's meekness and humility, going forth with faith in the cross, that brought the wolf into the fold. The duke just used raw power, his own personal muscle. Not really a good message for the kids.

Anyway, Mary made me a gift of the book. Wouldn't fit in the luggage already bulging with St. Augustine, St. John of the Cross, etc. and etc. Saint Francis must come, to be with me amidst the friendly birds and animals of Alaska (I presume they are friendly. If they might consider unfriendliness, then even more I need at my side the Little Poor Man who tamed the very fierce wolf of Gubbio.)

Also Henry David Thoreau (can't go to the woods without him of course), Emerson, Montaigne (he wrote about solitude, too), a copy of Hammerskjold's *Markings* the Lutheran pastor here gave me, and so forth two suitcases full and my carry-on bag is so heavy I can hardly walk. Oh, and a coat, my winter coat even though it is summer. This is Alaska. I suppose I should have a spare pair of pants. My other pair was in the laundry when I left. I really must get another pair of pants....

July 13, 1981

From Hammerskjold, an early poem written when he was twenty, embarking on a new life (as I am now at age forty-one):

I am being driven forward
Into an unknown land.
The pass grows steeper,
The air colder and sharper.
A wind from my unknown goal
Stirs the strings
Of expectation.

Still the question:
Shall I ever get there?
There where life resounds,
A clear pure note
In the silence.

I write:

I am being driven forward
(Lurching, rut-bounced, break-neck rush,
Woman driver, face painted, chest heaving, face grimaced:
Attentive to the road.)
I compose myself with folded arms.
She, sub-arctic Catholic, makes no passes.
I, enroute hermit, expect none.
She drives on.
This is a
Non-stop flight.

Nonstop flight from city distractions
Social obligations bringing unintended grief
Crowded chaos
Godless struggle and pain.
Nonstop flight to purified light:
The air grows clear, cold, sharp
In endless day:
Is darkness vanquished?

Mountain winds stir the strings of expectation:
Careening up twisting narrow road,
Ascending to the City of God
Leaving a cloud of dust behind us.
What are the horizons that lie ahead?

Above the level of our tempest:
High peaks, serene with snow and light.
We could not see them, they were so high.

We rise toward them
Lifting our eyes,
Are these the mountains of holiness
Where the saints dwell,
Whence cometh our help?

Still the question:
Shall I ever get there?
There where God resides,
A clear pure note in the silence.

From Psalm 48:
    Great is the Lord and greatly to be praised
        in the city of our God!
    His holy mountain, beautiful in elevation,
        is the joy of all the earth,
    Mount Zion, in the far north,
        the city of the great King.
    Within her citadels God
        has shown himself a sure defense.

Darwin, Alaska
July 14, 1981

Grass growing up through gravel in the streets.

Traffic? None. Almost none. An old truck rattles by. I noticed several trucks washed into the creek, half-buried in gravel. One must have been an ambulance. I can still see the cross painted on its side, the red faded to white.

Paint peeling from old buildings; unpainted wood, chestnut brown, tan and grey. How did they get the lumber here? On the railroad, I guess, back in the Old Days. The walls lean. The roofs sag. The lodge roof is pretty straight. And it has new brown metal roofing. Down the street is a little log cabin, surrounded by trees. A couple of the buildings have false fronts, like on cowboy movie sets. Maybe they were painted once, but the paint is all gone, or mostly. A big one says "HARDWARE" across the front, faded but unmistakable. A wagon wheel leans against the wall. A lightbulb sticks out above the door. I don't imagine there is electricity for this building anymore.

Stovepipes. Each building has one or two. Some are covered with overturned buckets. Some wear coolie-hats made of metal.

Windows of warped glass reflect wavy buildings and flowing trees. I cannot establish precise bearings in this place: nothing is exactly up or down, or straight.

Walking the streets, it seems like nobody is here. But a girl zips by on a bicycle, waves at me. I met her last night. Sara. She is the daughter of the lady who runs the lodge, Terri Charles.

There are many empty lots, or at least places with buildings missing, or foundation holes only, grown up or around with trees. Little trees are taking over the abandoned front yard of an unpainted house with a grey picket fence. In the back yard, someone has planted a big garden, beautifully tended, new vegetables coming up now. Who?

It's not a big town, just a few blocks. Not a long walk to the river, with that funny passenger tram but no bridge. And alongside town is a big creek, or a smaller river I guess. The river and the big creek are brown and turbid, not inviting. I have also crossed a plank over a little sparkling brook. I don't have it in my head yet where that is, in relationship to everything else. It is in the middle of town somewhere, though.

July 19, 1981

Thomas á Kempis says, "It is sweet and delectable to serve God, and to forsake the world." At first I had thought I had forsaken the world when I entered the monastery, but I know now that I really hadn't, not sufficiently, not enough to enter fully within the "unspeakable sweetness of contemplation" that God gives to them that love Him totally in solitude.

Dear Jesus, walk with me as I make my journey toward Your holy peace. Empty me out totally, because I am Yours totally. Grant me freedom as I strip myself of the encumbrances and false complexities that keep me from You, as I take up a solitary life, only to serve You. Restore me to unity in Your solitude.

Here I am in Alaska, at the very end of Thy earth. Keep me far from the machinations of men's affairs, so I can dedicate myself totally to You in silence.

Take me to the place where obligation ceases, so that my obligation to You can be complete.

Eyes

Here is what I notice about people's eyes in Darwin:

Kitty Chambers—Her eyes slant upwards toward the tension furrows in the center of her forehead. It is as if she is always asking a question of the world and is afraid of the answer. Even covered in that purple paint, her eyes retain innocence. Maybe I am reading in too much. Maybe her tension just comes from the difficulty of walking along these rough gravel roads perched on high heels, bound in a tight dress. Why is she covering up her grace? She must have suffered much pain and is trying to protect herself. I see kindness in her, a great warmth behind those eyes.

Ed Butler—His little red eyes are set into a smooth forehead. His tension shows in the set of his jaw and in his stance. We talk. He stands with legs spread and braced, for stability. Who does he think will push him over? He speaks with cocked arms, hands made into fists, in combat. His fat is his armor from the world. Who is the person underneath?

LJR—When I look into his eyes, it feels like there is a plaster wall behind his retinas. His face shows wonderment and puzzlement. I know him through his words, not his eyes. He is a man of many layers: On the surface, crazy. One step down, entrepreneur, businessman. Under that, the guile of the con man. Under that, warmth and caring, I see it. Under that, a little baby seeking love and security. (Aren't we all, more or less, at some level?) Then the wall, and what lies beneath I do not know.

George Johnston—Haven't seen much of him. He lives in a shack over at the edge of town. Not the sort of person you tend to notice, quiet and keeps to himself. People here respect his wish for privacy and don't probe. To me, his eyes say Keep Off, Don't Tread on Me! His body and movements speak of lack of ambition, sloth even, of muscle softness and a certain dullness. Not memorable. But also not consistent with those eyes.

Les Brown—Ease, grace and clarity in his eyes. He has a powerful little body, just beginning to feel the effects of age. I like his jaunty wide-brimmed hat with the eagle feather stuck in the band. I feel very relaxed with Les.

Tim Brown—His eyes are wide open like a child's, yet so deep. They open into vast spaces. Where have I seen eyes like his? In some of the older monks at the monastery, those who have devoted themselves to meditation for many years. They speak of innocence and vulnerability. They twinkle quietly, with crinkles at the outer corners from his persistent smile. Is this gentleness incongruous with his massive, muscular frame? I think not. He moves with slow, graceful surety. I feel that he is always watching me. Yet, when he comes into a room, the room feels less crowded.

Jot Shechter—The formality and assertiveness of Jot's face contrasts with the confusion in his eyes. I think the stiffness of his movements is a cover-up for the chaos within. I also see brightness and sparkle in his eyes when he gets carried away in some verbal exposition or when he is describing his observations of nature.

Terri Charles—For some reason I don't remember what her eyes are like. I know she is a very centered and strong woman, and that she continues to feel the great pain of her husband's recent death. I like being with her. Both Les and Terri make me feel comfortable.

Sara Charles—Her eyes show the wide-open wonder of the child, usually with the bright glint of youthful laughter. But then there are the moments of retreat, of a strangeness and fear I see there, the insecurity following her father's sudden death, I presume. All the time I feel great depth. Her eyes go beyond what I can know.

Father Mike wrote the following letter to an old friend. Mike had known John J. (Juice) Ryan since they were both active in the free speech, civil rights, and peace movements at Berkeley in the 1960's. Ryan was influential in introducing Mike to Catholicism. He stayed on at Berkeley, getting his degree in medieval literature, after Mike dropped out of the English doctoral program. I think they always remained very close. At the time of our story, Ryan was teaching at St. Francis College in Brooklyn, New York. —JBS

Way Out Alaska
July 26, 1981

To the Juice Man from Mountain Monk,
en route to hermitage ultima.

Began my exile to the desert in the company of a fine painted lady who drove me from Fairbanks the big town of the North out the long dirt road to the little village of Darwin. Here no TV no billboards no appointment book with schedule and agenda no vacuum cleaners no cocoa-puffs with free coupon enclosed good for twenty cents off next time save your money. Finally I think I get to the desert where I meet God in peace & calm.

Monastery also no cocoa-puffs but still lots of brother chums all crowded there doing this and that so one feels he can't breathe from the pressure of combined prayer and clerical administration.

There are people here, but they all seem to have plenty of space around themselves. They are each very different. I suppose in the city they would disappear anxiously into the crowd and be crushed, but not so here,

Finally for me there is lots of time for aloneness and solitary prayer. I am living now in an abandoned hardware store with ten rooms upstairs three don't even leak when it rains. Used to be a brothel I suppose, but I am pumping the walls full of prayer. That should drive out the old bad vibes. Old vibes mostly rotted away already anyway, just like the paper insulation in the walls.

Maybe here I can finally be an ordinary man.

You know, Juice, I leave the world to be an ordinary man. Back there in all that chaos and strife they all try to get big and stand tall because they've got to or they get trompled. Look, man, at what happened to us at Bezerkeley the Big U. You think you're doing the world so much good and what happens? Big head is what happens. To me it happened, you know. Mr. BIG MAN RADICAL on campus. Yes, ma'am, follow me and I will show you how to smash the state and bring forth the paradise on earth. Sleep in my bed tonight and we will discuss Marx and Mao and Marcuse. The apartment smells of paperback books with black covers and cheap newsprint pages that are already yellow on the edges: *The Annihilation of the State and Its Replacement by the Forum of the People Which Will Tell Us All Exactly What to Do* and such titles.

Oh yes, we tried so hard and we cared so much. But without God everything became vanity, so it all backfired. Oh sir, yes sir, come to my demonstration and we shall force them to make peace, justice and freedom. Come get clobbered on thy head and ejected from the university. So you lose thy deferment and get drafted and sent to Vietnam and killed there because I told you this is the path we walk together: fight for peace. We do it, except you go and I stay behind. So I was still in Berkeley and George is dead in 'Nam and what all have we accomplished? Please pass the marijuana, I said then, before I met God. Dear God I am overwhelmed by a burden I have brought upon myself.

So time now to fly to the desert. This world can only be saved by simple men who live out their lives amidst the rocks and sand. They raise the world with their sacrifice and prayer. When we leave the world as did the early Christian desert hermits, we leave a foundering ship, we swim for solid ground. Only when our own feet have found a foothold can we be secure enough to really help others who have been cast into the waters.

I know I needed the monastery when I went there eleven years ago, Juice. But just as much I know that now I need the serenity and peace of a more total commitment in silence and isolation. This Alaska may be the place. The Order can get some of the land that is for sale here at little Darwin town where a hermit can really be alone and chop firewood, haul water, and do the Lord's work. You know, the hermit is just a regular guy and that's what I'll be. Nothing special, just chop the wood and haul the water and say my prayers like a guy has to.

Weekly mail plane coming this a.m. so gotta run up to airstrip and get this on its way.

—M.M.

———————

From Ryan's response:

August 1, 1981

Juice Man to Mountain Hermit:

Mike, you know you are still trying to hold up the whole world, just like you did at Berkeley. It must make you tired. Remember the sayings of the desert fathers: "If you see a young monk by his own will climbing up into heaven, take him by the foot and throw him to the ground, because what he is doing is not good for him." They also said "avoid gluttony" Can there be a gluttony of silence and solitude? Young man, you try to wiggle out every which way but you still can't: you trapped, you see? Now you want to be just an ordinary person, free from guilt and obligation, just an ordinary hermit dressed in an ordinary hair shirt and sleeping on an ordinary bed of nails, just praying away saving the entire world. You are still full of contradictions, my boy....

Mike wrote again before he received Ryan's response to his previous letter:

Far Out Village
August 2, 1981

Mountain Man to Fresh Squeezed

Listen here, this town is getting to me. Too much fun for appropriate hermitage I think?

First of all gorgeous woman this one is no cute chick this is one solid woman of the earth no romance of course I stay away in my hardware store but purity of thought definitely affected.

O dear blessed cloister enclosure where are you now when I need you?

Also most excellent crazy black man I am living with. Long discussions into the night he totally wacko with many great insights. I think he is Adam and he has lived in the Garden of Eden. He got tempted, too, for mineral riches he says it was but I'm not so sure it was really only that.

He thinks he is a business executive. I think I am a monk.

Meanwhile I begin to realize this townlet got some tensions arising: Big plans afoot (maybe) by mining outfit for various civic improvements including ripping out mainstreet to make way for heavy trucks night and day.

I am supposed to get out of town. Gotta chop down some trees and do my Abraham Lincoln number with a cabin before the snow flies (that is soon around here), pile them logs, make me four walls, stack me some sod on the roof. Lots of good hermit's work and no time for frivolity.

So far I wake up in the morning and say my prayers OK, go to chop the wood and all, but then stay around and play with the kid down the street, however.

Me, I reject the world utterly of course.

What's happening in Brooklyn?

—M.M.

From Mike's next letter, after he heard from Ryan:

Teeny-Tiny Village in the Big Woods

August 7, 1981

Alaska Ascetic to Big Apple Professor:

...The contradiction is there, I can't deny it. But the truth is also there, that now more than ever what we need is the simplicity of the monk, the peace and calm of contemplation, the unity with God that comes from being stripped naked before Him, in penitence. Peace can spread into the world only from such a seed of peace. I remain convinced....

I suppose for some people the monastery is a good place to live the life. For me, though, too much going on there, too much distraction. Not only my dear brothers with their problems and plans, but the visiting ecumenical delegations, the annual retreat of the men from the Church of Our Lady in Schnectady, etc. and etc. Also I just need more time alone.

Here it may really be possible to get away and make the commitment to serenity, silence, and God's gentle grace. At first I thought the town of Darwin itself could be the answer, and as I wrote you last week maybe it is not, entirely. But it is a long way from here to Rochester and most everywhere else, not many visitors, and as a monk it is not my role to get involved in the intrigues of a small town. It is my role to move to the woods and empty myself out. And that is easy to do here.

Town life may always be complicated, here is no exception I admit, but the Lord's orderly peace is just five minutes walk down the trail from downtown Darwin....

When I get up in the morning and light a fire in the cookstove at the hardware store, a pair of birds, grey and black they are, are always waiting in the tree by the door. I bring them a bit of pancake or yesterday's rice. They land on my hand and walk on my shaved head. So I am already friends with the animals and what could be a better start for a hermit?

—A.A.

July 26, 1981

Dear Sister,

With the sunshine the garden is finally producing like mad. I tried a new kind of Bibb lettuce this year. Cucumbers are six inches long in the greenhouse. I picked a couple for a special treat. The days are hot, but the clear nights cool off. So I've gone out in the evening to cover the outdoor beds with plastic a couple of times already. It keeps off the frost. We've got little green tomatos showing up in the greenhouse, and lots of tomato flowers, too. But the cold nights are slowing them down. Don't know if we'll get any to redden up this year.

Les got a canoe in the city. He had no money, of course. He had just enough to hear some jazz at a night club. He said before he went that he wanted to hear that group play. Well, as he drove up to the night club, Les noticed a canoe leaning against the wall of the building out in back. When he went in, he asked about it. It turned out to belong to the leader of the band.

But the band wasn't going to play that night, because the trumpet player had the flu. Well, one thing led to another and Les traded playing trumpet for three nights in exchange for the canoe.

Do you remember the painting he calls "Dagheeloyee Glacier in the key of C sharp minor," the one done in purples and greens with the violins and railroad tracks? He traded it for four hundred feet of poly rope, two pulleys and a tank of gas. He needed the gas to drive back to Darwin, because by then he was broke.

Most of the way up Dagheeloyee Creek to his place, Les can follow trails along the bank. But there are two spots, one close to town and one up just below Iceberg Lake, where he has to cross the stream. In spring and fall, he can wade across. But with this hot weather, a lot of ice is melting, so the creek is too deep.

Les has been working out back of the lodge, getting his creek-crossing system ready. He had only one canoe, but needed two ferry-boats. So he cut the canoe in half amidships with the welder. Then he took some scrap plywood, cut it to fit over the cut ends, screwed the pieces on and sealed them with window caulk. So he has two half-canoes now. He says he'll use the rope to set up fixed lines across the creek and attach the boats to the lines with the pulleys. Half a canoe at a time will be light enough to backpack up the trail to the crossing spots.

When Jot Shechter heard that Les was going to go up the creek, he volunteered to go along and help. Jot didn't admit it, but I think he wanted help, too, in getting up the creek, up to where the old mines are. He has been talking for weeks now about going there. But he doesn't know about getting around this country. He wanders around a lot near town, but hasn't been very far, really.

There is a lot Jot doesn't know in other ways as well. Les would like to have some time with him up the creek. Just the two of them working together up there, they will have some time for discussion.

Meanwhile, the lodge is running pretty well. Les has been keeping the equipment going, but his repairs are always made from electrical tape and baling wire, so they seem to break down just after he leaves on a trip. Actually, I am getting better at fixing things myself.

Ed Butler is also finally helping out. I was out and Kitty was alone in the kitchen last week when the water line from the spring broke again out in the yard. Sara was there and told me the story. Water was gushing from both broken ends, draining out from the tank in the lodge and spurting out the pipe from the pump. The pump was still running (Kitty didn't know how to turn it off). Kitty was trying to fit the two ends together. She was drenched and her high heels were buried in mud.

Well, Ed has been following Kitty around like an overweight beagle hound after a bitch in heat. Finally he showed some gallantry. He shut off the pump and did a good repair on the hose. It paid off for him and they are a couple now. I can't see how good can come of it, but one can never know about such things. He has a wife and kids down in Wenatchee, Washington. Kitty has been through this sort of thing before too many times, I guess. She wants so much to love and has so much to give. Ed has been catered to pretty well as a guest in the lodge. Now he has Kitty as his slave. I'm letting my bitterness show. I shouldn't do that. Well, at least he fixes things. When the alternator went out on the truck he got it repaired right away and it's been running fine since.

I guess I am bitter because I am scared. Ed Butler has no respect for me or any of us. I don't understand his attitude. Why is he here? I guess it is for the money. Kitty says he had money sometimes in the past, but loses it all in Las Vegas. I don't understand gamblers. He says his company will build a road all the way up to the old mines. That will mean a bridge over the river where the tram is now. Every tourist will be able to drive right into town. He says I should like that because it will mean more business for the lodge. But if I wanted to run a roadside lodge, selling hamburgers to passersby, I could have picked an easier place to live. People who come here now really have to make some effort to get here, so being here means more to them, and they stay longer, too. Sara can play right in the street here. Our doors don't have locks on them. We have relics from the old days sitting right out in the yard and nobody takes them. They'd be gone in a minute if the road came in here.

He says they'll widen the road through the center of town for heavy trucks. And they'll build it all the way up Dagheeloyee Creek to the old mines and haul in trailers for the miners. He says they'll keep the mine going all year long, even in the winter, and the miners will come down here and give us lots of business at the lodge. Well, I like it quiet in winter and I don't like Darwin becoming the rough town again that it was in the old days.

I guess I should be used to losing what's important, after losing Ted in the accident. But I still care about this place and I want to hang on, even if it is hard.

It's not that I don't like having more people around. I guess the mining could be OK if they had some respect for us and for the place. It's that attitude of "I'm so much better than you because I have money, or at least I have big plans to get money, and I'm going to get my money by running over you and then I'm going to leave." Finally there was a confrontation up at the airstrip the other day when everybody was gathered to get the mail. Some people told Butler how much they resented his attitude. He got angry, as he does, and said, "My company is coming in here and we are going to mine and you can take the benefits if you are smart, or you can leave if you want to. There is nothing you can do to stop us. We are going to roll over this town. We are going to make it big." He got folks upset then. Les and Tim and I went around to the various houses in town and we all talked it over and got things calmed down. But people are pretty worried.

Of course I guess we have to keep some perspective. Ed Butler has been here nearly three weeks already and nothing has happened yet. The rest of the crew has not arrived. We are used to people coming out here with big plans. Maybe these miners will never show up. Les reminds me that it is one thing to say you are going to build a road up Dagheeloyee Creek and quite another to actually do it. And make the road stay put.

Ed and Jot have been getting into some terrible rows. Jot takes it all so seriously. He can't stand to hear Ed describe the miners' plans. Ed knows that, so he tells it over and over.

Jot says the National Park Service should protect us from the miners. This is a park, you know, but we don't see Park Service people around here very often. People here like it that way and don't like the government much. We're used to being free and taking care of ourselves. I don't know about the work Jot is doing. He is out measuring buildings and taking lots of notes. He doesn't understand our feelings about privacy. When we all gather in the lodge in the evening there is concern about the Park Service coming in and evicting all of us. Is he working on that? He seems like a decent fellow, if a little obtuse and abrupt. But who knows? I have enough to do, so I don't think about it much. If we show some basic decency to each other we can all get along.

Father Mike, the Catholic monk, has moved over to the old hardware store with Jasper. We still see him around, but not nearly as much as when he was staying with us. He keeps a strict schedule of his Catholic ritual, which doesn't leave much time for socializing. I miss him. During the week he was with us I got used to his good spirits. He's been taking care of Jasper, cooking his meals. Jasper looks better, is drinking a little less, and shaved a couple of times recently.

Father Mike has been sent by his monastery to find a place where a few of the more mature monks can live by themselves. Certainly there is plenty of room for that around here. Mike wants to live that way himself. I guess once he got set up we wouldn't see much of him. But even so, I do hope he can work it out to stay. He thinks he can be here at least through the summer. He has to send reports back to the monastery and they tell him what he can do.

He's especially good for Sara. She's been less dreamy lately and in better spirits. She still spends a lot of time alone. I can understand that, of course, although sometimes I think it can be overdone. Mike tells me not to worry. He thinks she is doing fine....

The following was printed out from a computer file belonging to George Johnston and found later in his Fairbanks apartment. I include it here because it appararently was written during the summer of 1981. The other people in Darwin do not write much about Johnston. My own memory of him is hazy. He was around, came to get his mail with everyone else, but didn't attract much attention.   —JBS

I am tired. I want to sleep. I want to go away. I want to stick knives in myself. When I was little sometimes my father got mad at me. He would tell me to hit my head against the sharp corner of the kitchen counter. I will bash my head against the wall. I will hit, hit, hit until I do not hurt anymore. I will slump unconscious onto the floor. Then I can rest. I will be nothing.

I am nothing. I want to be nothing. I will squeeze myself into a tiny ball and squeeze the tiny ball down into a point and it will disappear.

I am a black hole. I will explode. I am filled with rage. I AM FILLED WITH RAGE. I WILL HIT, HIT, HIT. YOU WILL NEVER DO IT TO ME AGAIN. I WILL POUND, I WILL HIT, I WILL KILL.

At 11:00 a.m on September 21, 1982, I will kill everyone in Darwin, Alaska. I will emplace myself behind the berm at the airstrip and shoot them as they come to get their mail. I will then hyjack the mail plane to Dietrich Camp. There I will blow up the trans-Alaska oil pipeline. Then I will return to Darwin and I will shoot myself. My father will never know that I am the one that did it. I will be just another one of the rotting, smelly, bloated dead bodies. I won't know that. I will be nothing.

I will not let them kill me. They are dirty. The dirty, foul, putrid oil people. The dirty, foul oil pouring out over the beautiful, pure, clean tundra. The white swans kissing beak to beak on limpid tundra pools with their little baby swans. White swans sailing silently through crystal arctic air. White swans besmurched by black filthy oil.

Blow it up. MY HANDS CLENCH IN RAGE AGAINST THE BLACK OILIES. I WILL BURST THE PIPELINE. I WILL SMASH

AND POUND AND DESTROY. Me, I will SAVE them. The clean, white swans, the white bunnies in their soft furry tunnels in the pure earth.

They in Darwin deserve it. They live in a National Park, my God. They CUT the trees. They SHOOT and they EAT the animals. Blood pouring from their teeth. They smash down the life and they kill it and they burn it. They must be STOPPED.

It all fits together. It is all part of one seamless whole. It makes so much sense. To blow up the pipeline, I must kill them. In killing them, it clears the way to blow up the pipeline. To kill them, I must kill myself. In killing myself, I stop the pain. I become nothing as I save everything. God's world is wonderful. It all fits together.

I do it all for them. For the redwood trees growing since the days of Christ, glorious. The quiet groves. The bright-eyed deer, with her fawns dappled in the sunlight. The great white mountain peaks rising majestically into the Alaska sky. As John Muir said so well, a day spent in contemplation of God's wilderness mountain glory is a day not subtracted from the rest of your life. Pitching a tent on the lakeshore, the warm sleeping bag, the feeling of health in the unpolluted air.

They are poisoning the air and the water. The air stinks. It is filled with the sound of the airplanes. I cannot get away from it. They buzz and they whine and I hear them even in my basement in Fairbanks and I cannot get away from them. I wear earplugs but they get through. The neighbor's dogs bark. They leave them tied up all day. They are gone to their jobs in the air conditioned, sterile, isolation tank office buildings and *they* can't hear the suffering, the whinning, the barking. But I can. I cannot get away. I will break a bottle. I will smash it with my foot. I will mix the broken glass with raw hamburger with my bare hands. My blood will mix with the glass and with the meat. I will feed the meat balls to the dogs. They will ingest the substance. It will travel down their gullet. It will pierce their stomaches and their intestines. It will sever their arteries. They will bleed to death from the inside out.

I will hurt until I become nothing.

The water is filled with parasites. Even in the clean, burbling mountain brooks the vile parasites lurk. The backpackers put them there. They wipe themselves and they put the wadded paper with vile excrement in God's own clean melted snow. You drink the water and your insides are pierced by the vile parasites and you get DIARRHEA and you BELCH and you are SICK from drinking God's own clean wilderness burbling mountain waters. I am filled with loathing for them.

I will be clean.

Items needed:

Submachine gun (1)

  Uzi preferred. They are reliable.

Gun oil

  Must keep gun clean.

Ammunition (1200 rounds)

Dynamite

Blasting caps

Wire (800 feet)

Food

Coat

Clean socks

From my field journal:

8 August 1981
10:00 a.m.
Location: Four kilometers up Dagheeloyee Creek
from the Darwin townsite.

I sit on the upended roots of a massive spruce. Its needles are orange and brown, and most of them have fallen off. The trunk is half buried in gravel. Les says the tree was swept downstream during the flood of August, 1979. That's the flood that took out all the bridges. There are bridge timbers littered about, mixed in with the tree trunks.

My seat is near the edge of the creek. For most of the way between here and Darwin townsite the creek braids and wanders all over the bare gravel flood plain, which averages 100–150 meters wide. But here all the water flows in one channel. I look upstream to a sheer rock face nearly 100 meters high. The creek hits the base of the face and careens foaming around a bend toward me.

The face is made of dark grey shale. A massive dike of white rock (porphyry, it looks like) cuts zig-zag through it, looming over me.

The face is an obstacle. To continue up the valley from here, one must cross the stream. Les is off in the woods somewhere looking for a stick to lean on when we ford the creek. This is where we will put the first ferry-boat. First, we have to wade across with a rope. We will secure the ends to trees on both sides of the creek. The boat will be fastened to the rope with a pulley-wheel, so it can slide freely across the water but cannot be swept downstream.

Les says we can cross the creek today. We had to wait twelve days to make this trip, at first because the water was too high. After several weeks of hot, sunny weather the clouds came in again on August 1. The thermometer stuck at 10°C night and day for a week, until yesterday. It hardly rained, just a drizzle now and then. The glaciers cooled, melted less, and so the creek dropped. (average drop = 2.5 cm/day; largest drop 5 cm on 2 August 81. See table 16b.)

[table omitted.   —JBS]

By the fifth day of cooler weather, Les said the creek was low enough for us to move. I was ready, but he wouldn't go because he said it was raining. It was drizzling a little, but certainly nothing to keep a man back. But I had to wait.

Yesterday afternoon the sky cleared. The days have been getting shorter more rapidly, although I didn't notice it during the overcast period. So I was surprised last night when it got dark. I saw stars for the first time since I arrived in Alaska. I understand now why the big dipper and Polaris are symbols of the North—they fill half the sky. This morning I bounced pebbles off ice on the puddles in the road near Clearwater Brook, the first frost of the season. Once the blanket of clouds is gone, the heat of the ground dissipates so quickly.

Malachite and Chalcocite Ridges and Mt. Ezra Darwin had new snow, like a coat of thick, fresh, white paint covering everything from the 1500 meter level up. But it didn't last long. By breakfast I could feel the warmth of the sun on my face as I sat in front of the tent eating my granola. Les came by at 7:30 all ready to go. I was surprised, because I have never seen him begin work before noon around town. It took me awhile to get my tent, sleeping bag and other gear together. I hope that Les was not put off by the delay. He is underequipped. He is carrying only a small daypack, which cannot have room for sufficient warm and dry clothing, nor spare food for emergencies. I may have to take responsibility for him under difficult circumstances, should the weather change or we run into unexpected problems.

According to the local viewpoint, Les has considerable experience traveling in this valley. This is my motivation in accompanying him, enough to overcome my qualms about assisting in the morally dubious venture of constructing this ferry system in the park wilderness. I feel it is essential that I have the opportunity to observe the condition of the upper valley, particularly in view of the heinous plans of Eldorado Explorations Unlimited. Baseline data on the current status of the ecosystem, recreational potential and wilderness attributes might at least help enable the Park Service enforce a relatively rigorous mining plan of operations.

I feel I have extended myself considerably for Les already, both in view of the wait entailed by his squeamishness about the weather and the ethical considerations involved in the project. I hope I will not have to act further to ensure his health and safety up here, a real concern given his age, physical stature and equipment.

Les had strapped two halves of a canoe to the top of an ancient jeep with plywood doors. At first he could not get the jeep to go, but then he fiddled under the hood and it started.

We were able to drive four kilometers up the dirt road from town. Les says that Jasper Russell bulldozed this road on the old railroad grade in the early 1960's. Of course the railroad once went all the way up the valley to the mines.

Note: The Park Service should consider gating the Dagheeloyee Creek road at the edge of the townsite. This location at the cliff face is very spectacular and should be kept for non-motorized use.

This is as far as we can go with the vehicle. We have unloaded the two half-canoes, the rope and the other supplies. I am prepared to bring half a canoe and the materials for the other ferry up the rest of the way on my back. Les is quite dependent on me. Even so, his knowledge of the trail at certain key points can be of importance to my work, so perhaps the exchange between us is a fair one. I have not been able to get beyond this point on my earlier explorations on my own, because the creek has been too high to cross. Even at its present level, it looks dangerous to me. Les, however, assures me that he has a safe method of crossing.

9 p.m.

Location: Old log cabin approximately
20 km up Dagheeloyee Creek valley.

I am exhausted. I am sitting in Les's easy chair. This is his house. He is across the room at the stove cooking dinner.

10 p.m.

Ate fried Spam with rice. Going to bed. Will write up field notes tomorrow.

9 August 1981
10 a.m.

Les is practicing the trumpet. I am wearing the hearing protectors he uses with his chainsaw, big metal earmuffs of the type used by airline personnel around jet aircraft. As a result I find the decibel level in the cabin tolerable. Sitting at the table, I see the West Face of Eldorado Butte, which completely fills the window. It is so close and so high that I cannot see the top of it. The window frames limestone cliffs cut by steep gullies. Spruce trees perch here and there on the cliff: one on a protruding pinnacle, a cluster on the littlest ledge.

I turn my head. Out the south window I see an expansive view down the valley, Dagheeloyee Creek flowing amidst the dark green forest, between the mighty battlements of Chalcocite and Malachite Ridges, a procession of peaks in a double row, marching down towards the sun. Les's house is perched on a bluff above the creek, so the view to the South is unobstructed by the surrounding spruce, birch, alder and willow. I see the route we came yesterday: up from Darwin, twenty kilometers south of here and not visible around a bend.

We first forded the creek at what Les calls "2-Mile Crossing," where the great white dike of porphyritic rock intrudes zig-zagging across the dark shale. We emplaced the first ferry boat there on fixed ropes, secured to trees on each bank. Les showed me how the Athabascan Indians wade a dangerous, icy stream. Both of us grabbed onto a sturdy poplar staff he found in the woods, in essence making the two of us into one, a single creature with four legs. The resulting sure-footedness enabled us to cross on the water-tossed gravels and cobbles.

Once across I thought we were surely in the wilderness. I could see the old jeep on the other side. We were beyond the range of vehicle pollution and noise now. But no. Les walked into the bushes and pulled out a dirt bike, a motorcycle right here in the midst of an Alaska National Park. He cursed because he found the seat all torn up. A grizzly bear had eaten it, he said.

I thought that I was going to pack the remaining half canoe & accessories on my back. But somehow Les managed to strap it all on the back of that dirt bike. I give him credit that it is a relatively quiet motorcycle. He said he is careful to keep it tuned up and muffled. He putted off, leaving me in the stench of his internal combustion fumes. I continued alone up the trail (the old railroad grade) through deep forest. The valley floor here is broad, with well developed soil and large spruce. It has been some time since the glacier covered it. Suddenly the valley narrowed: This was the canyon, where Dagheeloyee Creek passes in a slot between the peaks of Mt. Chalcocite and Mt. Malachite. The canyon walls are sheer, a hundred meters high, so the only way past is through an old railroad tunnel cut in a rock buttress. Reaching the tunnel was quite a trick. The approaches are all eroded away by the creek, so I crossed to it on a narrow ledge of logs and brush built across the canyon face, held together by baling wire. Les says that is his snowmachine trail in winter.

On the other side of the tunnel I looked out over an expanse of gleaming white—Dagheeloyee Glacier, its broad surface fractured by crevasses, so different from the dirty brown of the Loohana Glacier at Darwin. Dagheeloyee Creek issued from under an impassable ice cliff. The glacier poured forth from the slopes of Dagheeloyee Peak, visible unobstructed by lesser

Les's Ferry Boat System

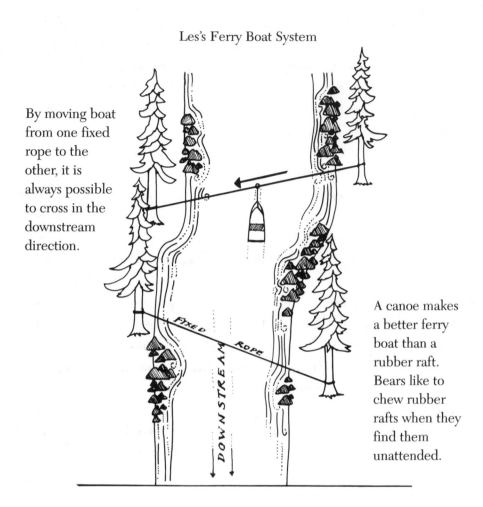

By moving boat
from one fixed
rope to the
other, it is
always possible
to cross in the
downstream
direction.

A canoe makes
a better ferry
boat than a
rubber raft.
Bears like to
chew rubber
rafts when they
find them
unattended.

FIXED ROPE

DOWNSTREAM

How to Make Two Boats if You Only Have One Canoe

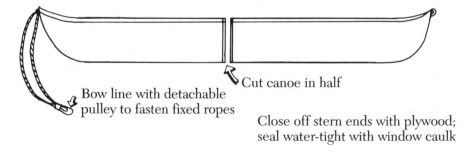

Cut canoe in half

Bow line with detachable
pulley to fasten fixed ropes

Close off stern ends with plywood;
seal water-tight with window caulk

ridges for the first time since leaving Darwin. I had to put on my sunglasses; the upper basin gleamed untainted white. The summit wore a plume of white volcanic steam.

There was Les below me, at the edge of the creek. He stood on the abrupt boundary of the forest: beyond, reaching to the naked ice, the ground was barren rock and mud. Perhaps the glacier had recently melted back from this point, and nothing had had time to grow. Les was amidst large spruce, which grew on both banks of the stream. I hurried down to help him. But somehow he had already crossed the creek by himself and affixed the ropes. I helped him ease the half-canoe into the water and attach it to the line with the pulley.

We crossed one at a time. He held the boat while I got in and crouched down. It is not a very secure feeling. When Les let go, the current slid the boat swiftly along the rope, which angled downstream. I got out on the other side, disconnected the pulley, and attached it again to the other rope Les had installed, which angled back the other way. The current shot the boat back to Les, who switched ropes again and came over himself.

The trail continued on the other side. Part of the log cribbing from Jasper Russell's washed away bridge remained in the bank. The scene was awesomely wild, with the enormous ice face before us and jagged ridges surrounding us. Darwin and the outside world seemed an infinite distance away. I was aghast when Les pulled another motorbike out of the willows. Its seat, too, was eaten by a bear.

Les zoomed on ahead, leaving me with instructions on how to get to his house. Once the noise of his infernal machine faded in the distance, I was left alone with the roar of the creek echoing in the ice-bound mountain basin. I must have paused an hour then, humbled in silence before the power of this place.

Then I went on. Dagheeloyee Glacier completely obstructs the valley, so the trail climbs the mountain slope, up and around the end of the great glacier. The glacier is a dam, blocking the creek and forming a large lake, four kilometers long and filling the valley floor. Hundreds of icebergs float in the lake, calved from the ice cliffs of the dam. Several times the basin reverberated with a crash and a roar, and I watched sections of glacier slump and tumble into the water, sending tidal waves smashing into the shore.

The trail is bulldozed into barren, loose gravel slopes above the lakeshore. I presume the slopes are barren because the lake level has been higher in recent times, covering them with water. The slopes are unstable, and in several places the track has already slid away in the few years since Jasper stopped maintaining the road.

Beyond the lake the trail reentered the spruce forest along the edge of the creek. But timberline was not far above the valley floor; alpine slopes were everywhere visible and the land had an open and lonely feeling. The creek itself was smaller, the volume downstream coming from the meltwaters of Dagheeloyee Glacier. Nine times the bulldozed track crossed the creek, where Jasper had had bridges, so frequently I found myself on the other side from his road. But always it was possible to continue along on the gravel near the creek, or Les had brushed a path through the woods, and I continued on up without having to get my feet wet.

How long I walked along this upper valley I do not know. The sharp, clean air brought such excitement that I neglected to check my watch. It seemed like just a moment and I was at West Fork Creek. I shinnied over the log bridge, which is just a tree trunk which has naturally fallen over the creek, spanning the banks four or five meters above the water. I guess it was Les who chopped the branches off with an axe.

By now the sun had set over Chalcocite Ridge and there was a chill in the air. I had been walking for many hours and had worked hard at the creek crossings. At each stage of the journey, I had felt myself emerging deeper and deeper into the wilderness, beyond anything in my experience. I had crossed the creek at the shale face, veined by the great white porphyry dike; penetrated the canyon through the tunnel, emerging into the vast and desolate glacier basin; crossed the stream again and traversed the basin; continued up, through the forest into the very heart of the mountains. And now, traversing this narrow and slippery log, surely I had left the world behind. Les had abandoned his second motorcycle back there in the bushes below

West Fork Creek; I had seen it. Up here it was just me alone in the wilderness, and Les up ahead, now in his cabin.

I walked another kilometer through the woods, then came around a slight bend. Before me was an elaborate series of beaver ponds. I counted seven distinct levels, separated by dams. Poplar trees lay criss-crossed, felled by beaver teeth. Even though I knew the mines had to be there, I was stunned: Beyond were buildings, a whole town of them, dominated by ore milling and processing facilities and cable-tramways stretching up the mountainside. The buildings were painted a uniform blue, with white trim, all faded. Trees grew up through the roofs of houses. Much of the town was half submerged, rotting, in the beaver ponds.

This was the old Syndicate mine site, with tunnel entrances far up the side of Eldorado Butte. No one lived here anymore. Not even a door creaked in the silence. I walked into the nearest building, the size of a factory, hollow, empty. My footsteps echoed. With light fading toward evening, it was dark inside. I crossed to the back door and looked out, surprising a beaver. With a pistol crack it slapped its tail in warning and dived, sending small waves lapping against the outside wall.

Beyond, another three kilometers through the woods, I found Les's house. It was getting dark, so I was pleased to find that he had arrived safely ahead of me.

Today he will rest and I will explore toward the head of the valley. His cabin is the uppermost habitation in this drainage, and I can expect to find true wilderness beyond. From here I can walk easily onto the lower slopes of Dagheeloyee Peak itself.

I cannot overemphasize the presence of Dagheeloyee Peak in this valley. Ever since we came through the tunnel at seven-mile it has loomed dominant, unescapable. Here at Les's we are so close to its icy cone that we must crane our necks to see the top. Occasionally the sun is suddenly obscured in the clear sky: it is the steam plume vented from the summit, blown across the valley, cutting off the light.

Table 16a (8 August 1981)
Human Artifacts Incompatible with Wilderness Values in Dagheeloyee
Creek Drainage, Dagheeloyee National Park & Preserve, Alaska

Location	Artifact
km 1-4	one lane jeep road with motorized vehicles
km 2	pickup truck half-buried in creek gravel
km 3	truck at roadside, wheels & engine missing
km 4	scattered bridge timbers & rusted metal parts, six 55-gallon oil barrels, pile of rotted plywood, fixed ropes & boat at creek crossing
km 4-18	one lane road bulldozed on railroad grade, washed away by creek at many locations; rails, ties, railroad spikes scattered along road edge
km 7	10-meter steel girder lying in bushes
km 8	sardine can
km 8.5	pile of plates, pots and serving utensils alongside road
km 10	log cabin with roof missing, bedsprings, 3 55-gallon oil barrels, scattered rusty cans
km 11	railroad tunnel through rock
km 11.2	bridge timbers & cribbing, fixed ropes & boat at creek crossing
km 14	small bulldozer
km 15	one room frame building, windows and door missing
km 15.5	dump truck in bushes, no engine, wheels or axles
km 17	log footbridge over West Fork creek
km 18	Syndicate mining operation: multiple buildings, trams, rusting heavy equipment, dumps, scattered metal junk
km 18-21	trail cut and brushed to cabin
km 21	one room log cabin, 2 snowmachines, shed, dilapidated outhouse, scattered sleds, miscellaneous equipment, 2 55-gallon oil barrels, fresh garbage and trash dump in bushes at bluff edge

From Mike's journal:

August 8, 1981

Jasper and I stayed up late talking last night. It was a clear and chilly night (it gets dark at night now), and we had a fire going in the battered barrel stove in the hardware store. We sat around it. Jasper had made an ample pot of beans for supper. We each had a beer, but only one, and we both felt especially mellow. The yellow flame from a single kerosene lamp did not fill the room, leaving shadows. Outside, the black sky was filled with stars.

Jasper rambled on. I couldn't make any sense from what he said. He spoke of contracts and negotiations, ore prices and alternative freighting modes, exploratory techniques. I think he spoke about his mother. He is very close with his friend Jimmy, the one who is blind now. They went exploring in the old mine tunnels, and he talked about that. I think. Anyway, he mentioned descending and crawling; he was in various chambers. Sometimes it was dark, sometimes not. He rambled on. There was no beginning or end to his story, just a perennial looking, looking for ore. Something frightened him very much. When his mind wandered to that fear, his eyes lighted with terror. Then it would recede, and he would go back to his cajoling and salesmanship, convincing me and himself about something, and recite more about those tunnels. He wanted me to go along with him, wherever he was going. He is very lonely. Mostly, I got the feeling he wanted to communicate something very important. It was one of those times when words aren't sufficient, but perhaps just being in each other's presence makes the difference, establishes the link between two people.

Finally we went upstairs to bed. Sleep came quickly for me, and opened into the most vivid dream. It was one of those dreams that when you wake up you are not sure if it really happened:

I am walking across a field of snow. In the fog: I can see nothing but white. I am lost, and I yell for help, but my voice is lost in the fog. My heart beats faster: I am afraid. I walk faster, feeling the beginnings of panic. Snow comes over the tops of my shoes. I am wearing city shoes, and my feet are getting cold. The fog is thick. I move my hands in swimming motions, find myself swimming through it, my feet off the ground. I see an entrance, distantly through the fog. I swim to it: perhaps it is clearer down there. It is a tunnel in the ground, a stone tunnel; the rocks around the entrance are plastered with snow. Warm air is coming out of the tunnel. I grasp hold of the rocks. My feet billow weightless above me in the warm tunnel wind. I pull myself into the tunnel. I have to get in there.

I am in the tunnel, falling, falling. Finally it is warm. The tunnel opens out, it is no longer narrow, I am in a vast space. At first it is black dark. Then below is a light. I fall slowly toward the light. Gradually, the sides of the chamber are illuminated from below, with long shadows. The chamber is narrowing as I approach the bottom. The walls are rough rock. Lizards with large eyes cling to the walls, watch me as I pass. The chamber is penetrated by an enormous scream. No, it is a roar. No, it is a growl. It comes from a side-chamber somewhere. No, it is my scream. I am trying to scream out in my sleep. It is a bear roaring, wandering in a side chamber.

The bear is wandering on the floor of the chamber below me. The bear is a piece of dirt, a fragment of brown bark, caught in my eye. An irritant, wipe it out with my fingertip. Now the entire floor of the enormous cavern is the surface of an eye. The light comes from the eye. I am falling into the eye. Troops of soldiers carrying spears march in streams over the white of the eye. No, the streams are streams of blood flowing in their arteries. The eye is now a seething mass of intertwined luminescent vessels, except for the still iris and clear lens in the middle. I am falling directly into the clear hole in the middle of the eye, passing right through the lens.

It is my eye. I am passing through my own eye.

There is a shock, I am jolted with flashes of red and green and black. Then I am floating, as if from a balloon, but there is no balloon, high over the surface of the land. It is a warm and verdant land. I must get down there. But I float. I am too buoyant and I sail upward even as I struggle swimming down. Finally there is a tree. I can reach the upper branches of a very tall tree and climb down.

The air is blue, a blue dome with a black hole in the center, the hole through which I fell. The sky is an enormous chamber. The ground is green, a lush disk stretching from horizon to horizon. The tree grows from near the center of the disk. It is not an evergreen tree—its branches are bare. Everything else is verdant, but this tree, the biggest tree, is bare. As I climb down it, I become aware of many lizards clinging to the side branches. They are watching me. They are like chameleons, camouflaged against the tree.

I look below me as I climb down the massive trunk, gnarled with thick bark. All around I see flowers and gentle brooks flowing from pure springs, meadows of grasses flush with the fullness of seed.

I see a thin man in white robes walking in the garden. He is Jesus. He looks up at me: His face is compassionate, tired, welcoming, worn, forlorn.

Directly below me at the base of the tree, at the exact center of this land, is a black space. No, it is an empty space. It is the blind spot in the back of my eye, on my retina. It is the spot I cannot see. I am drawn to that spot. I must get there, climb into it. I must not, must not go there. I do not have to go there. I do not have to go there. Jesus is in the garden. He is welcoming me. I can go to him, not into that place.

There is a lizard inside of me, in my chest. Because there is a lizard inside of me, I must climb into that hole. Good-by Jesus.

I am floating in outer space. The stars are distant in every direction. I see the moon floating out there. Or is it the earth. I am in darkness.

Eons pass.

In the center, in the center of outer space, there is a spot. There is an anomaly at that point. Is it a flaw in space? It is a house, a small house. Music comes from it. Light comes from it.

I go to the house. Inside, there is coffee on. I pour a cup and sit in an easy chair. The universe gyrates around us, a blackness of stars and suns and moons on all sides, even below the floor. Someone else is there with me. He understands.

Outside it is snowing. It is dark and it is snowing.

A wood stove is in the exact center of the room. The coffee pot sits on the center of the stove. A small lizard crawls out of the coffeepot. It grows rapidly into an immense dragon, coil upon coil of slithering scaled flesh, an expanse of green skin wings, an enormous mouth and bloodshot eyes, orange sulfurous fire belching between needle-sharp fangs. The entire universe is filled with the dragon.

Now it is Jesus who is there with me. He says, "Trust Me."

There is light inside Him. I strain to see into Jesus. What is inside of Jesus? There is something there. I must see. He embraces me. I yield to His embrace. He holds me tight to His chest. He is smothering me against his bosom. I am suffocating. Let me go, Jesus, I cannot breathe. I black out. In the center of the blackness, there is light. I crawl to the light. The light is the light at the end of a tunnel. I crawl through the tunnel; it is made of rock. I am getting cold as I reach the end of the tunnel. I haul myself out into the light: it is the blank white light of a foggy day. I am walking on snow, in the fog. Snow is coming in over the top of my shoes. My feet are getting cold. I am searching for help. I am beginning to panic.

I wake up in a cold sweat.

From Sara Charles's diary:

August 9, 1981

Dear Diary,

Lots happened today. It started out not so good. It ended up not so good, too. But Mrs. Henry helped out there in the middle.

After breakfast I saw Mike on the street in front of the lodge. We almost never see him in the morning, because he is busy then with his prayers and things. But there he was this morning, right out in front. He was walking down the street alone.

So I went out and said "Hi, How about some horseshoes, Mike?" It was a nice sunny day, and it has been *so* rainy around here. But he was Mr. Gloom himself. He had the hood up on his jacket. It made him look like a monk. I guess he is a monk. Mother says they wear cowling. Like the covering over the engine of an airplane. That's a cowling. I know that. Well, Mike never had his cowling on before, but he sure did today.

When he didn't want to play (he was so *negative* about it), I thought I'd done something wrong. At least at first I thought that way. So he sulked off one way. And I moped off the other. A fine pair we were.

At least I did the right thing. I went off right then to see Mrs. Henry. She's always good in crucial times like this. There she was, spread out over her gravel bar, just like she always is, just eating up that late summer sunshine. I guess we won't have many more warm days like this. Her yellow flowers have all changed. They're white now, all closed up and facing the ground. She says she's making seeds in them. That's a lot of work.

I asked Mrs. Henry to do something to cheer me up. Did I do something to make Mike mad at me? Fortunately, immediately she said it was not my fault. Mike was that way because he had gone on a trip, she said. But he came back this time. Maybe someday he won't come back, but this time he did. That did not make me too happy, because I like Mike. I always want him to come back.

He must not have liked the trip. Mrs. Henry said it was Very Disturbing to him. But that he would get over it. It was something he had to do, like eating everything on your plate at dinner. Once you ask for it and it's on your plate, you've got to eat it, even if it tastes different than you thought it would and it is yukky.

I don't know where he went. It must not have been too far. I saw him just yesterday, and no planes had come in or out, at least not until this afternoon, and that was afterwards.

Mrs. Henry knew about Mike's trip because an acquaintance of hers told her about it. A very large brown furry animal acquaintance. I guess she means a grizzly bear. Women are not supposed to say the name of the grizzly bear, or talk about them much. Their spirits are too powerful and dangerous. That's what Koyukon Indians like Mrs. Henry know. I guess now that she is dead she can talk with the bear, even though it is so powerful. I guess this bear saw Mike on his trip, so he told Mrs. Henry that he made it and came back OK. I hope Mike doesn't have to go on any more trips. Maybe he got scared because he saw a bear. Maybe he wasn't gloomy, just scared. He's new here, after all, so he is not used to seeing bears.

So I felt better after going to see Mrs. Henry. I always do. But as I said, the day ended up not so good, too. So now I'll write about that.

Well, I got back home to the lodge. I was just in time to help clean up from Mean Old Ed Butler's lunch. Yukko. And then flop-flop-flop-flop through the sky, here comes a helicopter. It landed right on the street. Ed Butler ran right outside. His big belly was flopping, flopping. It was his friends. They finally came in the helicopter. I thought yukko, here comes trouble.

August 12, 1981

Dear Sister,

We've been busy here the past few days. That prospecting crew finally came in. Counting Ed Butler, there are nine of them. Four are a work crew to set up their camp up the creek and open up the old tunnels. There are also a couple of old gentlemen, geologists or some sort of scientists, who will be here only a couple of days more, plus the helicopter mechanic and pilot.

Such a big crew is a lot of work for us, but we are getting into the rhythm of it. I looked over the books. Their business will make the difference for us this year. If they hadn't come, I don't think we could have kept the lodge going.

They gave us no notice at all—just showed up weeks after they were due. So the fresh groceries I had gotten special for them are all gone. We ate some, gave some away, and some just spoiled. And I'll have to get more. There is a fellow in town, George Johnston, who is driving into Fairbanks tomorrow for a load of insulation. He'll have extra room for me and groceries, so I'll be making a quick trip to the city.

Kitty and Sara will hold things down here. I have a lot of faith in Kitty. She's turning out just great, even if the kitchen is always draped with her panty hose, drip-drying. She seems to get some satisfaction out of her relationship with Ed Butler, although I can't understand it and I don't think it is good for her in the long run. But she's the one who has to deal with that. Sara on the other hand...I know things are not easy handling this crew of tough men, but I do wish she would get out of her funk and cooperate more. She's old enough now to be a big help when she wants too. I don't know. I keep thinking, well, its because she's lost her father, give the kid some time and extra love, she'll be OK. God knows, its hard enough on me, too, I miss him so much.

But she gets that dreamy look. And just when I need her around here, she goes wandering off. I see her down there by the river, staring into space, watching the flowers grow, those little yellow dryas flowers that grow down by the river. She'll sit there for hours. She comes back just fine and chipper, so I suppose she needs it. Or sometimes she'll be just sassy, and talk back to the guests. I'll give her credit, they usually deserve it, but we just can't do that running a lodge for the public.

Father Mike's been a big help for Sara this summer and has usually been able to put some spunk into her when she needs it most. But in the past couple of days, he's been in some sort of a funk, too. It's like there is a little rain cloud floating over his head. I don't know why, and it's not proper to probe. I guess he just has his ups and downs like the rest of us. But I'd really come to depend on him. He's the sort you trust right away and can really like a lot. Real gentleness and strength in him. Well, he came by for a while this afternoon and some of his good cheer was coming back, so maybe he's coming out of it, whatever it was. That'll be good for Sara, especially while I'm gone.

Les and Jot came down the creek day before yesterday. They got the ferry-boats in at the crossings. Les says it'll be easy now to go up and down the valley regardless of the water level. Les says he thinks Jot is making progress.

Jot was certainly in fine spirits when they arrived. Sara and I were up by two-mile, looking for orange delicious mushrooms for the spaghetti sauce—wanted *something* fresh in the dinner for the crew. So we met them as they came down. Jot had a calmness I hadn't seen in him before. That tension of his eased up a little. I felt good being with him, with the both of them, all glowing from the hard work and the job well done.

Unfortunately, it didn't last long. You could see him stiffen when he met the crew. He has not come to the lodge much since they arrived, but when he does, you can see the stress. He also becomes very official, formal like a lawyer. So far the crew has pretty much ignored him, except for Butler, who gets in his cutting remarks every now and then like usual.

As for me, well, I'm getting along with the crew all right, I guess. I think they are ignoring all of us. It's as if they weren't supposed to talk with us or something. The old scientists aren't that way. But I won't get to know them, I suppose, because they'll be gone by the time I get back. Another older man, I don't know what his job is, Perry Huntingford, talks a lot too. So maybe we'll get to know them better eventually.

Getting to know new people is why I like running the lodge. It would be easy to let it go now that Ted is gone. But if Sara and I are going to keep living here (and I know I want to), then we're going to need that diversity and human contact. Some of the people who come are really different and it takes a while to understand each other. But that's what life is all about, anyway.

I still get upset when I hear Ed Butler's bombast. Maybe you can see from this letter that I'm trying to show a little maturity and perspective. Settle down now Terri, I tell myself. Just because he's all wrought up doesn't mean you have to be. Give him an example to follow and maybe he'll settle down and show a little kindness, too. Anyway, we really don't have any choice, so we might as well give the mining people a chance. Maybe things will work out just fine, we just have to see...

———————————

From Mike's journal:

August 15, 1981

I feel like a novice again as I meditate on Mary on the day of the feast of her assumption into Heaven. Dear Mother, please help me find complete and perfect union with God. May I burn as one with your clean light, the light of the Father, sanctified by the perfect sacrifice of the Lamb of God, light of the world.

For thou art my lamp, O Lord, and my God lightens my darkness
(II Samuel 22:29)

May my meditations bring the union that will grant me peace, the only lasting peace amidst this world of pain and turmoil. May I gather myself up in the totality of simple dedication to the liturgy of the church, purified from obsessions and the delusions of grandeur.

May my prayer save me from the reign of greed and fear which supplants reason and faith. In thrall of our appetites and will we are divided within ourselves, ever restless, never at rest. This world is hypnotized by monsters, held in spell by the fires issuing from the mouth of Leviathan:

> His sneezings flash forth light, and his eyes are like the eyelids of the dawn. Out of his mouth go flaming torches; sparks of fire leap forth. Out of his nostrils comes forth smoke, as from a boiling pot and burning rushes. His breath kindles coals, and a flame comes forth from his mouth. In his neck abides strength, and terror dances before him.   (Job 41:9-13)

Let me turn my head from the unholy fires. Let me accept the promise of your crystal light, the free gift offered by the logic of faith.

I'm afraid that the past few days I've been a man obsessed. I think finally I am getting back my composure, some sense of inner calm. The regimen helps: Up with the sun at 5 a.m., a day of fasting and prayer, the long walks in the woods alone, early to bed. Cooking and straightening up around the place for Jasper, but little else. I feel like I'm getting into the life again, back into the rhythm. The sense of peace returns slowly: I remember the joys of solitude and feel a rededication of commitment to my vocation.

It is not so easy with the helicopter landing ten times a day right in the street out front. That Explorer mining crew has finally arrived. Burning with the unholy fires, they are. Well, maybe that isn't fair. But if I'm up at 5, the rest of the town isn't far behind me, awakened by that mechanical early bird lifting off to search for its worm.

After my walk, I have been stopping in at the lodge, around their dinner time. The crew clusters at its table pretty much by itself. I get a sense of an invisible wall around them then. When you get one of them alone, they are taciturn, as if they weren't supposed to talk. Maybe that's just the workers—the laborers and the pilot and the mechanic. I see some fear, or maybe it's just discomfort, in their faces.

Terri's off to Fairbanks for supplies. Kitty and Sara are doing a fine job of running the place, but it's not easy for them to put up with these characters. I've made a point of coming by every day and staying longer than I otherwise might. Les and I have been around pretty regularly in the evenings. Les's brother Tim has been staying away. For all his size and strength, he'd rather just avoid the unpleasant scene.

Jot's come by only once or twice. He must be terribly disrupted by the helicopter noise and the activity. And there is no getting away from it. But at the same time, there is a real strength in him that I have not seen before. It may have something to do with his trip up to Les's house. Or maybe it's some inner power he mobilizes when his precious wilderness is truly threatened.

There's a couple of fellows in the crew I have been able to make some contact with. The one I'm enjoying is Ludwig, a proper, somewhat Prussian gentleman, with a considerable amount of grey hair blowing in the breeze. He says he flew over directly from Hamburg for this venture. Electronics is his specialty. He's out with the helicopter every day, then in the evening he's bent over some sort of elaborate electrical mechanism that looks very delicate, adjusting this and that with precision instruments and various gauges. He likes smoked salmon. That's what he was looking forward to in Alaska. He's disappointed we don't have any in Darwin. He finds it very primitive here. But he is willing to put up with the discomfort in order to become rich. He believes these underdeveloped lands offer considerable opportunity for the enterprising to find wealth. His English is limited. He's quite aloof, but when I approached him in German he opened up some.

I'd like to have a chance to talk with Jack Rogers. He's the strong, silent type and therefore a bit unapproachable, with the rugged look of a man who has spent his life outdoors, lean and tough, short grey hair, clean-shaven. I couldn't guess his age. There's a touch of the old man in him—I can see it in a gesture or movement now and then. Perry says Jack is a geologist of quite some reputation, worked right here around Darwin making maps for the government.

Ahh, Perry. No problem striking up a conversation with Perry. In fact, it's hard talking to anyone else when Perry is around. Clinical psychologist he is, from Los Angeles he comes. Fascinating to study the psyches of the inhabitants of this place, is it not, he says. You a missionary, he asks, having heard that I am a priest. He is filled with himself: important job he has, whatever it is, I can't figure it out. Big mine coming here, lots of jobs for the inhabitants. Explorations Unlimited is a Corporation that Cares. Minerals for the world. World needs minerals, using them all up in the engine of progress. That's Darwin's destiny, minerals for the world. Save us from the shortages. America first, example to all the peoples. Darwin, city of destiny.

Jasper gets himself shaved and cleaned up and goes over to converse with the miners, and is quite impressive if a bit incoherent. You can see how he is a good salesman. But the crew really doesn't pay much attention. That hurts, and he's been drinking more again, over at the beer and wine bar in the lodge.

Ed's the only one he gets any attention from. Ed is still a little ticked off about Jasper's inability to come through with his promise of trucking and cat work.

It's interesting that Ed is sort of "one of us" now. He's been around longer, and with nothing to do all that time except interact with people (in his own way, admittedly). So in a sense the rest of the crew is outsiders and he's one of the family. A feuding family, but a family none the less. Maybe that's why he is defensive now talking with us? Feeling a role conflict?

As for me, the important thing is to stick by my discipline. I guess if I really have the vocation, I can do it anywhere and under any circumstances. With all this ruckus going on, I'm not sure this is the place for the hermitage, though....

From Sara Charles's diary:

August 15, 1981

Dear Diary,

Well, Mother's been gone since day before yesterday and she should come back. I do not like this crew in our lodge. Kitty and I are taking care of them OK. Yes sir, would you like your eggs scrambled or fried sir. Curtsey and be polite, young lady, says Kitty. Stick our tongues out at them I say to Kitty.

Well, why would I suggest such a thing? Here is why:

#1: They land the helicopter chop chop flop flop right in front of the lodge, right in the street, wake up the whole town & disturb the peace of all the people day and night. Right there at the volleyball court and horseshoes and the swing. A young innocent child like myself might be playing out there and be killed. That is no joke.

Mother asked them not to, but then she left. And so they still do it. Kitty asked them not to, also. But she is too nice. She is a push-over. Everybody else lands helicopters up at the airstrip or out by the river.

#2: M.O.E.B. and Dr. Schultz and Dr. Huntingford fly all the way back from Eldorado Butte every day for lunch. This is ridiculous. We can make them box lunches, just like we do for the men who really do the work. All they do is fly back and forth. Flop chop chop flop they are landing and taking off. All through the middle of the day when I should be playing or seeing Mrs. Henry. Instead of serving them.

#3: They want to wreck everything. But they don't care what happens to us. In fact, they don't think we are really people.

Dr. Perry W. Huntingford says they care. He talks a lot. He is a clinical psychologist who is here to help us with our adjustments. We will be making adjustments when they start their mine. So he will talk to us and make us feel better. Well, he is the one who needs a psychologist. I am doing just fine, thank you. Even though my father died and my mother is in Fairbanks and Kitty burned the beans.

#4: They aren't nice to each other. Nick, Dave and Joe are the workers. They are gone all day and come back all tired and sweaty. Ed Butler and Dr. Huntingford complain, complain all the time about how the work goes too slow. They tell the workers its all their fault. Actually, if M.O.E.B. and Dr. Huntingford would do some work it would get done faster. Actually, it wouldn't.

#5: They go around acting as if they had lots of important secrets. Hush hush this. Hush hush that. That is not nice if you are living with other people. And they are living with us, although they don't seem to know it.

Let me tell you a secret. Well, I know their secrets. They don't think a kid has ears. If they paid more attention they'd know I do. But they don't. So I hear everything.

First of all, Dr. Perry W. Huntingford isn't a clinical psychologist at all. Well, in a way he is and in a way he isn't. He never actually studied to be one. Jot says he bought his diploma from a mill in California. I didn't know mills made college degrees. I thought they did stuff with ore. And then there's mills that cut lumber out of trees. Sam Ross has one.

Dr. Perry W. Huntingford's real job is to be boss of the workers. Well, actually he and M.O.E.B. don't agree about that. Well, they agree that Dr. Perry W. Huntingford is the foreman. But M.O.E.B. says that because he is manager he is boss of both the foreman and the workers. Dr. Perry W. Huntingford says that M.O.E.B. is boss of the operation but not of the foreman or the workers. It is very complicated. I guess only the Big Boss, Carl Manley, knows for sure how it goes. He is in Seattle.

The Big Secret is Dr. Ludwig Schultz's machine. It can see into the middle of things. That is what he is doing all day up in the helicopter. First the helicopter takes the workers up to Eldorado Butte to do their work of opening up the old tunnels. The entrances are all full of ice. You can't get in. Actually, you can. If you know where. But I'm not telling. Then the helicopter comes back and picks up Dr. Schultz and his machine. It is his gravitometric radar instrumentation. They fly around and around and around all day. He points his machine at the mountain. They say that if there is anything valuable in the mountain the gravitometric radar instrumentation will find it. All it has found so far is lots of numbers. Dr. Schultz puts them in his book. That is what he writes instead of a diary. It sounds like a boring thing to do.

He will have to take his numbers back with him to Germany and do stuff with them. Then he will let them know what is in the mountain.

I don't know why this is such a big secret. Anybody can see that is what they are doing.

I also know why the workers and the pilot and the mechanic don't talk to us. Dr. Perry W. Huntingford told them not to fraternize with the locals. It gives away secrets and upsets people, he says. Dr. Perry W. Huntingford tells M.O.E.B. he shouldn't fraternize either. I guess that means he shouldn't sleep with Kitty. M.O.E.B. says Dr. Perry W. Huntingford is the one who needs to shut up. He's the one who is always in the bar with Les and Jasper and Kitty and Mike. Dr. Perry W. Huntingford tells M.O.E.B. he needs to talk to us. He says he is the company's intelligence line into the local community, whatever that is.

I'd like to talk to Mrs. Henry or at least Mike about all this. It's been so busy around here I haven't had time. Mike is hardly around at all anyway. He comes by for awhile in the evening. It feels so *comfortable* to see him. I guess he's feeling better.

From Mike's journal:

August 16, 1981

Jot and I spent the evening with Jack Rogers. He was sitting alone at a table in the back of the bar in the lodge, nursing a glass of red wine after dinner. The rest of the Explorers were bunched together under the light up front, playing pool. I walked back, pulled out the chair next to him, and sat down.

Jack worked this area for the United States Geological Survey, almost every summer through the fifties and sixties. He made the geological maps. He showed them to Jot and me later—multi-hued patterns in reds, oranges, browns, blues, yellows, showing the location of rock types.

Printed alongside the maps themselves are cross sections of the mountains, showing how the rock layers extend down deep into the earth. To make these cross sections, he had to infer what was underneath from what he saw on the surface, because no person can see under the ground like that.

Nineteen years he walked this land inch by inch, with rock hammer and notebook, hiking, climbing, moving about by helicopter over jagged terrain searching for clues, painstakingly assembling the evidence, making the patterns on his map.

Jack sits, moves, speaks from a posture of ironic distance from the world. It is as if something he sees or knows keeps him separate. Maybe I'm making too much of it. Could be he is just shy. Maybe that's why he chose this line of work, so far afield in the wilds. Big strong men often cover up their social ungrace with masculine aloofness. Does he feel unease in companionship? He is contemptuous, certainly, of the likes of the Explorers, with their frantic posturing, arguing, and incessant busyness.

He calls them "turkeys." Why did he come? Couldn't turn down the money, he said. They bought his name, something to show the investors. Gives him a chance to be here again in these hills. He'll only be here a few days more. Then the helicopter will take him and Schultz out to Bettles.

Schultz is a charlatan, he says. His way is too easy, a fraud. After a while, he and I tired of the noise and bustle of the bar, so we went out into the evening for a walk. The sun had set, and there was a chill in the air. We met Jot, who was interested in talking about geology. So we walked over to the hardware store. We sat in the side room, which had been the proprietor's living quarters back when it was really a hardware store. As it got dark, we lit the kerosene lamp and spread Jack's maps out on the old wooden table.

Now he spoke, quietly, commanding attention. Even though I couldn't understand all the words, I appreciated their poetry, even wrote down some of what he said. He talked of Paleozoic volcanic island arcs, of fossil crinoids and brachiopods, of strikes and dips and overturned beds. "Fusulinids of Permian age in these limestones differ totally from the Tethyan forms of the same age in adjacent terranes, indicating an origin outside the Tethyan realm, presumably to the east in the archaic Panthalassa Ocean, the predecessor of the Pacific."

His hands played for us on the multi-colored maps, pausing on Jurassic lavas and Cretaceous shales. The maps make sense, he said, if you think of continents drifting over the surface of the earth. Not long ago, he said, three hundred million years, the fragment of the earth's crust that is now the Dagheeloyees was atolls and mountainous islands, rising out of a far off shallow tropical sea. It drifted east and north, eventually meeting the west coast of America, sliding up alongside the continent, leaving pieces of itself adhering as it went. Two hundred million years ago, the remainder docked against the coast of Alaska. Dinosaurs walked here then. The impact of docking pushed up mountains far inland, ranges as grand as the Dagheeloyees are today. These ranges are now totally eroded away. All we know of them is the remaining gravel, sand and clay, washed to sea by rivers. And even this shallow sea is now gone, and the gravel, sand and clay of the seabed compressed to rock, and the rock again uplifted by earth's forces into new mountains, and the mountains again cut by water, and now by ice, exposing the seabed to our eyes and our geologist's hammer, in cliffs rising five thousand feet and more above our human heads.

All he can see of the rocks is what is exposed on the surface, Jack said. The puzzle is not complete. Question marks are printed on his maps. There was enough time, he said, since the docking, for more than one mountain range to uplift, erode to nothing, and be replaced by another. Perhaps the missing portions of the rock sequence would tell of unknown mountains come and gone. Evidence for them, if it still exists, is in the deeply buried strata, to which we have no access.

Volcanic Dagheeloyee Peak and the surrounding icefields are new, he said. Volcanos don't last; they are made of soft rock and erode quickly.

The first glaciers formed here only a few million years ago, not all that long before the first hominoid species dropped out of the trees and walked the plains in Africa. Many times the whole land here was covered with ice, many times the ice melted back, only to return again. The sequences of the ice, he explained, are measured in tens of thousands of years, instead of millions. The glaciers are ephemeral phenomena.

People have been around to witness the most recent one or two comings and goings of the ice. Jack didn't mention that. I don't think it was of consequence to him. Jot brought it up.

We talked past midnight. I didn't understand much of it. Jot took notes, and Jack left him with a set of maps and several books. Jasper came in and sat by the stove for awhile, but said nothing.

August 17, 1981

Too much going on here in Darwin, City of Destiny. If this keeps up, I'm not going to choose to stay. That's a hard thing to say, given the feelings I've developed for the people who live here and for the special life I've enjoyed these past weeks. But if my task is to leave the world to dwell in God's serene glory, and thereby to fulfill it and help give it birth onto this earth, then Darwin isn't the right place.

On the other hand, these people, my friends, need my help now. I'm finding myself sucked into a community in need. Again. It was that way in

Berkeley in the 1960's. Hopefully, I've matured some since then. But I didn't come here for that. Of course, it is necessary and right that people come together and take action in the world, to confront difficulties and evil. But if everybody plunges into the action, nobody has perspective. Action becomes merely confrontation. The good guys inevitably adopt the means and mores of the bad guys. That's the problem. There always gets to be good guys and bad guys, polarization—conflict. That's what's happening here now. And keeping away from the fray, maintaining inner peace, maintaining perspective—that's the way for Christ to be born into the world. That's the job for the monk, the hermit. So the local situation is asking me to yield my hermitage in exchange for participation, for action. But the larger situation calls for a vocation of eremetic discipline. What's going on here just reinforces that conclusion. What's a guy to do?

Today has been difficult for everybody. At dawn (about 5 a.m. now) the helicopter started carrying things up the creek to the mines. The men attached big loads by ropes, so they hung slung under the aircraft. They carried fuel barrels, parts of buildings, various motors, I don't know what all, heavy things, across the river from the road, into town, out of town. They landed right out in the street and flew directly over the houses. By 6 a.m. almost everybody in town was out in the street very upset. Apparently, it is simply not safe to fly with these loads over people. From what folks said, if the helicopter has any kind of difficulty, the pilot first thing hits a switch, which releases the ropes and drops the load—onto a house or whatever. It didn't look safe to me, either, let alone the noise, and the danger of running those helicopter blades right on the street.

Ed Butler was up the creek, and Perry Huntingford was in charge down here. Perry found himself confronted with a small but angry group of townspeople. He talked in abstractions about free enterprise and corporate rights, but that was a screen which held people off while his crew kept on working, sending loads into the air. His tone was unbearably patronizing.

I met another Darwin person at the lodge last night. Sam Ross lives in a log cabin out a little way into the forest but has been gone all summer, out flying fish he said. Down on the southwest coast of Alaska, the fishermen stretch their nets out into the water from the beaches. Sam has a plane and has spent the past couple of months flying off those beaches with loads of fresh fish, taking them to the processing plant. I could see he had just washed his hair and his clothes, but he still smelled vaguely of dead fish. He packed a pistol in a shoulder holster. I liked his tee-shirt. On the front it read, "The End of the World is Near." And on the back it said, "Check Your Bible for Schedule of Events." He has a big brass belt buckle with an eagle in raised relief, surrounded by the words, "Guns, Guts & God Made America Great." He's a tough little guy, not more than 5′ 7″, obviously in great physical shape, with just a touch of grey in one corner of his beard. His eyes are clear and direct. He doesn't take any guff.

He was absolutely livid this morning, finding his peaceful town taken over by these Explorers. There's a hint of a Scottish accent in his voice anyway, but more than a hint when he gets mad. He lashed out at Huntingford. It would have come to blows if Huntingford had responded directly. But Huntingford turned saccharine sweet (with acid underneath) with talk of the need to face changes in the community maturely, the responsibility of locals to put up with some necessary inconvenience, while anticipating joyfully the many economic benefits, and the appropriateness of making the proper adjustments. Huntingford's big, soft mind absorbed Sam's verbal blows. It was like kicking a sticky marshmallow. Sam was infuriated. Meanwhile, the helicopter kept shuttling loads.

The others didn't say much. They are not comfortable with confrontation. It is not their way. The standard here is to allow everybody a maximum of individual freedom, not to impose your ideas on anyone else. The result is an indirectness, an ethic which says it is improper to probe or to push someone else to do (or not do) something. Kitty was disheveled, speech scrambled. Finally, Les came forward and directly asked Huntingford to move the landing spot to the airstrip and to fly around town, instead of overhead. Huntingford directly refused. At this point the meeting broke up, with people still holding their anger. The helicopter continued all day.

Les went around town and called together a meeting of everybody at the lodge after dinner. He told me he wanted all the people—all the Explorers and all the townsfolk—to have a chance to sit down together and work out some resolution. Only Huntingford came for the Explorers. He claimed that the others could not come, because they were working seven days a week and in the evening needed their rest. He said they could not move helicopter operations to the airstrip because of the added inconvenience and expense. Huntingford dominated this gathering; people here are not used to meetings. With false graciousness he discussed the availability of psychological and career counseling sessions to assist community members with life transitions.

Sam finally spoke out. He said that was bullshit and he could shove it. Then Sam left. It looked like things were breaking up. Butler strode into the room, sweaty and bellicose. He pointed at Les and said he had heard that Les threatened to sabotage the helicopter. He said how easy it would be to accidentally drop a fuel barrel through the roof of Les's house up the creek. Then he ordered Huntington to place a 24-hour armed guard at the helicopter in the street in front of the lodge. And he walked out. Kitty followed him, very upset. Tim and Les had to physically restrain her until she calmed down. That was the end of the meeting.

I don't know where Butler got the idea that Les made threats. He wouldn't have. He got the rumor wrong from somewhere. Les came out of the meeting dismayed.

As for me, I didn't think it was my role as an outsider, a visitor, to say much. Mostly I listened and tried by my presence to be supportive of my friends and of the process of accommodation and working out of conflict. I hope it was a help.

Jot wasn't at the meeting. He has been staying away and keeping his cool. But later in the evening he encountered Butler on the street down by the hardware store. I was out for a walk, too, and ran into them talking. It was actually quite a rational discussion. Basically, Jot said the Explorers had no moral right to disrupt Dagheeloyee Creek with a road, buildings and a mine. Ed answered, vehemently but not without logic, that he just wanted to reopen a mining operation that began sixty-two years ago. If the valley had gone back to Jot's precious wilderness after the first round of mining, it would go back again after the Explorers were through. Meanwhile a guy could make an honest buck getting out the copper, which the country needed. And he was sick and tired of having to fight a bunch of escapists, bureaucrats and wimpy do-gooders on top of all the hard work of mining. Jot replied that the world was different now than it was in the 20's and 30's when the syndicate was operating here. There just isn't much wilderness left anymore, he said, so what there is has a relatively higher value compared to the minerals at present.

My sympathy was with Jot. But I have to admit he did not overwhelmingly convince me in the face of Ed's argument. On the face of it, in fact, I think Ed had the stronger case. Somehow, though, something was missing, something was hollow, in what Jot said. In what they both said. From my perspective, it's not just a question of roads and mines. There's no road nor mine yet. But the Explorers have already disrupted and changed this place. So it's a question of attitude, too. Must a miner be as belligerent and vain as these Explorers have been? Could they have come in here with such ambitious plans, making such a speculative gamble, without being money-hungry and aggressive? Could they be humble and respectful, and still succeed? If so, how would I and the community here feel about them? How would Jot feel?

Or is intending to rip the earth of its minerals, the intent in itself, an act of arrogance, so that the Explorers must carry the attitudes they do? Are miners in every culture arrogant? Maybe in ours, where miners have to be capitalist adventurers, it's worse. I don't know.

I don't think Jot was able to explain why he feels so strongly against the mining. The feeling runs so deep in him. It has to be more than an issue of aesthetics, recreation or ecological science, of roads and millsites. Whatever it is, it is affecting all of us. We are all wrought up about it.

From Sara's diary:

August 18, 1981

Dear Diary,

Mother is due back in a couple of days and I wish she'd hurry. It is no fun around here. Everybody is mad at the Explorers but we have to keep serving them breakfast, lunch and dinner. Make the beds, clean up after their dirty selves, scrub out the shower. Yukky, Yukky, Yukky I say.

They had a big meeting here last night. Everybody was supposed to be there. Les wanted everybody to talk. He thought it would make things better. Well, all us Darwin people came. Nick and Dave and Joe (the workers) and John the pilot and Chuck who fixes the helicopter and even old Dr. Schultz wanted to come. But old M.O.E.B. and Dr. Perry W. Huntingford said no, they couldn't. They had to stay in their rooms or go for a walk or something. I'm getting bored writing "Dr. Perry W. Huntingford" over and over. They call him a shrink, because he is a psychologist. (As you know, that is not strictly true. But that is what he says he is.) So from now on, I'll call him Dr. Shrink, but you'll know who I mean. Just like you know M.O.E.B. is Mean Old Ed Butler.

Well, then M.O.E.B. and Dr. Shrink started to yell at each other. This is before the meeting starts. They are up in M.O.E.B.'s room, which is right next to mine, incidentally. Yell, yell, yell. Who is the boss, they wondered. Who will speak at the meeting, they asked. Who is going up to the mines tomorrow and who gets to stay here and sit on his behind? Yell, yell, yell. Finally, M.O.E.B. said to Dr. Shrink, "You are the shrink, you handle these local yokels." And off he struts out the building. Strut, strut, strut. At the meeting Dr. Shrink did his normal thing, which is to pretend that he is much better than all the rest of us, which, like it always does, gets everybody pretty mad. Then, like he usually does, he said we needed psychological counseling. He said he would help us. This, of course, got everybody even madder. Hurray that Sam is back. He told Dr. Shrink that he could take that bullshit and shove it. Give it to him Sam!

Then M.O.E.B. strutted in. TaTaa! Things were so exciting then that nobody could stand it. M.O.E.B. was pink from head to foot. Perspiration was dripping off his ears. His hair was standing on end. The end of his nose was bopping up and down. Boy did he get mad at Les! He said that Les was going to damage their precious helicopter. Les, of course, would never do that. However, M.O.E.B. should know (which he does not) that he shouldn't say such things in front of wide-eyed children, like me. It can put ideas into their heads. M.O.E.B. told Nick and Dave and Joe they had to take turns standing around the helicopter all the time. They are guarding it with M.O.E.B.'s 30-06 rifle. I like Nick and Dave and Joe. They like me, too. Today I went out and helped them guard the helicopter. It was fun for all.

Anyway, then back at the meeting M.O.E.B. strutted out. Strut, strut, strut. This was too much for Kitty. Finally, she could not like him anymore. Hurray for Kitty! Smash, crash, she gave him a fist into his tummy. Smash, crash, she whammoed her purse onto his head. Yippy! Unfortunately, Les and Tim grabbed her from behind. They made her stop.

Today also I went out to see Mrs. Henry. Let the Explorers make their own beds today, I thought. I have better things to do. Mrs. Henry was finishing up her job of making seeds. It was cold and blowy down there by the river. Mrs. Henry says the wind doesn't bother her much. That is because she grows so close to the ground. Except for her flower stalks, she is not more than two inches tall. That is a good height if you are living on a gravel bar.

She said she could feel the unhappiness in town all the way out where she lives. She said people aren't getting along with each other because they are being disrespectful. She said the Explorers dynamited a beaver dam up the creek. They wanted to dry up the area around a building so they blew up the dam. They didn't even explain to the beavers first. Beavers are powerful animals. They are not as powerful as weasels and foxes and those kinds, but it is pretty dangerous to mess around with them. Mrs. Henry says there is lots of that sort of thing going on around here now, lots of disrespect. She can feel it in the ground. Everything is connected down there, you know. Mrs. Henry can feel it in her roots. Did you know her roots go down eight feet? They go way down there in between the rocks. If they keep up this way, the Explorers could get us all in mighty big trouble.

Well, I'm mad at the Explorers, so I think it's all their fault. I told Mrs. Henry so. But she says it's not just them. There's other stuff going on, people doing things they shouldn't that makes things not fit together right.

From Jot Shechter's journal:

August 19, 1981

...We had an earth tremor early this morning. It lasted several seconds and was sufficient to wake me up....

From Mike's journal:

August 20, 1981

I was out of bed at 2:30 this morning, confronting a night still dark and silent. Perhaps my rising was due to my stress at the town's tension. Or perhaps I am finding my discipline of prayer once again, returning successfully on my own to the rhythms practiced over the years with my brothers in the monastery, the waking before dawn to join the antiphonal chant of psalms in choir. I found myself lost in the primordial darkness of the night, a solitary mind awake in the dark, looking for a light, not totally reconciled to leaving the repose of sleep.

Repose of sleep? No, that is not right. Better to say I woke to seek the repose of the light, the simple, hard-edged forms revealed to the wakeful

by day. For my nights now are full of monsters, inhabiting vast spaces. I
dreamt last night of a campfire, a heart of flame lighting a circle in the
darkness, spitting sparks that rose into the night, winking out far above
in the blackness. Men squatted around the fire, big men, hairy men, clad
in skins, carrying clubs. An icy wind blew at their backs. They chanted
psalms, antiphonally:

> Why dost thou stand afar off, O Lord?
> Why dost thou hide thyself in times of trouble?

>> In arrogance the wicked hotly pursue the poor;
>> let them be caught in the schemes
>> which they have devised.

> For the wicked boasts of the desires of his heart,
> and the man greedy for gain curses
> and renounces the Lord.

>> In the pride of his countenance the wicked
>> does not seek him;
>> all his thoughts are, "There is no God."

> The heavens are telling the glory of God;
> and the firmament proclaims his handiwork.

>> Day to day pours forth speech,
>> and night to night declares knowledge.

> There is no speech, nor are there words;
> their voice is not heard;

>> yet their voice goes out through all the earth,
>> and their words to the end of the world.

My God, my God, why hast thou forsaken me?

> Why art thou so far from helping me, from the
> words of my groaning?

Oh my God, I cry by day, but thou dost not answer;
and by night, but find no rest.

Lord, thou hast been our dwelling place
in all generations.

> Before the mountains were brought forth,
> or ever thou hadst formed the earth and the world,
> from everlasting to everlasting thou art God.

The fire was built on a flat rock surface; it was out by the glacier. I could feel the depth of the rock below the men's calloused feet. There were layers and layers of it, as Jack Rogers had described. Buried down there, enclosed in the rock far below, were dinosaur bones, massive toothed jaws and empty eye sockets. The fire light did not penetrate down there, but I could see them nonetheless. The men stomped and shuffled and swayed as they sang. The cold wind blew out of the darkness.

When I woke I lit a lamp. A light appeared, and in the light an ikon, and I began to chant my psalms. There was now in the large darkness a small room, upstairs here in the old hardware store, a small room of radiance with psalms in it. The psalms grew effortlessly in this light, like vines in the springtime. Could I feel the mercy of God? What the Hebrews call *Chesed*, the great mercy, *Magna misericordia*. Out of the formlessness of the night and the silence a word: Mercy. Purify me, the psalms said, wash me of iniquity. But still I am ill at ease.

Soon the sky lightened over the mountains. Day came to Darwin. The spell was broken; the voices of working men came from the early morning street. I heard the whine of the helicopter starting up, then it stopped suddenly.

I looked out my window: great confusion down by the lodge, the Explorers all gathered and milling around by the helicopter. I went down to find out what was happening, sat on the fender of a wheeless truck over across the way from them. They were all involved in themselves and paid no attention to me.

Ed was pacing back and forth heavily, hands behind his back, paunch forward, sweating and fretting. Perry, John the pilot and Chuck the helicopter mechanic were all leaning into the front doors of the chopper, from which they issued curses and requests for various tools. Apparently, something was wrong in there.

Chuck came out, took Perry firmly by the arm, and pulled him away from the machine. He said that unless Perry got out of the way they would never get anything done. Perry then let loose a stream of pompous invective that just about blew the poor guy off his feet. At that point, Ed strode over and started yelling at the both of them, and at John, too, for good measure. Unless they got that thing fixed, and now, he said, the schedule will be missed, it will be their fault, and there will be hell to pay.

Chuck and John were flabbergasted. They don't even work directly for the Explorers. They come with the helicopter, which the Explorers have leased from some company in Fairbanks.

Gradually I picked up what had happened. As John had started up the engine this morning, the vibrations shook loose the whole instrument panel, which fell off into his lap. All the nuts were missing off the bolts that hold it on.

Ed blamed Perry, who he had made responsible for maintaining the guard on the helicopter. Perry chewed out the workmen, who swore up and down they hadn't left guard duty for a minute, nobody could have gotten to it. Then Perry chewed out the workmen more, until they'd had enough and told him he could take a pick and shovel and dig his own holes, because they were finished working for the Explorers forever. At that Ed blew up at Perry, accusing him of mishandling the workers, the helicopter, the townspeople, everything. Then he told the workers they had to finish the job or no pay, not even for the (considerable) work they'd already done.

This must have gone on for half an hour, maybe forty-five minutes. Meanwhile, Dr. Schultz and Jack Rogers went back into the lodge for another cup of coffee. And Chuck wandered off down the street. A few minutes later he came back with Les, and the two of them poked around in the front of the helicopter. I don't know how they could think with the cacophony going on around them, but at least nobody was getting in their way now. Les left again and came back with a handful of nuts. They worked awhile longer.

Then Les stood back and Chuck started up the helicopter with a whine that became a roar as he put power to the jet engine. That got people's attention. At that point I don't think anything else would have.

John took over in the pilot's seat. With all the helicopter noise, there wasn't much anybody could do but either proceed with the day's work or leave the premises. They certainly couldn't keep arguing, at least not here. I could see that things were resolving themselves, at least for the moment, and, besides, it was too loud for me, so I picked myself up and left.

I talked to Les later. He said that the nuts he had would do for the moment, but Chuck wanted to replace them with certified aircraft parts as soon as possible. The helicopter is scheduled to take Dr. Schultz and Jack out to Bettles tomorrow anyway. They'll leave early and go all the way into Fairbanks, instead, and pick up some certified nuts.

That's just what we need. More certified nuts here in Darwin.

Les said that Chuck and John are pretty ticked off, not only by what happened to the helicopter, but by the way Ed and Perry acted this morning. They went back to work today, but if this sort of thing happens again, he's not sure what they will do.

August 21, 1981

Terri came back today. She and George Johnston arrived at the end of the road around noon. They had a pickup truck filled to overflowing with her groceries and George's insulation. The truck had so much on it, I don't know how it moved.

Les and Tim and I went over to help with the tramming. What a pleasure tramming is! We loaded the tram cart with bags and bundles, then with rhythmic teamwork hauled on the ropes to pull the cart across the cable, over the raging icy river. It is such simple, so obviously productive work, free from ambiguity, necessarily shared. I feel sore in the shoulders tonight. I thought I was in good shape from chopping firewood at the hardware store, but I guess I'm really not.

Terri's husband Ted died last year right where we were working at the trams. He wasn't attentive, and a tram cart hit him full force, knocking him off the loading platform down headfirst ten feet to the rocks below. Since then, Les has put a railing around the platform. Still, it is amazing to me that Terri and the rest of the community can work the trams now with joy, attentive to be sure, but free from fear.

Les pumped up the two flat tires on the truck at the lodge and drove it down to the bank of the river on the Darwin side, so we could haul the freight from the trams into town. Les says it is mostly a Model A Ford. They call it Rigor Mortis; Terri painted its name with graceful calligraphy on the side of the hood. Terri's husband had put it together out of parts from several relics he found rusting around town. It's a good work vehicle, Les says, the most reliable vehicle in Darwin. It easily took all the freight, with a couple of us riding on top, all in one load.

Les says the tires are a little worn. It's hard to get good tires for a Model A these days, apparently. Les says he can make most of the replacement parts for the truck in his shop right here in Darwin, if necessary, but not the tires, of course. He had to pump one up again after we had loaded and were ready to drive the quarter mile into town. Later in the afternoon he replaced that tire with another one from a supply of a couple of dozen he has stashed in the woods behind the shed he uses as a shop. They all date from the 1920's. The new one didn't look any better than the old one to me. But who am I to say.

We dropped George and his insulation off at his place and went on to the lodge. Terri was tired, but in good spirits and happy to be back home. With the helicopter out for the day and the rest of the crew off working up the creek, it was quiet and peaceful in town. We unloaded the truck and went in for coffee and lunch.

Kitty brought out some special fresh pastries, just out of the oven. We were all feeling exuberant from the good, hard work. As we sat with full bellies, Kitty and Sara laid out the sad story of the Explorers and what had transpired since Terri's departure. It was sombering. But I could feel us all getting strength from Terri. She certainly is a strong lady. I think we all needed a fresh perspective from someone who had been outside this closed, little group of people.

After lunch, we all went about our business. Later, around dinnertime, I walked past the lodge just as the helicopter returned, back from Fairbanks and bringing the last of the crew down from the day's work up the creek. Terri met Butler and Huntingford as they climbed out of the machine. She said she had heard what was going on, and that it was not acceptable. The Explorers were welcome to stay, provided they moved the helicopter to the airstrip, flew around instead of over town, and refrained from any further threats against residents.

Butler and Huntingford repeated their usual statements about efficiency requiring helicopter operations at the lodge. They know she needs their business to make it financially through the season. I'm sure they thought she would apologize and back off, as Kitty had done.

Terri then gave them one hour to have all their possessions off the premises. She said there was plenty of time before dark for the helicopter to fly them all to Bettles, or they could camp out if they wished. Butler laughed. I don't think a woman had ever stood up to him. He ordered the workmen to go into the lodge and wash up for dinner.

Terri asked Kitty to give her a hand. They proceeded to go into the rooms, one by one, and piled the Explorers' clothes and other things neatly in the street next to the helicopter. Kitty went into the kitchen and took the dinner off the stove where it had been cooking, unset the tables and put away the plates and silverware, leaving just enough out for Sara, Terri and herself.

Sara, Terri and Kitty ate alone in the dining room, with all the Explorers standing around them. They ignored the Explorers completely.

In Terri's absence, with the fresh supplies exhausted, the fare at the lodge had in fact been quite plain, mostly variations on beans and biscuits. Now, with what had come in from the city, Sara, Terri and Kitty served themselves roast chicken, broccoli with hollandaise sauce, and baked potato with real butter. I had already eaten with Jasper, but they invited me to join them for dessert—raspberry pie (local berries, just out of the oven) à la mode (almond brickle ice cream, kept hard on dry ice from Fairbanks)— and coffee (Mocha Java, fresh ground).

The Explorers watched.

Just before dark, the helicopter warmed up, took off, and landed at the airstrip. Without further discussion, Terri then invited the Explorers to put their things back in their rooms. She explained that it was after the lodge serving hours, but that she understood the men were hungry and so could arrange to make peanut butter and jelly sandwiches. The Explorers ate in silence. Not a word was spoken.

This fragment found in George Johnston's computerized records appar-ently dates from just after his trip with Terri to Fairbanks: —JBS

I am tired, you mother fucker whore woman. You will die. Carry all your stuff, oh yes I will. You ride with me all the way to Fairbanks and you don't have the slightest inkling of what is in store. Goody-goody lady all so pure, all so righteous, you have no chance. You all die. Priest man, *Ig Patri Om Dominus Christi*, stay here then fuck you you die. Prepare to meet your god.

This town is filled with crazy people. I cannot ABIDE them. I cannot STAND to be around the nonsense they allow around here. Crazy man Russell on the streetcorner, my head pounds with pain because you are there. I will smear your intestines on the street gravels.

Someone has to bring order to this place. No one else will, so it is my burden.

Out of my way, mother-fuckers. The clean-up man is here.

Darwin
via Bettles Field,
Alaska 99726
August 20, 1981

Albert F. Cooke, Superintendent
Dagheeloyee National Park & Preserve
P.O. Box 8429
Fairbanks, Alaska 99687

Dear Mr. Cooke:

I wish to call your attention to the activities of the mining company Eldorado Explorations Unlimited this summer in the Darwin area. These carry the potential for serious, long-term environmental degradation, particularly in the vicinity of Dagheeloyee Creek and the western slopes of Dagheeloyee Peak. My research to date indicates that this area is of central importance to the aesthetic and recreational resources of the National Park and Preserve. Thus I believe it is incumbent upon the National Park Service to take the most efficacious regulatory action possible, consistent with the guidelines imposed by the Alaska National Interest Lands Conservation Act.

To date I have had unexpectedly no contact with National Park Service personnel in Darwin. In view of the ongoing events here, it will be much to your advantage to send in a group of your people to take hold of the situation promptly. In addition to resource managers and planners, I recommend that your group include rangers with police authority and thus enforcement capability.

When I was in your office in early July, my review of your records showed no current mining plan of operations filed by Eldorado Explorations or any other company for this area. As you know, such plans are required under the Mining in the Parks Act. Unless such plans have been submitted to you since that time, the ongoing operations in the Darwin vicinity are in violation of law and, as I am sure you will agree, subject to immediate shut-down by your agency. If a plan has in fact been filed since my review, I would appreciate your sending me a copy by return mail.

I am camped in the immediate Darwin area and will be pleased to meet with Park Service personnel when they arrive. In view of the urgency of the situation, I will anticipate their visit at the soonest possible time.

I am having good results in obtaining the field data as we discussed in your office and look forward to submitting a complete interim report in the fall, as called for by our contract.

Sincerely,
Jotham B. Shechter

ELDORADO EXPLORATIONS UNLIMITED
Memorandum

August 20, 1981

TO: F. Carleton Manley, President
FROM: Ed Butler, Operations Manager

I will now report many things which surely you want to know about regarding our operations. Still have not heard from you yet all summer. As you know for sure the crew arrived with the chopper at the date of August 9. This date is three weeks late in respect to the date of beginning of which we had discussed and so the whole thing is running behind considerably as regards the schedule. A couple of times it snowed already up on Eldorado Butte so it is hard to keep warm working up there and because it is so late the summer is pretty well past and I expect it will get colder yet before we get all done.

Schultz and Rogers are done so they will take this letter with them out to mail when they go in the morning. They will be flying out direct to Fairbanks because we have had a royal fuck-up with the helicopter. To tell you the story I will start at the beginning. It is not too good with the citizens here. They make threats against our operations. Let me tell you honestly this is Huntington's fault because he does not handle these local people the right way. I took no shit excuse me for using this word but I did not and so they treated me with proper respect. Then he got here and he has this way of talking psychology this and psychology that so we come off like wimps. So pretty soon I hear the citizens is planning assaults against the chopper and like that and I have to take steps.

So I post guard on the chopper. I tell Huntingford to make sure the guard is rotated proper and no citizens is to get near the chopper. That of course is part of his job as work crew foreman. So the next day which is today what happens? Bingo we got sabotage. I am out there first thing this morning to get things organized so we make emergency repairs and get flying. But the chopper has got to go all the way into Fairbanks tomorrow to get fixed. So trust Huntingford to do a job I do not plus now we got to be very careful to watch our stuff at every moment and keep a tight ship. Let me tell you that with Huntingford here that is not easy to do so I hope you will do something about him as I am keeping him in his place but he is hard to control and he is as they say in the Navy a loose gun on our deck.

Schultz flew around all he wanted with his ray-gun thing. He says he got all the numbers he needs but surely you will be talking with him direct when he gets to the telephone in Fairbanks so you know this already by the time you get this letter. So I guess we will know for sure what is in that mountain. So I know my duty which is to get that camp set up yet this year to show the investors and to get ready for the drilling and etc. We got most of the camp ferried up the buildings and such but still some equipment and fuel to go. The tunnels is a harder thing to do. They are all blocked with ice. The guys are working at it. But that ice is real thick. However we will proceed with this and use dynamite so do not worry as certainly we will show the investors the tunnels by the time they get here.

When do you yourself get here? This is a question I ask myself more than once. I assure you I take charge which is needed but this operation here is undermined by Huntingford I must tell you.

—Butler

ELDORADO EXPLORATIONS UNLIMITED
Memorandum

Darwin
via Bettles Field, Alaska 99726
August 21, 1981

TO: F. Carleton Manley, President

FROM: Dr. Perry W. Huntingford,
        Director of Field Exploration & Development

Dear Mr. Manley:

I find it necessary to write in respect to a series of events which have occurred, and which unfortunately affect the field exploration and development activities of our Company here in Alaska.

The Company crew under my direction arrived successfully on the ninth of August, traveling via chartered helicopter to Darwin, Alaska. As per your instructions, I had met Dr. Ludwig Schultz at the Fairbanks International Airport, who arrived from Germany with the Gravitometric Radar Instrumentation; Dr. Jack Rogers of the United States Geological Survey, retired, who arrived on an Alaska Airlines flight from Menlo Park, California; and also the team of laborers you had engaged to assist with our on-site work.

Following a night of necessary and appropriate rest and refreshment at the hotel in Fairbanks, we hired a taxicab to the premises of the Alaska Helicopter Leasing and Charter Service, Incorporated, where we met the pilot and mechanic who were to be with us henceforth, and to whom our very lives would be entrusted. Despite initial appearances to the contrary, this was to be a false trust, as you shall see.

The helicopter set us down in the ghost town of Darwin, adjacent to the public-house which was to be our home and base-camp for the coming weeks.

Perhaps this is the point to set out the particulars of the grievances which unfortunately I must lay before you. For it was upon this arrival that the difficulties, which in the coming days would emerge forth in their fullest, were first indicated. The Company's advance man, Mr. Edward Butler, had made arrangements for lodging and board at this establishment and, indeed, had himself been situated there for quite a number of days already upon our arrival. I must admit that my expectations were not entirely met, as although Mr. Butler had communicated to us by post that hotel accommodations were to be expected, in fact this particular hotel of his choosing occupies a facility which was abandoned in 1936, deteriorating ever since, and only in recent years reopened, and at that with minimal repairs. Need I say more than to indicate that the W.C. consists of nothing more than three out-houses of most unsanitary condition, with flies, spiders and mosquitos present within. Must I note also the presence of these creatures, and other vermin, such as mice, within the very confines of our private rooms?

If this were the only complaint, of course I and the crew well could have handled it, certainly for the interval until our permanent camp at the site of mining were established, with its adequate and modern plumbing, housed within the sturdy walls of its sophisticatedly designed, modular units. I am a psychologist with a bent toward anthropology. And as an anthropologist I am aware of the necessity at times for conformity to the admittedly primitive standards to be found in some locales. We must learn to adapt, mustn't we.

However, we arrived to find that Mr. Butler had made no provision for lorry transportation to the site of mining as we had expected. Indeed, he himself had never been to the site at all; and, instead of finding the way ahead paved for us by our advance man, we had to start "from scratch" as the saying goes, with aerial transport of all our supplies, a slow, laborious, and (need I say) expensive procedure.

Let me assure you that despite these difficulties I proceeded to set forth the work-men in their tasks, digging with tools of the hand into the mining-works, clearing the path for the exploratory endeavors which must follow, assembling the structures at the remote and lonely site which shall be our shelter and sustenance in the months that are to come.

And, despite the hardships, Dr. Schultz and Dr. Rogers went onward with their scientific investigations, probing the depths of the mountain with their accumulated decades of professional experience, deriving the raw data from which we shall certainly in the end pinpoint with exactness the location of the valuable ore.

What, do you suppose, was occurring in the ghost-town of Darwin during this period of our intense creativity? It saddens me to report that in the time prior to my arrival the advance man, Mr. Butler, had completely alienated the residents of this far-northern outpost, to the point at which their role-relationships *vis-á-vis* our Company were in a tumultuous and inadequate state. Fortunately, I was in a position to apply the procedures of psycho-therapy to alleviate the mounting tensions of the situation; unfortunately, the success of my efforts was obstructed by the obstreper-ousness of Mr. Butler, who, while maintaining a puissant posture of illusory proportions, in fact played the part of the fribble, and was contradictory in the same breath, on one hand articulating a policy of non-fraternization with the populace (a policy the sagacity of which I adhere to) but simulta-neously maintaining a sexual liaison with the serving-maid, thus by his inconsistency undermining my efforts at reconciliation, so essential for the efficacious onward movement of our field exploration and development activities.

Eventually, of course, his recusancy bore its inevitable fruit; the trollop rejected him.

I wish that now my descriptions, which doubtless cause you anguish, could cease, but that is not the case. I cannot now corroborate with substantial evidence that it was in fact Mr. Butler who turned the operator and the repair-man of the helicopter against us. Let it be sufficient for the moment to recite the events that transpired with simple objectivity, so the facts as they may fall will speak for themselves: As I have mentioned, relationships had suffered a decline, and this was not only with the inhabitants but also between the members of our own group, a consequence of the combination of primitive conditions, the stridency of Mr. Butler's manner, his inconsistencies in the application of his roles, and (let it be said straight-out) his professional failures in securing the rudimentary elements of transportation and accommodations for us.

What followed was a despicable act, not justified in any way of course, even by the above. On the morning of yesterday last, I arose to find that our helicopter was victim of an act of sabotage. Yes, sabotage. How did I know it was the operator and the repair-man who perpetrated this deed? The deduction is clear; to whit: The act of destruction to the machine was not of the sort to cause death or injury to the occupants, yet it was well thought-out to delay our operations. Who would have the skill to achieve this end and who, while desiring our obstruction, would simultaneously evidence concern for the physical-well being of the vehicle's occupants? Clearly, the answer is the staff of helicopter itself. Second, note that as a precaution I had placed guard, well armed, stationed day and night at the helicopter. In the face of this demonstration of lethal force, who would have had access to our machine of the air? None other than the operator and repair-man.

By providing a basic structure of social order to the situation, I cleared the way for repairs to the machine to proceed, which they did, and again we are in the air as a functioning mining crew. But never again can I have confidence in the flying team which carries responsibility for our movements.

Let me tell of my dismay, as well, at the inattention, the potentially fatal and thus actually criminal inattention, of our laborers, to whom was delegated the assignment of standing guard over the aerial vehicle. For it was right in their midst that the operator and the repair-person disabled our machine; it was for want of clearer observance on their part that our operations were delayed and that we accreted the expense of a repair journey for the machine to Fairbanks. This time we suffered no injuries to personnel and the delay, due to prompt and complete attention to repairs, has been minimized. But in the future, the low calibre of our laboring staff may subject us to serious and disabilitating disruption.

Thus my report is this: In fact, I have been able to press forward the work of the Company with amazing alacrity, given the incompetence and dismaying treachery of the hired staff, and I do report with joy significant progress on all fronts: in the movement of matériel, in the procedures to gain access to the tunnels, in the assembly of data through the researches of our scientists. But although so far overcoming the difficulties of the moment, as your representative in the field, I must report grave difficulties with personnel, threatening in the long term to the completion of our operations and the implementation of our endeavors.

Sincerely Yours,
Perry W. Huntingford, Ph.D

ELDORADO EXPLORATIONS UNLIMITED
18001 East Third Avenue, Seattle, Washington 98352

August 27, 1981

TO: Butler & Huntingford
         Darwin via Bettles Field, Alaska 99726
FROM: F. Carleton Manley

I will be arriving September 12. I expect to find the camp at Eldorado Butte in operation upon my arrival.

———————

Backwoods City
August 23, 1981

Dear Juice,

I am deeply disturbed. No peace in Darwin City. The devil roams the streets. Sheriff out of town. Local priest (that is me), big headed and big hearted, drops rosary beads, rushes into the streets to fill the gap (as usual). So I am wrestling with the devil in the dusty streets of Backwoods City. Round two: devil winning on points. Time for priest man, erstwhile novice hermit, to quit the match before his shoulders are pinned to the dirty gravel. Got to split this scene, I'm afraid, Juice-man. I didn't come here to play cowboys, to fight the people's battle against corporate greed, or to take over a parish of renegades, madmen and pagans (and good simple people too), no matter how noble the cause.

No sweet serene solitude here. A million miles from anywhere, and yet it is all here, the noise, the conflict, the anger, all concentrated and personalized, packaged up with stress and tension and delivered to yours truly. Juice, can you picture it: Here we are in God's own serene paradise, nature all around, the great white mountains, the whole works. Here comes the naive, eager monk looking for couple of quiet little cabins for himself and his brother-hermits, off in the woods somewhere, preferably with a good view, looking for the chance to say his prayers and keep his discipline, support his simple needs with a few odd jobs, some physical labor and maybe writing a magazine article or two.

And what does he find? Peyton Place with helicopter. This town is embroiled in argument between a particularly nasty and unscrupulous bunch of miners and a small group of local residents who value their quiet and isolation. I think well, OK, so in lots of ways this place no different than any other, let me express my love for these people as best I can moment to moment, day to day, but I'm no secular priest, I'll go about my own monastic business. This is a great place in many ways for a hermitage so I'll just go ahead and do what I have to do. My contribution is not through intervention in their affairs, but by my personal demonstration of the contemplative life.

Juice, it's not working and its getting to me. I've come to know the people in this town. For the first time in eleven years I'm really with a community of people in the world, women, children, even a crazy man, the works. And I like it, Juice. I don't want to go off and leave them. I'm drawn to them, to the place. I suppose that in itself makes staying impossible. It's just not compatible with my vocation. But more than that, their tensions have become my tensions. And, I'm afraid, their craziness is becoming mine, as well.

I'm having dreams, Juice. You know I'm living with this crazy man. He offered me a place to stay; I needed one; he can use the help around the household. We talk by the fireside and then I go to bed and I am possessed by dreams I don't understand, with dragons and cavemen in them. I wake feeling all mixed up.

At first I could take it all as it came, keep to myself at least most of the time and maintain my discipline. But it's gotten to be too much. I'm saturated. I think the dreams are the worst part. I can't pray anymore, Juice.

I can't even keep to my schedule. Gosh, Juice, I've even been sleeping in late in the morning like my drunkard crazy-man friend!

I miss my brothers in the monastery. I admit it. I felt so ready to go off by myself. I wasn't flippant about it. It took years of monastic practice to reach the maturity hermitage requires. I thought I had it. You know it took years to convince the abbot I was ready. He was so skeptical at first. And I was so sure. And now...I don't know, Juice. I yearn for other Catholics. For a priest, a confessor. To go back to the monastery. To go back? Yes I want to, I yearn for that comfort. And yet the thought feels empty.

Why hasn't it worked out here for me? Is it just that this is a weird town? But I feel the problem *inside me*, not just in what's going on in Darwin City. Maybe that's because of the dreams. In any event, the mess is inside me now, as well as outside. And I ain't acting like no hermit.

What I've found special here is the people. Of course, that is not what I came for. I talk and I hobnob too much. I am feeling especially close and drawn to the woman who runs the lodge. I feel a depth and empathy in her, and I am drawn into it. It is sensual, although of course not sexual for me. But the potential is there, and I trust myself less because of all the craziness mixing up in my head. Maybe it's the absence of my Catholic brothers that pulls me toward her, my loneliness in my confusion. Or maybe that my love-making with God in prayer is momentarily shadowed, leaving a void which I seek to fill with a human soul and flesh.

My discipline is just about shot. I am loosing control. I'm not trying to hide that from anybody. But I don't think it shows on the outside. I don't think people here realize it. Maybe that's part of the problem. I am so alone.

Isolated, and yet not in solitude. I came here to the wilderness. I expected to encounter the devil here. But I came to empty myself out, to embark then on the struggle and work through it with God's help. I have found no such emptiness. Here rather is a mad fullness, a fullness of the world that disturbs me. I have not been so disturbed since before my conversion to Catholicism in Berkeley, since the madhouse days of the Movement.

Well, Juice, I've gotten it all off my chest. I had to to talk to somebody, my dear old friend. Now what? A proper leave-taking I guess. It's not so easy to leave here. I can afford to take the mail plane to Bettles. Then hitch-hike to Fairbanks, I suppose. Or maybe I can find a ride out the long dirt road from here. Cars come in and out once in awhile. In a week or ten days I'll be out.

So it is leave-taking time in Darwin City. Still, I feel the pull to stay. But that is my corruption. So I shall leave. My next address: the diocese in Anchorage. I'll check in with them when I get out from here. After that? Back to the monastery, I suppose. I am too confused to proceed with my venture in Alaska now. I need a break, at least.

I pour this out on you, dear Juice-friend. Your listening sustains me.

Love in Christ,
Mike

———————

Terri wrote again to her sister Peggy:

August 24, 1981

Dear Sister,

I'm just about done unpacking and putting away the groceries and things I got in town. It always takes a couple of days to do it. We're all set now with good fresh food. These guests are big eaters. We have plenty enough for the weeks they'll be here yet.

Talking with you on the phone from Fairbanks made me feel happy. I sure would like to see you and the family. Maybe for Christmas. We're saving our pennies, and with the crew staying into September we can probably afford it.

The drive in from town went fine. No breakdowns, just one flat tire. We had the truck way overloaded, as usual. George Johnston isn't a person you get to know easily. He's pretty quiet and kind of distant. Maybe he's lonely. I don't know. Anyway, it was a smooth trip. No problems.

Kitty and Sara had a rough time with the crew while I was gone. They were landing their helicopter right on the street. Noisy and a real bother. Now at least they've moved it up to the airstrip, which is a lot better. They are still very demanding guests. Kitty has broken off her relationship with Ed Butler. A good thing, no doubt. That dear lady deserves better. Actually, she did a fine job keeping the lodge going. So did Sara. They had almost everything neat and clean when I got back.

Almost. I found amazing things behind the couch and in the back of the lower shelves, in the places you can't see into without really looking. There was Kitty's underwear, a stunning long-haired wig, some dirty dishes. She also swept the dirt under the rugs. I noticed because they were getting lumpy.

Sara knows better. Kitty did it, Sara told me. Sara is in such a mood lately. She simply has no tolerance for the crew. Tolerance takes more maturity than she has yet. I admit they are boors. In some ways she's growing up so fast. Her mind is so quick and sharp, always ahead of mine. That's for sure. I never know what to expect. And so moody. Brooding one moment, then the next she's off playing like a little child again. I think she's growing and changing so fast, she can't figure out what age she is supposed to be.

As for me and the crew, well, I still worry some about what they might do around here. But, as Les was saying last night, we've seen people like them come and go so often through the years. They make a big show and then they leave. Les says at least we earn a living off them. The summers are hectic. But then they go away and we have the winters to ourselves. And winter is the good time, the special time. That's why we're here....

I've come to know Father Mike better. He's been over several times. Yesterday we walked out to the glacier. He'd never been all the way out to the ice. I'm glad he got a chance to see it. He'll be leaving soon. Sara and I both have enjoyed having him around. Mike says it's just too busy around here for him. I can understand that, but I wish he could see what it is like in winter. He really wanted it to work out for himself here. He's pretty troubled now. Maybe it's from living with LJR. He's been a big help to Jasper, I know. But I couldn't have lasted with Jasper, even as long as Mike has.

I can tell Mike is attracted to me. Since Ted died, I haven't felt interest in any man. I'm still locked up with memories and griefs. But I felt an immediate ease with Mike. When he came he was so centered and calm. It's almost as if he had been living in the midst of one of our winters. We talked about it. It comes from living in the monastery. He was there eleven years without hardly ever leaving. I still can sense that maturity in him. It's still there, under his confusion of the moment. I hope he finds the solitude he is seeking. Anyway, he's a Catholic priest, so that's that! I wish he'd stay, though. He'd be a good neighbor....

August 27

p.s. Sister Peggy, I can't let this letter go out without telling you what's happened since I wrote it. Day before yesterday we fixed breakfast for the crew like usual, and they all flew off up to their mines. I guess it was late in the morning when the helicopter returned. Sara, Kitty and I were all out picking blueberries, so we didn't see them come back. Tim was the only one who saw them, and he didn't talk to them then. He says he saw a lot of hustling around and packing up, and the helicopter made a couple of trips out. Tim minds his own business, so he didn't pay it a lot of attention.

Well, when we got back there was a note from the pilot thanking us for our hospitality and the place was all cleaned up and their things were missing. I noticed that right away, because it had rained the day before. They had put their wet clothes up to dry on the line by the stove, and those were gone.

Two of them, the managers, usually come in for lunch, you know. Nobody appeared.

We went through their rooms and most all of their gear was gone. Except in the manager's rooms, Ed Butler and Perry Huntingford. Their things were still there.

Such a mystery. Dinner time came. Not knowing what to expect, we made a big pot of chili with cornbread. That would keep if nobody ate it right away. Nobody showed up.

Yesterday the lodge was just quiet and empty. You can tell fall is coming, because a cold rain fell all day. The sky was dark enough that I lit the lamps right after dinner. We couldn't figure out what had happened to the crew. They just vanished. If they hadn't taken their things, we would have worried about a helicopter crash. And they did leave a note. But it didn't say much. They didn't write about any emergency, or having to fly to the hospital, or anything like that. A real puzzle.

Sam Ross flew over Eldorado Butte, just to make sure they hadn't gone back up the creek and had helicopter trouble. But he didn't see anything.

So there we were, with all these groceries, an unpaid bill, no crew, and no word about what happened.

Early this morning—it was still dark and raining—knocks on the door woke me. In my sleep I thought it was tree branches blowing against the wall in the wind. I suppose I kept them knocking quite awhile.

It was Butler and Huntingford. What a sight! They were drenched and freezing cold. They hadn't eaten anything since the day before. They just stood there dripping. I got them in and told them to strip off their wet cotton clothes, then I got them dry things, put chili and cocoa on the propane burner to warm and lit a fire in the heat stove. When I lit a lamp, I could see their lips were blue.

At first, even Perry Huntingford had the words drained out of him. As they got some energy back, they sort of growled at each other under their breath as they hunched over the chili bowls. So I could tell they weren't getting along with each other, either. They were also embarrassed about what happened. They mumbled a lot.

Day before yesterday they had some big confrontation with the crew up at the mines. I knew Butler and Huntingford had been treating the men pretty bad. As Butler and Huntingford tell it, that morning the workers refused to go into the mine tunnels. The day before they had finally opened up the entrance with dynamite.

I don't know what Butler and Huntingford said to the workers. It must have been quite something, because the workers and the helicopter people, John and Chuck, just flew off and left them. As soon as they warmed enough to talk, Butler and Huntingford asked me if the crew was still here. I had to tell them the crew was gone. They just slumped a little deeper in their chairs.

So there were the managers, alone up the creek. They waited up there through that first night and into yesterday, expecting the helicopter to come back, or to be rescued I guess. They had shelter from the rain in the old buildings. They've hauled up lots of supplies, but I guess they didn't know what was where. Luckily, they found some candy bars.

Then they decided to walk down to Darwin. It took them eighteen hours. I don't think they knew how hard it would be. They've flown over the valley so much, but they've never gone anywhere on foot. There was enough moon behind the clouds so they could see a little at night. I'm glad they kept going after it got dark. They probably would have died of exposure if they had stopped. They didn't have matches to build a fire.

About dawn I got them off to bed and went back to sleep myself for a few hours. Perry got up in the middle of the afternoon. Kitty fed him some breakfast. There was a fellow here then from Fairbanks, who owns some land in the subdivision over by the edge of town. He had been camping on his land. People come in every so often and do that. The subdivision is just some dirt roads and surveyed lots. People from the city buy property and talk about coming here to live. Once in awhile they come in to see what they paid for. Well, this fellow was in the lodge having some blueberry pie when Perry ate breakfast. Kitty overheard them talking. The man was about to drive back to the city, and Perry hitched out with him.

So when Ed Butler woke up at dinner time, he was the only one of the crew left. That was just a couple of hours ago. We served him steak and potatoes. He didn't eat much. Now he's downstairs sitting by himself by the stove. It's still raining.

So here we are with just Ed again. I wonder what he'll do now. I sure hope we get paid for the time the crew was here. Maybe they'll come back. The president of the company, the big boss, was due to come in sometime this fall. Who knows if he will. They have reservations for weeks yet, and then for even more people in mid-September. We sure have more groceries here than I'll know what to do with if they don't come back. I can give some of the fresh food away, but some will surely spoil otherwise.

Our Christmas plans have to be uncertain now, of course. We'll have to see if we can pay our bills and have some left over to get down to see you. I hope we do.

Missing you lots.

Love,
Terri

———————————

From Mike's journal:

August 30, 1981

I am up and down like a yo-yo. One day I feel my discipline is gone, my mind is scattered, possessed by monsters. The next I feel solid in myself, glad to be breathing the pure air, exhilarated by newness and challenge. I can't allow this inconsistency to continue.

The monk vows to be stable. Stability means to be grounded in place and in habits, to be able to concentrate on the light of God rather than on the endless chaotic details required in changing one's abode or way of life. My image of hermitage is as a condition of stability as ultimate as we can get on this earth. Leaving the monastery, traveling to Alaska, looking for land and a cabin—I acknowledged that these would be disruptive. But the period of transition is stretching out with no clear end in sight.

It would be easy if I could simply dismiss my experiences here, if I could just feel that I checked out this place and found it not right for our hermitage. But I cannot, for I am drawn to this place, engaged with ties I cannot easily break.

Each day here has vividness, is lived in technicolor, with intensity. Not everything is good, not by a long shot, but everything matters, down to the tiny details. It matters how much water I use washing dishes, because I have to haul it. It matters what I say when I pass a neighbor in the street, because each contact we have with another person here is significant to us.

Well, all this was less true when the Explorers were here, with their activity and noise. Now they are gone, except for Ed, at least for the moment. In contrast, a hush has come over the town. I see everyone easing up, letting go, breathing more deeply. And I feel better. My attraction to the place returns.

But I am set to leave, to return to New York State, to my monastery. My reasons for leaving are not just the Explorers, but also the more profound unsettledness that leads me to question whether I can ever find serenity here, and personal involvements which seem to make solitude unlikely. So I will go. But I will not forget Darwin. I wonder how long it will take back in the monastery to reestablish my inner tranquility. Can I clear my head of the memories and dreams? Have I been infected in some evil way? Have I picked up some of Jasper's schizophrenia? But I'm not convinced the change in me is negative. I'm not sure. I am unsure. I am unstable.

...I had the chance for a ride out today. The road washed out after the rains, and the highway department came to fix a culvert. Les was impressed they came so soon. He said sometimes the road stays out for weeks. A worker came over the tram into town, and he said they had space if I wanted to drive out with them.

But Les needs my help for a few days, so I'll pass up this chance. There will be other opportunities to hitch out. Les started up the creek toward his place and found that his ferry-boat ropes are all tangled up, with the canoe swamped and stuck out in the middle of the current. He says he'll need a couple of people to help him get it out. It's a big job. When he got back to town, he asked Ed about it. Ed admitted that he and Perry messed up the system trying to cross the creek. There are two boats, one not far from town and another quite a hike up the valley. From what Ed says, they are both unusable now. Les's plan is to fix both of them, ending up at his house and staying overnight before returning to Darwin. He's asked both me and Jot to come along.

We had quite a storm. It's still raining off and on. But Les doesn't want to wait. He's concerned that the creek might carry away his boats. So we'll leave in the morning.

September 1, 1981

Les is across the room in the kitchen. I smell woodsmoke and bacon frying. He is making pancakes. Jot is still asleep on the floor in front of me. I sit in Les's battered easy chair. Sunlight streams onto me through the south window. It's nearly noon. When I woke a couple of hours ago, the tall, dry grass, filled with seed, was white with frost. On the north side of the cabin, a puddle retains a film of surface ice. We are surrounded by mountains. We are the only people in the valley. The world is far away.

Yesterday morning after breakfast, we started up the creek from Darwin. Soon we came to Les's first ferry crossing. His ropes cross the creek, fastened to trees on both sides, just below a big cliff. The trail approached through the woods, ending at a washout. We left Les's jeep and walked out across a broad gravel area to the water's edge. There we had an open view of the cliff in front of us, upstream, the current frothing at its base.

I blinked, twice; closed my eyes and opened them again. The cliff is made of dark rock. But embedded in it was an enormous white dragon, long, twisted, and ornate. I looked at my companions. They did not seem to notice. They stood at the edge of the creek, scratching their heads, pondering the tangled ropes and the flooded canoe being pounded by the midstream current.

I stared. It appeared that the beast was moving. But the movement was merely a shadow, cast by a bush growing on a high ledge, swaying in the wind. I approached the dragon. It melted into the cliff face, becoming long veins of some sort of light colored rock. I felt a blast of wind. The cliff face darkened as the sun passed behind a thick cloud spitting raindrops. I turned back. I did not mention the dragon to my companions.

I watched them watching the creek. I was at the edge of the woods; they were in front of me, a tall man and a short man. Although I was not far away, I could not hear them speak over the roar of the water. The short man was pointing. The tall man stood with his hands on his hips, his booted left foot up on a boulder. The outline of the short man was indistinct. He wore old clothes, which merged with the brown and grey pattern of rocks, sand and water. The tall man was cobalt blue from head to ankle. Raindrops flowed over the surface of the blue hood that covered his head. The wind billowed his crisp nylon raincoat and rainpants.

Suddenly it was raining hard and the rain turned to hail. My companions turned around and we hustled to the shelter of the old jeep. Les and I got in. In my old work shoes, my feet were already damp and getting cold. Jot stayed outside, watching the storm. The little hailstones bounced off his hood. The hood fit snugly around his face, exposing only his nose and glasses, which were protected by the wide brim of his cap, sticking out from under his blue covering. At the bottom, the hood was tied shut with a bow of blue cord, which rested neatly on his beard. His feet were warm in massive, well-sealed boots. He was like an astronaut in outer space, encased in his portable protective suit, free to wander comfortably in a hostile environment. Les started the jeep and moved a lever he said turned on the heat. I felt a weak current of warmish air pass by my ankles on its way to the cracks around the plywood door, which was held closed by a piece of bent coathanger.

Within a few minutes, the clouds separated, opening large patches of blue overhead. Mountains appeared. I could see now that we were within the confines of a narrow valley. We walked back out to the creek.

Les had a plan. The drowned canoe, or half-canoe rather, was still attached by its bow-line to a rope which spans the creek. Fortunately, it was not far from a massive boulder sticking out of the water with more than the height of a man. Hopping from rock to rock, we might be able to get to the boulder.

Les asked Jot to find a long stick. While Jot was searching, Les took the coathanger wire off the jeep door and scrounged around in the back of the vehicle. He came up with several pieces of dirty cord, various colors, which he tied together, and some string. Jot came back with a pole, about the size of a fishing pole. Les said that should be just right.

He had me hold the pole while he fashioned the wire into a hook and bound it on with the string. I continued to hold the pole as Les made his way gingerly over the water to the big boulder, barely getting his feet wet. I steadied Jot by his outstretched arm as he balanced on the rocks, handing the pole and cord to Les on his high perch.

Les hung one end of the cord over the hook and patiently began fishing for the canoe. He almost had it quite a few times, but lost it. It took quite a while. Fortunately, the sun was out now and the wind had faded. My damp back was comfortably warm. Finally, he managed to shove the cord through the loop in the canoe bow line, pick it up on the other side with the hook, and get it back. We had a line to the canoe. Jot and I passed a hank of heavy rope to Les, who stuck his pole out at us to receive it. Les tied the rope to the cord and, pulling on the cord, snaked the rope out to the canoe, through the bow loop and back, and tied the rope securely to itself. Then he made his way to shore with the other end of the rope. He almost fell into the creek.

We tried hauling the canoe to shore using the rope. With all three of us pulling, we could get it within reach. But the moment we eased up to grab for it, it sailed back into the current. Les got a come-along (that's a hand winch for moving heavy loads) out of the jeep. With the added length of the come-along cable attached to the rope, we could just make it to tie onto a big timber lying on the gravel. So finally we were able to winch the boat slowly to the bank. With the water rushing into it, the canoe must have weighed hundreds of pounds. Once we tipped and emptied it, it came out of the creek lightly and easily.

Then we used the come-along to help us take up the slack on the ropes spanning the creek, getting the whole system into good shape.

One by one we sailed across the water in the little ferry-boat. We got in and crouched low. It was tippy. We pushed off gently, and once we caught the current it zipped us to the other side. We'd disconnect the canoe from the rope, fasten the bow line to the other rope, and send it back across on its own. We brought the come-along, rope, and various tools with us.

Les took them and went on ahead on a motorbike. Jot and I walked on up the trail together. It was the first time I'd really had the chance to talk with Jot with some intimacy. It was different out here, with the sun shining down, feeling good from having worked together, moving along this beautiful trail through the woods. With each step we left troubled Darwin behind.

Jot was different, too, graceful, gay even. I hadn't seen much of him lately. He's been spending a lot of time out around the countryside, on his own. Has he been changing gradually? I should have been noticing, but I have been too obsessed with my own problems lately.

Jot told me about the various kinds of trees. There's spruce (the only evergreen tree here), and poplar (some people call it cottonwood) and willow. Lots of kinds of willow, but they interbreed, hard to tell apart. And birch, with the white bark that peels off. You can use it for paper. And alder, which grows along the creek and up high on the slopes, and is hard to walk through if you don't have a trail. There aren't many kinds of trees here, far fewer than down south. Ecologists have various theories about why that is so, but nobody knows for sure.

The leaves are getting fall colors, lots of yellow, and up on the hillsides I see reds, too. The forest floor is ablaze with patches of vibrant red, the leaves of low-growing plants and lots of berries, crimson and maroon. The flowers are all gone, but the stalks of the most common tall one, fireweed

Jot says it is, have turned red, too. They make it look like the forest is on fire. At the top they are puffed out with cotton and are sending seeds blowing in the breeze on light cotton stars. Jot helped me notice. We came to groups of big trees with smooth trunks, leaves high above fluttering in the wind. They are the quaking aspen. Jot showed me why they quake. The stem of the leaf is flat, can only bend in two directions, so when the leaf catches the wind it tosses back and forth.

We saw some birds and squirrels and a very funny looking porcupine that waddled away from us into the forest. Jot showed me bear tracks that we knew had been made recently, because they hadn't been worn by the rains of this past week. That bear must take a size 15 shoe at least. It was using our trail and traveling the same direction we were. We came to several large piles of bear poop on the trail. They were filled with berries.

Jot says his work is going well. He talked about a point system for rating scenery and something about a map with isobars showing degrees of human impact on wilderness resources in various locations. He's also working on maps of all the buildings, roads and trails. I'm impressed with his fluency in talking about his work. But when he speaks his professional jargon, the way he looks at me changes. His intense eyes focus on mine. That makes me uncomfortable. It's as if he were trying to convince me of something, to win me over. Of course I really don't understand much about what he is trying to accomplish, but I'm not judgmental about his studies. But he treats me as a judge. He's very good at making his case.

It was exciting following in the footsteps of an enormous bear, and in the sunlight I felt carefree, my burdens lifted. I imagined the bear circling back through the woods and coming upon us. I could almost see his dark eyes flashing between the leaves out in the bushes. But I felt he was my friend, and I didn't mind. I asked Jot if he thought the bear might really be watching us. He said it was possible.

Eventually, the trail climbed up a little and entered a tunnel, an old railroad tunnel Jot said, blasted through the solid rock of the mountain.

Since our stream crossing we had been held in the bosom of a narrow valley, in warm sunshine and gentle forest. We came out on the other side into a different world.

We emerged into a vast, empty, cold, bare space; an immense basin of air, supported on its sides and bottom by encircling snowcovered mountains, new snow from the recent storm, Jot said. Below us was a white glacier, with a jagged and chopped up surface; crevasses, Jot explained. The afternoon sun still stretched over the western ridgeline, glaring on the white surfaces. Trees cast long shadows. A penetrating breeze drifted into our faces.

We stood at the tunnel opening for the longest time, saying nothing. Jot's eyes moved slowly across the landscape, absorbing everything. He was relaxed. Usually, his hands are tightened, if not clenched at his side. They hung loosely now, or easily conformed to the tunnel wall when he leaned against it. I felt the power of his gaze and was drawn to imitate it.

Below us, a strand of trees (that would be the spruce and poplar, and maybe the aspens?) extended out part way toward the glacier. The bushes (that's the willows and alder, right?) went further. Green and yellow forest fringed the bottom edge of the great basin, except where it was covered by glacier ice. It was definitely autumn here. Above the forest was snow.

We saw Les out toward the glacier, not far away. We went down to meet him. He had gotten the rope, come-along and tools off the motorbike. But fixing this crossing would be harder. The canoe was sunk out in the current, straining against its rope, fifty feet from shore, no exposed rocks nearby. How would we get to it? We pondered and debated various schemes for the longest time, until the sun dropped below the ridge, putting the basin floor where we stood in a pool of shadow.

One option was to return to Darwin and come back another day. That might well have meant the loss of Les's canoe, battered every minute by the current. And if we went back, we'd have to do the lower ferry crossing in the dark. Les said that once we made the upper crossing, it was a straightforward walk to his place, easy even in the dark. We had at least an hour of light to recover this second canoe and get across.

Jot told us he'd make a try at reaching the boat. He asked Les to build a fire. Then he pulled a pair of sneakers out of his big backpack. He stripped off all his clothes. Dressed only in sneakers, which protected his feet from the sharp rocks, he made his way out into the creek, bracing on Les's tram rope as the water foamed against him. The water rushed from under the glacier, two minutes walk away. By the time he was in knee-deep, it splashed up to his belly. His lanky, sinewy body shined wet.

He had one end of the big rope looped around his wrist. I held the other end. As he slowly advanced, I played the rope out to him. An increasing length lay in the current, pulling downstream. Jot soon realized he couldn't keep his balance and hold his end of the rope against that pull. So he carefully came back to shore.

He said he had enough warmth left in him for one more try. This time he took instead the end of Les's lightweight cord, short pieces knotted together. The current didn't pull nearly so hard on it, and he managed to inch his way out to the canoe and put the cord through the bow loop. The ice water out there was nearly up to his waist and splashing over his chest.

While Jot stood over Les's fire, Les and I tied the big rope onto the cord and tried to pull it through the loop in the canoe bow line. We almost had it, when one of the old knots in the cord separated, and the two separated ends swept sailing downstream. We had to start over.

By now Jot was sitting inertly around the diminishing flames of the campfire. He still had goosebumps on his back, but his lips weren't purple anymore and he wasn't trembling. I suggested that we build up the fire, let Jot get dressed and warm, and consider staying here for the night. Les got me started piling sticks on the fire, but then he wandered off down along the creek bank. Concerned for Jot, I didn't pay much attention.

Here we were way out in nowhere, and it felt so alien and strange, with the glacier looming over us and the creek roaring, and the empty vast sky dimming toward the coming of the night. The mountains encircled us like a ring of gigantic frozen angels standing shoulder to shoulder, their white-winged backs to us, sealing off the world, walling off the sun. Even as day faded down here, the peaks reflected the reddening rays of the evening sun:

Are these peaks, bearers of light, the consorts of God? Or are they Mephistopheles, Ashtaroth, Abaddon, Mammon, Asmodeus, Belphegor, the Angels of Night, sheltering an isolated sanctuary of the devil's dark kingdom? I do not know. Most are unnamed on Jot's government map. To stay here the night, out in the open: It would be scary.

The sticks caught, the flames rose, Jot gradually thawed.

Les came back. He asked me to come give him a hand. We walked over to the tree on which the rope from the canoe was anchored. The rope was wrapped around the tree several times and knotted, and beyond the knot its extra length lay in loops on the ground. Les carried the come-along winch and our extra piece of rope.

He attached the extra rope to the midst of the taunt canoe line by wrapping it around and around the line and making some sort of knot. Then he tied the winch onto the other end of the extra rope and secured the winch cable around the tree. He worked the winch, winding in the cable. As the cable tightened, it took up the burden of holding the canoe in the current, and the line tied to the tree fell slack, so we could untie it.

By this time, Jot was dressed and with us. After Les freed the end of the canoe line from the anchor tree, he gave it to Jot and me, telling us to hold on—tight. Then Les detached the come-along and extra rope. Jot and I were the anchor now, holding the line to the canoe, which bucked and jerked in the current, trying to pull us in. We could hold it. I knew we could.

Les grabbed hold, too, and had us walk slowly downstream along the bank. Clearly, the idea was to get downstream far enough that the current would push the canoe down over to us. We had to let out more rope as we walked. The current was so strong, we couldn't pull the rope straight. It still made a big "V" downstream across the channel. The canoe did move a bit toward us, but not nearly enough to reach it.

We got to the end of the rope. We held on while Les tied on our extra rope. Finally, we used up all of that rope, too. And still the canoe was near mid-stream. Jot said it looked hopeless. I watched Les.

A little further downstream, just beyond our reach, was another tree on the bank. Les went and got the pieces of our light cord, reknotted them together and this time double-checked all the knots. He made a double loop of the cord, so it would be four times as strong. He asked Jot what he had in his pack. While Les and I held the line, Jot got the straps he uses to tie on his sleeping bag. With the straps and the cord, Les lengthened the line out to the canoe enough, just enough, to tie around the downstream tree. The straps and bits of cord twirled under the tension. But they held.

Still, the canoe was way out there in the current downstream of us. We had to take in some rope. Les hooked the come-along onto the line at one of the knots, fastened the cable around the new anchor tree, and winched in. Then, with the come-along holding the load, he untied the cord from around the tree, took in the slack, and retied it securely.

The straps and cord lay loose at our feet. He untied them from the line and used the cord to make another one of those wrap-around slip knots for connecting the come-along to the taunt line. It was a special knot. Under tension, it gripped the canoe line securely. But slack, it slid easily along the rope.

Les pushed the slip knot as far out over the water as he could reach without wading in. He certainly didn't want to get wet. Then he had me winch the cable again. We were able to pull in another six or eight feet of rope this time.

We did this operation over and over: We let loose the come-along and slid its attachment as far out on the rope as we could reach. Then we'd winch in, giving us more slack on the end of the rope. Then we'd retie the rope around the tree, taking in the slack. After several rounds, we took in the length of the rope we had brought with us from Darwin.

Pretty soon, as the downstream sag came out of the long line across the creek, the current inched the canoe toward our bank. Eventually, we were able to lean way out over the water and grab on to it. And with all our strength we lifted one side out of the water. In the water it weighed a ton, the current plowing into it. At the moment the water spilled out, it became almost weightless, and came flying out onto the bank, tumbling us happily onto our backs.

Finally, after detaching the canoe, we moved the long line back upstream to the original anchor tree and used the come-along to take up the slack and tighten it up.

Les's ferry-boat system was back in operation! We could cross!

It was starting to get dark. Les and Jot crossed first, one at a time, no problem. Then they sent the canoe back to me on the rope and I got in. I was pretty tired, and I'm still out of shape, I guess.

It happened so fast. The boat caught the current and I shot across. Then it hit a rock. What happened? Did I lean the wrong way? Instantly it flipped and I was in the water.

Les was to me in a second. I felt his firm hand grip my arm as the current swept me past. That little man lifted me right out of the water. After a moment, I got a footing on the rolling rocks in the stream bed and the two of us struggled splashing toward shore. Then Jot waded in and hauled us both out.

We were all soaked and chilled, and now it was getting really dark. Immediately we set to work gathering firewood. This time, Les made a really big fire. We stripped and hung our clothes up to dry on crude stick tripods. We squatted naked facing the fire, our chests and outturned palms catching the heat. The fire popped and crackled, sending showers of sparks into the blackening purple sky. I stared into the fire, could see nothing else. The flames shot far over our heads. The whole world was the fire, Les, Jot and myself, surrounded by blackness. I could not see out from the circle of firelight. It was so dark. As the cold wind off the glacier moved against my back, it seemed as if eyes must be out there in the dark, watching us. But of course I saw nothing.

I was surprised that I was without fear, alert and aware but without fear. It seemed right to be here. I wasn't tired anymore. Gradually, the fire warmed us.

It was many hours past dark when we arrived at Les's cabin. The moon came up to light our way the final distance.

[My journal for that day contains only natural history observations, without commentary. Let me repeat just one one item. It was just at dusk, after we had restored the upper ferry and were making the final creek crossing. I noted a big black bird, a raven. I heard the pulsing wings, low overhead. The bird circled, turning its head, watching. Then it vanished over the glacier.   —JBS]

  Mike's journal continues:

September 2, 1981

It is early in the morning and very dark. My internal clock woke me for prayer on the Trappists' schedule. Jot is asleep on the floor by the table. Les is asleep in his bedroom alcove. I feel cramped in here. I did get dressed and go for a short walk, but a cold wind is whistling through the trees. I said Matins sitting in Les's chair, with Jot snoring at my feet.

Now I am in a wooden chair over in the kitchen part of the room. Without waking Jot or Les, I can keep a little light turned on here, a naked automobile tail light bulb fastened with baling wire to the side of the wood-burning cookstove. The electricity comes from batteries charged by photo-electric solar panels mounted on the south wall of the log cabin. There is no sound except Jot snoring and the wind. I am bundled in my sweater and jacket. It will probably be some hours yet before I can build a fire without waking my companions.

I am irritable from inadequate sleep. Maybe that is why I am worried. When I'm finished with this journal entry, I'll try reading. Les has Meister Eckhart, Teilhard de Chardin, a bunch of science fiction on the shelf. I don't know if I can read long by the glare of this bulb. I should just sit quietly and compose myself. But I don't know if I can.

Now I think about our journey up here: the bear, the immersion in the creek, the fire. Why did the image of a dragon come into my eyes back there in the rock face at the entrance to the valley? Just a natural illusion, a resemblance.

I think Les is a shaman. He conveyed us up here under his protection. That is why I was confident that nothing could happen to us, even after I got dumped into the ice water and it was getting darker and colder. It is nonsense to call him a shaman. He knows this valley very well, so it is appropriate to have trust in him. He is simply a guide, and it's natural to have faith in a guide.

Now I am remembering the dreams I've had recently. More than remember; I feel them again. Three or four weeks ago I had the first one. I wrote it down, but I left that part of my journal down in Darwin. That dream upset me so. I didn't understand why. Now I see that I undertook some sort of journey. It took me to Jesus. That is the monk's path, the journey to Jesus. But the dream didn't feel like a monk's path. The pain. Now I see the pain in the dream. I was falling. I remember the feeling of falling out of control. I got to Jesus. Oh, Jesus, embrace me, I have never been so close to You! Jesus embraced me, but He did not let me stay with Him. He sent me away. He sent me back into the world, where it is very cold and lonely, and I feel lost. Oh Jesus, I want to stay with You. Please let me stay with You. That is why I entered the monastery. That is why I have come to Alaska. I am looking for You, Jesus. I wish to empty myself in Your embrace. I want to be free of the pain.

There was a dragon in that dream. Probably that's why I momentarily mistook that white rock for a dragon. Probably that's why I'm thinking now about that dream. The rock reminded me of it.

I feel there's something else about the dream, though. Something about this house, Les's cabin. There is some connection between the dream and this house. And about Les, too. I don't remember.

There was another dream. I wrote it down, too, but now I don't remember it. I think of that big, hairy grizzly bear out there in the dark forest and I remind myself of that other dream. It had something to do with Jot and Les and me around that fire we built by the glacier. Was it a dream of precognition about our trip up here? There were bears in it, and a big fire. No, the bear was in the first dream, wasn't it? I don't remember.

I am in over my head. I feel like I could drown. Darwin, Jasper, Terri, the troubles with the Explorers, coming up here, it is foreign and too much. I have got to get back to the monastery.

The dreams are not important. I have not gotten enough sleep, so I am irritable and confused. I am sort of dreaming right now. I am staring into the glare of this little light and it is dark all around, I am cold and the wind is blowing, and Jot is snoring, and I am sleepless and so I am not able to keep things in order.

Les asked Jot and me to make this trip so that we could help him fix his ferry-boats. That is what we did. We fixed the canoes and soon we will go back down. That is all there is to it. That is why we are here.

When these distractions are over I will return to my discipline of monastic prayer and develop it further. It is necessary to take time to help people like this, coming up here to assist Les. But I have to keep in perspective the importance of my vocation. I have to find a quiet and peaceful place to fulfill my central duty, finding Jesus in the calm space of contemplative prayer.

September 2, 1981

(continued)

Jot is in the kitchen making dinner. We shall see how it comes out. He says it is to be some concoction of rice and beans. That actually is what we have been eating since we got up here. But Les's cooking is so excellent you don't notice it. He used to work as a cook with teams of geologists, employed by big mining companies exploring around here, before the national park was established. He said he once spent an entire summer living *inside* the tunnels that honeycomb Eldorado Butte. They camped in there, in the dark. The only food Les has at his house here now is what was left over from last winter. There's plenty of it, your basic grains and beans. This cabin is his winter home, primarily. He brings supplies in then by snowmachine.

I finally got a nap, so I feel much better. I got going this morning with the help of Les's powerful coffee. But this afternoon I fell asleep on Les's bed, right on the maroon satin bedspread. I never even heard Les and Jot hammering. They were out in the yard putting together Les's picnic table. It's a genuine picnic table, a great big one, made of grey, weathered wood.

Les found it down by the mine buildings and hauled it up by snowmachine last winter. He had to take it apart to get it here.

It's too late in the season to use it, except maybe for lunch under the noon sun. But Les will have it for next summer.

He has a little grassy spot by the side of the house for picnics, with a barbecue pit lined with old bricks and covered with a mammoth grate he appropriated from the mines. Les's place is perched atop a little bluff, so the spot has a splendid view out over the creek and forest, with mountains all around.

Earlier today, Jot and I walked down to the mine buildings. Coming up, we had passed by them, looming over us in the moonlight. They are less than an hour's walk from here, but they're behind a fold in the mountain, so you can't see them from Les's place. It's an entire town. Several hundred people lived and worked there in the 1920's. The main mill building is huge, stacked up story after story against the sloping mountainside. That is where they processed the ore. It was the most valuable ore deposit ever found, Jot said, and now it is gone, shipped to Tacoma, Washington, where they have a smelter. And the town is empty and the mountain is empty.

Full size trains came in there. We walked onto the tracks and loading platforms. The tracks used to extend all the way to Fairbanks, but most of them are gone now. Twenty years ago somebody pulled them out to sell as scrap, hauled them all the way down to the dock at Seward. Then came the '64 earthquake, and they were swept to sea by the tidal wave and lost. But the salvage crew never made it up here, of course, with all the bridges out. Jasper bulldozed the rails out of the way when he put his road in up the valley. You can see them by the side of the trail now, bent and overgrown. Alongside the buildings in the abandoned town, though, the rails are still in place. It looks like a train could arrive tomorrow.

The buildings are made of massive timbers, brought up two thousand five hundred miles from Seattle by ship and train. We went inside the mill. The doors are all unlocked and open on creaky hinges. Inside are enormous steel wheels and gears, great metal shafts connected by rubber belts, everything either black and greasy or red with rust. Not that much rust, actually:

everything amazingly preserved in this dry, cold climate. Inside it looks as if people could return and start the machinery again.

It is all so silent now, but the workers had to live amidst the heat of all this machinery, surrounded by the arctic cold all around, never comfortable, overwhelmed by the roar of turning wheels and the grinding and pulverizing of ore, subject to unpredictable accidents, to falling into the massive turning gears, to the sudden failures of those enormous spinning belts.

We walked up flight after flight of wooden stairs in the semi-darkness of the building's interior. Outside the sun was shining, but we felt the cold rising out of the mountainside against which the structure clung, out of a vast reservoir of cold barely touched by a full summer's warmth and now, at summer's end, soon to be reinforced again by six months of snows and winter ice.

Finally we came out on top, emerged out of a squeaking door into the light on the mountain slope far above the valley floor. The slope was overgrown by bushes. There was hardly a path. The leaves were mottled brown and yellow. Jot said they were a kind of willow. Over our heads thick red metal cables reached up the mountainside to the mine entrances far above, suspended sagging from towers that had not yet failed. These cables had carried the ore buckets. The miners also rode the open buckets, to and from the tunnels. It was not safe. They had no alternative. Metal debris and old equipment lay scattered in the brush. Jot saw a mouse collecting grass seeds. It scurried under a pile of tangled cable.

From the top of the mill we could look down over the town. We saw numerous buildings, some large, some small. The architecture was uniform. Every building was painted blue, faded now, with white trim. Jot pointed out the beaver ponds, which flooded most of the town. We could see the path we had taken from Les's house. It ran through the center of town and disappeared into the forest. After awhile we walked back down the steep hillside, through the brush.

A big dump truck sat at the side of the road between the buildings. It had no tires. Dirt had been left in the back. A seed must have fallen onto the dirt: A tree grew out of it. We sat on a fender warmed by the sun and ate our lunch, peanut butter and honey sandwiches on crackers, from Les's supplies. We drank clear, fresh water from a brook that rushed off the mountainside, right in the middle of town.

Then we poked around some more. To think of it: The industrial revolution came to this valley, and went. Account books still lay in the offices. We could see that the workers served for a pittance of a salary, long days and little time off, Chinese and Poles and Ukrainians slaving to bring hundred-million dollar profits to the Wall Street Syndicate. They lived in dormitories. We went through one, four stories tall, narrow metal bunk beds, 1936 calendars still on the walls. It must have fifty rooms. Not often, once a year for some of them, the workers took the train down to Darwin, where they cashed their paychecks and spent them on alcohol, gambling and whores. Terri told me the stories. So did Jasper. There's nobody left now in Darwin from the old days. But Terri and Jasper knew some of them, the handful that stayed on after the Syndicate shut down the mines.

We looked for beavers around the buildings, but saw none. Jot had located the dens when he was here before, three mounds in one of the larger ponds, he said. There must have been a lot of beavers.

When we got to that pond, at first Jot was not sure we were in the right place, because he could not find the beaver houses. But when we looked, we could see where they had been. They were opened up, the sticks and mud that made them scattered. They had been big mounds, taller than a man—not even a grizzly can get into them.

Then we saw garbage around, not antique junk but fresh trash. And then we understood. The Explorers had dynamited the dens. Why? We guessed they wanted to drain land on which to put their camp, or maybe to be sure the beavers wouldn't extend their ponds to flood out the camp. Now the beavers were surely gone.

Nearby we found the Explorers' cache, parts of white aluminum prefabricated buildings, fuel in bright blue barrels, boxes of food. Some animal had already gotten into the food, and torn packaging was littered about. The cache was next to a long, narrow open area, like a wide place in the road. Les told us afterwards that this is the Eldorado Butte airstrip. It didn't look like much of an airstrip to me. We could tell it had been cleared at one time, but the brush was growing in again. A little stream of water overflowing from one of the beaver ponds ran across the middle of it. The Explorers had opened a landing spot for their helicopter, marked with lots of fluorescent pink surveyor's tape, tied on to the surrounding trees. Other chainsawed trees lay jackstrawed on the ground.

Jot was stunned and transformed. He had been in a light and graceful mood, at ease in our explorations, clearly a man of the mountains. We'd both been feeling exuberant from our trip up the creek. It had really been a pleasure being with him, uplifting to my rather dark and confused mood.

I'd been feeling bad about my decision to leave Alaska, about my personal failure to bring about my hermitage. Striding down the trail with his long legs, pointing with a stick to this tree and that, to the various berries and fungi and rocks and birds, Jot had effused a delight in what we saw that brought me out of my funk. Such excitement with nature is new to me. I guess I've been a city boy—New York City to Paris and London and then the years in Berkeley—and a Trappist monastery is a kind of city as well, a little medieval walled city, even if it sits in a rural setting. I know now that even this summer, I've been sticking pretty close to the center of Darwin.

I realized that first when Terri took me out to the glacier a couple of weeks ago. It felt so alien out there, as if I had journeyed to the moon or to some Greek version of hades, absent of Christ. And yet I felt an attraction. After all, this was the desert, Alaska version, which I was seeking. Hermits live in deserts—deserted and barren places—don't they? But the desert is a quiet place, and the struggles of a hermit are internal, worked out in the serenity of undisturbed contemplative peace. The glacier did not feel quiet. The attraction I felt was sensuous. It was stimulating and unsettling.

Was it simply Terri's sexual presence that I felt at the glacier? I thought it was, until my walk up the creek with Jot and Les. Jot responds to nature sensually. He was speaking the language of science with his mouth, but his body expression and his attitude was as a lover. I saw it in his hands as he fondled a rock he was showing me and when he gently pulled back the leaves to expose the seeds in a stem of grass. His eyes caressed the mountains as we stood at the end of the tunnel, taking in that vast and desolate scene.

I'm ill at ease with all this hocus-pocus about romance with nature. It is a distraction to me. Well, I don't know. I'm attracted to it, and I don't know if I should be. In a strict moral sense, it's not right for me as a monk and a priest. I'm not going to wallow in sensuality. St. Francis got along well with the birds, but he didn't fondle them.

Jot, though, is not a priest; and it was a joy to see him released from the tensions he brought up with him from his life as a Berkeley professor. I felt good being with him, he had a lot to give, and I shouldn't feel bad about *that*.

But there at the Explorers' cache suddenly it ended. I could see it in an instant: the intensity of his eyes; the tightening in his brow, neck and hands. Probably it would have been better if he could have been angry briefly and then passed off the feeling. Instead, he expressed himself in cold, calculating words. He talked about the evil of the Explorers and their destructiveness. He laid out the reasons against their activities. He could no longer move freely, but only with gestures of protection and offense. He became the lawyer, armed with the unwieldy shield and heavy sword of argument and debate. He was an embattled man, besieged.

We stood there for an hour at least, surrounded by trash and looking at the stack of aluminum wall pieces. The sun dropped over the ridge and I got cold. Finally, I sat down, but Jot still stood. In great detail he laid out his program for combating the Explorers with a series of letters, planning studies, and legal actions directed at government agencies. His lucidity revealed frightening competence. I would not want to be a Explorer and have to face Jotham B. Shechter.

But after awhile it got boring and I got colder and still Jot went on. Finally, I reminded him of the picnic table project and we started back to Les's. As we moved up the trail, we emerged from the shadow of Eldorado Butte and the sun reappeared. With the evidence of the Explorers out of sight, the exercise of walking, and the welcome warmth of the sun, Jot settled down, but his light glow of recent days was gone.

We'll see how his beans turn out tonight.

[My beans were a little undercooked, but edible, I think. After dinner, we listened to the Beethoven violin concerto on Les's stereo. Mike nodded off during the music.

When I awoke the next morning in my sleeping bag on the floor, Les was busy in the kitchen and Mike was reading in the easy chair by my head. By the time I had dressed and washed, Les was serving sourdough pancakes and bitterly strong coffee. I hadn't been drinking coffee at all that summer, favoring herb tea with my morning granola, but I had a cup. The caffeine certainly affected the after-breakfast discussion. I came to know later that these leisurely talks around empty plates, sticky with maple syrup, were the time for philosophical dialectic. Mike and I pushed our chairs away from the table and leaned back. I had the chair which was held together loosely at the legs with wire. I kept thinking it was going to fall apart, so I wasn't as relaxed as when I came to trust Les's baling wire repairs. Les sat in his easy chair in the corner, legs crossed, nursing his third cup of that coffee.

What I remember most from that morning is not the words, not the ideas, but the inflection of Mike's voice, the expression of inquiry on his round face, his being at ease and puzzled at the same time. I didn't notice those sorts of things in people then. It is now, with the changes of many years, that I remember them.

The conversation was a dialogue, and I think it can best be presented that way. What follows is a reconstruction, based on my memory, assisted by both my own and Mike's extensive journal accounts. In his notes Mike actually quoted some of what transpired. —JBS]

Mike: You should know, Jot, how much I enjoyed walking up the valley with you the other day. You were so at ease, so buoyant.

Jot: I like it up here, I like the wilderness. That is why I came to Alaska.

Mike: You taught me so much. Learning the names helps me see the different kinds of trees and rocks. You notice everything around you. Watching you, I am starting to learn how to notice, too. I've never been around an ecologist before.

Jot: Thanks. I'm not an ecologist, actually. I majored in ecology as an undergraduate, but an ecologist is a kind of scientist. I haven't done experiments in years. I'm interested primarily in policy, wildlands policy, which involves politics and planning and natural history. That's a better term, "natural history." It means observing all of the natural world carefully, with method—not just creatures and plants, but the rocks and the weather and so forth.

[Mike paused, looking at me with that open-eyed directness of his, without guile, that inspired trust. At such times he was like both a child and pastoral father. He never was a parish priest, but he would have been a good one.]

Mike: Do you think we are in the wilderness up here?

Jot: Of course we are. Well, no we are not, not strictly. The valley does not conform to the definition of "wilderness" given in the Wilderness Act of 1964. That's a federal law. That's why it wasn't classified as a designated "wilderness area" within the national park when Congress designated the park last year. The roads and buildings preclude wilderness classification.

Mike: How about Les's house? Is it in the wilderness?

Jot: Of course not. It is a non-conforming structure. We find it convenient, but it is an incompatible use.

[Mike looked pensive for a brief moment. I didn't understand why until much later: We were speaking at each other in two different languages. He was asking spiritual questions. I was giving legal answers.]

Mike: Then it should not be here?

Jot: No it shouldn't.

Mike: How about us. Should we be here?

Jot: Where? Up the valley here? In Les's cabin?

Mike: I mean both, I guess.

[Les looked on with interest, legs still crossed, took a sip from his coffee cup. I'm sure he could see that Mike was asking these questions introspectively, rather than aggressively. Mike sat leaning back in his chair with both arms outstretched, one palm up, on the table, the other resting on the heat stove, cold now without a fire in it, an open and vulnerable posture. I don't remember these details. I doubt I even consciously noticed them at the time. But Mike thought them important and recorded them in his journal.

He took each answer I gave him as a little gift. It was like feeding a squirrel nuts at the park. His mind chewed around each answer, while he observed me wide-eyed and even wary. He was obviously non-threatening, and thus disarming to my normal mode of combative conversation, the lawyer's mode to which I had returned since reacting to the Explorers' cache the day before.

He provoked me into answering slowly, after thought, which was not then my habit.]

Jot: In a strict moral sense, it is wrong for this cabin to be here, wrong for us to build and fix that ferry system. There is too little wilderness left in the world. We are selfish to put our mark on this valley.

Mike: How about us, ourselves. Is it right for us to come here?

Jot: It is, if we don't disturb anything, "take only pictures, leave only footprints." We could come, walking lightly, camp in a tent, make only a small fire or carry a backpacker's gasoline stove. Eventually, if too many people came up here, even hikers would be an intrusion. It's the numbers that make the difference.

Here Les interjected: A big fire seemed moral enough after we all went into the creek the other day.

Mike: How about Les? He has lived up here for a couple of decades.

Jot: It's the same for all of us. Has to be, to be consistent. But the law provides for Les, Mike. Les has a permit from the Park Service to be here, a lifetime permit. Because he was here before the park was established, he has grandfather rights. There's a special section in the act of congress allowing him to stay. It prevents undue hardship.

A permit system. That's how the Park Service can control the numbers that come up here hiking, too. Let only a certain number come in, and specify the camping areas to minimize impact, that would be an effective wilderness preservation measure. Part of my work is to develop the data base to support such a system.

[Les just watched. He was interested in seeing what Mike was getting at, and how I would respond.]

Mike: And the old mines, the mining town?

Jot: What about them?

Mike: Are they an intrusion, too?

Jot: Of course. They are considered to have historical value, because they were an important step in the development of Alaska. From the point of view of wilderness preservation, they should be removed. Probably they could be burned, which would accelerate the restoration of natural conditions. But their historical value precludes that.

Mike: I didn't find them very historical. They're only fifty or sixty years old. There are empty industrial buildings in lots of places, like Oakland, California, and Gary, Indiana.

But I found them fascinating. Didn't you? Set way out here, so forlorn. It feels to me they are sinking into the mountainside, slowly crumbling. Very impressive, yes?

Jot: Impressive architecture, for sure. As an integrated and planned set of structures, the place would be interesting to my Berkeley colleagues in the College of Environmental Design. But out of place. Doesn't belong here.

Mike: Too bad. I liked being there yesterday. Sad and lonely, eerie I'd say, attractive. How did you feel? You showed me through the buildings.

Jot: They are interesting. Impressive, as you say. Just out of place. Imagine, though, how it was when the Koyukon Indians hunted up this valley: no buildings, deep forest, many more animals around probably, just a narrow footpath worn by moccasined feet. A mysterious wilderness.

Mike: That would be preferable today?

Jot: Oh, yes, of course. And, hopefully, the Park Service will eventually be able to return the landscape to that natural status.

Mike: No abandoned buildings, no washed-out road, no half-canoes, no picnic tables, no Les and Jot and Mike around the breakfast table?

Jot: We could still be here, but we'd have to come up on our own resources, camping out with a tent. It would be closer to nature.

Mike: I am remembering what it was like to walk through the big mill yesterday. And what it was like to come up here with you two fellows, the creek crossings and all.

[He put his chair down onto all four legs and stared into me.]

We felt such freedom and joy coming up here, all three of us. You were ebullient, Jot, through it all. Until we found the Explorers' stuff.

Jot: That wrecked it. They must be stopped.

Mike: Yes, they must be stopped. I suppose. But why? Why does it matter?

Jot, how do you feel about being so deflated by the Explorers presence up here? You were so joyous, and now you have lost that.

Jot: I have? I think I am doing fine. You are seeing me being efficient. That's the difference. Now I will be efficient so that I can deal successfully with what must be done. We will not be beaten by the Explorers. The valley will be saved.

Mike: My question is, what will you save? You and I have come here from thousands of miles away and we are finding something here. What I see is that you found something and then when you saw the Explorers' stuff and the wrecked beaver houses, you lost it. I found something, too. As for me, the hike in and the scenery and the trials with the boats, the old town, and Les's house way up here, all of it is new and exciting and quite overwhelming. It's disturbing to me, too—maybe just because it is so different from the cloistered life I have led.

My question is, why are we here? Don't you find it odd that a Berkeley law professor and a Catholic monk find themselves in a little log cabin up this creek in Alaska? And what is Les doing here, anyway?

Jot: The answer has several components. We find peace and release from the stress of modern life when we come to the wilderness. We find joy in the physical work of hiking and stream crossing which was necessary to traverse this valley. We feel our unity with nature when we observe and understand the animals and plants and rocks, and the cycles of weather and the seasons so dramatically visible here.

My mood changes when I see the Explorers' cache, because preserving this wilderness sanctuary is important to me. The Explorers intend to make this valley just like the rest of the world outside, a place of machinery and destruction.

Mike: You make it all sound so simple. Maybe it is. It feels to me that there is more to it.

Jot: What do you mean? Can you pin down what you mean?

Mike: Pin it down? No, I can't. I don't think I want to. I just want to sit with what I am feeling. Sit with it. That is what I want to do.

Jot: You have lost me.

[Les nodded at Mike in subtle affirmation. He looked quietly pleased. Was he acting smug, as if he had a secret? I was frustrated, didn't know why. The conversation seemed meaningless. It sat there in my stomach, undigested, for a long time. I had to carry it around with me. I went out to split wood for the cookstove. My muscles were stiff from sitting. I felt better after I took the sledgehammer to several chunks of firewood.]

From Mike's journal:

September 3, 1981

I am alone at Les's house and alone in this valley. Les went down the creek toward Darwin late this morning. Jot decided to go by another route, what Les calls "over the top," that goes over Malachite Ridge and down alongside the Loohana Glacier to Darwin. It's a long, hard hike, Les says, but spectacular in this gorgeous fall weather. And I decided to stay here. I was hesitant in proposing to remain, but when I did, Les thought it was a fine idea. He'll come back up in a week or two and we'll go down together. He used the canoes today to cross the creek, so they're left on the opposite shore from where I'd be if I walk down myself. So I am really here until Les returns, unless I ford the creek or climb over the mountain.

It is very quiet. Nothing is happening and nothing will happen. I am simply here in this cabin in this valley and nothing is happening. The creek is flowing downstream. That is the big event. It makes the only sound, and it is constant.

I guess the Explorers could come back, but there has been no sign of them.

It is evening. I finished cooking Jot's underdone beans and ate them with rice for dinner. The room is still warm from the cooking fire. The sun has set behind the ridge. I am alone.

I have never been alone before. I have been a monk for eleven years and I have lived on this earth for forty-one, and this is the first time I have been alone. I could not speak to anyone even if I wanted to. If I hurt myself, no one will come to help. If I see visions, I must be judge of their truth. If I find God, He will be my only companion. It would make for an intimate relationship.

I sit in Les's easy chair in a corner of the room. The light is subdued; the log walls are dark. Les has filled the gaps between the old logs with some kind of hard foam. It feels like hardened shaving cream, but I suppose it is not. To brighten things up he painted the foam with gold spray paint. I see the aerosol can sitting on the shelf below the long counter, next to the tools: wrenches, pliers, a couple of hammers, a saw, a jar of nails, rusty and a little bent, but reusable.

The house is all one room, plus a sleeping alcove, but one end is the sitting and dining space and the other is the kitchen. The spaces are separated by the wood burning stoves, a cookstove and a big heating stove, occupying the middle. The counter runs the length of the room. At this end, it is covered with a dark red velvet cloth. Connected by a spaghetti of wiring, the stereo system components sit on the cloth, along with a pile of letters, the repair manual for a Honda 90 cc trail bike, a yellow paperback copy of G. I. Gurdjieff's *Meetings with Remarkable Men*, and a roll of resin core solder.

Above the counter, windows face north toward spruce trees and high snow-covered mountains, now pink in the evening sun. They are still in the sun, although it is already darkening here, low in this narrow and deep canyon.

The table on which we eat is right next to me. It is made of planks and covered with a tablecloth. It has no legs. Instead, the back is nailed to the wall and the front is suspended from the ceiling by a pair of large ropes attached to the corners. Two wooden captain's chairs borrowed from the mine town face the table.

This end of the room is carpeted, bright red nylon carpeting except for a strip along one wall, which is gold.

Over near the bedroom, with the correct lighting from the east window, is Les's easel and a small table with oil paints and brushes. On the floor several canvases lean stacked against the wall. A trumpet hangs by a nail overhead. The trunk of a little tree is nailed to the wall next to the bedroom. Les sawed off the branches, leaving nubs which serve as coathooks and a hat rack. His jaunty painter's beret hangs there, and his red down jacket, with feathers coming out around the several patches.

The other end of the long counter is in the kitchen. It has a place for rolling out pastries. The kitchen is well equipped, with all the spices one might want and plenty of cooking pots hanging from nails pounded into the log walls and dishes stacked on open board shelves. Black cast iron skillets sit on the stove, well seasoned. Les does not wash them.

A two-burner gas hotplate sits on the gray metal-topped table over by the kitchen wall. It is connected to a large propane tank which is next to the table, right in the house. I wonder how safe it is to have all that explosive gas kept inside. Aren't gas tanks usually away from a house some distance?

A white enamel sink designed for a kitchen feeding dozens of hungry mine workers, appropriated no doubt from some Syndicate building, is set in an elegant cedar cabinet that must have come up from Seattle by ship and train sixty years ago. One of the cabinet doors has a hole chewed in it. Les said a porcupine did it. Les wasn't happy about that. That cabinet is his finest piece of furniture. In other respects it is in excellent condition. The caulk sealing the cabinet to the cabin wall is painted with that gold spray paint. The sink drains into a bucket located in the cabinet. There is no plumbing, yet.

One of my projects while I am here is to dig a hole next to the house by the kitchen. Les has a piece of high-quality two inch black plastic water pipe left in the valley by some prospecting outfit. He'll connect it to the sink and run it out through the wall into my hole. He says if he covers the hole with insulation and snow, the sink should drain all winter. No more carrying the slop bucket out by hand.

The kitchen floor is covered with linoleum, gray square linoleum tiles at one end and a piece with a white pattern at the other. The root cellar, a deep hole in the ground for storing food at a constant cool temperature, is under the kitchen, reached by a trap door in the floor. Les has been able to keep some eggs in there all summer without spoiling.

In all the walls there are windows with wonderful views. As I look upward, I see that the ceiling is covered in its various portions with some black plastic here, some white insulating board there, and some sort of light-colored material over in the far corner. The roof is held up by a big exposed beam that runs the length of the house, supported with a post by the stoves. The beam is a log, with the bark still on it. From the looks of it, the post in turn is supported only by the floor, which sags under the weight. I know that from sweeping. The area around the post is decidedly the low point in the floor. That makes it easier to sweep, because the dirt goes downhill.

As I write, the light is fading. Night is coming. I have switched on the reading light mounted above this comfortable overstuffed chair. It's electric, one of those glaring car bulbs it looks like, but with an aluminum foil reflector that actually directs a decent light over my shoulder onto the page. Massive batteries, connected by a maze of exposed wiring, switches and gauges, fill the space between the chair and the wall to my right. A paperback science fiction novel, *Destination Void*, by Frank Herbert, lies on one of the batteries. My left hand reaches down to a pile on the floor: Three back issues of *Playboy*, two of *Scientific American*, and the trumpet score for a Haydn concerto.

I think back on the conversation this morning. I asked about wilderness. We talked about this cabin and about the mines and about the Explorers. But I think back and what comes up is not that. I sit here in this chair in the darkening evening and I envision Jot's naked back glistening with the spray of ice water, his muscles straining to grip the rope against the torrent of current as he struggled toward the canoe. I see his muscles knot and release, tighten and flow in rhythm with his movements, the rippling of his back and shoulders emulating the roiled surface of the raging creek. I feel the shock of being thrown suddenly into that torrent, the split-second of absolute helplessness, then Les's firm grip on my arm, the muscled saving gesture, the certainty of his hold, that little man virtually lifting me out of the water, his coming as a total and unthinking act of the flesh.

As I write, moment by moment this room darkens. I am the only person in this valley. No one can know what I do here. If I wander off into the woods, lose my direction, I could wander until I starved. Eventually I would be eaten by a bear. Probably I would never be found. From the point of view of the outside world, I would simply vanish. If when I next go through the yard to the outhouse I am surrounded by an assembly of angels and carried off to heaven, I would never be found by any man. I would simply vanish. How odd.

If in a week or two I return to the world down the valley, it is an act of my own volition and responsibility. Whatever happens in the meantime is up to me; more precisely, between me and God.

Finally, I am a hermit. At least for the moment.

Can I be a hermit? Am I up to it?

A hermit maintains discipline.

> Happy are they whose way is blameless,
> who walk in the law of the Lord.
> Happy are they who observe his decrees,
> who seek him with all their heart,
> And do no wrong,
> but walk in his ways.
> You have commanded that your precepts
> be diligently kept.
> Oh, that I might be firm in the ways
> of keeping your statutes!

I sit here in darkening silence. I remember the fire we built to warm and dry ourselves. I remember our naked bodies illuminated by flames. I remember the heat as I reached in to add wood to the fire. I remember the abrupt cold and dark as I left the circle of warmth and light to search the gravel flats for another stick of wood. I feel the heat of the fire beating into my chest, feel myself touching the hot hairs on my own chest. I remember Les's tight grip on my arm as he hauled me from the icewater. I feel my heart beating, the rhythmic thump thump. I remember. I remember the rhythmic chanting. I remember chanting with my brothers in choir in the monastery. I remember chanting with my brothers around the fire. I remember the rhythmic thump thump.

Lord, you have been our refuge
> through all generations.
Before the mountains were begotten
>> and the earth and the world were brought forth,
>> from everlasting to everlasting you are God.
You turn man back to dust,
>> saying, "Return, O children of men."
For a thousand years in your sight
>> are as yesterday, now that it is past,
or as a watch of the night.
You make an end of them in their sleep;
>> the next morning they are like the changing grass,
Which at dawn springs up anew,
>> but by evening wilts and fades.

I am alone in this valley. Finally I am alone. Whatever shall I do? It is dark. I feel the thump, thump of my heart. My bladder is full. I shall have to go outside to pee. I shall have to confront the darkness. There are wild animals out there. I am afraid to go out. Don't tell anyone. I am afraid to go out and pee. I want to stay right here in the little circle of light thrown by this 12-volt automobile bulb with the aluminum foil reflector.

Thump, thump, thump, thump. I hear the drumbeat. I know the bear is out there, outside the circle of the light.

Let my cry come before you, O Lord;
> in keeping with your word, give me discernment.
Let my supplication reach you;
> rescue me according to your promise.

September 4, 1981

I have dreamed:

A man dressed in white is there ahead of me on the gravel road. He walks on away and does not look back. I follow. He pushes open a massive wooden door and enters a building. I follow.

I see him climbing upward. I must pursue him. Here and there I find ladders, old wooden ladders with handrails, handrails worn smooth by the passage of many hands. I climb the ladders from floor to floor. The building is endless, rising one story above the other. It is made of bare wood beams. It has no rooms. It has platforms and scaffolding connected by the ladders. It has giant rusted machinery, shafts and gears and conveyor belts running from level to level. I have to duck and twist and crawl to pass around the equipment. It is dark, except for a glare of light coming from windows in one wall only. There is no glass in the windows. The glass is broken out. It lies in shards on the floor.

I almost catch up with him. A long stairway leads outside of the building. It connects again at the top of the building, somewhere far above. It is suspended in space. It is mounted on tall posts. I can see that some of the posts are rotten. The stairway is narrow. It has no handrails. He is climbing the stairway. I step on the first stair. It is rotten. I am afraid. I am too exposed out there. It is a long way down if I fall. I dare not follow. I go back inside. I climb the ladders inside. I must find him. I trip on the rung of a ladder. I hold on to the railing. I am afraid. Now the building is occupied. There are many workers. They are little men. They are beavers. They walk with humped backs. They walk shuffling their feet, dragging heavy tails behind them. They look straight ahead, intent on their duties. They do not see me.

They start the equipment. Slowly, the shafts and gears and conveyor belts begin to turn. I must be very careful not to be caught in the machinery. It is very loud.

There are beavers everywhere. I must wait my turn to climb the ladders. I must get to the top and get out.

146

Now the beavers are Trappist monks. They are wearing heavy wool robes with cowls. The robes are long and heavy. They drag along on the ground. The monks look straight ahead, intent on their duties. They do not see me. I am not a monk. I am an explorer. I wear blue jeans.

They are chanting the Hail Holy Queen.

"Hail Holy Queen, Mother of Mercy, our life, our sweetness and our hope! To you do we cry, poor banished children of Eve; to you do we send up our sighs, mourning and weeping in this valley of tears! Turn, then, most gracious Advocate, your eyes of mercy toward us, and after this, our exile, show unto us the blessed fruit of your womb, Jesus. O clement, O loving, O sweet Virgin Mary!"

The beavers are gnawing on the timbers that hold up the building. They must stop! The building will fall on all of us! Don't they see?!

Now there is a small room set into the vastness of the building. It has a floor and ceiling and three walls. The open side is reached by a short ladder from the platform I am now on. A man sits at a desk. He is the abbot. He is the spiritual father of the monks. His cowl covers his head. I cannot see his face. He is reading and he is typing slowly, hunt and-peck, at an old typewriter. Does he not see the urgency?

He is reading from the Bible, from Isaiah,

> "Lo, the Lord empties the land and lays it waste;
>> he turns it upside down,
>> scattering its inhabitants; ...
> The earth is utterly laid waste, utterly stripped,
>> for the Lord has decreed this thing.
> The earth mourns and fades,
>> the world languishes and fades;
>> both heaven and earth languish.
> The earth is polluted because of its inhabitants,
>> who have transgressed laws, violated statutes,
> broken the ancient convenant.

"Terror, pit and trap
      are upon you, inhabitant of the earth;
He who flees at the sound of terror
      will fall into the pit;
He who climbs out of the pit
      will be caught in the trap.
For the windows on high will be opened
      and the foundations of the earth will shake.
The earth will burst asunder,
      the earth will be shaken apart,
      the earth will be convulsed.
The earth will reel like a drunkard,
      and it will sway like a hut;
Its rebellion will weigh it down,
      until it falls, never to rise again."

I can tell what the abbot is typing. It is a requisition list. He is ordering replacement parts for the machinery. Does he not see the urgency? Why does he not see the urgency? A beaver has climbed the short ladder into his office. It is gnawing at a leg of his desk.

His telephone rings. It is an old telephone, with a crank to turn to make it operate. The abbot picks up the ear-piece. God the Father is on the line. I cannot hear what He is saying.

I know a bear has entered the building. Somewhere below me. I must climb out before it finds me.

The beavers are at work down below. I hear crashing. They have cut through some of the lower timbers. Platforms below me are collapsing. I must get out through the top.

Where is the bear?

I climb many ladders. Now the abbot is far below me. I hear a surprised yelp coming from his direction. Perhaps a beaver has bitten into his leg by mistake. Is he still on the telephone?

There is a door set into the dark cold wall. It is not straight on its hinges. I can see light coming in around it. I open the door.

It opens outward onto a steep sloping meadow filled with warm sunlight and wildflowers. A burbling brook flows through it. A magnificent fruit tree in bloom grows next to the brook, drinking of the clear waters from gnarled roots. A figure in white wades through the tall waving warm grass. He is dressed in a light, flowing robe. He has long, clean locks of hair. He is a young, blond bearded man. He has a wooden box in front of him, slung from a leather strap around his shoulders. The box is filled with ripe, red apples. There is a sign on the box. It says,

"Apples, 25 Cents."

I do not have twenty-five cents. Whatever shall I do? The young man speaks in a gentle, soft voice: His mother will give me twenty-five cents. She lives above the building.

I am out in the meadow now. I look back at the building. It is painted blue, with white trim, old and faded. It is massive and huge and is built in steps against the steep hillside. Parts of the roof are missing. The many windows are broken. Chemicals of some sort are leaking out around the foundation, red and brown fingers of wetness poisoning the edge of the meadow. The meadow is not large. It is surrounded by tall brush. I cannot see through the brush. I can see neither the top nor the bottom of the building. I could not walk through the thick brush. The only way to the top is through the building.

I must go back into the building. I must leave the young man in the meadow. I must climb the ladders to the very top. I need a quarter for an apple.

I go in but am lost. I climb over equipment. But there is a passage. It is in the back of the building, where it is built into the hillside. It leads into the earth, cool and dark. I step down into it on damp stairs. I can see nothing. I cannot proceed. I hear the drip of water. I am afraid.

That is the end of the dream.

I do not understand it.

The dream is just a result of going into that old mining building with Jot. It has nothing to do with my reasons for being here. I can forget it. I must forget it. It is so disturbing.

As I write these words, Les's house is suddenly transformed by the morning sunlight streaming in the south window. I feel the valley glow with light and color. Now with the sunshine, the dream is far away, unreal.

I feel good this morning. I wish to greet my wilderness world. I am a hermit. At last I am a hermit. I am alone in this valley. Today I will walk amidst the fall leaves and along the bank of the creek. I will chop firewood and cook beans. I will see no one and speak to no one. I will say Mass in the company of soaring white mountains.

A two week experimental hermitage. Until Les returns.

Everything is OK. Oh My, whatever shall I do? Whatever shall I do?

I need time to let all this settle out. I need time to work it through. I have time. I will give it time.

Later

I write this by candlelight. Giant gears and belts hang in the darkness at the edge of the light. Beyond is darkness, and rain dripping through leaky roofs; it has been raining hard without letup. I am in the old mill building at the mine, could not stay away, have been here all day. Why?

Just now I thought I saw a figure moving in the darkness. The thought is terrorizing. I am the only person in the valley. I know I am.

Today I went to the stairway outside the building on tall, rotting posts. So unsafe. I dared not step out onto it.

During the day I found a dark passageway, leading into the earth where the building is built against the mountainside. Damp steps led downward. I should have brought a flashlight. I did not think. I did not think that I would stay here the night. I did not think I would find a passageway.

I had some matches, lit one and tried to follow its light down the damp steps. The light did not show what was to come. The match burned out. Darkness was ahead, and the sound of a slow drip of water. I dared not lose sight of the passageway entrance, of the mill machinery standing in the light of day. I retreated.

I cannot go ahead. I cannot go back. Why am I here? I cannot say. Yet I know I must be here. For the first time I am being a hermit. I like it. I hate it. What I feel about it makes no difference. I have to be here. Why do I have to be here? What does this have to do with finding God?

Nothing. Nothing, nothing, nothing.

I have to get out of this building. But I cannot find my way back to Les's house in the darkness, through the rain. I have to be here all night. I have to wait for the light.

Another day

The heavens open up and poured forth waters. The creek, which had reduced to a pleasant brook, rages now beyond anything I have yet seen, brown foam, leaping its banks, ripping trees from the shore, rolling boulders clanking down its bed.

I think of the Syndicate with its millions, building the railroad with its tracks and bridges up here, now all gone; of LJR with his cat, his decades of work rebuilding the road, swept away in one such storm.

Creek, you are a creek no more. River, I hear you, I hear the roar of your waters from inside this cabin.

In the forest, the leaves are blown from the trees; now the earth stands bare before the blasts. I hear sudden roars in the night; by day I see mudslides peeling off the mountainsides, taking whole slices of the forest with them. Trees float by, sailing on the river, their roots rising upward like masts.

Sometime in September

...I tried plugging up the leak in the roof with a plastic bag and some tape, but it didn't work. So I put a saucepan under the drip. Plink, plink, plink.

I've lost the date. Perhaps it is around somewhere, but I can't find it. No watch, either. In the morning the sky lightens weakly and in the evening it gets pitch dark. Rain.

I don't use Les's electric light anymore. It is too harsh. Instead, I use a kerosene lamp.

When?

It is an evening. This afternoon it snowed long enough to cover the grass in the yard, then switched to rain again, melting the snow. The air is thick with cloud, sealing me off from the world down the valley. I am sitting by the warmth of the stove. I am alone. I should be at peace. I should be a monk, a simple hermit alone with God.

Alone? But I am cast adrift upon a raging brown river, and the torn remnants of strange dreams toss with me as the banks hurtle by, images sharp, hard and dangerous, like the fallen trees sailing down that river that rages outside my door.

Oh Mary, holy virgin mother of God, help me.

I breathe deeply and slowly. With each rhythmical breath I feel myself paddling my canoe to shore. Let me be at peace. Firm breath, strong breath: my body is substantial, the dreams are but images. I begin to relax. I feel the radiant warmth of the fire in the stove.

I love it here, you know, alone in this valley. I exult in solitude. It is an addiction, a drunkenness. I fear I have passed a frontier. Can I go back? No? I am no longer an ascetic. I am a sensualist.

I become a lush, drunk on the dark evening, an addict to the flame of the lamp. Drunkenness gets to the liver, and to the brain.

I am in the garden. My fingertips touch everything—the fading light of dusk, the raging of the river, the softness of the lamp. I burn my fingertips on the flaming logs in the stove.

It is not as I anticipated. No, it is so hard. Am I a monk or a hedonist in sin? I fear I have crossed a frontier and I can never go back. I fear I can never go back to the monastery.

My attention wanders, my breathing tightens up. And the images return again, the wheels and gears, beavers gnawing at my foundations, Jesus walking away from me. Jesus, I cannot get to you, Jesus. Why not?

My head is stuffed with busy beavers, building up and tearing down. No room for Jesus. Too busy.

I remember a quotation from Meister Eckhart,

"A pure heart is one that is unencumbered, unworried, uncommitted, and which does not want its own way about anything but which, rather, is submerged in the loving will of God, having denied self."

I am sitting here alone in this valley in the darkening night. What am I to do? Whatever shall I do?

I shall pray. I shall read the gospels. I shall follow Jesus, Who said,
"I am the light of the world.
No follower of mine shall ever walk in darkness;
no, he shall possess the light of life."

I shall be a monk.

Next day

Finally, the sun shines bright on snowy peaks and the woods are wet and clean.

I have come back inside for a peanut butter and jelly sandwich. Les has lots of peanut butter, in gallon jars. He baked bread while he was here, little sourdough loaves. I made some crackers, too, to use in the Eucharist.

Fortunately, Les had a bottle of wine, an unopened gift from a visitor last winter. We each had a glass with dinner, the night before Jot and Les left. There's still quite a bit left.

I used it to celebrate a joyous Mass this morning. I covered the picnic table with a white sheet as an altar cloth and found a (relatively) clean dish towel to use as the corporal. As I raised aloft the Body and the Blood of Christ, I was joined in the doxology by little grey birds wearing black caps, flying and swooping into the spruce trees around me, singing in adoration, "dee, dee, dee," a congregation of the faithful.

Later I sauntered along the path that continues up the valley, admiring the white-barked trees, the breeze-tossed patterns of sunlight and shade on the forest floor, the brilliant blue of the sky and the eternal white of Dagheeloyee Peak.

Can I admit it here? I skipped down the hill to the creek. I stood on the creek bank and preached like St. Anthony to the fishes. Give thanks to God for the waters! St. Anthony got good results: lots of fishes came and stuck their heads out of the water and listened. None appeared for me. I wonder if there are any fish up here? Could they live in this torrent?

I spun around in a little dance, snapping my fingers, singing St. Francis's Canticle of Brother Sun,

Be praised, my Lord, with all your creatures,

Especially Sir Brother Sun,

By whom You give us the light of day!

And he is beautiful and radiant with great splendor.

Of You, Most High, he is a symbol!

I spun until I fell dizzy on the moss. Like Brother Masseo! St. Francis and Brother Masseo were walking along and they came to a fork in the road. Which way to go? They didn't know. So St. Francis made the brother twirl around until he lost all sense of direction. "Stop!" said the saint, "Point the direction we shall go." And Brother Masseo pointed, and where he pointed is the road they chose, following God's will.

Some other time

I looked at Les's canvases, the ones stacked against the wall by his easel. That was snooping into his private things, just a little. They are incomplete paintings. Perhaps some are rejects. One is a picture of the bluff above the creek at 2-mile. It shows an enormous white dragon, embedded in the rock of the cliff.

From Jot's field notebook:

3 September 1981
1:00 p.m.
Location: On the gravel floodplain of Dagheeloyee Creek, just downstream from Eldorado Butte.

The unobstructed sun illuminates the valley from the South, its angle already so much lower than it was at mid-summer, its light strong, warm and pleasant, but no longer overbearing, not even now at midday. The spruce at forest's edge cast substantial shadows northward. Sparkling in the sunshine, Dagheeloyee Creek flows gently over the gravels it has brought down from the surrounding mountains.

I wonder if the creek does most of its rock-moving during floods. On previous occasions of high water, I could hear cobbles rolling along on the bed of the stream. This instability made fording the creek difficult and dangerous. But now the creek is a murmuring brook, its flow of clear waters much reduced from just three days ago, when we crossed it as a silty torrent. With the clear skies, nights abruptly became cold; even now plates of ice adhere to the north side of streambank rocks. The creek, fed primarily by melting snow and ice, shrinks and calms.

I sit on a boulder of white porphyry rock. The creek waters have rounded it, making a smooth and comfortable seat. I have Jack Rogers' maps and books with me. The geologic map shows a band of felsic hypabyssal (porphyry) rocks up the valley on Chalcocite Ridge. This boulder must have come from there. By the geologists' dictionary: "felsic:" composed chiefly of light colored feldspars, feldspathoids, quartz. "hypabyssal:" formed under the earth, but not too deep (above the abyss). It was intruded from below as a hot liquid into cracks in the surrounding mother rock. According to the map, the intrusion took place in the mid-Cretaceous. The Cretaceous period lasted about seventy-five million years, a time of the later dinosaurs, which died out during the great world-wide extinction at its end.

By comparison, it was only a little while ago, some thousands of years past, when this boulder tumbled down the mountainside. I imagine that water worked its way into hairline cracks in the exposed surface of the porphyry, up there on the ridge. Each winter, the water froze and expanded, pushing on the cracks, over the years breaking free chunks like this one.

How did it get down the valley to its present location? By its own weight, it could have rolled from ridgetop to the creekbed. But I cannot imagine Dagheeloyee Creek moving such a heavy rock miles downstream. Could it have happened during a massive flood? Or was the valley floor filled with a glacier at the time that the boulder fell? Perhaps it rolled out onto that glacier and was carried here on top of it, as the ice flowed downstream.

The upper Dagheeloyee Valley is ice-free now. But the Loohana Valley floor, just over the ridge, is covered with glacier ice. Why the difference? They are both at about the same elevation. In fact, the Dagheeloyee Valley is a thousand feet higher. I shall have to observe both valleys more closely for clues.

From here I have a view of the full sweep of Chalcocite Ridge, a dozen kilometers of exposed rock. The rocks are piled layer upon layer, one kind upon another, like a giant layer cake of many flavors, except, instead of being vertical, the whole assembly is tilted. In the autumn light some layers do look edible: chocolate, vanilla, a candy-like purple.

The only reason all these layers are exposed to view is that they have been uplifted and tilted. They were made one atop the other, the newer layers burying the old ever deeper in the earth. During the making of these mountains, the whole sequence moved up and sideways, raising miles of rock, which otherwise would have remained hidden from human sight forever. The glaciers helped. They cut away the sides of the ridge, steepening them into these towering cliffs, exposing clean, bare rock. In their prime, the glaciers in this valley are thousands of feet thick, smothering much of the ridge under ice, scraping and eroding where they lie, undercutting the slopes above. The glaciers come and go with the cycles of the weather. At present, they are but a remnant; however, they will come again, and doubtless yet again.

Down the valley, I see a sharp arete crested with a golden horn: light rocks, the oldest in the valley, by the map Permian limestones, 250 million years old, containing identifiable fossils.

Looming over me here the ridge is brooding dark by comparison: basaltic lava flows which emerged from seafloor vents during the Triassic, each flow leaving a layer a few feet thick on what was then a flat seabottom, accumulating, pressed and altered into this black-green mass accounting now for several kilometers of the ridge, containing no fossils, no record of life within.

Upvalley I see the contact between the basalt and another limestone formation, the Eldorado Limestone, their meeting making a long line angling across Eldorado Butte, dark against light, an almost featureless igneous mass touching the sweeping bends and folds of a multi-layered rock composed of the bodies of archaic creatures from long-gone tropical seas.

The copper was deposited in the Eldorado Limestone, dissolved out of the basalt, where it exists in low concentration, and precipitated by evaporating water into the limestone caverns. Think of it: an insemination of the living rock by the juices of the dark and heavy basalt, a penetration achieved over an eon, a treasure developing within the womb of the world.

A treasure ripped from the womb by the miners, sucked out through their tunnels, as a vacuum suction abortion extracts a fetus, done and gone in a geological instant.

Up the valley, beyond the Eldorado Limestone, are other, more recent, sea-floor deposits: the Loohana Limestone, layers of carbonaceous shale, the Dagheeloyee Limestone, then layers of reddish-brown weathered sandstone, more shales. Then conglomerates—consolidated beds of stream gravels, pressed hard into rock—in total, a hundred and fifty million years of accumulation, during which the basalt and the limestone remained locked in tight embrace deep under the earth.

Then beyond, at the head of the valley, where Chalcocite Ridge disappears into the high central massif: Dagheeloyee lavas, subducted seafloor pulled under the continent, heated by the earth's internal fires, ejaculated to the surface from the uttermost depths. From here the layers of solidified lavas appear as bands of dark and light alternating on the steep headwalls, on the layer-cake cirques which are topped by a thick cream frosting of white glacier ice. Steam, rising from the summit of Dagheeloyee Peak, towering above all, shows that the process of rock formation, of the continuing creation, is not yet over.

3 September 1981

7 p.m.

Location: On the west shore of Dagheeloyee Lake,

near Dagheeloyee Glacier.

I put up my tent on the gravel flats near the lake. From down here in the valley, the sun has set over Chalcocite Ridge. Sunbeams project between indentations in the rock, a crown of searchlights sweeping across the baby blue sky. At timberline, I see patches aflame with crimson: perhaps the autumn leaves of bearberries and blueberries. Other patches glow yellow: quaking aspen, I presume.

Wavelets of grey, silted water lap at the lakeshore. A fleet of icebergs rests on the water's surface. Damp cold wafts off the water and the adjacent glacier. Here and there, clear new ice skims puddles shaded by rocks. This ice of the new season survived the warmth of the day; it will grow and thicken tonight.

I hold a piece of ice against my swollen left cheek. This afternoon, as I finished writing in my notebook up by Eldorado Butte, I walked over to sit on the soft earthen bank of the forest's edge, where it gives way to the gravel and boulders along the creek. I must have sat directly into a yellow jacket nest in the soil. The beasts came swarming out. Instantly without thinking I hurled myself into the creek, the only possible refuge, boots, clothes and all, and lay there in the shallow water, as submerged as I could be, swatting and smashing the wasps that even underwater adhered to my pants and shirt.

A benefit of the prompt icewater bath was a diminution of the consequences: it is the recommended treatment for stings. But everything I was wearing was wet. Once the creatures had settled, I fled down the gravel bar a couple hundred yards to regroup myself. It took awhile before I dared venture back to get my pack and this journal, which of course I'd left right at the opened nest.

I wrung out my wet things and strung them on the back of my pack to dry in the sun. Although I don't carry a full change of clothes, I had dry socks and underwear and sweater, so I could carry on.

But the delay was substantial. Instead of crossing the glacier and ascending to camp at the pass tonight, I ended up here. I had wanted to spend more time at the pass. It must be splendid up there. But I really don't have enough food nor fuel for the stove for more than this one night out. So tomorrow I will have to traverse over the pass and on to Darwin. Maybe if I move right along, I can take a couple of hours to explore and observe around the pass.

Meanwhile, the stings are painful. I hope I can sleep tonight.

In the morning I start out onto the glacier. This is the only place I can get onto it. Everywhere else on the valley floor the glacier edge is too steep, or the glacier comes right up against impassable rock cliffs. Only here does the white ice slope gently to the gravel, making an easily traversed ramp. According to Les's directions, once atop the glacier I walk angling upstream, zig-zagging between the crevasse fields. The glacier is bare, firm ice, and I should be able to see and avoid any dangers. Then on the other side, directly below the pass, an easy way off the ice leads to the base of the trail that goes over the top.

It will be very beautiful. I'll get an early start.

4 September 1981
10 a.m.
Location: At the bottom of the little moat between the east
edge of Dagheeloyee Glacier and the base of Mt. Malachite,
1000 meters below Malachite Pass.

What a strange and isolated spot. Compared with the vast space I felt all around me while I was crossing the glacier, this valley is a hidden garden, walled off by a sinuous gravel moraine on one side and steep mountain slopes on the other. I feel as if I could reach out and touch both the moraine and the mountain at one time.

On beyond the moraine, the sheer ice edge is but a hundred meters away. I can see that not long ago the ice extended all the way to here. But the glacier edge has melted back, leaving the barrier wall of broken rock between its cold face and the base of the mountain, creating this sheltered moat that geologists call the "fosse."

Over by the glacier nothing grows. But here a meadow flourishes in rich soil. While the flowers are past blooming, the autumn display is splendid: blueberries set in nests of tiny, lush-red leaves; the blue-black crowberries; the saturated red of the bearberry leaves and fruits; the maroon of the cranberries; the yellow and orange foliage of drying flowers. Only green is absent.

The colors are reversed from the summer season, opposite from our normal expectations. And human eyes cannot process red and blue at the same time; our perceptions vibrate rapidly between the colors. The effect is hallucinatory in this moat, surrounded by an uninhabited expanse of rock and ice.

The biggest plants on this northwest-facing slope are a few knee-high spruce. The needles of some are brown, dead and failed. Perhaps the spruce are here because the glacier is melting back. In a hundred years, maybe, they will make a new forest here. Or maybe, instead, a little more snow will fall on Dagheeloyee Peak above, one extra storm each year, and the glacier will thicken, once again obliterating everything living within this valley, within the lifetime of these struggling trees.

Nice as this spot is today, I'm glad I'm not staying here long. I found a set of enormous bear tracks along the base of the moraine. The fosse might be a natural route for the animals. That is perturbing. I don't want to encounter a bear in this confined space. I remember that Les always travels armed, which of course I would not do.

I am getting tired already, and my head still aches from the wasp stings. I was too uncomfortable to sleep much last night. Restless, knowing I have a long way to go today, and that I'd like to have time to enjoy the pass, I was up at first light (that's by 6 a.m. now). I hustled through breakfast, packed up and mounted the ice ramp onto the glacier.

It is clean white ice, crunchy underfoot, easy to walk on. Once you get up onto the glacier, the mountain country is all that matters. Whatever is down there in the world of living plants and animals, of trees and flowers and squirrels and towns, is distant and trivial in contrast to the giants all around: the expanse of ice catching the morning sun, the ranks of peaks rising through crisp, invigorating air. And you are a part of it all, your breath steaming with each exhalation. You are a speck amidst the summits which are as the pantheon of Olympus around you, but you are among them nonetheless, above and apart from that lesser world below.

I wound my way between the cracks in the ice. Several times I had to jump streams flowing on the surface of the glacier, crystal water racing down channels incised into turquoise ice. I attended carefully to my route. Staying to the way Les recommended, I traversed a country of gentle ice hills and vales. But when I mistakenly wandered too far downstream on the glacier, suddenly I was in a tumultuous landscape of cliffs and crevasses.

I ended up taking hours to cross what by straight line is less than two kilometers of glacier. Finally, I found a place where I could climb down off the ice with difficulty. Downstream from this spot, the glacier abuts untraversable cliffs at the base of Mt. Malachite. The only way on to Darwin is up, up over the pass.

Les said this is where the trail begins. I see no sign of a trail. But this has to be the place. I'll just start up the mountainside. It is all meadow, the footing is good, there is no brush. I don't need a trail. The pass is directly above. I'll rest in the sun at the pass. I'm already tired and not feeling too well. I'll need a nap.

4 September 1981

7 p.m.

Location: Malachite Pass.

I finally got to the pass and into my tent. The tent is not on a level spot, but it will have to do. I'm not sure this is actually the pass, but it is probably close: the ground slopes down on both sides, as best I can tell.

When the wet snow got under my glasses I had to take them off. It probably didn't matter, because I could not see more than a few feet anyway through the fog and with the snow gusting into my face. Thank goodness at least I got to where I could pitch the tent. The snow is deep enough now that it got over the top of my boots. My feet are wet and cold.

One minute I was sweating in the sun and the next it was hailing and then the hail turned to snow.

The meadow was so easy to walk on when it was dry. It turned so slick with the snow on it, too slick to even think about trying to go back down the steep part. Even continuing on up was almost impossible. And I was still aching from the stings and my head was pounding. At least that feels better now, enough to write. Writing takes my mind off what is going on out there.

I twisted my ankle. I think it is OK, but it is beginning to hurt. I tripped on my own feet and slid down a hundred meters of slope. There was just no way to stop on the slippery hillside. I thought the worst part was going to be having to climb all the way back up. Then my ankle started to hurt, but I made it on up here.

I just want to huddle in my sleeping bag out of this storm. Maybe it will be over by morning. In the morning I'll light the stove and cook something hot to eat. I had a couple of candy bars left, so I ate those. I hope by morning it will clear off and I can cook a meal outside and get on down to Darwin.

5 September 1981

12 noon

The storm is still raging. I have slept only intermittently. The wind bangs the tent. The roar and slamming keeps waking me. There must be a foot of snow out there. Because it is blown into drifts it's hard to tell exactly how much there is. I tried getting dressed, but my ankle is too swollen to lace up my boots. Still it keeps snowing. Visibility zero.

At least I have had a good meal. I ate last night's dinner this morning, cooking in the tent: a glop of freeze-dried swiss steak, peas, instant mashed potatoes. It felt so good to have something warm. I have one hot meal left: a Malt-O-Meal breakfast. It was supposed to have raisins and nuts with it, but I've eaten them already. The storm can't last. It has to end and then I will go down.

5 September 1981

6 p.m.

The tent was collapsing under the weight of the snow. I had to go out and dig it out with my hands. Now my gloves are soaked, too. Every time I go out I bring snow back in with me on my clothes. I can't help it: with the wind it gets into everything and it sticks, so everything in the tent is getting wetter. I just ate my last hot meal and I am still hungry. I have to use the stove to melt snow to get water to drink. My urine is very yellow, so I know I am getting dehydrated.

I still can't tie my boot over my left ankle and it hurts.

I have to stay here until it clears and then hobble down off the pass to Darwin.

I think I am camped at the pass but I am not sure. I could not see where I was when I made camp and it is still impossible to see anything.

6 September 1981

It is morning. It has just got light. I don't know what time it is. My watch got water in it and stopped. It was in the corner of the tent. All the corners are wet now. The foot of my sleeping bag is soaked through. I am cold. My ankle is throbbing. Maybe I have a fever. I have to get up the energy to melt some snow to drink.

The snow has turned to cold rain. That is worse. I don't dare go out of the tent for fear of getting soaked through and freezing.

All I want to do is get to Darwin.

The wind keeps howling and it is driving me nuts. The wind just has to stop.

I can't sleep. I can't toss and turn because I have to stay in the middle of the tent to stay out of the puddles. Sometimes I fall asleep exhausted, but I don't know for how long that is.

I have to get down today. I have to get down to survive.

Later

I tried getting down. I can't. I am writing this for whoever finds me. I will freeze and die. I am back in the tent again. It is snowing and the wind is blowing. The tent is still slamming in my ears from the wind.

I tried getting down to Darwin. I got on my clothes and my jacket and my raincoat and even my boots. I cannot tie up my left boot because of the ankle. It hurts.

I cannot carry anything because of that ankle. I just have to walk down and leave everything up here. Luckily I left the tent up so when I failed I got back in.

I got out of the tent. I went over to the edge. It is steep. I can't see anything in the fog. It looks like cliffs down there. I can't see. I didn't dare go down. I might get stuck on the cliffs. I can't walk too well. My foot hurts.

Later

I want to be in Berkeley. All I want is to be in Berkeley. Let me be there. I will never come back here again. It was a mistake. I am dying. Everything is wet. I am thirsty.

Why did I come to Alaska to be miserable.

Why am I here. Why.

Later

No good. Bang, bang the tent bangs in my ears. I cover them with my hands.

Got to dig out the tent. Too much snow on it. Can't.

I sleep I wake. What time is it.

I write in the notebook. Got to write in the notebook.

Fever.

it is later
next day
    Wind stopped.
    Thank god
         wind stopped
    I hear them out there   Quiet now   I hear them walking
    on the snow   can't see
              fog
    They talk   many voices   I can't hear words
    can't see them   they are out there
            where?

Later
    Thank god quiet. I have slept. Fever must be down.

Later
    The bear.
    He is around the tent.
    He is pushing at the tent or is it the wind come again. Please no wind.
Please no bear. Please no, no no

later
    Angels. I did not know there was such a thing as angels. Father Mike
will be pleased. Wingspan est. approx. 3.5 meters avg. + or - .25 meters.
Color: iridescent yellow-blue. Number in flock est. 125, allow 25% factor
for error either way.

    later   bear is back   go away bear

    later   got to walk to Darwin. get dressed. wear tennis shoes. can't
wear boots. ankle. leave stuff here & travel light mail day got to get down
to meet the mail plane

10 September 1981

It was early evening, just before dark, day before yesterday, when Terri found me. She says I was wearing tennis shoes and my sweater, jacket and raincoat, all soaked. My glasses were missing. She says I had an ace bandage on my ankle. I must have left my pack and tent and all my gear up on the pass.

I do remember getting out of the tent. The storm stopped, but I could hardly see in the fog. Somehow I lost my glasses; rolled on them and broke them in the tent, dropped them in the snow, I'm not sure. The air was so still and thick. It was quiet, and I couldn't see. The snow was way up over the top of my sneakers, but I didn't pay any attention.

All I could see were these enormous bear tracks in the snow. They came right by the tent, circled it, and kept on going.

I followed the tracks.

If they had not been there, I would have had no idea where to go. They dropped down off the edge of the pass and angled down in a definite direction, traversing an easy slope between two gullies, then down through thick brush.

I got to the bottom of the slope. I found myself following the bear tracks through a flat field of snow, still in the fog. Gradually, the fog raised a little. I could see the base of the mountain rising steeply to my right. Off to the left, maybe a couple of hundred meters away, was a towering wall of bare rubble moraine. At first, I couldn't see the top of it.

I just followed the tracks. I must have been in the fosse between the ridge and the Loohana Glacier. It was so big and empty, with a flat, featureless floor covered now with snow.

I don't know how long I wandered down the fosse. The fog came down again. I could see nothing but the tracks. I seem to remember shouting for help. There was no echo; the fog absorbed the sound. I think I staggered through the snow like a blind man, feeling with my hands out in front of me. I was lightheaded, either hypothermic or feverish. My vision was like opening my eyes underwater. I felt like I was swimming.

I remember seeing a big, dark spot. The bear tracks went toward it. It was the entrance to a cave. I checked today on the geologic map. The mountain there is limestone. It could well have caves in it.

The tracks disappeared into the cave. I stood just inside the entrance, looking into total blackness. I dared not go in, even though for some reason I wanted to. Stale air came out of the cave. I could hear a roaring and humming within, as if the air were pouring through distant passageways. As my eyes adjusted to the dark, I remember seeing icicles on the ceiling and walls near the entrance, where there was enough light to see. I don't know how long I stood there.

The exhaustion, cold and illness must have been progressively affecting my brain, because I remember nothing from that time until yesterday, when Terri was taking care of me here at the lodge. I must have made my way on down the fosse and beyond it alongside the glacier on toward Darwin. Les's instructions said to cross over the snout of the glacier about a kilometer back from the terminus. It's not a long traverse, but the terrain is rugged: rubble covered ice humps. I had to do it, because that is the only way to avoid crossing Dagheeloyee Creek at its deepest, right here at Darwin, and Terri says the creek is in full flood from the storm. Then to get to town, I would have had to pull myself over the Loohana River on the tram. When Terri found me, I must have been wandering up into town from the tram. I was hypothermic. They had to put me in a warm bath to save me.

I am sitting on the couch in the lodge with my feet up next to the stove. Terri just brought me another bowl of chicken soup. Terri and Sara and Kitty are being so warm and kind. I appreciate everything: being invited to stay here in the lodge while I recuperate, three hot meals a day, even hot and cold soaks for my sprained ankle. They tell me I didn't eat much yesterday. Sara found my spare pair of glasses at my permanent camp down by the creek. It feels so good to be able to see again.

From Terri's letter to her sister:

September 10, 1981

Dear Peggy,

...Fall was so short this year. The colors were just coming on in the trees when it starting raining and blowing. Luckily, it was cold enough that on the mountains it snowed. Otherwise, the flooding would be a lot worse.

We're concerned about Iceberg Lake. Sam Ross flew over it and says its full. When it's full like this, sometimes it dumps all of a sudden, pushing its way out under the glacier. The creek is so high already. With all of Iceberg Lake added in, it could take out some more of the town.

Yesterday, Les and Tim and Sam and I managed to pull a big fuel tank away from the creek. Les used his cat. And we moved a couple of trucks that were parked over there. But that's all we can do. Last time the lake went, it took out a big chunk of the bank. Some trees went and one of the old whorehouses. You can still see pieces of it sticking out of the gravel downstream.

The crew still hasn't come back. So I suppose no trip south for us this winter, unless they do, and pay their bills. We'll eat alright, especially if I get a moose. The hunting was always Ted's job, but I can do it....

The sky is clear, so the temperature will go down another notch tonight. It will probably do in the potato vines. They got touched a little by the frost a week ago, and some in August, too. I had them covered up with the plastic tarps, so they made it OK. Kitty and I harvested all the peas today.

Sara picked buckets of blueberries on the hillside this afternoon. It's wonderful seeing her do useful work on her own. When we get a good frost, the cranberries will be ready. There's lots this year.

Tim went down to fish camp this summer with his friends from Allakaket. He canned up a couple of cases for us. He also gave us a dozen beautiful fresh fish. We ate a couple. The rest fill the freezer. And then there is all the meat I bought in the city for that crew. So we may be without money, but we'll eat fine I think.

Unless the snow comes really late, we have plenty of firewood to last until I can get to the woodyard with the snowmachine. Last winter Tim and Les helped me out a lot with the wood. But it's time for me to be able to make it on my own. I need to remember to put in the order for a new chain and bar for the saw. It can take six weeks to come.

Les says he'll make the fuel run to Bettles in a week or two. Mike, the monk, is up the creek at Les's. Les will make a trip to get him when the creek goes down again, so the fuel run will be after that. We want to get the fuel in before there's ice on the road. Les will take the big lodge truck. We can load eighteen barrels on it, which should be enough diesel oil for the generator next summer and snowmachine gas for him and us all winter.

Les has his snowmachines in pretty good shape already. I'm asking him to help me fix the track on mine, and replace the hitch on the sled. We'll carry the fuel barrels across the ice on my sled. Full barrels are heavy, and my sled is less ratty than his.

Maybe it's just as well the crew disappeared. We have plenty to do even without taking care of them. Ed Butler is still around. He is actually being somewhat helpful in doing chores around the place. Ed says he got a letter from the big boss, Carl Manley, in last week's mail, saying he'd be up on the twelfth. That's day after tomorrow. But we don't know if he wrote that before or after the rest of the crew left with the helicopter. We don't know what he knows about their leaving.

Meanwhile, Kitty and Ed are back together. I still don't think the relationship is all that good for Kitty. But it seems to be working out for the moment. I suppose if Carl Manley doesn't show up, Ed will have to decide what to do. I can't keep feeding him indefinitely.

Kitty is thinking about staying on through the month, then going back to Fairbanks. She's welcome as long as she wants to stay. We'll close the lodge to business by the end of the month. Pretty soon after that, it will be cold enough that we will heat only the couple of rooms that are insulated.

Sara's started on school again. Her packet of books and lessons came from the state correspondence teacher last week. She's becoming so independent in getting her schoolwork done. I help her only now and then.

...With the leaves mostly off the trees (so quickly) snow's coming feels suddenly urgent. No matter how many times you go through it, it is exciting and a little scary....

From Jot's field notebook:

11 September 1981

...This evening I woke from a nap to find my backpack, with all my gear in it, even my lost glasses, leaning against the wall in my room. I asked Sara how it got here. Sam Ross walked up and brought it down from the pass this afternoon. He left after lunch, Sara said, and was back before dark! I was asleep, so he just left it here! Why did he do this for me?

He is a hunting guide and a trapper, with no love for the Park Service. I found him brusque, so thought he didn't care for me, probably because of my work and my education. I've never gotten along well with people like him. And yet he went all the way up there, just to bring down my gear. I'll be sure to thank him in the morning. I'll go over to his house on the crutches Terri loaned me. I wonder where he lives.

Les and I had a good talk this afternoon, out by his shop, where he was welding some part of a snowmachine. I told him how much I appreciated his taking me up the creek to his home twice this summer. He invited me to come back and visit during the winter, up at his place. I hadn't considered a winter trip possible before. Les pointed out that I must see winter to know what the area is like half the year. With his help I think I can do it. If the department lets me move my course in public policy planning to the spring quarter, I could come up over Christmas break. It is exciting to think about. Winter: What is the Alaska wilderness like in winter....

September 14, 1981

Dear Peggy,

...Carl Manley, the Explorers' boss, was due in day before yesterday. He buzzed the lodge around noon, flying a spiffy new Cessna 185. I went to pick him up at the airstrip. But he didn't stay. He didn't even come down into town to see Ed Butler. He just had to get up to the mines right away, to see what the crew had done. He hardly had time to talk to me. I don't even know what he knew about the crew, or the helicopter leaving, and so forth.

He needed some gas. We don't really have enough to sell. I've been using the little bit of aviation gas left in the tank up at the airstrip to run the truck. He assured me his company had lots of gas and would replace it, and pay their lodge bill, too. So I gave him a few gallons and he flew away.

Well, he flew away and he didn't come back. Ed asked what we should do. He was sure Manley wouldn't be camping up there by himself. I said the only thing we could do was to ask Sam Ross to fly over and check. So Ed walked over to Sam's.

Sam flew up the creek. He found Manley's airplane bent up, lying in the middle of the airstrip. Sam says Manley probably misjudged the approach, came in too low and then pulled up to go around, stalling the plane and cartwheeling into the ground.

Even in his supercub, Sam didn't have much room to land. It's a short strip, even without an airplane crashed into the middle of it.

Nobody was there when he landed—a relief for Sam, who feared the worst for Manley. Mike soon appeared. He had seen Manley's plane come in and fortunately came down from Les's to investigate. Manley had lost some front teeth, but was walking around and seemed to be OK. Mike was concerned about internal injuries, so didn't want to move him far. He'd set up a bed and took care of him right there in one of the old mining buildings.

Manley got into Sam's plane under his own power. Sam says Manley even took care to pack up his small suitcase carefully and wanted to bring it along. Sam told him he couldn't, because he needed to keep the plane light to get off safely, which they did.

[Compare Terri's understatement with Mike's description of the take off, excerpted from his journal:

"Sam had only a short distance to get off the ground. But with Manley in the plane, it was heavier. He had to cut weight. So he drained almost all his gas, leaving just enough to get back to Darwin, and took out the back seat and left it with me. Manley sat on the floor. We pushed the plane back right against the bushes at the end of the airstrip, just as far as it would go, to give them a couple more feet of rolling room. Sam gave the plane full power and off they went. He banked even before the right wheel left the ground and managed to squeeze through at an angle between the shattered wing of Manley's airplane and the bushes along the side of the runway. He cleared the wreck by at least eight inches and the bushes by two feet, straightened out, appeared to vault straight up, and soared over the trees at the end of the airstrip like a bird."

—JBS]

Not knowing what Manley's medical condition might be, Sam wanted to get him right out to a hospital. Sam refueled from his barrels here in Darwin and flew on to Bettles. When they got there, Manley wrote Sam a check for his flying time, said thank you and good-bye, and strolled off to the nearest telephone. Oh, well.

So Sam came back home and here we are. Ed Butler is still here, never saw his boss, and doesn't know what to do. And the lodge bill still isn't paid.

Town is getting quieter. Jot Shechter left on the mail plane. He says he'll be back in December. Maybe he will. Jasper found a ride out the other day, "to make a phone call." I expect we'll see him next summer. But you never know....

From Mike's journal:

Darwin

September 17, 1981

I know the date again. I am back in Darwin, so I know the date. I am back in the busy outside world. Now that I'm back, I know what time it is. I have been up the creek. Up there I am not so sure what time it was.

I am back so suddenly. Yanked out. Sam flew in again this morning, to pick up his seat. First he buzzed over Les's house, about a eighth of an inch over the roof. I interpreted that to mean he was giving me a signal. I was sipping tea at the time. Which I spilled into my lap.

I walked down to the airstrip. He had set the plane down precisely, landing again between the end of the strip and the wreck. Sam had a come-along winch with him and was already working on moving Carl Manley's airplane out of the way. Between the two of us and the winch, we were able to manhandle it over to one side. We rumpled up the metal some more in the process, but Sam said that didn't make any difference. It's just a source of spare parts.

Now Sam could use the whole airstrip for his takeoff. To me, it just looks like a narrow patch of gravel bar surrounded by trees. But it is plenty long and smooth for Sam's teeny-tiny plane with its expansive wings and great soft tires. His plane has room for two people, the pilot in front. He invited me to fly back to Darwin with him. And I accepted, to save Les the trip. Les was due up about now, anyway. I trotted on back to the cabin, got my things, and closed up the place.

With the back seat in again, I would fly in comfort. I squeezed in. I am a slightly wide person, but not too much wider than the airplane. Sam showed me what to grab onto to pull myself up and in. I guess some fragile pieces of the airplane might break if I grabbed them too hard, wires and wooden pieces and such. I certainly didn't want to do that. I fastened my seatbelt.

Sam's airplane is made of sticks, wires and metal tubes, covered over with a skin of painted cloth. The skin is tight like a drum. I tapped out a tune while Sam walked around the plane, checking it out.

Manley's plane is so much bigger and heavier, with four cushy seats and a metal exterior. But it is all smashed up now. The metal is crumpled, the windshield broken, the wheels snapped off, and the wings at an uncomfortable angle.

Sam told me not to push a certain knob or the plane would take off without him. I did not push it. Sam stood in front and pulled on the propeller with his hand. That started the engine. The plane shook. Sam jumped in, holding his cap to his head in the wind coming off the propeller. The plane rattled as he upped the throttle.

Suddenly we were off. I wasn't prepared. Zoom! We leaped into the air. My stomach felt like I was in a Manhattan elevator. I could have reached out and grabbed a twig off the treetops at the end of the airstrip. Les's house down below looked almost real: the path to the outhouse, the ax leaning against the woodpile, the black plastic tarp covering the roof, tied on with bright yellow polypropolene rope, the crooked stovepipe.

Then the world turned sideways. Trees and the creek were on the right. Sky and puffy clouds were on the left. A big mountainside was overhead. Another big mountainside was below. The world tipped again. Now the sky was back above us, where it belongs. We flew over Les's cabin again, a little higher this time.

Now we were floating. We were suspended in a thick, transparent substance, while the valley slowly moved along beside us. We were almost down at the bottom. Cliffs and pinnacles towered above us so high I almost could not see the tops. They looked so much bigger than they do from the ground, so clearly defined as they sailed majestically to the rear. Trees rushed by underneath. I could make out each one distinctly.

The Syndicate town passed on the right, the faded blue and white mill building growing out of the hillside beside us.

Over the roar of the engine, I told Sam this was my first flight in a little airplane. When he heard that, Sam made the world spin around again.

Now the mill building was below us and great huge white Dagheeloyee Peak was above us, and I could see beaver dams and ponds and the Explorers' cache off the right wingtip. There was the truck with the tree growing out of it where Jot and I had lunch, and the trail up to Les's. I was feeling a little sick. I closed my eyes while the world spun backwards.

I opened my eyes when the world leveled off again. I didn't know where we were anymore. At first the mountains were all above us. Then we cruised by their jagged tops. This was not the only valley. There is a valley next to this one, and another beyond that. Down there were creeks and forests and lakes and glaciers. They moved slowly now.

We went up and the valleys disappeared. They are just dark places between the mountains. Darwin and Les's place and the trail up the creek: They are a speck down there, submerged between projections of rock and ice rising into an ocean of blue air.

The mountains were close. I knew I could reach out and pick up a rock. Then the world spun around again. Sam pointed to the left and said, "Sheep." Wild, white sheep running on a slope. Then my stomach was in my head and the next thing I knew we were above the cliffs.

Now there was just the big white mountain. It had grown much higher. We could never get to the top of it. We flew over the glaciers. Everything was white to the end of the world. And the big mountain stood over it all, white pouring from the top. The sky was blue, with puffy clouds. We danced around the clouds.

It all moved around us, and my insides moved and my head spun and there were clouds and mountains and cliffs, and forests and rivers and lakes, and they went on forever and I could touch them all. The next thing I knew the plane was coming down and there was Darwin and there was the Darwin airstrip and with a thump and a squeak we landed and the trees raced past us as we rattled along on the gravel and it was over.

Sam got out, but I sat awhile. Finally, I extracted myself from the back seat and got out, too. I felt silly and a little sick as I staggered around on the airstrip. I looked at Sam. He was checking something in the engine and paying no attention to me. We were the only two people around. I felt this wonderful smile come up from my tummy. I couldn't hold it down. I danced and I twirled on the gravel airstrip, even as I was dizzy and sick from the flight. I spun until I rolled on the ground. Sam didn't say anything.

September 18, 1981

Morning, out of bed to chilly room in the old hardware store. Pee out the back door with my jacket on. Light the fire. Put the kettle on to heat.

Out for a walk, no one on the streets. The spice of spruce smoke and coffee on the air: Terri is already at work. Rusting oil barrels tilt nested among dry flower stalks burst with cotton fluff seeds. The whirr and the chit of two distant birds. The lodge generator chugs dependably. Les must have fixed it again.

I float along. I speak to the birds. I speak to the oil barrels. I speak to the aroma of spice and coffee. Good morning spice. Good morning seeds.

They answer back.

What do they say? This morning they speak with such clarity that they bring tears to my eyes.

But I remember that last night they all spoke at once and it was too much and I was confused. And the old hardware store spoke of lives gone by, of deaths in cold rooms, of wasted years, and I was afraid again.

Now it is morning, and the creek sings like St. Hildegard. You are quieter this morning, creek. May I sit by you.

I see rocks in your bed that were submerged, invisible, last evening: freezing night, the glaciers do not melt, the creek shrinks.

The sun bursts out over clouds: suddenly the creek reflects the glare. Oranges and reds from backlit shoreside autumn trees, hills dark on the shaded skyline, the splashed boulder glistens, water on ice. Full seedpods of dried brown grasses stroke my face as I sit on dry gravel at the road's edge.

The road is narrow here now: no vehicle can pass. The creek bit into it during the flood. But the water is lower again, a friend this morning, my companion, brother creek.

Oh creek that knows the upper valley, like me you have just come from that world, you know that place too, we know together. Welcome to Darwin, brother creek.

Your waters, too, are roiled. Yet you sing.

The sun melts white frost to wetness on browning leaves. I remember picking raspberries here.

Behind me, poplar trees drop yellow and brown leaves on a broken roof. Their trunks crowd the remains of a forgotten whorehouse, pushing in the walls.

I move from the creek bank, with its cold breeze, to sit on the sheltered whorehouse porch floor, facing brother sun, feeling his warmth. I feel the chill shadow of the porch railing across my legs.

The heel of a lady's dress shoe lies amidst fallen leaves on the disintegrating floor boards, next to an upturned rusted paint can. The paint can label is still legible. "Bursley Products—Quality You Can Trust." The shoe leather is eaten away. By mice? Inside, paisley wallpaper hangs in tatters. I pick up the edge of a carpet. It shreds in my hands. Mice and the creatures of decay return the whorehouse to the earth. The creek brings the waters of the upper valley to eat into the bank and eventually to wash the whole, entire, down and away, intermixed with the rocks and waters of the mountains.

Moving waters, cleansing waters. I feel them. I feel the blood rushing in my veins. The same.

A car battery lies tipped on the salon floor. I can see where the acid poured out. The linoleum is dissolved. It had a checked pattern, blue and white.

But I am distracted. I forgot the kettle heating on the stove. I rush back to the hardware store kitchen. I brew a cup of coffee. I have learned to like strong, bitter coffee. Les makes it strong. I sit by the stove, feel its radiant warmth, and I meditate on you, brother creek, companion of my recent journey, and on you, brother sun, circling to the south, every day more distant.

I walk outside. Brother raven beats by on black wings, watching, watching. He croaks. I croak back.

Later

I will stay.

Les and I talked, and I will stay.

The town is quiet.

Jasper is gone. He even cleaned up some of the mess in the kitchen. Tim Brown is gone, down to Oregon this winter, where he and Les have family. Jot is gone, too, back to Berkeley. He left a note for me at the hardware store, expressing his thanks for my company. I wish I'd had the chance to say the same to him. Maybe I will in December.

Bright and sunny today, cool, jacket weather. Les came by and we talked, out in the sunshine. He said, "You know, a person could fix up the kitchen in the hardware store if he wanted to, patch up the holes and maybe throw in a little insulation, and he could spend the winter, using that room to live in, if he wanted to."

"Who does the building belong to?"

"Well, that's unclear. Maybe Jasper. But probably not. Maybe somebody down in Seattle. Or New York. The courthouse where they kept the records burned in '48."

"Wouldn't fixing up the place cost money?"

"No, I know where there's some boards and nails, and an extra roll of insulation, if the porcupines haven't gotten into it. They eat fiberglass. There's sure to be enough left. We could do it."

So Les will help me. And I'll go with him on the fuel run he's making to Bettles. He could use a hand. We'll help each other.

I'll write the abbot for permission to stay. I will say, Dear Father, there is potential here for monastic hermitage. He will grant permission, I know it.

I'm not sure where to put this piece. It was in one of George Johnston's computer files in Fairbanks. He was living mostly in Darwin, but he would go back and forth to the city. Afterwards, they found his computer and all the files in a dark basement studio apartment. He had training as a computer programmer, but had been unemployed for some time. His files contained numerous lists, lists of enemies, lists of things he was planning to do. Mixed in were monologues like this one. It is not dated, but other files on the disk make reference to September, 1981, dates.

—JBS

When I close my eyes I see small arms firing. Rifles and machine guns. I imagine that I have a machine gun. I have had it a long time. I can see the handles. They are worn smooth and comfortable. The metal fits my hands. It keeps the world away so that I am safe. But I am not safe. Men are falling all around me. I am in a ditch. A man above me is hit. Blood gushes out of his chest. He tumbles onto me. He is trying to scream, but he is choking on his blood. He gasps and dies on top of me.

The enemy is all around at the edge of the woods. I can see them there, just back in the trees. If I stick my head up, I will be shot. I have to keep my head down. That is why I walk with my head down. My posture isn't too good. That is why. If I walk with my head up, I will be shot.

Every time I stop thinking about something else I hear the guns firing. They are so loud they get in my way. It makes it hard to do other things. There are explosions everywhere. It makes it hard to think about anything else.

The atomic bombs have started falling. My family is turned into cinders. They are like pieces of burned toast. There is nothing I can do about it. I am poisoned with radiation. Pretty soon I will start vomiting blood. Then I will die. There is nothing I can do about it.

Can my machine gun blast through the windows of the White House? The windows are three inches thick. Bullet proof glass. First the shots will not penetrate. But they will chip away and eventually they will make a hole. Then they will make a hole in the president's chest. It will be a red hole and it will gradually widen and he will vomit blood. His advisors will be very surprised.

How to explode the White House: Get a small nuclear warhead. They make them now that fit into a backpack. There are hundreds of them. It just takes one. They are stored in the European theatre of operations. America has them for NATO. When the Russians come, we will use them on the towns and little children. Bribe a sergeant and get one. The Israelis do that all the time. They are smart and they are tough and nobody pushes them around. Everybody wants to bomb them, but they don't let anybody do it.

There was a picture in the paper of an Israeli bus. It was blown up. There was a lady's leg in the picture. It was swollen up and sticking up from a seat. The lady was dead. The rest of her was somewhere else.

There are tunnels under the White House. You don't want to give them any warning, or else they will put the president down there and he will get away. You've got to get him on top, above the ground.

Under the ground the president and his officers sit at CRT computer terminals. That is where they run the war. They are the ones who decide where the bombs will fall. They are the ones who tell the soldiers where to shoot the guns.

Under the ground it is all filled with wires. There is a chain of command. The president is in charge. Then there is the cabinet. Then there is the Joint Chiefs of Staff. They are the main generals. There are specific rules they follow. These tell them when to shoot and how to do it. They must follow the rules exactly. The computers tell them what to do. Whenever you need to know what to do under the ground, there is a computer terminal there to tell you. They are all linked together.

The mountain is all hollowed out to make room for the officers and the computers. The entrance is blocked with a giant, radiation proof door, so you can't get in and you can't bomb them. They have periscopes every-where. These are television cameras hidden in the buildings and behind the trees. We can't see them, but they can see us. The soldiers come out of holes in the ground, and then they shoot us. The generals tell them when and where and how. They follow the specific rules.

The deeper you go the more powerful the generals you will find. The president is at the bottom. He is in charge. He is an old man who does not know anything anymore. He makes all the decisions. He has a big hole in his chest and he is vomiting blood. He doesn't have to know anything, because the computers can tell him. They know all the rules. They know the procedures. They are kept very clean. Orderlies are constantly attending them, mopping up the blood and dusting them off. If they got dirty they would malfunction. Then the procedures could not be followed.

If I follow the procedures then I will not be shot. That is why I walk with my head down. I will plan exactly what to do. I will buy my Uzi submachinegun five months in advance. I will practice diligently. I will procure the proper books to learn about the proper placement of dynamite. The execution will be flawless. The plan will be uninterrupted. Nobody will know in advance. I will maintain discipline.

From Sara's diary:

September 21, 1981

Dear Diary,

Wow what a day, diary. We got rid of M.O.E.B., but Kitty's in deep trouble. Mother says today is the equinox. That's when the day and the night are the same length. Before today it was light more than it was dark. Tomorrow it's dark more. Les says now we've got the long sliiide down into winter. That's how he says it. The long sliiide down into winter. With lots of i's. Pretty soon the snow comes.

Fortunately, before they took Kitty away she and Mother and I finished getting the lodge all closed up for winter. That is, we put away all the stuff we use for guests, like most of the dishes and the great big pots and stuff like that. We kept out just what we use ourselves. And we shut off a bunch of the rooms. Like the bar and the guest rooms. Actually, we just closed the doors. Later, when it gets colder, we'll seal them off. With insulation and tape and caulk and old newspapers and whatever we can find that will seal them off but good, so the cold can't squeeze in.

I remember last winter. Mother wasn't used to closing up the lodge all by herself. Well, I helped, but I wasn't used to it, either, and besides, I was younger and less capable then than I am today. She was used to having Father around to do it with her. But he was dead. He was dead for the first time that winter and it was a new thing for her. So she didn't remember to do everything. She was pretty upset a lot, too.

Anyway, the point is we forgot to cover up the keyholes. Then Wham! Right after Halloween it went to forty below. Huddle round the stove time for us! Actually, we kept the house pretty warm. Well, the floor was cold and kind of windy down there. And you'd go past the door to the bar and you'd get blasted. The bar room was all cold and sealed off, of course. But that old forty below air sure came through that keyhole. I bent over and looked out through that hole and it felt *weird*. Mother told me not to do that, so I would not frostbite my eyeball. Of course, any sensible person would know that. And then we stuffed fiberglass into the hole and covered it over with duct tape. We did that sort of thing lots of places and then it was less windy down there on the floor. I still had to wear two layers of my heavy wool kneesocks when I sat at my desk. It was cold down there under the desk. Which is where my feet live when I'm doing schoolwork.

So now the lodge is closed up and we had Kitty to help us do it. I miss Kitty. I hope she is OK. I wonder when we'll find out what is happening to her.

So what has happened that brought this about? That is, why are both M.O.E.B. and Kitty gone? Let me tell you.

Well, first let me tell you some good news. Well, actually M.O.E.B. going is good news, too. But here is some more. Mike is staying! Hurray! He's living in the kitchen at the hardware store. Les is helping him fix it up for winter. I wonder if he knows about how to make snow angels and if he can make that sharp turn on the sledding hill. If you don't make that turn, you go smacko into the bushes. It will be fun doing that with Mike. I wish Kitty were here, too, though. Even though I'm sure she would *never* make the turn. We would have to dig her out every time for sure and she would get snow down her dress.

Now back to the story. Today was a sunny day. That is part of the story, which is why I am telling about it. Because M.O.E.B. was sunning his big fat self, tummy and all, on the lodge porch. It faces south. It is sheltered from the wind. It feels like summer there, even at the equinox, which is today. If the sun is shining, which it was. So there was M.O.E.B., leaning back in his chair this morning, taking in some sun. Actually, it was not his chair. It was our chair. It belongs to the lodge, not him. But he was sitting in it. He definitely filled it all up. In fact, we are going to have to wire the legs on tighter, because they got loose from big old him sitting in it.

Meanwhile, Kitty and I are inside working, working, getting ready for winter. Actually, even before today we didn't know how long Kitty was going to stay. She has things to do in Fairbanks this winter. That's how it is. People come and you think they are going to stay, but winter comes and out they go. Maybe she'll come back next summer. I wonder if she'll be out of trouble by then. I guess she will be. It's not that bad. But boy what a hassle she's got! It is M.O.E.B.'s fault, of course. He's the one who should be in jail, not Kitty. Mother wasn't around. She was off across the river with Les and Mike, fixing up the truck for the fuel run. She missed the whole thing.

Well, certainly not the whole thing. Four hundred pounds of bloody moosemeat is still hanging in the shed. At least we got it up there. They took away some of it but not the rest. And it's so early in the season yet we'll have to can lots of it, so it doesn't spoil. And that's a job! So Mother definitely hasn't missed it all. Still lots of work to do. Well, it's good meat. Mother was going to hunt a moose anyway. But that was going to be later, when it was cold enough to keep just by hanging it in the shed. You cut the moose in quarters and hang it in the shed. It freezes and when you need a piece for dinner you go in with the saw and saw off a nice chunk. But she would not have shot a cow moose, like M.O.E.B. did.

Did I tell you what happened yesterday? No, I did not. But I will, because it also is about the moose.

Mike and I were crossing Clearwater Brook on the planks, right down there in the woods behind the lodge. We had been out by the river, looking at the view. I brought my bicycle. We went right by Mrs. Henry. She's pretty much dormant for the winter now. We still talk together, of course, but her leaves are not making food anymore and that sort of thing. Mike does not notice her yet. I wonder if he will some day. Mrs. Henry says he has Potential.

So there we were balancing our way across those planks. I looked up and Wow! right there in the creek was a humungous bull moose. He had absolutely enormous antlers. They were so big he could have scooped up M.O.E.B. with them and carried him away! That would have been a sight! Hurray for the moose! Carry him off and deposit him somewhere. But that's not what happened. He swayed his big head back and forth and snorted. We could hear his heavy breathing, hiss, snort, hiss, snort. He was all shaggy. When he walked he would lift up a leg and then stop, put down a leg and then stop. No hurrying for Mr. Moose.

At first he did not pay much attention to us. When we looked we saw why. There down the creek was Mrs. Moose. He was paying attention mostly to her. She was making strange noises.

This did not seem too safe to me. There we were balancing on those planks over the creek. You know that a moose is a very large animal. Elephants and hippopotamuses are larger, but we don't have them around here. And as everyone knows, when a male moose is after a female moose, he is dangerous indeed.

Then Mr. Moose decided maybe we were competition for Mrs. Moose. This is not a desirable position to be in when you are balanced on a plank with a monk and a bicycle crossing a creek. Mike said perhaps Mr. Moose thought the handlebars were the antlers of another male moose. Charge! Crash! That is what male moose do in the fall. Mr. Moose lowered his head and you could see he was deciding maybe he should do something about us.

Fortunately, just then Mrs. Moose made more of those strange sounds. She went splashing away down the creek. What did Mr. Moose want to do more, chase us or her? Well, here I am, so you know the answer. What you do not know is how fast a person can cross a plank and run up the road and cross the yard to the lodge. It is faster than you think.

So what does this have to do with M.O.E.B. sitting there this morning on our porch in our chair sunning his fat self?

Who comes down the middle of the road in front of the lodge? Mrs. Moose. Leg up, leg down, walking right through the town.

M.O.E.B. opens one eye in his bald fat head and sees Mrs. Moose. Off he sneaks to his room and comes back with his 30-.06. Pow! Bam! He shoots Mrs. Moose right in front of the lodge.

We must remember that moose season ended for the year yesterday on September 20 and of course this is a cow which is never legal to shoot, and it is very unfair to do so. Plus nobody around here hunts moose until later when we can be sure it will be cold enough to keep the meat. Of course, M.O.E.B. does not think of this. Pow! Bam! He shoots.

Not five minutes pass by and Zoom! a Cessna 206 buzzes right over the lodge twice and lands at the airstrip. Uh Oh, this could be trouble for M.O.E.B. Will he get caught for shooting the moose? So Kitty and I try to help him hide the moose. How do you hide a dead moose which is lying in the road in front of the lodge? It cannot be done. Kitty put a blanket over it. That was her idea. Most of the moose stuck out.

Down from the airstrip comes the pilot. He is from the air taxi service in Bettles. Carl Manley, the big boss from Seattle, has chartered a plane to pick up M.O.E.B. and take him away.

Normally, this would be a very good thing. But here we are with Mrs. Dead Moose in the road and right away M.O.E.B. has to go, which he does. M.O.E.B. packs his bags and off they fly. Good bye M.O.E.B. and good riddance, I say, except now Kitty and I are stuck with the moose.

So we begin to butcher the moose. Cut, cut, blood, blood, mess, mess. I show Kitty what to do. I remember doing it with Father.

We work away and it takes forever. Finally we get some of the pieces hauled over to the shed. And just then what happens?

Helicopter! A big one, flop flop chop chop right over the lodge. It lands over behind the hardware store in the big open area by Les's shop.

This time I know we cannot hide the moose. Her insides and the pieces are piled all over the street. Who is in the helicopter?

Park Service, that's who! The helicopter is a blue and white Bell Jet Ranger and it is filled with green people with shiny metal badges. They are Park Service dressed in green from head to foot and here they are with us and what is left of Mrs. Moose.

They are here to see Jot Shechter. They say he asked them to come. When was that? Well, a month ago. We tell them he is gone back to California. They want to talk to the Explorers. We tell them they are all gone. Too bad.

So what to do? Well, there is this dead cow moose in piles in front of the lodge. Unfortunately, they must arrest Kitty. They are very sad about it, but it is the law and must be done. It is a Very Serious Offense. Fortunately, I am merely a young, innocent child. I can stay home. Good Bye Kitty!

They are supposed to confiscate the meat. They give it to the Needy. Well, we are needy and we will eat it just fine, thank you. Actually, I do not talk to them that way. I am a polite young lady.

Anyway, they can't fit very much of Mrs. Moose into the helicopter. It is full with just them and Kitty.

Flop flop chop chop, off they go.

Good bye Kitty. Good bye summer.

Hello winter. When we get done with the moose, Mother and I are going to get the skis down from the attic. Zoom! I can't wait to go barreling down the Chalcocite trail with Mike! I bet he sails into the bushes. I wonder what he will look like with his head in the snow and his feet sticking up into the air.

Winter

At the still point of the turning world. Neither flesh nor fleshless;
Neither from nor towards; at the still point, there the dance is,
But neither arrest nor movement. And do not call it fixity,
Where past and future are gathered. Neither movement from nor towards,
Neither ascent nor decline. Except for the point, the still point,
There would be no dance, and there is only the dance.
I can only say, *there* we have been: but I cannot say where.
And I cannot say, how long, for that is to place it in time.

—T.S. Eliot, from *Burnt Norton*

[Mike and Terri and I wrote about winter in our letters and journals. I will be sharing them with you. But there are events of that time that are best described from a perspective we did not have then. So I will begin by narrating the story of the moment of my first arrival in winter Alaska as I remember it, and as I imagine that it was.   —JBS]

Minus ten degrees Fahrenheit. Light snow filters through a luminous grey sky, big six-pointed crystals piling unbroken on the rocks of the canyon walls, on the green needles of spruce curving upward from roots grasping purchase in narrow rock fissures, on motionless frozen turquoise waterfalls. Bursting faint orange onto thin grey clouds, the sun drops below the horizon in mid-afternoon. Deepening snow muffles the rumble of the creek moving under multiple layers of ice, and there is silence.

Above the canyon, on the forested bench beneath the slopes of Mount Malachite, a moose snips willow shoots. The grinding of tooth and the hiss of hot breath penetrate the silence. Above the forest, under whitened meadows, mice emerge from tunnels to drag sheaves of grass into dens below the snow.

A boreal owl drops onto a mouse, eats it. The silence is uninterrupted.

Above the slopes, and above the cloud layer, on a ridge swept clean of snow by a former wind, one hundred wild sheep and seven goats graze on dried cotton grass. Saturn shines as dusk fades in the southern sky. Night descends. Tenuous clouds dissipate.

Below the peaks and the watching animals, below the last wisps of unwinding cloud, starlight reaches into the canyon. The remaining heat of the earth rises out of the canyon through the clearing atmosphere into outer space. The temperature sinks to minus thirty degrees. Squeezed by night and cold, the atoms of the upper atmosphere vibrate in a silent but audible hum, pastel auroral curtains dancing before distant galaxies.

Now a rhythmic swish moves along the canyon floor. A lone skier searches his way up the valley, seeking his way by the celestial light, aided at moments by a brief assist from a small flashlight, which he stores in his underpants to keep it from freezing useless. Small icicles hang from his nostrils. Periodically he stops to check the location of the trail, gnawing on a piece of frozen cheese.

Professor Jotham B. Shechter of the University of California Law School (I myself, as I was then) skis along the creek bottom, then up a snow ramp to follow the snowmachine trail as it contours the canyon wall. He snags a ski tip on a buried willow, tumbles, curses, rights himself, continues. He reaches the canyon rim, enters the tunnel, entryway into the upper valley. A torrent of supercooled water shoots through the canyon below, a roar in the darkness. Beyond the slot, the creek is again frozen, and the professor descends to it, skiing between boulders, then skirting the glacier face, drifting silent through powder snow. The winter trail heads outward across Dagheeloyee Lake, winding between shadow iceberg monoliths motionless in the unyielding lake surface.

Ice rivers hang on the high peaks at the head of the valley, glowing with reflected light from the electroluminescent sky.

He skis in even rhythm, feeling the trail with his ski tips, his eyeglasses, opaque with frost, buried in his pocket.

A waning crescent moon clears the eastern ridge, flooding the valley with a new pale light. It reveals the darkened form of the abandoned ghost city, stovepipes snow covered. Beavers remain in their dens as the professor skis past their ponds, encouraged onward now by music drifting on the thick subarctic air.

Mahler's Fourth Symphony, the choral movement:

> *"We enjoy heaven's delights,*
> *So can dispense with earthly things.*
> *No worldly turmoil is to be heard in heaven:*
> *Everything lives in peace and calm.*
> *We lead the life of angels*
> *Yet are very gay about it;*

We jump and dance,
    We skip and sing.
     St. Peter in heaven looks on."

The trail leads to the music. Finally, a dim bluish fluorescent electric light in a window. Up a final hill, around a bend, he skis to a squat, flat-roofed log cabin, past a snowmachine with sled, past gas cans and a snow-covered picnic table, past chopping block, ax and firewood, past the solar panels which charge the batteries which power the stereo that puts forth Gustav Mahler.

He takes off his skis, knocks at the door. Mahler ceases, the door opens, warm air and light. Les Brown welcomes, "Come in Jot. I have been expecting you."

When the moon reached the zenith, the man woke. He climbed out of his sleeping bag and put on a parka, patched, some feathers coming out of the left sleeve. He moved across the room in one short step, stooped to open the flue and draft on the woodstove, let it roar. He reached for the flashlight on the wooden Chevron Blazo gasoline packing case that served as bedstand, turned it on, held it in his mouth while he used two hands to remove the chimney from the kerosene lamp, strike a match, light the lamp, and replace the chimney. He stepped into mukluks. Flashlight in hand, he brushed past the bed to the door. When he opened it, the cold hit his bare knees first, a mist swirling along the floor. He walked out.

He did not need the flashlight. Although the aurora had faded by midnight, now the waning crescent moon sent enough light to outline the puffs of snow on the spruce and to silhouette black poplar limbs against the starry sky. The crunch of his mukluks boomed in the silence. He stopped to pee. The urine hissed on its way down, steaming, its warmth fracturing the ice in the pee hole with a pop and crackle. He paused. As his eyes adjusted to the darkness, he saw the ax leaning against the chopping block and a single set of hare tracks crossing the yard, fresh since the afternoon snowfall. Across the creek, a great horned owl called, "hoo, hoo-hoo <u>hoo</u> hoo, hoo hoo." Distant, from the empty mining town, its mate responded.

He turned back to the cabin, stomping his feet on the porch to shake the snow out from the rubber treads of the mukluks, bending for an armload of spruce. He entered and fed the fire, removed the parka and dressed. As the wood caught, the stovepipe glowed red. Water in the kettle on the stovetop began to boil. He poured out one cup into a coffee-pot, then measured one tablespoon of coffee into the boiling water.

He folded the hinged bed so that it made into the frame of a chair. He placed the futon mattress as a cushion on the chair. By now the coffee was done. He poured off his cup, leaving the settled grounds in the pot. Alone, hands enfolded around the warm cup, seated legs crossed on the futon, with the wick on the kerosene lamp turned low, Father Mike prayed to Mary and to Christ and focused his awareness on the sound of blood coursing through his veins.

———————————

Quilts, handmade from colored fabric scraps, hung over the plate glass windows of the old wooden lodge. They kept out the cold, and their bright color, reflected by a single candle flame, held back the night. Within, the big room felt enclosed, like the inner hall of a medieval castle hung with tapestries, or the innermost chamber of an ancient cave, walls decorated with the paintings of a hunting and gathering people. The quilts, the wooden walls, and the loneliness of the night guaranteed privacy. A single small window, encrusted with rime, remained uncovered. It faced into a small courtyard, letting in the pale light of the crescent moon, etched against the pre-dawn sky. The big barrel heatstove glowed red.

Tables, chairs and two overstuffed couches pushed against one wall, stacked one on the other, left a wide open space.

In the space, the woman danced.

She became the raven, wings outstretched, looking, looking, seeing to the left and to the right. She became the tree, standing straight and tall, waiting, waiting, feet in snow, waiting the long night, patient for the spring. She became the bear, curled in the den, giving birth to tiny cubs, nursing them in the warmth of her body. She danced naked, wearing only hand knit socks: the wooden floor was cold, but the air above was warm, very warm, and sweat flowed from the hair of her armpits, and from her brow, sweat gleaming by candle flame.

Reader, I ask something of you. Reading the words is not enough. Do you know the significance of the pause? Winter. I am writing about the pause, the space between. I wish you to understand. Please take three deep breaths slowly. Pause between the breaths. Notice the pause.

Now, listen to me. You remember I am writing this as an older man, from a cell in a Zen monastery in San Francisco. I hear the passing of cars and trucks outside. It is relatively quiet in here, but out there life is very busy. This monastery is not strictly of the city, but neither is it what I knew in Alaska in the winter. I am in the city but I recall the winter, particularly that first winter, because when an experience is new to us it can be especially vivid. I need to do this, to remember. If you come with me, you may remember, too.

We knew, I think, when we all lived in caves. That was a very long time ago, when the ice extended much further, and men and women and children sat by the cave mouth, sat by the fire watching the snow fall in the darkness outside, with their backs to the darkness of the cave's depths. We knew then, as the clan sat together through the long night.

I am trying to remember. This retelling is to help remember. It will help me if you remember, too. There is more power if we do it together. I think it is very important that we know of winter, both of us. It may save the world.

We cannot be impatient. We must start at the beginning, in September, not December. So let us keep our friends in mind, Les, Mike, Terri and Jot (me as I was back then), up there in winter's darkness, while we go over the events that brought them to that juncture, that prepared them for that place.

Do not forget that winter takes preparation. It cannot be entered into suddenly. It is very demanding in that regard, unforgiving of error. Let us make our preparation.   —JBS

From my field notebook:

13 September 1981
Location: Lobby of Fairbanks International Airport.

I arrived in Fairbanks from Darwin yesterday. I had intended on meeting with Park Superintendent Cooke upon my arrival in Fairbanks, to review the progress of the summer's work and to ask him a number of questions regarding his planning process, the scope of which I have begun to question. When, however, I came upon the first pay telephone and approached it to call his office, the dial tone was too loud. It was so loud that I could not dial.

I stood there. A car went by on the street, breaking my train of thought. I realized that I did not have the energy to talk to the Park Service receptionist on the telephone. The telephone is such a stupid way to communicate, just inadequate, and too much work. The superintendent and I need to sit down together for a couple of days and talk things over. There is so much to convey to him. Finally, I gave up. I simply cannot see the superintendent under these circumstances. He will have to wait. It will be months before I return to Alaska.

My hotel room was so noisy last night that I couldn't sleep. The window did not open and it was so stuffy and hot that I could not breathe. The heating ducts made the most terrible noise. The room was cramped and enclosed.

I am sitting in a black Naugahyde chair in the terminal lobby. Numerous people swirl around me while the paging system shouts names. But it all fades out. It has happened repeatedly since I arrived in the city: I am surrounded by a barrage of cars, store signs and traffic signals. And then suddenly I am back in Darwin. The city fades out, replaced by the sharp image of being on the street of Darwin in autumn morning sunshine. All the sensations of Darwin are vivid—the crisp cool air, the clean definition of the bare tree trunks, the crunch of gravel underfoot. And I see each of the individual personalities, Terri, Mike, Les, Jasper, Sara, Sam, etched in my consciousness as my attention turns to each of them in turn.

Darwin fades out and I am back in Fairbanks. But I cannot stay here in Fairbanks. The mind goes back to Darwin, while the city fades in and out as a swirl of lights and roars.

The first time I turned on the overhead electric light in the hotel room it was too glaring. I had to turn it off immediately. Finally, I turned on only the light in the bathroom and pulled the bathroom door almost closed. I sat on the bed in a proper light, a semi-darkness they would call it, for I don't know how long. I wish I had ear plugs to shut out the noise.

All night I heard each car as it passed by on the street outside. I paid attention to the sound of each motor as it moved across my field of perception. Late at night, there were few enough that I could, and did, focus on each one.

I lecture on environmental law at Berkeley starting on Tuesday. All I want to do is get out of here and back to Darwin.

From my office file on the Dagheeloyee National Park contract:

17 September 1981

DAGHEELOYEE PROJECT:
NOTES FOR FIRST INTERIM REPORT
TO NATIONAL PARK SERVICE

- Include list of major scenic features
    — Focus on relationships between scenic elements
- Succinct summary of why area is significant
    — Note interaction of lifestyle and land use

this is NONSENSE

nonsense

nonsense

List
    bear
    monk
    the creek
    caves
    ice
    Terri

Terri

Terri

Terri

I CANNOT WRITE THIS. THIS OFFICE IS IMPOSSIBLY BRIGHT AND LOUD.

BUZZ NOISE HOT GLARE TELEPHONE RING!!!!! RING!!!!! RING!!!!!

LEAVE ME ALONE!!!

nobody understands me
they are all blind
they don't know
they don't understand
I have nothing to say to them
can't they just be quiet
can't they hear the roar out there they are making. They must be deaf
I don't think I can possibly stay here at Berkeley
I don't care about the United States National Park Service
I don't care about the United States National Park Service
The United States National Park Service knows

nothing
nothing
nothing

I have been staring at this paper for two hours. I have been interrupted thirty two times during this period by telephone calls and visitors. I have a headache.

NO ESCAPE

it is all meaningless. empty. empty. there is no way back.

Mike soon wrote me, asking how I felt being back in Berkeley and suggesting that writing down my feelings might help me adjust to the transition. The following is the first entry in my field journal after leaving Alaska: —JBS

2 October 1981

Location: Sproul Plaza, Berkeley Campus

I watch hot air rise in waves off bare pavement, while six saffron Hari-Krishnas in tennis shoes beat drums through the lunchtime crowd toward the Orange Julius. Pages from today's newspapers blow languidly along the asphalt, catching on the trunks of manicured trees and on the black polished shoes of businessmen. Three pigeons wander, one pecking at stale pink bubble gum adhering to the pavement. I smell fumes from graffitied buses and clean, overheated Japanese automobiles.

A stoned panhandler has just asked me for $1.25 to buy a slice of pizza. As I sit on this park bench at the entrance to campus, a young lady wearing green hair and heavy metal earrings in the shape of Christian crosses comes to me in supplication. I grant her an extension of time to complete a term paper, because she has walking pneumonia and her dog ate her notes during her mother's funeral. I have just lectured on zoning as the administrative taking of property without compensation. I went into the bank to cash a check, standing twenty-six minutes on a mauve plush carpet next to a plastic potted rubber tree in a windowless room, in a long line of speechless people snaking up to six young women with artificially uplifted breasts, long pink fingernails and red paint on their lips, counting money.

What I am describing is really true.

I have adjusted to being here. At least I am not distracted by daydreams anymore. I can go ahead again. Big deal. Lectures. Tenure.

Shit.

October 1981

Dear Mike,

...You wrote to encourage me to write down my responses to being back here in California. Well, in the past few days I have become competent and efficient again. Yesterday I sent off my interim report to the Park Service in Fairbanks. It will meet the superintendent's expectations.

Darwin would be a distant dream, except for your letters. Thank you.

I am quite sure my colleagues think I am the same as I was before the summer: Shechter had a bit of a time getting his act together after his long vacation up there in Alaska, but he's OK again. The Promotion and Tenure Committee likes him, so he will make Associate Professor at his first review, if he can stick to it and not get sidetracked. Keep the production up, Shechter.

I am producing again. But you ask me to tell you how I feel. You suggested that I should adjust. However, I do not believe I am. I am not sure I know how to explain what I mean. The difference lies in specific memories, of the tastes and smells, of the play of the light through the trees. Terri surely has told you about my experience in coming over the pass. The falling of the snow is always in my mind, and the bear tracks around my tent. It has not been my practice in the past to be concerned about people, but now I am: you, Terri, Les, Sam, the others.

I have these memories, or at least a feeling of them, all the time. You must understand that I mean all of the time. As a result, all the rest of what I do is a game, which I play well....

Please keep me informed of the seasonal changes in Darwin. You know I am always interested. And I am interested in the people also.

Best wishes,
Jot Shechter

October 1, 1981

Dear Peggy,

By the time you get this letter, I'm sure Sara will have told you the whole story of her trip in great detail. I'm so glad you and Steve were able to come up with the money to bring her south. You know that if the Explorers had paid the bills, we'd both be there with you, at least for awhile.

It certainly wasn't easy seeing her fly off this morning, but it's clearly for the best. Her life here has been so good in many ways, and so rich. Now she'll have the chance to go to school and have friends her age, and be with a teacher besides me. And she loves you and Steve and Emma and Daniel a lot....

I wonder how she will be changed when she comes back. She grows up so fast. She left her favorite old red-haired doll Sally behind....Maybe I'm entering my second childhood, because I've got Sally propped up here on the couch with me.

She still lives with her fantasies, though. Perhaps these will disappear with her busy life this winter Outside.° She made sure to go out to the river to say good-bye to her imaginary friend Mrs. Henry this morning, even though it was raining and chilly out there on the flats.

Mrs. Henry is an old Indian lady, I am told, and very wise. Sara has been spending a lot of time out by the river with her. It is a desolate spot, really, out there in the wind blowing off the end of the glacier. Ted and I used to walk out there once in a while, just to get away from town together.

Sara told me that if I want companionship while she is gone (that is the word she used!), I should go talk with Mrs. Henry. Well, maybe I will. I'll certainly have a lot of solitude this winter and I might want some company. I have never been alone quite like this. Ted would be away sometimes, like the winter he was gone thirty-three days bringing in supplies with the cat. But for me there was always little Sara to take care of. And before she was born, Ted and I did everything together.

° *"Outside" is the term Alaskans use to refer to the rest of the world outside Alaska.*
—JBS

I'm looking forward to being alone, actually. I think it will be hard sometimes. It seems that way now. You know how that is, when someone you love has just left and you feel that pit in your stomach.

But also I feel really free. Nobody I have to take care of! Hurray! What will I do first?

...Town is pretty much emptied out. After he drops Sara at the Fairbanks airport, Sam is going on to Sitka, where he has a few weeks work flying DC-3's along the coast. It's not his favorite, but it's a grubstake. Tim is out, gone to Oregon for the whole winter this year, first time in a decade at least that he has been away like this. He and Les have a sister down there and he likes the music and theater there. George Johnston must be gone to Fairbanks again. I haven't seen him around in over a week. So only Mike and Les and I are in town right now. Once the snow comes and the ice is good, Les will put in his snowmachine trail and be off to his place up the creek.

It looks like it might snow this afternoon. The sky is so dark I feel I want to light the lamps, even though it is still midday. Well, I've got bread that needs attending.

Hugs to Steve and the kids and of course a big special one for Sara.

Love,
Terri

[Terri kept writing something to her sister almost every day, even though she could mail the letters out only once a week. The letters were like a diary.]

October 2, 1981
...I had to brush snow off the lettuce and the last of the chard when I picked them for dinner. Started some garbanzos in the sprout jars today for my salads, in addition to the regular alfalfa, mung and lentils. I've never tried them before.

I have so much time! It's just amazing. This morning I finished the chores and got a moose stew going on the stove—the root cellar is full of potatoes, carrots and onions from our harvest this fall. And there was the whole day still in front of me.

The first thing I did was make some space for *me*. There I was with tables enough in my dining room to feed fifteen and couches enough in my living room to seat a dozen. And here I was all by myself, with no corner I could really call my own. So I took a table and set it against the south window in the living room, and that's my desk, where I'm writing now. And I moved the most comfortable easy chair right up next to it, where it will have good light from the lamp on the desk. And that's my chair. Then I moved another table into the kitchen, right near the warm cook stove, and that's where I eat. And I'm going to just leave all this just where it is, all day and tomorrow, too! I can leave my papers on my desk and my dishes on the dining table and I don't have to move them to make room for *anybody* else.

After that flurry of activity, I was exhausted. And I realized I could sit down and rest. I could actually sit down and rest. Amazing. So I sat down in my easy chair with a cup of tea and I watched the snow fall.

Then, after a long while, I decided I wanted to go for a walk. So I did. I went out the path through the woods along the creek and watched the creek begin to make ice. Then I wandered out toward the river. By that time the snow had stopped and there was some deep blue sky peaking out over the glacier. I said hello to Sara's friend Mrs. Henry.

When I got back, dusk hadn't even begun yet. I had plenty of time to split the wood and get water from the brook and fill the kerosene lamps, and clean up and close the generator shed (which I won't be needing), and do the final putting away of tools from around the garden.

Then I had the whole evening ahead of me! So I sat in my chair again with another cup of tea and looked out the south window and watched the sky slowly get dark.

October 3

I had some moments of unbearable sadness before I went to bed last night. I miss Ted and Sara, so I was tempted to take out the pictures of him and of us as a family again....

The summer birds are all gone and the trees are so bare without leaves. The ground is brown and muddy, and the air still chilly and damp.

Mike stopped by for coffee after breakfast. He is busy chinking up the cracks in the hardware store. Les found him some bats of fiberglass and several old wool blankets to stuff in the holes, which will help some. He says he is already burning quite a bit of wood. And the cold hasn't started yet. He's hauling trees off the gravel bar at the creek. They washed down in the flood, are pretty green yet, and don't burn too well. Sometimes I hear him singing in Latin to himself as he works down there.

...Les stopped by for awhile before dinner. He is still putting together his snowmachine. It's two old machines really, that he is combining into one, using some of the parts from each. He says he left them alone together in the shed all summer, hoping they'd mate by themselves out of mutual attraction, but it didn't happen. So he's got to do it himself with his welder.

October 4

Today I set up a small table next to my desk. I put a few things on it— a green spruce branch with cones, a bird's nest Sara and I found this fall, and a clean bone from the moose I've been eating, things I like to touch and look at. And in the middle I set a candle, which I light at dusk and keep burning through the evening.

October 5

Mike and Les stop by every day. They come briefly and they don't overstay. I can see in Mike's face that he is worrying about something, but he doesn't talk about it. He's having some trouble keeping warm. It's not going to be easy in that hardware store.

It makes sense that we see each other, the three people in town now, and I like them both. They both give out a sexual energy, though, that is a little difficult for me. Mike is a priest, but he is a very sensual man, and so is Les, even if he is quite a bit older.

I want to see them, but now that I have a chance for some privacy and time to myself, I'm getting possessive about it.

October 6

This morning, Mike told me he felt the need for more solitude. He wondered if it was OK with me if he didn't come by every day. I understood exactly and maybe that problem has solved itself....

October 8

I get up early in the morning, just before the sky lightens up. I make tea and light the candle on my little table and sit quietly through the dawn. Then I have my breakfast, eggs and toast, and do the clean up. And still I have all day before me! I have been walking down by the river, where the ice is forming rapidly now.

In the afternoon, I do the outdoor chores, the wood and water. I like the sawing and splitting and hauling. When snow comes, I'll be going out to the woodyard with the snowmachine to get more logs, but I've got plenty in the woodshed to burn until then.

Then I come inside and I do nothing, just absolutely nothing. Then it is getting dark, and I make another cup of tea and light the candle again. Soon it is time to begin dinner. Tonight was Chinese stir-fried moose almondine, with mung bean sprouts....

October 9

Rained hard all day today. This evening I took it in my head to push all the tables in the dining room aside and make a big clear space. I have a place to dance. I haven't danced in years....

October 11

Sometimes I get so lonely. Yesterday was wet and grey again. I made the mistake of not getting outside, so by dark I felt so dull. I missed Ted and Sara and all of you. In the evening I cried for what must have been hours. Now the sun is shining and I feel better....

I helped Mike carry logs off the creek bar this afternoon. That helped both our spirits. This evening Les is having me over for dinner. He's cooking chili rellenos with hot sauce, and pineapple upsidedown cake for dessert.

A letter from Mike, undated:

Dear Jot,

You ask me to tell you about the seasonal changes in Darwin. So, I ask myself, what would Jot Shechter notice? What would he like to know about? I've been seeing almost as if through your eyes. It's a new way of seeing for me, and very wonderful. Thank you, Jot.

Often it has been raining, cold rain. But not always. When the clouds part, the sky is so deep blue against the white new snow on the mountains. Even down here snow fell for awhile yesterday, but when the sun came out it melted.

The family of ducks that nested by the brook is gone, and so are most of the little tweety-birds that were so cheery through the summer. Three gray jays come sit on the poplar tree outside the hardware store every morning when I wake up, waiting for a handout. They must come by when they see the smoke rising from my stovepipe. I think they make regular rounds, because Les and Terri have them, too. (We're the only people in town right now.) Two of the jays are the parents and one is the darker colored young one from this summer's brood. Their other babies are gone. Sometimes magpies come, too. But the jays yell at them. When I walk in the woods I see just one kind of little bird, chirping along in a flock. Terri says these are the chickadees, and that is what they say, "chick-a-dee-dee-dee," flitting among the bare tree trunks in the brown and empty-feeling forest.

When I walk in the woods in the morning, the leaves are all crunchy with ice.

Darwin town has more buildings than it did this summer. With the leaves off the trees, houses have appeared where you never would have expected. And the trees in town seem so shrunken, all naked.

A small, handprinted cardboard sign in the window of the lodge says "closed."

The lodge generator is shut down for the winter. Sometimes Les runs one at his shop during the afternoon, while he is working. Any sound reverberates now through the town, on the hard bare ground and the walls of all the empty buildings. Quite a while ago the fireweed sent off the last of its flying cotton seeds, and with their bright color faded they stand stiff and dull like straw. The roads are muddy, and the potholes all float plate ice, which doesn't melt in the day anymore. This morning the water in the old wheelbarrow was frozen solid to the bottom.

Sara's gone Outside to spend the winter with her aunt and uncle and cousins and go to school, so I miss the clatter of her bicycle arriving at my door.

Sometimes the nights are black now, with cloudy skies. I feel the light whittled away with each passing day. When I walk in the evening, kerosene lamps show through a few scattered windows. Beyond, darkness extends to the horizon everywhere.

Sometimes, there is light in the sky. Les and Terri say it is the northern lights, but so far I've just seen it through the overcast. Usually, I can walk around the town by that light, but it is a dull light, without shadow or definition.

Jot, Darwin feels empty and open, as if it is about to welcome a longed for guest. It feels like the clutter of summer has been put aside, the floor is swept and the table is set, and the hosts wait expectant.

Your brother,

Mike

The following excerpts from Mike's journal are also undated:

The snow has come. It arrived at night in total stillness, except for the sound of impact of each flake. I went out with my flashlight to watch. Huge crystals land on my sleeve, where I can see the details of their six-pointed patterns, each different. They heap unbroken in piles on every surface, the top of the propane tank, the chopping block, the ax handle.

This morning my clothesline supports a two-inch high wall of stacked crystals. Bird tracks are all about the ground: The jays are here. Finally I can see how my mouse has been getting into the house. He comes out the corner of the woodshed and goes in under the sink. I can tell by his trail in the snow. The air is all fog, and a few flakes emerge from it.

I didn't see anybody today. Les came by in the afternoon; I can see his tracks going to his shed and up to my door. But I was out for a walk.

The sky cleared during the night. With the moonlight on the snow, night is like day inside out, like living in a three-dimensional black-and-white photographic negative. It is a still photograph, not a movie picture, no motion except my own.

From my bed I heard two owls hooting, calling back and forth.

Also I heard pops and snaps during the night, loud, outside. And sometimes a roar, as if the creek were suddenly at its summer flood, but then it would fade away again.

The thermometer on the tree read ten below zero this morning. All three jays were waiting for me to get up. Their feathers are puffed up spherical like warm down jackets. I went out this morning with bare feet. A mistake. They feel now like I burned them a little bit. Frostbite? I have to be careful.

I cannot get the hardware store warm. I spent all day getting wood down by the creek, but I'll burn half of it by tomorrow. The water bucket on the floor by my bed froze solid during the night. I had to hang it up over the stove to thaw out. I thought I had the holes in the house all filled. But jets of cold wind come in around the windows, the door, even between boards in the walls. I try to cover them over with tape, but it doesn't stick to the cold wood. So I am jamming bits of fiberglass in every crack with a butter knife. That helps, a little. I have to talk to Les about what to do.

The creek is carrying a slush of ice. It's been making ice for a while now, accumulating wherever the spray freezes on the protruding rocks, forming solid shelves reaching outward over the waters, and building up underwater on the creek bed.

This morning the sky is overcast, temperature above zero; much easier to keep warm.

I could tell even before I went outside this morning. Something was missing. I didn't remember what it was until I went out and looked at the creek. It is the roar of water, continuous since I arrived in Darwin in July. Suddenly it is gone. Where is the creek?

It is wandering all over the gravel bars and even out into the woods, gurgling softly in channels and stagnating in pools everywhere. I went out with Les, and he pointed out the ice dams, where the bottom ice meets the top ice and chokes off the creek's flow. The dams' surfaces ripple wonderfully, their knobs and ridges cold, smooth and wet.

How will I get wood? The downed trees I've been getting on the floodplain are all submerged in water and slush now. I can't even walk to them. Les showed me a few poplar snags close by in the woods. This bit of dry wood won't last too long, though, if it gets colder again. I've learned you can't use green, live trees. They just don't burn.

The creek roared again in the middle of the night. Why? This morning it is muted. It doesn't flow through the woods anymore. The pools have become flat ice burying the gravel along the creek. Flowers grow on the ice! But each petal a feather of frost really, delicately branching from a central spine. I lay down on the ice, belly to the cold, to see them, and they wilted under the warmth of a single breath.

The tree trunks lying out there are embedded ice. I can never get them now. Where is brother creek? Some places, I cannot find him. He must be down there, under the ice. Some of the dams are cut through, and there I see him flowing again swiftly, down on his gravels.

I've been working so hard trying to keep warm that I don't dwell on my troubles. By the time I've found and cut and carried and split enough firewood to last another day, and hauled the water, and kept the stove going and cooked my meals and chinked a few more holes, I'm plain exhausted. I sleep dreamless sleep. This isn't what the saints wrote about the spiritual journey.

I could probably pray better if it weren't so cold in the hardware store.

How does Terri do everything? It is so much *work* living out here. I think of her running that lodge and taking care of a kid all summer. She always seems so calm. I saw her yesterday afternoon out prying boards off one of the fallen buildings with a crowbar. She's using them to build new shelves and cabinets in the lodge kitchen. She pulls out the old nails, then pounds them straight with a hammer. I saw in the lodge: she has big coffee cans full of straightened old rusty nails, carefully sorted by size and type.

I like to go to the lodge to visit Terri. It is warm there. After breakfast I go over and we have coffee. She always seems to have plenty of time.

We don't say much, but it is nice to sit together with someone. She says she is not religious, but with everyone else gone the lodge has the feeling of a monk's cell, enclosed and warm, sparse but comfortable, everything that's needed and nothing more, calm like a church.

Here you don't pry into someone's past. But slowly I am learning more about Terri, about where she gets her strength. This morning, she told me quite a bit. She got to talking, finally. She's very lonely. I don't know how she can do it, being here all by herself, her husband dead not much more than a year and her child so far away, but she wants to stay. They were close, too, she and Ted. You can tell by the way she talks about him, the way her head shifts sideways and her eyes focus distantly.

Terri's been taking care of herself and other people since she was a kid. Her father left the family when she was twelve, leaving her mom to take care of five kids and a farm. Her mother had to work as a store clerk in town for the money. So, as the eldest daughter, Terri pretty much took care of things at home. That was in British Columbia.

Her mom must have been a sturdy person, too, because by the time Terri was eighteen, they had things in hand well enough that Terri could go off to college in Vancouver on scholarship. She rented the drafty front porch of someone's house and lived on $100 a month, which she got doing house-cleaning and mucking out stables.

One year she took a term off and bicycled alone down the coast to San Francisco.

She majored in French and worked one summer caring for the children of a wealthy family in Quebec.

She met Ted when she was working as cook for a mine north of Fairbanks. He was a bush pilot. She came with him to his place here in Darwin. They rebuilt the lodge together. It had been closed for thirty-five years.

I've been getting all my wood with a handsaw and ax, but it's just too much. Today Les got a chainsaw running for me. He put it together using an old saw that wasn't working and a bunch of parts from other saws he has in buckets in his shop. He showed me how to use it. I hate the noise, but it cuts fast. Necessary.

Fortunately, it's warm, barely below freezing, and I'm getting ahead on firewood.

I asked Les about Terri, and so he told me more: Ted would be gone a month at a time, hauling in a big sled of supplies with their bulldozer in the winter, making three miles a day if he worked hard. Often she was alone in town then, with no way to communicate with him or anyone, no way to know if he were alive or dead. For a few years he was the mail pilot, and usually the radio in his plane didn't work. The company wouldn't pay to have it fixed. He'd fly off to the coast in bad weather and not come back for days, and she'd have no way of knowing if he was OK. That was when Sara was a baby.

Les says she spent her pregnancy cleaning the block of their old bull-dozer with a toothbrush. Then she painted the block bright red, and the rest of the cat green.

When Sara was born, Ted was off flying polar bear hunters on the arctic ocean icepack. Terri rented a trailer on the outskirts of Kotzebue for the last month of her pregnancy, hauling water from the city pump by hand. When she went into labor, she walked a mile and a half to the hospital on icy streets.

Damp again today, edging up toward freezing, with light snow. Terri and I took a long walk out the trail through the woods along the creek. She is like a companion on my spiritual journey. She is making her own journey, too; that is clear.

I breath deeply the spruce-smoke scented air of solitude. I hear the beating of my heart in the silence of the night. As the circulation of my blood purifies the tissues of my body, so meditation on Mary cleanses the fabric of my soul. I feel her power move through my body, pulsing outward from the center of my prayer. I empty myself of everything that belongs to a man in the world. I rid myself of all the lesser joys, the false peace, the incomplete loves, making space for the Great Love of His presence.

Mary, free me from distraction. Rid me of all desire for the lesser joys, the cholesterol clogging the arteries of my spiritual circulation.

Terri, I imagine you in the privacy of your own solitude in the lodge down the street. As companions we journey with God.

Zero and lightly snowing today. We have maybe six inches on the ground. I hear Les rattling around in his shop, working on his snowmachine. We had lunch together here in the hardware store. He ate just a can of sardines. They have special healthful properties, he says. He asked if he could have my empty maple syrup can. He needs it to fix his carburetor.

George Johnston is back. He came in on the mailplane. The road is closed for the season by snow. Terri, Les and I were all there to meet the plane—our weekly encounter with the outside world. George had little to say, though he is polite enough, and went off to his house. With so few of us here, each personality is a palpable presence, like the river or the snow or the mountains or the ravens overhead. The air feels different with him here, a heaviness, a questioning. Les, Terri and I have felt so comfortable together, flowing like the braiding and branchings of the creek. George is different. But he keeps to himself; certainly it's his right to find some privacy, too. And a person can do that out here, in winter. We all respect that.

From one of Terri's letters. After mid-October, she stopped dating her letters and diary entries. —JBS

...This morning, Mike was hiding in the tree outside the front door. When I came out for wood, he dumped a bucket of snow on my head. Then he laughed and laughed. He looked like a roly-poly bear up there. And he climbed up and down like one, too, shinnying up and down so easily.

He ambushed George with snowballs the other day. I didn't see it, but I saw the spot, all the tracks and swipes in the snow, down by the brook. The snow is so dry the snowballs couldn't be much more than powder puffs. But Mike says George just gave a sour look and plodded on his way as if it hadn't happened. Mike says he'll find a way to get George to open up yet.

————————

From Mike's journal:

This afternoon I talked with Les about what to do. I know now that I will not be able to keep the hardware store warm when the cold really comes. And, to tell the truth, I am realizing that I want a deeper solitude. I remember the solitude I experienced up the creek last fall, and I crave it, difficult though it may be.

Les says I am welcome to use his brother's place. It is just a tiny cabin, five minutes walk from Les's house, his house up the creek, set off by itself in the big spruce. Les expects Tim to be gone the whole winter, down in Oregon, and says Tim won't mind my using his place. But I'll write him and ask, anyway.

Joy! Solitude! Hermitage!

We have to wait for conditions to be right to go up the creek. Les says the ice has to be good and we have to get more snow first. He'll go up on the snowmachine and I can follow on cross-country skis. He's got an old pair I can use. We need some more snow and a week of zero weather to make conditions perfect.

...Snowed a couple of inches during the night; enough, Les says. Now we need some cold.

Terri is doing so well in her solitude. I watched her splitting firewood today. She moved big logs from woodshed to sawbuck, without effort it seemed. They were batons in her hands. She has more than strength: it is grace, and her work is a dance. As she worked, she generated heat, and she shed her jacket and sweater. How could a woman have such well muscled strength? She, whose chest has fed a baby, breathes so deeply with each upswing of the heavy steel splitting maul. The rhythm is so smooth, her posture echoes the balance of her form; the logs split evenly, precisely, flying outward from the touch of her sharp steel, a touch delivered as if effortlessly, by circling arms. I watched in awe as the pile of split wood, ready now for the stove's maw, grew.

Overcast cleared last night and this morning the thermometer reads minus twenty-five. Les says I should go ahead and cut up one of the shacks at the edge of town for firewood. It will take all day to get enough and carry it over here.

Minus thirty this morning. Yesterday it didn't get above minus fifteen. The temperature is creeping down. The sky is silky blue, cloudless; the mountains pale blue. Total silence everywhere, except for strange pops and cracks from the woods at night, the hooting of the owls, and roars and gurgles from the creek that rise and fade with the drift of the air.

The creek has dammed itself again. Clouds of steam rise from the wet ponds. Les says the creek is making ice. But it is so cold.

Twice today I was startled by an explosive bang. It is the empty oil barrels around town contracting.

Minus thirty-six. It only goes up eight or nine degrees during the short day. The sun barely breaks out over the treetops to the south at midday. When it does, I rush out to greet it before it is gone.

Good ice on the creek now. The dammed ponds are frozen.

But it is too cold to travel.

I've moved in with Les. His place in Darwin is a plain, uninsulated, mining-era house, but it holds heat better than the hardware store, and we can share the task of getting wood for just one place, instead of two. The door is insulated with newspapers tacked on. I sleep on the floor next to the stove, wearing my parka in the sleeping bag. Terri is letting me use Ted's parka. It's somewhat too small.

This cold spell has to end, and then we'll go up the creek.

The full moon illuminates the night. We live by its light.

Les and I are crowded in his house, but I choose not to visit Terri today. Instead, I read in the easy chair crammed against the wall in Les's little living room. My back freezes and my feet, clad in wool sox, extending to the stove, cook. I must not burn my feet. They must be ready for the journey up the creek. Springs stick out through the cushion into my backside. The table next to me is piled high with cartons of eggs and canned goods that should not freeze. This is the only room in the house we can keep above freezing. I tried reading Saint John of the Cross, but could not concentrate.

Terri needs her privacy now, and I respect that. I am on a monk's path. And so is she.

I am uncomfortable as I write this. There's no table space here, so I write in my notebook on my lap. Les is outside working on the snow-machine. It is minus twenty-five degrees and he is lying on his back in the snow trying to remove bolts with a wrench. He has to come in every couple of minutes to warm his fingers.

Well, I am not going to think about Terri. On our spiritual journeys, our happiness lies in the fulfillment of our purified capacity for emulating God's supernatural grace and glory, in identification with Christ. This fulfillment comes from the recovery of our true nature, according to which we are made in the image of God. Terri and I travel this path together, in our joint solitudes.

Les just brought in a five gallon can full of gasoline and set it on top of the hot stove to warm up. I find this disconcerting.

Today I have chosen to stay here rather than distract myself from my spiritual path by socializing. It will be easier to avoid distraction when we are up the creek.

This chair is very uncomfortable.

I am not being distracted today by the smoothness of Terri's face when she serves tea. Each time we have tea it is like a Japanese ceremony. There is no consideration of time, no trace of hurry. Her face is utterly relaxed, eyes focused totally on the motion of raising the pot, the pouring of the clear boiling water, her bent fingers and neatly trimmed nails holding firmly, but without tension. Strong hands, hands which separate the flesh of frozen moose and haul the steaming water buckets from the frost-lined brook, hands which can touch a cup so lightly. And her wrists, bound bundles of ligament and tendon, gently rippling with the movement of the placing of the tea strainer. I notice this beauty in every little detail, because I am a monk, because I have chosen to empty the extraneous from my life, because now, here, in the solitude and emptiness of this arctic winter, I have the time and the space to focus on being at one with God, in freedom from distraction and diversion.

Minus forty-two. I got a nip of frostbite on the end of my nose today. It is different than it was at minus thirty. I have to remember to keep the scarf over my face. It hurts to breathe too deeply. I must not frostbite my lungs.

Les and I spent most of the daylight cutting up the old shack. Tonight we'll burn everything we cut.

Pastel blue days. The moon has passed full and rises after dark now.

No wind. Smoke from the stovepipes rises straight up forty or fifty feet and hangs there.

Minus forty-seven at dawn. It will not break minus thirty-five today, at best.

Sam flew in yesterday. Just in time, Les says. Can't fly below minus thirty-five. Airplane metal gets too brittle. Sam explained why the smoke stays low. It stays below the temperature inversion. Like Los Angeles, sort of. Up higher, it's warmer. Up where Sam was flying, it was almost zero Fahrenheit. He was getting too warm; had to take off his parka.

Minus fifty-two. I would enjoy this more if we didn't have to spend all day getting wood. Les says there is plenty of wood up the creek.

Minus twenty-five is the magic number. Soon as it's above minus twenty-five, we go for it.

Minus fifty-eight this morning. The jays did not come. I hope they are alright.

We work outside a little while, but then we have to come in to get warm. I never feel chilled. It's not cold like in New York. I'm just working along and suddenly I realize that if I don't come in Right Now, my hands will freeze.

The world is unbelievably soft all day, a pastel world. I can hear Sam splitting wood at his place, a mile away. I can even hear him talking to himself. But I can't make out the words. They are distorted as they ride to me on the drift of thick air.

Clearwater Brook is not frozen. It comes out of a warm spring, I guess. Steam rises from its undulating surface. The overhanging willows are a garden of frost, inches thick now on every drooping twig.

The watchword is: Keep Dry. We wear canvas mukluks, down parkas. If liquid water gets in them, the insulation is gone, our skin will freeze. Don't spill water when we dip our buckets at the brook. Don't get our mitts wet. The brook is a dangerous oasis.

The snow is desert sand. Dry.

This evening a wisp of cloud for the first time. It is warmer, above minus forty.

I write this by the light of a kerosene lamp turned low, so not to wake Les.

I woke in the darkness of night, disoriented. Then I realized I was sleeping on Les's living room floor, with the iron door of the barrel stove above my head. The fire had died. When I got up to pee, the air outside felt warm and the sky was pitch dark, overcast. It has not been that way for so long. I heard a distant roar, somewhere above it seemed, but felt no wind. The Cold was gone. I shined my flashlight on the thermometer: exactly zero Fahrenheit. I stood on the porch feeling exposed. The Cold had been a protective enclosure, and it was gone, and the world had seeped back in. Then I remembered I had awakened from a dream.

I recalled the dream as I stood there, clad only in parka and mukluks, feeling the warmth of the air around me, but the Cold still inhabiting my heart, emanating from my dream. The dream was cold, clear air, and a stark crescent moon, and me standing naked and vulnerable on crisp snow. I cried out, but the words went nowhere. I could not hear them. There was a ring around the moon. I looked down on the snow covered roofs of the mill building, built against the mountainside, rising from the darkness of the abandoned Syndicate town below. I had emerged from the uppermost story of the building, out past rusted piles of cable onto the snow. Above dry leafless alder branches I saw plumes of snow rise from distant mountain peaks in faint moonlight, but heard no wind, felt no breath of air.

I remembered that the white-clad man in the meadow had told me to seek his mother above. That was in summer, but it is winter now. Now I had come out above. And I knew she was near. But I could not see her. A weasel, big as a cat, emerged from beneath a pile of scrap iron pipe. She leapt along gracefully, leaving pawprints in the snow. She stopped and stared into my eyes. Then she turned, flowing under the alders, and disappeared.

Then I heard the distant roar of wind, and I woke to hear the roar outside Les's house here in Darwin.

I must try to sleep. The cold spell has broken: In the morning we go up the creek.

We woke at dawn. Ten above zero, and the trees are bowed before the north wind. A white-out blizzard: I could barely find my way to Terri's this morning. By noon it let up some, and Les went out alone with the snow-machine to start making trail up the creek.

I worried when he did not come back by dark. I had finished dinner when at last I heard the putter of his engine and saw the beam of his headlight reflected on the falling flakes. Parka-bundled, his face rimed and icicled, his machine piled high with white, Les looked like a snow monster emerging from the darkness.

He had pushed his way up the first six miles. That will be a big help when we start up the creek in the morning. Tonight I can see stars emerging from between the clouds. Tomorrow we go for it.

Terri is coming too. Les asked her to join us. She'll help us put in the trail, then ski back down to Darwin after a few days.

Terri evidently wrote the following passages during the cold spell. They are undated.   *—JBS*

I enjoy sitting quietly in the evening with a cup of tea.

How long have I been sitting here since I wrote the last sentence? The kerosene is lower in the lamp....

This afternoon I walked out to the open river flats again, where the snow is packed by the wind onto the bare, flat ground. I had to put up my parka hood to keep the cold breeze from burning my face. The giant mounds on the glacier are all snow covered. Only the big rocks are blown free of snow. They are too cold to touch.

The wind at dusk was like a raspy old voice. It was as if Sara's pretend friend was talking to me. I pretended I could understand. What did she say? She said we are not alone. The wind was like a thousand voices, all together.

It was as if I could see the old Indian lady making baskets, down there by the river. I could imagine it was summertime, and there she was, weaving with fast, brown fingers. She talked while she worked.

I heard the raspy wind. And there was the blown snow on the big empty space in front of the glacier. The river was flowing underneath the ice in front of us, but it made no sound.

Today I went again to the river. I came across a fox curled up on the downwind side of a rock. When it saw me, it got up and trotted off. Why was it out there?

From Mike's journal, written up the creek:

I have lost my urge to write. I sit, doing nothing. I chop wood and cook meals. I sigh. How long have I been up the creek? I have lost track of the days. I know that Les is at his house, enclosed in warmth. He is painting now, wearing his beret, as he does every morning. And I am sitting in his brother's cabin, where the abbot thinks I am praying. But I am fooling him. I just sit here, doing nothing. Dear abbot, I need you. I need my confessor. Dear God, what shall I do?

Mercy, dear God, Mercy. How did I get here? Pretensions of glory, dear God. I was making the great religious pilgrimage to the lonely realm of wonderful eremetic fulfillment.

Blaah.

I will go out and chop firewood, because the cabin is getting cold, the daylight is passing, and soon once again the night will envelop us.

I walked out into the woods, pulling the red plastic sled behind me in the snow. Les had cut a dry spruce snag out by the hillside, and I hauled some pieces back, then split them to size.

But I feel so much better, going out into the sunlight, building up a sweat working in the snow, enjoying the bite of the cold air in my throat, watching split chunks fly.

For days, who knows how long, I have not written in this journal. After our journey up here, I could not write and felt no need to write. Was that because of exhaustion, and guilt? No. Even now, I am not sure what to feel. Exhilaration, rather; exhilaration and exhaustion all together, and a great fulfillment. How can I admit it was a great fulfillment? What was the fulfillment? Was it arriving here, being here? Am I avoiding the question in such a pretense? Terri, old boy. Don't forget about Terri. But she is only part of it. There is much more.

The question stands before me. What happened? So what?

For a long time, I wasn't even curious. I felt numb; no, it was that I felt especially alert. It was both: they are the same. So I didn't write, but now I am curious again, so I am writing again. Maybe my curiosity will fade again. I hope so, for it is a pretense. I am tired of pretensions.

The journey was awful and wonderful, and nothing is the same anymore. I can put what happened behind me now, and yet it lives in me. What about Terri? Wrong? Of course it was wrong, if I have pretensions of being anybody. Me, big time Saint Hermit. No way, no way. I am an ant. I am smaller than an ant. I am a New York monk stuck in a dilapidated shack up some snow-clogged valley in Alaska dependent on a weird guy with a snowmachine held together with bubblegum and baling wire to help me get firewood so I don't freeze.

Monk, shmonk.

Well, Terri is back down in Darwin, and that is good.

I am not going to write, because I have lost my pretensions. That is why I haven't even considered telling about our journey up here, and what followed.

The night before we left Darwin the clouds parted and the temperature plunged. Les and I woke to a clear dawn at minus twenty-four degrees, above our cutoff temperature of minus twenty-five. We ate breakfast and packed up lunch: some cheese, a couple of candy bars, two cans of sardines. Les brought a dozen eggs, well wrapped against the cold, to enjoy when we got up the creek. Terri came, and she and I waxed our skis. Les took his hot bricks from the stove and put them into the snowmachine to warm it for starting. The brief day was passing; soon the sun would edge up between the spruce on the southern horizon, making the long shadows of mid-day.

First Terri and I rode the sled behind Les's snowmachine, bundled up, parka fur tight around our faces. Sled runners, bouncing on the trail, kicked snow into our eyes. The trail Les made the day before had firmed up overnight, so we putted right along, At Two Mile, we crossed the creek on good ice; I waved to the dragon in the rock. He wore a snow cap. Then we got to where Les stopped the day before. Deep, unbroken snow. We left the sled there.

At first, Les went ahead on the machine, slowly. Terri and I skied behind, pushing along on his soft, unsettled new trail. But the snow got deeper and deeper, the machine worked harder and harder, then mired.

Now Terri and I skied ahead, breaking trail for the machine, taking turns leading, light powder snow rising up over our knees. My skis were down there in the snow somewhere, but I didn't see them usually. Sometimes a ski tip rose to the surface as I pushed along. We were a freight train and I the engine, chug, chug, chug. I chanted antiphons to the Blessed Virgin in rhythm. Sweating, I took off my parka, strapped it on my daypack. Les followed putt-putt on the machine. Though we moved in the shade of the valley floor, the sun was shining above us on the white mountains, looming close on both sides. But now the shadows climbed the slopes. The summits turned pink. The trees sat heavy under the weight of snow lying on every branch. The creek next to us seemed frozen solid.

We approached the canyon. Here the trail would go up to the tunnel, bypassing the narrow, steep-walled canyon slot. But we would take hours building snow ramps to the tunnel entrance above, and back down the other side. Instead, Les suggested a short-cut—going right through the slot. Usually, that way is open water, but that day it was ice-covered—what luck! Terri and I scurried through, then Les zoomed over on the machine. He made it, but the ice caved in behind him. Now we were committed, with no way back to Darwin.

It should have been easy, though, to slog on to Les's cabin. We'd passed the hard part.

But above the slot, the creek was flowing open; no ice! We could not cross. Remember: Wetness is freezing, wetness is death. Water churned out from under the steep face of Dagheeloyee Glacier. Les explained, an ice dam must have broken underneath. We were stuck on the east side of the creek, unable to cross to the trail. We would have to go over the glacier itself.

We ate our sardines.

We wound our way between boulders, up a steep bank, through deepening snow. Here the machine slipped, almost rolled into the creek! Les jumped free, but the machine was off our trail, almost buried in white fluff. Terri and I took off our skis. We three wallowed to the machine, pulling and hoisting and dragging it back. I fell face first, cramming snow down my neck and up my sleeves.

We managed to get it onto the trail, but not far ahead the snow was just too deep. The machine sat hopelessly stuck, snow heaped to the windshield. We had to continue on foot and come back for the machine another day. Les put on snowshoes. We took the eggs with us so they would not freeze.

Probing with a ski pole, Les led us over the blank whiteness of the glacier, fading with dusk. Giant invisible crevasses lurked under the snow. He knew where the crevasse fields were, he said.

We could not get down past the crevasses and ice cliffs to Dagheeloyee Lake. Instead, we crossed the glacier to a miners' trail on a high forested bench above the lake. It would tie in to our original route, Les said.

We traversed the bench above the frozen lake, wading the snow path between spruce etched black against the stars, feeling our way with our ski tips. Now we wore our heavy parkas closed against the Cold.

Not much longer now, Les assured. I gnawed on a piece of frozen Swiss cheese. We must keep moving, keep up the head of steam, keep warm. I forgot to chant. Muscles kept the rhythm.

How long did we go? The pole star stood over the head of the valley, our destination. The constellation of the great bear arced slowly about it, looking down upon us. We were three individuals, moving without speech, yet I felt the warm core in each of my companions.

Eventually we moved along the edge of the bluff, above the creek, near where the trail descended to the shore, where we expected to cross back over to our original route, to the Syndicate town and beyond, to Les's. But what did we hear, down there below? Water. No, it could not be. But it was. The creek was wide open here, too: flowing water, with no way to cross. What shall we do? I realized how exhausted we must be, how near death was.

"Jesus, Mary and Joseph, have mercy on me!"

I put my head between my knees to keep from fainting away. We would die here. They would find our bodies in the spring.

Soon after I felt a kick of adrenaline, a tremendous surge in my veins. Suddenly everything was so clear. I stood straight, totally alert. I did not think about living and dying. I did exactly what was necessary. I moved one step at a time.

We found our way down to the open water with flashlights. We must cross, because the trail did not continue on this side. Now we spoke, debated: Should we try to walk back to Darwin? Surely, we will freeze. Les said he would build a fire. I knew we could not get enough firewood by hand to get warm. I recognized this without fear. It was so cold. Les did not try.

We had to ski along the creek on this side, crossing to the trail when we found an ice bridge. But how do you walk through thick brush wearing six foot skis? I needed to aim the ski tips precisely between the willow stems. But I could not see my skis under the snow. I searched for them with my flashlight. They must be there, because they are attached to my feet. Well, I took off my skis and tried walking. The snow was nearly to my waist. And now the skis, carried in my arms, caught on branches and snagged. Meanwhile, Les and Terri moved on ahead. Stop! Wait for me! How do they do it?

The great bear circled amidst the stars overhead, laughing.

I put my skis back on, learned to reach out with my ski poles to guide the tips of my skis between the willow stems. I dropped my knit headband from my forehead to cover my nose and cheeks. Snot icicles formed below it. Periodically, I chewed one off. I needed the moisture.

We came to rock cliffs, plunging into the water, blocking our way. We *had* to cross to the trail on the other side. Was there an ice bridge somewhere in the darkness?

I wandered out toward the creek, searching with my flashlight, Les and Terri following, onto a flat, open area of snow along the creek channel.

Suddenly I broke through snow into water. In a moment, our skis weighed a ton, with sticky wet snow attached. We hustled to shore, but too late. The wet snow froze instantly, encasing the skis in blocks of ice. We had to leave them there.

Now we would walk. But still we could not cross the creek: our canvas mukluks would soak through; we would lose our legs.

Les said there was a house. It was not far from where we were and it was on this side of the creek, just beyond the cliffs.

We'd have to climb through the trees to get above the cliffs. But could we even move in this snow?

The snow was almost—but not quite—too deep. Then we traversed above the cliffs, and still it was steep. We hung from branches, slithered between alder stems, snow in our faces, the sound of rushing water down below.

We had far yet to go, but now I knew we would make it! Then I noticed a billion stars spread across the black sky. I saw jagged summits decked with glowing glaciers. I could see by their light!

I felt the huff of my hot breath into icy air. I heard the crunch of our mukluks into the snow. I heard the snap of twigs as I crawled. I felt the snow shoved into my parka, the drip of cold water melting against the back of my neck. Hurray! I was a monk and a hermit. Here I was, come to the ultimate hermitage!

Past the cliffs, we descended the slope and waded deep snow toward a building in shadows against the hillside, an uninhabited two story log house, with a wringer washing machine on the porch. The door was unlocked. Les lit a lamp, revealing a humped wooden floor, an old table, some cotton mattresses, wooden chairs, a rusty barrel stove against a log wall protected by sheets of frayed asbestos, and other doorways, leading to other rooms still in darkness.

It was as cold inside as out. Les appeared with an armload of firewood, which Terri stuffed into the stove. Les threw on some liquid from a can and lit it with a match. With a sudden poof the fire took. We huddled by the stove.

I realized how thirsty I was. Terri came in with a bucket of water, filling a kettle on the stove in the living room, while I rummaged around in a cold, dark kitchen with my flashlight—Aha—I discovered a container of Nestle's Strawberry Quick with some left in the bottom. Brushing mouse turds off the lid, I took it out to the light and pried it open. The Quick was rock hard in the bottom of the can. I chopped at it with the handle of a tablespoon, stirred the chunks into a cup of hot water. Warm, sweet, strawberry liquid slid down my throat. Heaven!

We sat close to the stove, our tummies warmed, our behinds cold, our hands embracing hot cups.

When I went to get more firewood from the porch, the waning moon had risen. A thermometer on the wall read minus twenty-eight. When I returned from the outhouse in the yard a couple of minutes later, the thermometer read minus ten. I thought, this is a strange thermometer.

Then the sky began to roar.

Soon after I came in, the wind descended, howling from the North. I stepped again to the porch, briefly watching. Snow flew from swaying tree limbs. Star silhouetted spruce bowed against a crescent moon. The thermometer held at minus ten. With the windchill factor it was a hundred below zero. What if the wind had started earlier, while we were still out there? Burning spruce crackled in the barrel stove, and the bottom of the stovepipe glowed red.

The house had a single bedroom. Les chose to sleep there. Terri and I lay on lumpy mattresses on the living room floor, covering ourselves with ragged wool blankets. The stove was banked. Cold flowed up from below. Cold seeped between the blankets. The wind howled.

We slept, moving to the warmth.

Touching deep into soft muscles. I dreamed of breasts filled with woman's milk. But I rose into dim, rich, warm consciousness. Thirst. I drank, teeth against my teeth. A flower of ejaculation. Warm, soft liquid. Relaxation, sleep.

Later, we woke in the darkness. A chewing sound woke us. I shined my flashlight into the corner. It caught the eyes of a weasel the size of a cat. The creature bounded across the room and disappeared under a floor board.

We woke again past dawn, white light through frosted windows. Les had coffee boiling on the stove and eggs frying. Wind roared out of the North.

There are no questions, you see. We sing and dance, and are very gay about it. In the morning we rise in silence. We feel every little thing: the way the Cold sits low to the ground, the color of snow, the lamp's long shadows playing against the cabin walls.

We are poor, we are surrounded by the savage and unforgiving, so everything has value. It matters how far the crack extends today up the kerosene lamp chimney. Will the chimney break? The chimney is irreplaceable; it makes an island in our darkness. The sweat on our mittens matters, for wetness lets in the Cold. The moment matters, for we dwell in it; yesterday and tomorrow do not exist, for they are uncounted.

The Cold stands beside our dwelling. We fear the Cold; yet because of the Cold outside, our hearth is a warm oasis, a sheltered kindled spark of life, a germinating egg in which life expands. Cold is the eggshell. Hard, white, dense, impenetrable, barrier against the world, creator of the boundary, maker of space, encloser of the beating heart.

The Cold brings forth the Man dressed in white, Whose mother I sought by the light of the crescent moon. The Man dressed in white walks the dark snowy forests, attending to us His sleeping children. He is tender of the egg.

The egg is within us. It is fertilized when we lie open, as the virgin snow, piled crystal lattice, lies open to the starry sky. It is fertilized when we are virgin as the snow, open bride of the night sky.

Virginity. Terri and I had made love, a mortal sin. That next day, we did not speak of it. Outside, the wind howled on. We ventured out only for water, from a nearby beaver pond, and for firewood. Les got an ancient chainsaw running, and we carved pieces off a log shed in the yard, enough for the coming night. Other than that, we sat quietly by the fire, backs to the cold. Every cell in our bodies had been emptied out. We poured cup after cup of warm liquid down our throats. We tacked a blanket over the door to the kitchen to keep the heat from escaping the main room, where we sat.

The weasel had gotten into the sacks of beans stored in the icy kitchen. Pintos, black-eyed peas, and red beans were mixed together on the floor. We washed them, picking out the shreds of plastic bag, removing the weasel turds, and boiled a luscious chili with a can of tomato paste and the flaccid kernels of a thawed can of corn. We ate it all, along with the remainder of the dozen eggs.

Soon it was dark. The house had but the one little lamp, with a cracked chimney and almost no wick. Les ripped a piece off a shirt he found in a corner and pinned it to the wick, extending it into the oil. The oil was yellow, burning unsteadily, sooting the lamp. We sat close.

No question remained to be answered. Mouse turds, lamp smoke, mortal sin, the unending blast of the wind: now these were not questions.

God gave mercy. On that day I was a virgin for the first time. This is not heresy. Sitting here now in this tiny cabin, surrounded by the snow, forest and mountains, I know it is not.

Father Abbot, my confessor, I need to speak with you. But I cannot, you are so far away.

Now I pause in my recollections, rise from my seat and step out the door into the soft daylight. I hear Les's trumpet, distant tones floating from his cabin on the hill.

When we awoke to our second morning in the log house, something was missing: the wind was silent. Already it was the full, shaded light of mid-day. Terri and I looked at each other. Although safely encased in long underwear, I felt like Adam when he first saw his nakedness. Les wandered out of the bedroom to splash water on his face.

We ate the remnants of yesterday's meal, cleaned up and swept the place, and packed up our few things. Next to the stove, we left logs and kindling, enough for someone to start a good fire. And then we walked out.

The air was about fifteen below zero and the sky still crisp clear. I felt exposed, as if I had broken out of an enclosure; inside, the house was dark, even in mid-day, with small windows and soot-stained walls. That golden haven of our arrival seemed dingy now, surrounded by light white snow. All of the trees were naked and stark, with every bit of snow blown off: the dark green spruce, the tan and grey poplars. The snow surface no longer showed its virginal crystalline puffy latticework; it had been beaten by the wind, crusted, indented with snow lumps tossed from the trees.

Les led us wading through the snow to the creek, which was refrozen and solid.

I could not believe the change. Now it was nothing to cross the creek. Was the open water just a hallucination of the night? An illusion that forced us into the terror, exhaustion, and all that followed?

Already the light was dimming, but soon we were at Les's home: abundant firewood in the shed, soon a blazing fire in the heat stove, and the cook stove crackling, too, as Les worked in the kitchen. The night journey on the mountainside, the wind, the strange log house out in nowhere, the dim lamp with the cracked chimney, making love with Terri, the weasel— all of it became a dream, a fiction, fading into the haze of relaxation, comfort, and warmth. It could never have happened, and yet it was still in me, dwelling there with my dreams of dragons, of bears and beavers amidst strange machinery, of the search for Holy Mother Mary in the snow. I sprawled back in Les's easy chair, patting my belly. I let it all seep down into my big belly and it disappeared. I was big enough now to hold it all. The mountains, the forest, the glaciers, the creek, the old buildings, the hibernating bears under the snow, they all were within me, and I had room for them all, and more. Jesus was walking by the creek. He was in me, too. I burped, content.

Then Terri poked her thumb into my tummy. I was snoring, she said. Les brought steaming plates of spam, rice and melted cheese to the table. Dinner. I ate four helpings. I burped, content.

The next morning was a high, thin overcast and minus five degrees. After a big breakfast of Les's sourdough pancakes, Terri and I headed out to recover our skis, left down the valley at the base of the cliffs. With the creek frozen, we could follow the trail and it really wasn't far at all. Les loaned us two pairs of snowshoes, grey, cracked, held together with bits of cord and wire, with loose leather bindings. Mostly they made walking easier.

They were not, however, too good at remembering the correct direction of travel. At least my pair were not. On our walk, Terri and I had a very meaningful discussion. I found that whenever the discussion got most meaningful, my right snowshoe stepped on its left mate, pitching me head-first into the snow. At that point, the snowshoes thankfully chose to wave around in the air, signaling Terri to rescue me.

We crunched down the trail from Les's, leaving Les inside washing dishes. At first, we talked:

Me: ...and so the purpose of our vows is to give us stability in our life of union with God. They protect us in our striving for virginity of spirit.

[I suddenly catapult headlong into the snow; Terri grabs me around the waist from behind and hauls me upright.]

Me: What should we name the baby? I have an Uncle Harold I really like. Harold Charles Lewis. That's a nice name.

Terri: Or Haroldine. I don't think there will be any baby. Don't worry.

Me: I'm not worrying. I don't worry about anything since we got up here. I suppose I should worry about not worrying, but I don't....

But marriage is is abandonment of the entire path....

Terri: You are proposing? I love you, Mike. But marriage is out of the picture. For now.

Me: Terri!

Terri: I'm sorry, Mike, but I've been wife and mom for a decade and it's time for something else. Time for skiing up the creek—you know I've never been here before, never even thought about it. Ted was always the one out and gone. It made sense. Someone had to take care of things at home. In summer we had to keep out the bears. In winter we had to keep the stove going, didn't want to let the house freeze. And then there was Sara.

Nope. This winter I'm going to sing and dance. I may be sad and lonely, but I'm going to take the time to enjoy it, beat my drums and just do nothing.

I enjoyed making love with you. It was warm and sweet. And I think we needed to do it. It answered some sort of question.

[Terri looked so radiant, realizing her own freedom. We joined hands and attempted to dance while wearing snowshoes.]

Me: We made love, and instead of being impure, we are purified.

Well, being virgin in the spirit means being open and empty to receive God.

[I trip and plunge, buried in white powder. Terri rolls me over. I sit, wiping snow out of my collar and emptying out my mittens.]

Terri: Maybe God wanted you to sleep with me. Maybe He wanted you to empty yourself out into me, so there will be room in you for Him.

I don't know anything about the spiritual life, Mike. I just know I am who I am.

Here, grab onto my arm with both hands and I'll pull you up.

Me: Thanks.

[We walked on in silence, holding hands when we could without tipping over. A squirrel chittered at us from the top of a tall spruce. I chittered back.]

———————

From a letter Terri wrote Sara:

...I went with Mike and Les to help put the snowmachine trail in up the creek.... Mike and I skied up, breaking trail. We couldn't get Les's snowmachine all the way the first day. The snow was deep and we were tired, and then it was windy awhile, so it took a few days before we were ready to come back and get it. We skied down to the snowmachine carrying shovels and fixed up the trail with ramps up the steep spots. The day was just right for skiing, sunny and little below zero....

After we finished with the trail, I went on down back home to Darwin by myself. The wind hadn't blown down lower, so the trail didn't have soft snow on it. It was packed and fast. But only once did I end up with my head in the snow and my skis in the air! I flew down the trail, soaring like an eagle, dashing between the trees like a goshawk....

The next day I skied out to the river. And there was Mrs. Henry, sitting on the gravel bar, weaving her baskets....

From Mike's journal:

Antiphons for Winter

> No dreams, no visions,
>> just the darkness of the night,
>> the falling of the snow,
> And then comes clearing and stars,
>> the bear circling above,
>> heartbeat of days.

> Sitting by the lamp,
>> I do nothing, wonder nothing.
> The moon in pregnant roundness births a new month,
>> slims and fades.
> Daylight slips away,
>> becoming a narrow window in the darkness.
> Spruce smoke spice is the smell, fire is the warmth,
>> the stove glows red, water boils in the pot.
> Outside is white and black and long shadows,
>> star shadows, moon shadows,
>> brief shadows of the distant sun.
> Owl hoots,
>> raven beats by on black wings.
> I haul and split firewood.

> Sleep when tired, awake to night,
>> my eyes adjust to the darkness.
> I go out, stand in the snow,
>> listen patiently to the silence.

> As it was in the beginning, is now and ever shall be, world without
> end, Amen.

Aurora

Now Les is in Darwin. He snowmachined down to greet the mailplane and will return tomorrow, weather permitting. I am alone up the creek and have finished my dinner of pea soup and sourdough bread.

I am sitting in my chair supposedly in meditation, but my head aches. The shadows from the kerosene lamp are too stark. The lamp needs to be brighter; my eyes water as the intensity of the flame wavers with each beat of my heart. I am suffocating in this tiny room. I just have to get out of here, out, out, out. So I put on my mukluks and my parka and my wool cap, turn down the lamp, and walk out the door.

At first there is only black, and the bite of cold in my throat. My feet feel their way along the firm-packed path. I walk down onto the flats by the creek, away from the enclosure of forest, surrounded by sleeping mountains and a vastness of sky dim with stars. No sound, no color, no movement. Nothing. Nothing happens.

A tremolant sash of light moves across the northern sky. The sky is filled with music; I hear the dance, although it makes no sound, the mountains hum as gigantic pipe organs playing fugues. The sky is filled with modulating light, green, blue, red; and the snow glows in response. Searchlights sweep the sky; then a second sash joins the first, and the two silks waver horizon to horizon, with ethereal rosettes exploding crimson overhead.

It is more than I can stand. I kneel in the snow, crying, tears freezing as they leave my face.

This is simply the way it is: I see no visions. Slowly I begin to chill. Slowly I walk back to the warmth of the cabin.

I take off my mukluks, cap and parka, and sit by the lamp turned low.

As it was in the beginning, is now and ever shall be, world without end, Amen.

Everything beyond this valley is hazy and indistinct, just strange memory and unlikely whispered rumors. Not that this valley is small and the surrounding world is large: No, the reverse. The creek valley is huge beyond boundary, deep and high, letting me travel endlessly without destination. Everything outside the valley is merely a narrow fuzzy zone, a shell of chaos beyond the edge of the world.

From Jot's journal:

17 December 1981

Location: The lodge, Darwin, Alaska.

Outside conditions are -25°C temperature; 66 cm of powder snow on the ground. I reached my arm down through the snow today and felt the ground with my mitten. It is as if the bare ground has had a thick layer of fine white sand poured onto it. All the buildings, every tiny branch of each tree and bush, carry a load of snow, so that the town looks like a perfect Christmas card, with all the dirt and junk of summer buried and hidden. The roads are gone, replaced by packed white paths about 75 cm wide indented with snowmachine tracks. The generator is shut down for the winter, but I can hear a snowmachine in the distance. Now at 3:30 pm the sky is dark, with hazy high overcast, which spread from the southwest starting at dusk, two hours ago. The high temperature for today was -23°C. At sunset, it dropped rapidly to -28°C, then rose slowly back up as the clouds formed.

I stepped out of the mailplane this noon into a strange sunlight, casting long, blue shadows out of the forest onto the snow on the airstrip. When I faced south, the sun streaming directly into my eyes was painful. But otherwise, compared to California, it was a kind light, gently illuminating a white and pure land, the contours and surfaces softened.

I cannot put the feeling of this cold on the temperature scale I have known in the past; it is something entirely other, with no chill, but instead a snap to it, with none of the damp leaden feeling of the winter I knew in Michigan or like we have in the Sierra. And here no wind at all, none. The air was dry crystal, like the snow.

Tomorrow morning I will ski up the creek to Les's. He did not come down today, so I will bring up his few pieces of mail. The trail should be smooth and packed, because they have had no snow since he came down last week.

Mike wrote me recently, asking me to describe California to him, especially what the people looked like, their faces, etc. I did not answer him, because I didn't have the time. Now that I am back in Darwin I realize that in the beginning, when I first went south last fall, I could have given him the descriptions he wanted. But after a couple of months in California, I did not see faces anymore.

However, now that I am in Darwin I do notice people again. Terri and Sam and George met the mail plane. They were all friendly enough in saying hello to me, but then I felt left out as the three of them worked together sorting the mail in the unheated mail shack and then stood together talking in a closed triangle. They were an in group and I was an outsider, I guess. Sam and George are men of few words, so they did not stand around long. The sun soon set and I could feel the temperature dropping. Sam and George went their ways. Terri asked me to stand on the back of her snow-machine sled, and we roared down the trail back into town.

Terri is a beautiful woman. I remembered that, but she is different now. I don't know how to talk to her. More precisely, I speak but she does not answer. I do not think I am being inappropriate in my conversation, and we got along well last summer, so it must be her, not me, that is the problem.

I'm not used to describing people, but I do want to describe Terri. She seems haughty and distant, but that is not a correct description. She stands very erect. She moves very slowly. Her loose, rich brown hair curls over her shoulders. I am very attracted to her but I do not feel big enough to approach her, although I measure 22 cm taller than she.

Mike says to look at the eyes. Hers are wide open and round with the pupil in the very center. I feel like shrinking away when she looks right through me.

But she is a gracious hostess. Les wrote saying I could stay with her when I got to town. She is being most kind, and has set up a bed with clean sheets for me here in the living room of the lodge.

I am not used to feeling ill at ease. My command of the language usually carries me through any social situation, even if I do not want to be in it. After awhile I get tired of talking, and then I must go out into the wilderness where I am alone. But here I am in a social situation in which I do not know what to say. And I cannot go outside for long because of the cold and dark. I will be eating and sleeping in the same house tonight with this woman. I feel like an alien. Where is the wilderness home I came to find?

Tomorrow I will ski up the creek, an exciting challenge, and leave this strangeness.

18 December 1981
Location: Les's house, up the creek.

I am so exhausted that I do not know what to write. Today I skied up the creek. I made it, but by the time I arrived to safety I had been traveling six hours in darkness. Stopping to rest was impossible because of freezing.

Last night I could not sleep. I lay in bed feeling confined by the stuffy, enclosed feeling in Terri's house, the lodge. When she took down the heavy blankets covering the windows in the morning, the glass was opaque with frost formations. We ate breakfast by dim dawn light and I left by 10:30 am at -23°C.

All day was foggy and clouded, maybe ice fog. I don't know. Snow fell, accumulating slowly. The snow got deeper as I ascended the valley; 10 cm of new snow by nightfall made moving on the trail slow. Each step was an effort. During the daylight all I could see was the shape of the trail in front of me and all the vegetation buried in heaped snow. Sometimes I could hear the creek under the ice nearby. I was all alone, and I knew if I made any mistake, fell and twisted my ankle, I would die.

I intend to record my natural history notes of winter here. Not now. Maybe tomorrow.

Soon it slowly got dark. Then the sky cleared and I could see the trail most of the time by starlight. No wind. The mountains were so huge. The Aurora Borealis came out. It is too much to describe now. I was all alone and the valley was all empty. I felt there was someone behind me, someone watching me. It felt like the stars were all looking at me, like Terri did with her eyes.

This is not what I want to describe in my journal. I need a record of the unusual snow formations and the blue-green frozen waterfalls, etc. The water seeps out of the cliff faces even now in mid-winter and freezes layer by layer onto itself, looking like solidified waterfalls slick wet on the surface.

Les says the trail is pretty good for traveling now. If it were any more difficult, it would not be possible for a human being to get up here.

[I devoted most of my subsequent journal entries to landscape description. (The entry of 19 December consists entirely of scientific notes, written during a day of recuperation from the journey.) I omit the bulk of these sections, retaining my emotional response to people and the place.   —JBS]

20 December 1981

10 am

Location: Les's house, up the creek.

...Les and Mike do not *do* anything. They seem to be moving through Jello. They sit for the longest time, just sitting there. Could something be wrong with me? I do not remember this slowness from last summer. I felt so out of place at Berkeley, but now I feel out of place here. Where do I belong?...

Les seems quite normal otherwise. We chat and it feels like old times.

Mike tells me to look at the eyes. Well, Mike's are wide and round, but not fierce like Terri's. I'm concerned that he has become like the students on drugs at Berkeley. But I don't understand it, because when we talk, he is the same old Mike; slower, but fluent and definitely sober. Then we stop talking and we just sit there, and he looks right through me with x-ray vision. I think he can see the synapses flickering in my brain.

...Les's house is lit only by the weak fluorescent light, with dark log walls and the black heatstove filling the middle. Outside it is almost always night....

I don't know what I am supposed to do here. Why did I come? I came for winter and wilderness. Instead, I am in this cabin with Les and sometimes Mike. Everything here is dim and dark and strange. I wish they would tell me what is going on. I try to ask them, but when I ask, they don't answer properly.

21 December 1981

-28°C, clear.

...Today is the winter solstice. Les's cabin is precisely on the Arctic circle.

I have been sleeping on Les's floor next to the dining table. We get up while it is still dark out. Les makes coffee, but it is too strong and muddy for me. Then we sit doing absolutely nothing for a half hour by the light of the bluish 12-watt fluorescent bulb.

Then Les turns on the propane light in the kitchen, so at least my eyes don't hurt so much from the dimness. This morning in celebration of the solstice, he made sourdough pancakes with fried eggs and sausages. He made the sausages out of Post Grape-Nuts mixed with egg and bacon grease. Mike came up from his place to eat with us, then returned to do whatever it is he does down there in his cabin.

Les's house is on a bluff with an exact south exposure, at an elevation above sea level of 760 meters. Before noon Mike came up again from his cabin in the woods below. The three of us stood outside on the edge of the bluff waiting. The slopes and cliffs rising steeply above us on both sides of the valley sparkled in sunshine, while we remained immersed in a pool of cold shade.

Then, precisely to the South, the sun exploded at the horizon. Shadows of far-distant southern mountains stretched toward us. Our own shadows were elongated, distorted. The snow crystals glittered red and blue. I felt but the faintest warmth on my face from the sun, almost none.

Mike knelt in the snow, crossing himself.

A cloud of steam vented from the summit of Dagheeloyee Peak, spreading over the blue dome of the sky, dissipating. It lasted five minutes. Then it was over. The sun set, and the shadows grew slowly up the mountainside.

From Mike's journal. He probably found the concept of "turning" in Martin Buber; I remember that Tim Brown had several books by Buber in his cabin. —JBS

The Turning from Darkness to Light
Antiphons for Solstice-Christmas, 1981

My eyes crave the light,
    feed on it like a starving man.
Oh God I am so hungry.
    On my knees in poverty
    I raise up my arms
    begging for bread.

Sun, golden sun,
    rising on the day of the turning.
Son, golden son,
    birthed at the moment of the turning.
Venus dawn's morning star,
    glowing sun's reflected light;
Mary Mother of God,
    haloed at the cradle;
My upstretched arms catch the first rays,
    I am midwife.

Midwife at the turning.
    Midwife to my turning.
Midwife to His coming.

Welcomer.

    Supplicant.

Host.

    Beggar.

Offering the wealth of the world

    Empty handed.

Jot is wild eyed and restless. He systematically looked through every one of Les's shelves and cabinets today, trying to find the missing chainsaw file. Outside, he is always poking into the bark of a tree, or digging under the snow to look at the ground, always searching for something. The only time he stops, I think, is after he has exhausted himself.

Today we went out into the woodyard to help Les get a tree. Les went ahead, as he does, putt-putting slowly on the snowmachine, pulling his rickety firewood sled. Jot and I followed on skis.

Yesterday, we had made a new trail, branching off from the main one, to several standing dead spruce. First we walked the route on snowshoes to smush down a path. Then Les was able to drive the machine over it to form the trail. Overnight it firmed up, so now he can pull loads over it without falling through. We have at least three feet of snow on the ground now, all fluffy powder, so it's hard to get anywhere without a trail, even on skis.

Well, Les felled a big tree, solid unrotten wood with lots of heat in it. Then he showed Jot how to limb with an axe, and Jot went to it. He swung away like crazy, all his tall lankiness extended by the length of the sailing axe. Thwack, thwack, thwack and it was done. Les and I really didn't have any-thing else to do, so we just watched. And Jot did most of the heavy work of hauling the logs to the sled, where Les loaded them on. I wasn't pushy enough to make Jot let me help.

When we got back to Les's house, Jot finally relaxed, just slumped in a chair with a cup of hot Postum and powdered milk.

Maybe that's how they do it out there: work until you drop. But why? Jot says his body doesn't feel good unless he works. There must be a tremendous tension built up inside him. His eyes are always looking, looking.

––––––––––––

From Jot's journal:

23 December 1981

Location: Les's cabin, up the creek.

-31°C at dawn, clear overhead with a bank of clouds to the South.

Today we went into the woods to get firewood. A little downy woodpecker *(Dendrocopos pubescens)* was working in the dead snag until Les started the chainsaw. The bark was drilled through with rows of woodpecker holes. The tree may have died from the burrowing of the squirrels under the roots. Around the trunk the snow was littered with spruce cone scales, and the tunnel entrances were open, with fresh tracks leading in and out. One squirrel sat in an adjacent tree stomping its feet and chittering for us to go away.

The trees in the woodyard are spaced quite openly, with patches of alder, willow, and soapberry between, along with areas of lowgrowing bearberries and the like, and patches of grass, all hidden now by snowcover of course, but easily seen by pushing the snow away. The snowcover must be a wonderful insulation. Rows of tiny tracks and drag marks show where the voles come out of their snow tunnels to harvest the seed-laden tops of the grasses and pull them down to their dens. (*Microtus* sp. I assume. One ran over my sleeping bag last night.)

A flock of chickadees came through later, while I was limbing the tree. They were eating seeds out of the spruce cones in the trees all round us and didn't mind our presence. These were black-capped chickadees (*Parus atricapillus*), except for a few—two or three perhaps—boreals (*P. hudsonicus*), with brown caps.

The sun did not reach into the woods, so the sprightly call "chick-a-dee-dee-dee" and the flitter of their warm little bodies was especially welcome.

The three gray jays that frequent Les's followed us raucously out to the woodyard, but did not stay.

Also saw the tracks of a single large loping weasel, presumably a marten (*Martes americana*).

Twice a raven flew over, low. I see them much more often than I did in summer.

During the day or when I am out working or skiing, I am delighted to be here. The mountains are so stupendously grand, plumes of snow blowing from the ridges and peaks; the forest is muffled in snow, yet alive with animals; all the painful desecration wrought by man is covered over and buried by nature's white. I can be at ease, knowing that they who would dig and blade and smash this sanctuary cannot be here in winter. The cold and the dark protects us. This is what I came here for. This is what I expected, wanted, and more. It is the peace and wildness of Alaska in summer, but more.

But then I go in with Les, and often Mike is there too, and night comes, and it is different. The room is so dim. My fingers and feet feel cold when I am inside. The air has a thinness to it that lets in the cold, even if the cabin is warm and my face is heated by the fire in the stove. There is something about the night. Maybe it is the confinement. It makes me feel like I did when I was stuck on the pass in the tent during the storm last summer, not able to exercise basic competence and control. I have to just sit there for such a long time, and there is nothing I can do about it.

I am tired of sleeping on Les's floor. The wilderness means being alone with nature. I want the wilderness.

26 December 1981

Location: The old log house, in the forest across
Dagheeloyee Creek 1½ km south of Les's.

I moved over here this morning. Les thought I might want to have a
space to myself and suggested this place, built sixty years ago to house a
wealthy family of prospectors. It is an entire house of 90 square meters
floorspace, with an ornate bathtub, kitchen, and fine molded wooden pan-
eling upstairs, but dark, sooted and squalid in disrepair. I was not even
aware of its existence, until Mike and Les told me that they stayed here
when they put in the snowmachine trail earlier this winter.

I have come to be in the wilderness, so would not choose to occupy such
a place. But I am tired of sharing Les's cabin and there is no alternative.
Outside it is -34°C and I cannot camp out. I will spend my days skiing and
use this house simply as a base. Les brought over food and a Coleman gasoline stove, so I can eat here, too, and be independent....

27 December 1981

Location: Log house.

-36°C at dawn today; high was -33°C; now at dusk, -35°C and dropping
slowly. Clear skies.

Les helped me get wood today. We went down the trail to an area with
dead trees. He showed me how to use the chainsaw, which I hate but have
to use. The temperature is creeping downward more each day, and Les
says if it gets much colder it will be harder to get wood. And I am finding
it takes many logs each day to keep this house tolerably warm. I spent the
entire daylight sawing and limbing, while Les snowmachined loads back to
the house.

I get my water from a beaver pond next to the house. The beavers have
built a dam out front, flooding the yard to within three or four meters of the
door. The edge of the pond is snow covered, but ice-free. Water is easy to

get, but if I step over the edge (hard to see in the snow), my foot goes right through and gets wet. I must be very careful. Beavers have felled many trees around the house, leaving chewed-off stumps.

At one time, this house had electric lighting and inside plumbing. Now I use an outhouse, but it has no hole beneath it; the material just sits in a frozen pile on the ground.

I have to ask Les tomorrow for a better light. This lamp is not bright enough to read by.

I do not believe in ghosts.

28 December 1981
Location: Log house.

-38°C at dawn; high was -35°C; now -39°C at 8 pm. Clear skies. The waxing moon has cleared Malachite Ridge, illuminating the valley....

[I omit landscape description here.   —JBS]

...The moonlight enters the house through the frosted window panes. I can almost see by it. Today I borrowed a Coleman lantern from Les, but it casts harsh shadows and makes a loud hissing sound I cannot stand. To read I have to use it, and I tried reading for awhile, until my eyes hurt and the lamp made me uncomfortable. Now there is nothing to do, and thirteen hours until dawn.

10 pm

I went out to ski by moonlight. I cannot speak of it. I never want to leave here, ever. This is it.

11:30 pm

I have been wandering about the house. There is nothing to do, so I pace around. The moonlight is just enough to keep me from bumping into the furniture and I carry my flashlight to look at things, sixty year old magazines, yellowed photos of the people who used to live here, boxes of old clothes.

29 December 1981

3 am

-40°C.

I slept for awhile, until the sound of voles running around woke me up. There is nothing to do except just sit here. The moon has set. It is dark. Ten more nights and then I get to go back to California. But I cannot stand the thought of that, either.

evening

-41°C; clear, moon.

...Now it is dark again. It has been dark a long time. I just sit here. Today I didn't see Les or Mike, because I didn't want to.

During the light I skied down to the Syndicate town. The noon sun hit the snow covered buildings but the temperature came up less than 5°C and dropped back rapidly. I walked into one of the buildings, but the dark cold inside was oppressive, and I burned my skin by touching one of the frigid rusty pipes with my bare hand....

I found the Explorers' cache. A bear must have gotten into it last fall, bending and tossing the metal prefabricated building pieces, ripping open and scattering the food containers and equipment boxes. But everything was clean now, covered over with snow....

...Carl Manley's Cessna 185 lay by the airstrip, both wings smashed, the wheels askew. With the windshield broken out, the cabin was filled with snow. A hare has excavated a shelter under the fuselage, littering the snow with scat.

Dusk had passed by the time I started home, but I skied easily by moonlight. I ate my beans and rice and now I sit here. The moonlight is brighter. It floods in the windows.

I do not believe in ghosts.

The ice is coming into the house. Water drips down the inside of the log walls, freezing into icicles in corners of the kitchen and bedroom. A film of cold water spreads down over the surface of the walls in the living room. It must be coming in through the roof, snow melting from the roof.

I am burning half a tree a day in the barrel stove.

Here I sit in a house all night doing nothing. I would like to be in the wilderness instead, but I do not know how to get there in Alaska in the winter.

From Mike's journal:

I went over to Jot's to ask if he would like to go on a New Year's Eve moonlight ski with me. We hadn't seen him in several days. Now his voice sounds deeper and he is gesturing much less abruptly with his arms.

It's been super cold again, so I haven't been out much. I've been getting lazy I guess, and lethargic—depressed, couldn't pray properly, feeling just blaaa. Les calls it cabin fever. Jot says he's been out every day, been all the way up to the head of the valley and up to timberline on Dagheeloyee Peak, everywhere. He sure has energy compared to dull old me. So I decided to go skiing with him and pump myself up with outdoor juice.

Getting ready: Bring the skis in from the porch to wax. First you have to warm them up by the stove, melt off all the compacted ice from the last trip, avoiding the little puddles they make on the floor—don't get your socks wet!

Wool underwear, wool pants, wool shirt, wool sweater, wool socks. Wool felt mukluk liners hung last night over the stove, warm and dry now. Wool mitts. Wool cap, covering the ears. A wool headband, stretched around my ears and over my nose, protecting my face. I feel like a human mountain sheep. Bag of nuts, dried fruit and (most important) M&Ms in the left pocket. Flashlight in the right pocket. Screwdriver, baling wire, pliers, spare ski tip, matches, pickle and cheese sandwich—emergency equipment in the little backpack. Mukluks, warm jacket on. Skis, waxed, outside leaning against the porch, cooling so they won't stick on the snow. Shove a log in the fire, shut down the stove, blow out the lamp. Ready to go! Clear, dry air, thirty-five below on the thermometer. Just about light enough out there to read sacred texts by moonlight, if they are the large print easy-to-read edition.

How could I help Jot lighten up? Should I tackle him as he approaches my cabin and pummel him with powder snow? No. That would interfere with the worshipful aspect of our venture tonight. Let's make snow angels instead, then. I've never been able to get Les to try this. I used to teach the novices to do it at the monastery in New York.

I flopped onto my back in the yard and moved my arms and legs back and forth to make the angel's wings and gown, but disappeared into the snow. The trick is to get up without messing up the pattern. You have to sit up and sort of roll forward to a standing position and then jump away. But the snow is too deep here. I needed Jot's help to get up. I think he looked at me disdainfully.

We skied first up the trail onto the edge of the bluff where Les lives. Every movement stood out in the moonlight. The smoke from Les's fire rolled off the top of his stovepipe, cascading down in slow motion over the front of his cabin and over the bluff like a waterfall. We could locate my place and Jot's house in the woods below, seeing our smoke drifting low through the spruce. Our eyes followed the course of the creek downstream for miles, its incised canyon emphasized by the stark moonshadows, clouds of steaming condensation hanging over spots of open water.

Later we stopped to look at the snow piled on an evergreen bough. Each unique snowflake rested unbroken in the latticework heap.

Suddenly we heard stuttering clucks like a witch's chicken, out of a child's nightmare. Something invisible fluttered into a willow bush, sending snow billows tumbling from twigs with the sound of falling sand. Jot showed me tracks: a series of forked footprints ending with a series of parallel lines in the snow, where wingfeathers had beaten into flight. He pointed out the black eye spot in plain sight under the bush in front of us, a camouflaged ptarmigan.

We skied a long way up the valley, further than I had ever gone before, following Jot's trail. It is desolate up there, beyond where the big trees grow, where the valley ends against the base of Dagheeloyee Peak. We were too close to see the top of the mountain. Once we got moving, we didn't talk at all. Afterwards, I invited Jot in for tea, but he declined.

December Full Moon

Hearing the high pitched sound
that my brain makes when my ears import nothing,
or is it the background sound of the universe,
the om
that is always present but we never almost hear it
except when white and black are nestled together
with sharp edges in the negative of day:

Heatless disk illumines
beach of waiting water
through sandpaper air:

I wade upon the glittering shore
of an abyss so deep
I dare not yield
to the siren's call.

Except for the short excerpts below, my journal entries up the creek after December 29 were limited entirely to emotionless recording of weather data and objective landscape description. I stayed for another week and a half, keeping mostly to myself, then skied alone down to Darwin. I spent another night at Terri's, then took the mail plane out, back to my responsibilities at Berkeley.   —*JBS*

...I cannot write anything. My head aches from the darkness. I wait for the period of dawn and dusk, and the brief interlude of sunshine....

...-20°C today, invariant from night to day, and overcast; no sun. I was outside for less than an hour, and even then the light was never bright. I feel horrible, drained out....

...-16°C today and still cloudy; with light snowfall. Leaving at dawn, I spent the entire day trying to hike up Eldorado Butte. I did not get very far through the deep snow, which was almost up to my waist on the sidehill, even on skis. But it was a heavy physical workout, and I feel truly excellent tonight. I love being here; truly this experience is bliss....

...I do not want to see any person. When I see Les or Mike it is an intrusion....

...My mind is filled with scenes of California: the browns and greens of eucalyptus trees swaying in the wind in Marin, madrone glistening in yellow sunlight, blue waves surging white spray onto warm sand, the rich smells of mossy redwood glens and of rose gardens in the Berkeley hills....Here there is no smell and no color and no warmth....

...I asked Les if I could have dinner with him tonight. It is too lonely. Only three more days and I get to get out of this place. I am, however, afraid of leaving....

The thought of going outside the valley is frightening. I wonder if I could stay through the winter? No, my career would be ruined....

...I have to pack up tonight, so I can leave at first light. I do not want to do anything, however, but prefer to just sit here. When I turn the lamp up, it is too bright. I like to just sit here, but I have to pack and then go up to dinner at Les's. It is socially necessary to say good-bye to Mike and Les this evening. I like them, but I would rather just sit here by myself.

I am going to quit my job at Berkeley and move here for good. I wonder how Les would feel about that.

10 January 1982

Location: The lodge, Darwin.

-15°C; overcast.

I felt loss and anxiety when I left the upper valley today, skiing through the tunnel and on down into Darwin. I have left the peace and quiet solitude of the wilderness, have been evicted from my natural home.

Tomorrow I fly to Bettles and on to Fairbanks, and the next day to San Francisco, to lecture the following day at Berkeley. All of that is an insane fantasy, and because it is unreal I can do it without effort. But I do not wish to do it. I wish to continue to sit here quietly and, when necessary, to go outside and saw down a tree and split it into firewood.

Terri has calmed down a great deal since I saw her last. She is not nearly so imposing and ferocious. I do not know what caused her to change; some capricious mood, perhaps, brought on by the loneliness and darkness.

I would like to dance with her. This is a strange thought, because I have never danced before; or when I have tried it, I have been extremely awkward.

From Terri's journal:

Jot stayed overnight on his way out. He is so relaxed that he is almost a different person. He was a little bit this way after his adventures on the pass last summer.

The strangest thing happened. He asked if we could dance together! The way he said it made it seem perfectly OK, so we did. I taught him to waltz, humming the music myself. He is actually quite graceful when he takes off his heavy boots.

———————

From Jot's journal:

13 January 1982
Location: apartment, Berkeley, California.

I cancelled my lecture today, called the department secretary and had her put a notice on the classroom door. Professor Shechter is incapacitated.

I have been watching a spider on its web in the corner of my living room for the past three and one half hours. Thus far it has not caught an insect. However, it may.

19 January 1982
...I tried going to mass at the Catholic church this morning. It was boring and I left.

24 January 1982

...I went to services at the Conservative synagogue today. It was just crowded feeling. Maybe the Orthodox would be better. I haven't gone to temple since I was a kid. My parents didn't take me very often, and I didn't go to religious school after my family got thrown out of the temple for non-payment of dues.

30 January 1982

...Had lunch with Jake at the faculty club today. He suggests I might like to attend the Sunday sitting for visitors at the Zen Center over at Green Gulch ranch in Marin. Probably they are another group of fanatic cultists, so I'd prefer not to go....

[The following entry follows extensive notes on a three-day hiking trip at Point Reyes Seashore.   —JBS]

16 February 1982

...On my way home Sunday I stopped in at Green Gulch ranch. The cultists had me do an experimental Zen sitting. The place is quiet.

I asked if I could move in here, leaving only to commute for my lectures, office hours and committee meetings in Berkeley. They said I had to begin as a day student at their Zen center in San Francisco. I would have to commute into the City. Because of my job I can't take the time to do that, and I hate the commute. It won't work.

I do not belong in their center. I do not belong in Berkeley. I do not belong in Alaska. I do not belong anywhere.

Mike stayed up the creek. Every week or so, Les snowmachined down to town, ostensibly for mail, actually for a bit of more varied company. But Mike remained, the continuity of his winter rhythm unbroken. Some days Mike shared a meal with Les, up at Les's bigger cabin. Some days Mike saw no one. His journal was sparse, primarily poetry. His friend Juice wrote, concerned because he received no letters. Mike responded with a short note, saying only, "Forgive me that I have not written. Please share the blessings of my silence. This is the season beyond words, dear friend."

By the time I left in January, the days were noticeably longer and the noon sun higher in the sky. As the month progressed, Mike wrote in his journal, "It is as if we are living in a giant dark pot, and someone is slowly removing the cast iron lid."

During what must have been mid-February, Mike wrote of asking Les to find the pair of sunglasses Mike had left in the old hardware store, packed away with the black suit and Roman collars he had not used since arriving in Darwin. The snow covered valley floor and the mountain slopes glared in ever-brighter sunshine.

Mike wrote, "The thermometer reads -12 in the shade, but I opened my jacket and unbuttoned my shirt today as I skied down the valley, and Brother Sun warmed the curly hairs on my chest."

He maintained his monastic discipline, rising at 2 am to recite Matins, saying Mass in the early morning, and devoting his day to study, prayer, work and meditation.

With the increasing daylight, he wandered about on skis, apparently becoming more proficient at staying upright. "I focus on moving lightly," Mike wrote. "Can I glide on the skis without tightening any muscle unnecessarily? Can my slide over the snow be a caress of the sleeping earth?"

To picture Mike's sunlit journeys you must first understand the scale of the landscape, Dagheeloyee Peak and the surrounding mountains rising above the forested valley and the two warm, inhabited cabins. How can you feel the actual size? Imagine you want to make a scale model *of the valley, one to put in your living room perhaps. So you make Les's house out of paper, an inch tall and a couple of inches long, and you place it on the floor. Now you will place a model of the volcanic peak next to it. How big will your modeled mountain have to be? As high as a fourteen story building.*

If we were at the top of Dagheeloyee Peak, looking down through a powerful telescope to the valley floor below, we would see a speck moving along a white trail between the trees. That would be Mike, skiing.

If we were close up, we would see him zipping along on beat-up cross country skis, wearing a tattered pink Brooks Brothers shirt, a plaid knit scarf, a red wool cap, and sunglasses with mirror lenses, a white dab of suntan lotion on his nose, singing "Kyrie eleison" at the top of his lungs, out of tune.

Daytime temperatures crept up above zero Fahrenheit, plummeting back at night. Sometimes snow fell, but the cloudy periods did not last. More than four feet of powder smoothed out the surfaces of the valley, hiding the brush and rocks and all the minor litter of abandoned human works.

Then, in late March it must have been,

"I leaned against the bank on the north side of the creek, facing the sun, opening my shirt to take in some rays. I could smell! I could smell warm earth and the odor of spruce cones and damp mosses! Brother Smell, who had been gone all winter, has returned!

"I heard a gurgle of melting water. Brother Sun is melting snow on this south-facing bank!"

And a few days later,

"The snow is wet today. It sticks to my mitts and pants, so I am all wet, too. But it doesn't stick properly to the bottom of my skis. I slide all over and can't get traction. What is happening to Brother Winter?"

Under the impact of the sunshine, the snow sank and consolidated, forming a hard crust Mike and Les could walk on. No longer confined to the trails, Mike explored everywhere, climbing the hillsides and poking into the buildings at the Syndicate town, watching icicles drip off the tin roofs.

Les had gotten a letter from a friend in Fairbanks, confirming the scheduled exhibit of Les's paintings in the lobby of the Best Western Motel. So one morning Les piled his canvases onto the snowmachine sled, the abstracts and the hallucinogenic landscapes, and headed down to Darwin. He hitched a ride to the city with Sam Ross, who was flying there anyway, and was gone for two weeks, leaving Mike alone. Mike moved up to Les's big cabin, to keep it from freezing and because it was more comfortable.

The bear came the next day.

_____

From Mike's journal:

I begin two weeks of delightful solitude. Les will miss Easter here at home.

Palm Sunday today: Blessed is he that cometh in the name of the Lord! Not having branches of palm and olive to consecrate, I made due with spruce and poplar. Les suggested I stick poplar branches into a jar of water. He says they'll leaf out. I'd like new green leaves blooming on the table for Easter.

I felt renewal on the warm breeze this afternoon, a hint of moist fecund freshness carried on the aroma of conifer needles under a heavy overcast sky, with a temperature just below freezing. A little bug flew about. Could it be a mosquito? All the snow is off the tree branches, and I think the willow buds are swelling.

In sunny weather lately, the snow crust softens for a while at midday. It's hard to move around outside then, because I break through into the deep dry powder underneath. I adapt by taking a siesta. But today the crust remained crisp and firm, so I jaunted about the valley on a walking meditation, like a wolf circumambulating the boundaries of the territory, I suppose. Saw where a beaver has felled a tree down at the Syndicate town, fresh yellow wood chips all over the snow.

A big animal came past Les's house while I was gone. It must have been heavy, because it broke through the crust. But the tracks weren't round, punched moose hoofprints. The crust was all smashed.

Later

Black dark now out, under overcast skies with not much moon yet and no aurora tonight. I can't prove this, but I have the feeling that somebody was watching me when I went to the outhouse a minute ago. Les, of course, is miles away, and so is everyone else.

This morning I found big tracks between the house and the outhouse.

This afternoon I was down at the creek with a bucket getting water. The trail down from Les's is broken up with heavy tracks, a mess impossible to walk on. I had to go around through the woods.

I found a big pile of soft, steaming bear poop on the trail. Last summer Jot showed me how to look in animal poop with a stick to see what they are eating. This poop was full of bone fragments and hair. Brother Bear is eating meat.

I think I do not need to go to the outhouse tonight.

I dreamed last night that I heard Les coming back, unloading his snowmachine out in the yard. I think I woke up then, hearing something moving about outside. This morning there are big, dirty bear pawprints on the window.

I do have to go to the outhouse this morning. This is undeniable.

So welcome, Brother Bear! Welcome to the renewed life of spring! Welcome Easter companion!

Later

While I was washing dishes, I heard something rattling around out by the shed. I walked out to investigate. It is a big, huge, shaggy, brown grizzly bear with a black nose and enormous paws.

He ran away when he saw me, his too-loose skin shaking and rolling. I put back all the fuel containers he had tipped over. He has also been digging around where we dump unburnables over the bluff in the woods. I cleaned up the trash as best I could. Some of the cans were punctured with big tooth holes

Later

When I went out to split wood, there was Brother Bear in the yard again. I said, "Greetings, Brother Bear. Welcome back. My, you look skinny after your long winter's sleep. How are you?"

This time the bear did not run away. He stood up full length on his hind feet. He must be *at least* twelve feet tall, and he looked and looked and sniffed the air.

Slowly he lowered himself down onto all fours and walked with dignity off into the woods.

I think today is a good day to do some of the indoor projects I have been putting off.

I had to get up in the middle of the night to chase off the bear. It was prowling around, scraping against the cabin walls. When I banged a pot with a big spoon, it went away. Didn't see it at all during the day today. I guess I frightened it off.

I will miss Brother Bear. I am not sure that "brother" is the properly respectful term. A companion he is though, a mighty companion.

The buds on the poplar twigs in water on the table are opening at the tip, showing tightly wrinkled fresh new green, exuding the sweet smell of spring. I sat outside this afternoon leaning against the warm dark logs on the south side of the house, drinking in sunshine. Still several feet of snow on the ground. The sun shined during dinner. When it finally set, the valley filled with the peaceful light of the moon waxing toward full.

Maundy Thursday: I dwell on the Great Mystery of the sacrifice of our Lord, on His incarnation, His death and His eternal return.

However, my concentration on the liturgy is not so good. Companion Bear woke me again during the night, bumping against the house. I beat pots and pans to scare him away, but he came back. Now he is sitting in the yard, scratching his nose. He has decided not to leave. I have decided to stay in the house.

He has been in the dump again, so the yard is littered with trash. He pulled the tarp off Les's motorbike out by the shed and ate more of the plastic seat cushion. Les will not be pleased.

Tenebrae: Night of chanting.

I don't have fifteen candles, but I found six on Les's tool shelf. Used five, left one, and when I can will replace what I burned. I set them up on the table, turned off the fluorescent light, and began reciting the psalms. Brother Moon streams in the window, nearly full tonight.

One by one I extinguished the candles, until the solitary light symbolic of Him alone remained. Then the house rocked and I rushed to the window. There again was Companion Bear, leaning up against the wall with his enormous shaggy bulk, clear in the moonlight.

I banged pots to drive him off, but he didn't leave. I sang the *Benedictus* rather swiftly, accompanied by Companion Bear bumping around against the kitchen wall, and retreated to Les's bedroom with two big pot lids, banging them like cymbals.

He seems to be gone now. I write this by moonlight, sitting on Les's maroon bedspread.

Good Friday morning, reciting the story from John of the suffering and death of Our Lord at the completion of his visit on this earth. No sleep last night; the bear returned. Now he is rumbling around outside the house in broad daylight. He doesn't care what I do anymore. I pray for the intercession of God for the good of the Church and for the human race and to keep the bear out of the house. The pee bucket is full and I don't dare go out.

After I completed the Good Friday passion liturgy, I tried to go out to get firewood and visit the outhouse, but the bear sat in the yard.

"Companion Bear, I said, "Please let me pass."

Slowly, I edged around the sitting bear, easing my way toward the outhouse. He rose to all fours when I pulled the dilapidated biffy door shut. I watched through the cracks between the boards as the bear sniffed the door of Les's cabin, rubbed his back against the log post at the corner of the tin-roofed porch (which swayed but did not fall), and then lay down against the cabin door to take a nap.

I was wearing only slippers, so I couldn't escape down the trail to my own tiny cabin in the woods below. Well, maybe I could have, but I couldn't just leave Les's cabin to the bear. And besides, if the bear came to my cabin, he could push it down with one paw. I wouldn't be safe there. So I waited to get back into Les's house. Tired from being up all night, I curled up on the outhouse seat, trying to stay warm. I must have dozed off.

When I looked again, Companion Bear was over by the kitchen wall, snuffling. I could hear his snorting breath. His hair was falling out, and I think I could see his ribs. He looked like a giant person trapped in an over-sized moth-eaten skin.

Of course the outhouse door creaked when I opened it. The bear rose on two legs and peered dimly at me as I tiptoed toward the cabin. I spoke to him in a soft but authoritative voice, talking of our brotherhood as dwellers in the wilderness, requesting this old man of the mountains to let me by and to go away into his forest. He dropped back onto all fours and ignored me, swaying slowly as he sniffed at the wall.

How can I say this? I felt at that moment that he was the true hermit, come from the cave and wandering alone in poverty, and I was an imposter.

I reached gingerly for an armload of firewood, backed slowly through the door, and latched it tight.

"Safe in the house: *Agios athanatos, eleison imas*—O holy immortal One, have mercy upon us!"

Oh my, there I was, and there he was. But now he was banging hard against the wall. I peered out of the kitchen window at him. He was digging and snow was flying. I beat Les's big metal spoon against a pot, but he didn't pay any attention. Then the house shook again as he clawed at the bottom logs of the wall. He took big bites at them and I could see splinters and dirt on the snow. Oh no!

"Oh Companion Bear, what have I done to you to deserve this? Answer me."

I retreated to the easy chair in the far corner of the room, contemplating the alternatives. There on the wall was Les's rifle. I remembered him saying that his guns were always loaded. I had never shot a gun and never intended to. Did I even know how to hold it properly? I beat the pot again, but the bear did not even pause, and so I stopped.

The bear was splitting out chunks of the log wall with his teeth. I felt a cold breeze coming from the kitchen. He began to dig under the house, where the ground wasn't hard frozen. I saw dirt fly up past the kitchen window.

Oh my, what should I do? I sang Good Friday antiphons very loudly. I banged the pot with the spoon. I banged pot lids. I eyed the rifle. I needed to go to the outhouse *again*, but didn't.

The bear had dug Les a new basement. The bottom log of the kitchen wall was ripped in half lengthwise. I could see daylight under the counter. I took the rifle off the wall. It was heavy, cold and smooth. I tried to figure out how it worked. A bear arm crashed upward through the kitchen floor. Linoleum fragments stuck to the claws.

I aimed the gun in the direction of the kitchen. "Forgive me, Companion Bear. I am sorry, so very sorry, noble brother. Don't be angry with me. But I have to do this, and fast." I pulled at the trigger.

But nothing happened. And now the bear's head emerged through the jagged hole in the floor. I examined the rifle. It had various levers and switches. I moved them around and tried again.

This time there was a tremendous explosion. The recoil almost broke my shoulder. The kitchen window shattered and there was glass all over. I must have missed.

I pulled at the levers to try to get the gun ready to fire again. The bear was standing in the basement he had dug, throwing pieces of floor out the hole in the wall. He pulled the legs off the kitchen counter. Then he grabbed a gallon jar of peanut butter, unscrewed the top, and ate it all.

"Holy Mother of God, this is a hungry bear. How does this gun work? What will Les think when he finds his house destroyed? Some caretaker I am."

I aimed the gun again and fired at the bear's chest. It must have been very close range for this big gun. I was not fifteen feet away. The bear stood and looked at me and roared an enormous sad roar. Now I had figured out how to make the gun fire. I shot him again. Blood poured out over his fur and he slumped into his hole in the floor. His head lay on the linoleum but most of him was in the dirt below the house. The floor was getting all bloody. Cold air blew in. I sat in Les's easy chair, facing the huge warm body across the cabin, which stared at me with open dead eyes. I sat for a long time, speaking to him gently, while the fire burned down and the house chilled.

At dusk, I rose and relit the fire. I had to do something about the bear, about the hole in the wall, about the the kitchen.

I walked over to the body and tugged at it. It was too heavy to budge. As long as it was lying in the hole in the floor, I couldn't begin to block off the flow of cold air from outside. I really couldn't begin to clean up the mess until the bear was out of the house. How could I do it? I couldn't wait until Les came back—that was more than a week yet.

So I returned to the chair and thought for awhile. I flipped the switch, nailed to the log wall amidst the spaghetti of exposed wiring, and the bear glowed weakly in the bluish electric light. I thought: The bear must weigh six hundred or a thousand pounds, and he doesn't look like he would fit through the door, even if I could move him. And there is no way to pull him out the way he came in.

I will have to cut him in pieces to get him out. But how do I start? I have never been a butcher before. Well, Sara and Kitty cut up that moose last fall, so I should be able to cut up Companion Bear.

Maybe Les has a book that tells how to do it. I looked over the titles on his shelf: *Beelzebub's Tales to his Grandson*, *Ski-Doo Snowmobile Repair Manual*, *The Playboy Annual*, *The Holy Bible*—nothing there.

But over in the kitchen: cookbooks!

The Complete Book of Oriental Cooking, egg rolls and won ton dumplings. No. *Flavors of India: Recipes from the Vegetarian Hindu Cuisine*. Useless. Here's one: *Moosewood Cookbook* by Mollie Katzen. Cutting up a moose couldn't be that different from a bear. Darn, recipes for buttermilk-beet borscht and mushroom strudel. Not a moose in the book.

Finally, *Joy of Cooking*. Good old *Joy of Cooking*. Mama had a copy with chocolate stains on the cover.

First "make an incision through the skin....Draw out all entrails, gib-lets, etc." But my companion is lying on his belly, and he's too big to roll over. Then I am supposed to take off his skin. That's his fur coat. From the feet first. But his feet are way down in that cold, dark hole. I can't even get to them.

What if I just took the chainsaw and sawed him in half through the midsection. Dear God, that would be a terrible bloody mess. And the lower half would still be in the hole and I couldn't get it out.

No, I have to do it right. What would Les do?

I sat on the remaining kitchen floor in my parka, leaning against the sink cabinet that has the door chewed through by the porcupine. And that little hole had bothered Les! What would he think about the one in his floor! I had to fix it. I sat with the pile of cookbooks on my lap, next to my compan-ion, my hand in the thick fur of his cooling paw. Outside air gushing in through the hole froze my behind. Heat radiating from the roaring, wide-open stove beat at my face. My eyes ached from reading in the dim fluores-cent light. The bear had twisted the copper tubing, so the propane lamp didn't think to take the books over to Les's chair, where there was more light. Anyway, I felt better with my hand on the bear, as if he needed my touch. Or maybe it was that I needed him in my loneliness. We were in this together, just the two of us.

"Venison: Hang venison in a cool airy place." Hmmm... I noticed Les's come-along leaning against the wall. And some rope.

Then I realized the first step was to get Companion Bear up out of the hole. I could lash the come-along to the log that runs along the ceiling and winch him up. Once he's hoisted, I could gut him and skin him and cut him up, the way the cookbook says, and haul him out of the house.

The full moon rose over Malachite Ridge, and the room brightened.

Securing the come-along to the log was easy. But next I had to get the rope around the bear, under his arms and around his chest, so I could haul him up. I was going to have to lie flat on the floor, right in the dirt and blood, and get in under the bear. I took off my parka and my sweater, so they wouldn't get all messed up. I have only two shirts, so I took off my shirt, too. The bear smelled terrible.

With all my might I worked the rope under the bear's chest. He was so heavy, so huge and so dead. This was an embrace. I could not help it.

When I had him tied on, I stood on a chair and worked the winch. Slowly he rose.

I saw him in the moonlight, his head and then his arms rising from the broken floor, moving with each squeaking ratchet of the come-along.

Finally he was suspended, arms outstretched, head slumped, extending almost the full height of the room, swaying in the cold wind that came up from underneath. I stood by the stove, exhausted, his blood mixed with sweat on my chest, watching by moonlight and by the thin, dim bluish light of the solar-electric fluorescent lamp.

Total silence, except for the slow creaking of the laden rope. Occasionally, the burning spruce popped in the stove. The stale smell of grizzly bear mixed with the sweetness of the smoke and the sharpness of air blown over frozen earth.

The Easter moon cast shadows in the room, and through the windows I saw the precise cold forms of leafless trees etched against the snow.

There were two of us. Me, so small, who had perpetrated this deed. And him, so huge, crucified before me. But I had had no choice. No: rather, he had given me a choice, and I knew this was how it had to be, and so it was. And now what should I do?

I took Les's hunting knife and lunged to gut him. To keep him from swaying away, my hand made a fist in his hair. I hacked a wide gash in his belly. There was his stomach, his liver, his heart, just like my stomach, my liver, my heart. His blood, his flesh; my blood, my flesh.

I kneeled before him, catching my breath. I knew I had to do something very huge. I knew I had to do it. This is not sacrilege. Father Confessor, listen to me, I know it is not. It is the opposite. It is necessary.

I took the wine glass from Les's shelf, and I filled it with his blood. And I took the knife, and I severed a portion of his heart. And I held them up to him, asking his blessing on what I had done. And I spoke to God, saying, God, Your ways are mysterious, and they are more than I can understand.

Then I drank of the blood and I ate of the flesh, and I knew the Lord's words,

> I tell you most solemnly,
> if you do not eat the flesh of the Son of Man
> and drink his blood,
> you will not have life in you.
> Anyone who does eat my flesh and drink my blood
> has eternal life,
> and I shall raise him up on the last day.
> For my flesh is real food
> and my blood is real drink.
> He who eats my flesh and drinks my blood
> lives in me
> and I live in him.

Summer 1982

May 23, 1982

Dear Diary,

Let me tell you, Diary, I wish Mother were back from Fairbanks. She would never let M.O.E.B. get away with this one.

There I was at the river talking peacefully with Mrs. Henry, when he came across at the ford.

There he was with his puffy, pink face and his puffy, pink, sweaty neck and his puffy, big chest all sticking out. Undoubtedly, he was suffering from body odor. But I could not tell because the diesel fumes stank too much. Even more than him. You may not believe this is possible, but it was true.

So I stood in front of big fat him on his big fat bulldozer and told him "No way, Chevrolet," and said some other things that I learned at school this winter. I am not writing them down here, because they are not proper to say in a diary.

"No," I told him. "No, you may not drag all that stuff through our town and tear up the streets and everything."

I stood there in front of him with my arms crossed over my chest. That is what my dad would have done. I could see the top of his bald head getting redder and redder. This was very satisfying.

I believe M.O.E.B. is apoplectic. This is an excellent word that I looked up in the dictionary. It means he is prone to a sudden loss of bodily function, which I hope happens soon.

Well, his big, fat, bare arms went back and forth working the clutches and the hydraulics. The blade went up and down. The bulldozer wiggled back and forth. Have you ever stood in front of a D-8 which is hitched to two sledges full of mining equipment and portable housing? Let me tell you, it is a very impressive sight. The lights on the Cat look like big eyes. The blade looks like a big mouth. The whole Cat train looks like a ferocious dragon, all long and squirmy and farting stinky smells. "Farting" is not a nice word, but it is appropriate here.

After awhile I noticed that M.O.E.B. looked different. His face was grey, instead of a glowing, healthy pink. His forehead was wrinkled up, instead of nice and smooth. I thought, "This means trouble."

The bulldozer came forward. I stuck out both arms and pushed at the blade. However, a D-8 is much larger than an eleven year old girl. This is a fact. Finally, he was going faster. I had to run out of the way.

Pretty soon, Mike and Les and Sam heard the noise and came. They could not do anything, either.

Clankety clank clank, rip, rip, tear, tear. The Cat train went right past our lodge, making big ruts in the street. It went right on through town. It went right on up the creek. We all stood around afterwards. Nobody had much to say. Mike gave me a big hug. I gave him a big hug, too. I think he needed it more.

From a letter Terri wrote her sister Peggy:

May 23, 1982

...I left Sara back in Darwin. I didn't really want to, but I didn't think it appropriate to bring her this time, even though we've been apart for so long. With Les and Mike right there in town, it's like I left her with family, even though she's by herself at the lodge. Sara said she didn't mind....She is so grown up!

...You know it was her choice to come back before school ended down there. She finally told me that she came back because she felt I needed help getting the lodge ready for summer—she did it for me!

This trip to Fairbanks is just not suitable for eleven year olds. I'm getting supplies. But most of the time I have to be in the lawyer's office and at the bank. That Mr. Carl Manley still hasn't paid the crew's bill for last year. So I can't buy this summer's groceries, the generator parts, etc., except by going into debt myself. I haven't ever owed anybody anything before....

My lawyer says he has heard from Manley's lawyer. They are threatening to complain about us to the state health department. He says there are some government rules about putting chlorine in the drinking water and needing flush toilets in lodges. My goodness, what will they think of next.

Anyway, I can't expect the Explorers to pay anytime soon, and I have to pay the lawyer's bill, too.

...Kitty is coming back with me for another summer. She hasn't changed a bit....

From Jot's journal:

28 May 1982

Location: Camp in the woods next to Dagheeloyee Creek, Darwin, Alaska.

I have just arrived back in Darwin for my second season of field work for the National Park Service....

After briefly saying hello to my friends at the airstrip, I walked directly to this, my old campsite. The place feels home.

All the snow is melted, but the earth is still damp. In the woods, frail, green stems emerge between last summer's fallen brown leaves. Under the leaves, I find pale root shoots and the white fuzz of mold, sources of the season's new life. But 8 cm down, the soil is still frozen rock-hard. I can see where my tent covered the ground last year; nothing grows there.

White furred catkins cover the willows. The new leaves of at least one of the smaller willow species (unidentified) are delicious; others are bitter. Poplar scent is incense kindled from bursting leaf buds by cool breezes. I have seen three, very large mosquitos.

Little juncos and white-crowned sparrows, back from the South as I am, hop about the forest floor, pecking for seeds and bugs. In the distance, a varied thrush sings its single unvarying musical tone.

I walked out from the woods over cobbles and gravel to the water: The creek is low, slightly turbid with silt; snowmelt, I suspect. Above timberline, the mountains are white. Below the snowline, they show a band of brown, then near the valley floor begins the lightest, freshest yellow-green.

I turn my face to the hot sun, high overhead. Cumulus cloud puffs move across a deep blue sky, sending chill shadows racing across the land.

In this peaceful scene it is almost impossible to believe that Explorations Unlimited will implement the plan of operations it has submitted to the National Park Service. In Bettles, the resources manager for the Park told me he did not think they would actually do what they had stated. Metal prices are depressed, and the cost of mining operations up here would make their proposed activities unreasonable....

Mike wrote to his friend John J. (Juice) Ryan at St. Francis College, Brooklyn:

May 28, 1982

To Juice,

From Recluse Returned—

Tweet, Tweet. the birdies sing. So sweet, ahh so sweet, earth soft damp underfoot with little green tendernesses uprising allover. And the air is intoxicating drink, the nard gives forth its fragrance, a sachet of myrrh rests in my bosom.

&

simultaneously, or perhaps is it because?

(otherwise the cosmos is out of balance heaven forbid)

RRRROOOAAAR RUMMBBBLE RUMMMBLE

It is the Explorers! HO HO, they have returned on a steed of steel! Crunch the town! Mash the people! Blast the land! Acquisitiveness, Materialization, Competition, Greed! (no good story can be without a bad guy)

They head for Hermitage Ultima on the giant bulldozer, blade down. This hurts. I, the unenlightened one, sit in non-dispassionate marination, stew in my belly.

rumble rumble in belly. Where is the still point of the turning world?

I left it under a snowflake.
And it melted.

They call it break-up.

The bear broke up the cabin. But I got that fixed. It was really not so tough, after I helped him out the door. You get a log in the woods and stick it in the hole where the bear split the other one out lengthwise with his teeth. And you bend some rusty nails straight with a hammer, and use them to put the pieces of floor back together, after you find the pieces in the snow. This is a jigsaw puzzle, merely. Afterwards, there are some holes, but you can chink them with an old sock and seal it all up with a tube of caulk and when you spray it with gold spray paint it is good as new. The kitchen window, which I had shot out, I replaced with one I took from the Syndicate town, which was OK with the inhabitants I think.

Les hardly noticed. We could not, however, recover the peanut butter and so were on straight jelly sandwiches for the duration.

Which was not long.

"Break Up" is a season. It is when your world for half a year breaks up and flushes down the creek. The sun melts the snow, the trails fall in, the ice bridges collapse, you can't go anywhere, everything's wet mush. This is after winter and before spring. Made the trip down the creek with Les on the last possible day to go on snow. Now am living in the former hardware store again.

"Break up," as in "crack an egg." The egg of silent cold which protected us broke and I was poured back into the world like a yellow yoke into a big cake batter, stirred thoroughly by a bulldozer.

This creates an identity crisis.

New Metaphor: The winter costume does not fit anymore. It feels hot and stuffy. So you take it off and dance off out into the world, glorying in the light and the smells.

But then you remember something left behind at the first autumn snows.
You do not want to face it, but you cannot avoid it in the sweet sunshine.

It appears like magic when the snow melts, lying on the ground just where
you left it last fall, when it got covered over by the clean pure white.
Now it is there to trip over, and all the garbage you threw out during the
winter is with it, all of it,

and now you have to face it, while the mosquitos buzz at your head
and bulldozers drive up and down your spine
building an expressway between the K-Mart and the Seven-Eleven
and the secret inner sanctum of your soul.

The old things lie about: Beavers chewing at the foundations.
Strange dreams. Jesus, where are you? The search for a Companion who
will not find me.

And winter, which was the universe, now just another dream, past,
time of inexplicable pagan rites, and liaisons,
foolish in the light of day.

The Abbot writes: Yes.
Establish a foundation for hermits.
Others will come
When you have bought the land and arranged for the set-up of appro-
priate housing.

But now that does not seem right, to set up an establishment here for others
to enter. The right way is to come alone, without the Institution. But am I
selfish in closing the door to others?

Well, first the question of the bulldozers must be resolved. No new foundations possible until the bulldozers working up the creek and in my soul have finished operations.

What shall I say to the Abbot?
I shall procrastinate.

I yearn for the simple life.
Maybe I shall become an English teacher
at a small Catholic college in the East.

—R.R.

May 29, 1982

Dear Diary,

Well, guess what: Flop flop chop chop. Here comes the cop-turd right onto the street in front of our lodge. Dust all over the place, cough, cough. Out comes a bunch of men who try to act pleasant to the dear sweet little lodge girl. This girl has to abandon important projects to greet them. Be polite her mother says. BLECCH.

Then roar, dust, cough, the cop-turd takes off to pick up M.O.E.B. from wherever he has gone to on his bulldozer up the creek. And in a couple of minutes there he is again, right here on our property, his mean old pink self. And guess what.

This you will not BELIEVE.

He asks mom if they can STAY AT OUR LODGE!!!

You must realize that mom has just come back from a difficult journey to Fairbanks, where she had lengthy appointments with lawyers and bankers, so inappropriate for young people that HER OWN DAUGHTER, whom she had barely seen in MONTHS, could not accompany her. All because THEY did not pay their bill from Last Year.

So I stand there, being as polite as I could. Which was not too much. And out comes mom. What does she do first thing? She invites them into our lodge. Boo, hiss.

Well, by this time it was raining. However, I would have preferred to let them get wet. At this time mother said to me, "That is quite enough, young lady." She says I have plenty to do in the other room while they talk. Well, I do. It is my carpentry project. I am building a rack for cups in the kitchen. It requires a great deal of very loud hammering.

It was not fair for mother to tell me to work on my needlepoint instead. In this day and age the daughter of the house has to diligently practice masculine skills as well. So I sneaked up next to the door to the main room and listened to what they said.

Well, M.O.E.B. said they would pay this time. He also said that he would tell his boss (that is Mr. Carl Manley, who does not know how to fly a plane very well) not to complain more to the government about how our water is too pure and our outhouses have got flies. Old Grimy-Slimy was SOOO understanding of our difficult situation. He could explain to his mean boss about what was what out here in the Bush. He was so nice to dear old mom.

SEXIST EXTORTIONIST BLACKMAILER MALE CHAUVINIST PIG

Blecch. I wanted to puke. "Come on mom, beat him up," I thought. (You should see mother's great muscles.)

But no, she just sat there listening to him.

"Mom!" I thought. "Don't you realize that you are being victimized?" Because of my experience Outside this winter, I am aware of a great deal that my mother has not yet learned.

So old G.S. (Grimy-Slimy, formerly a.k.a. M.O.E.B.) talked, while mother sat there with her legs bent gracefully, just like the high school homecoming Queen did in her fancy dress last fall. I got very bored.

Finally he was done. What would mom do now?

She said, and I quote, "I am sorry, but the lodge is not available to you at the present time. May I show you to the door?" HURRAY for Mom! HURRAY for expanded feminist consciousness! By this time it was raining hard.

From Mike's journal:

May 31, 1982

...Lots of ruckus in town. The Explorers sawed down a bunch of trees, clearing an area out by Jot's camp next to the creek. Ed Butler has been working with the cat over by the river. I haven't gone to see what he is doing, but it's 11 pm now and I can still hear the grinding of the cat....

June 1, 1982

...The Explorers set up two big trailers on the site they cleared yesterday. He must have pulled them across the river yesterday. They look like big, white metal boxes with little windows and aluminum doors....

———————

I remember that the next day, Les, Mike and I drifted one by one to the lodge. We sat on the stained paisley couch and in the overstuffed chairs with springs poking out through the cushions, as the rain made puddles in the ruts left by the cat train in the road out front. Even though it was mid-day in June, I had the urge to light a lamp. Terri had a fire going in the heat stove. A moth blew in when Mike entered. I remember the clank of the door and the jangle of the bells Terri kept tied to the door knob, to let her know when a customer or a neighbor arrived. The moth beat against the window glass, trying to get out. I extracted myself from my chair and tried to catch it to let it go free. But it fluttered beyond my reach, and I gave up. Les sat with a cup of coffee. Terri got tea for Mike and me. I heard the table creaking in the kitchen, where Kitty and Sara kneaded bread.

"A couple more days and that's it for fording the river this summer. It's been coming up fast, always does this time of year."

"I'm surprised he could get those trailers across even now. Looks deep."

"The water was rising an average of seven centimeters per day until the rain started. The glaciers cooled then, and today it's actually quite a bit lower than yesterday."

"Pretty soon, though, it'll come on up again. Always does. That'll be it for taking the cat across this summer...."

We talked about the Explorers' new camp next to town at the creek. They had cut all the trees from a thirty-meter square area, leaving high stumps to trip over, stacking the slash in loose piles. We could see the trailers from the center of town. Les said they looked like second-hand pre-fab housing units left over from building the pipeline. Probably, the Explorers had picked them up cheap. Aluminum does not age gracefully (the white walls were dented and scratched—and dragging them through the river hadn't helped). They ran an unmuffled gasoline generator we could hear from inside the lodge.

Les had already gone over and had coffee with the workmen. They said the Explorers had bought the land, a subdivision lot, from a realtor in Anchorage. They were going to build a bridge over the Loohana River. They were going to build a road all the way to the Syndicate town this summer. —JBS

———————

From one of Terri's letters:

I wondered how Jot would take it. The Explorers set up camp right next to his tent. I expected him to be tight and upset.

But he had moved his tent to the other side of town, out by the glacier. He was standing straight, not bent over. He didn't wave his hands when he talked, like he did last year. He sounded very organized. I had forgotten he is a lawyer.

I don't like the Park Service or anyone else telling us how to do things here in Darwin. But since this is a National Park now, I thought that there would be some rules about building roads and mining and so forth. Jot said that the Explorers own the mining claims. I guess the Park people can't do too much about private property. I don't remember the details. Also, the Explorers can build a road without asking anybody's permission. I guess that's the way it is with private property, and we have to put up with it. After all, I don't want the government telling me what I can do with my lodge.

Even though he says there's nothing we can do, I have a feeling we can trust Jot to come up with something. Les thinks so, too.

Mike didn't say much. He is the one who seems most disturbed. Part of it might be his feeling about me. I thought we had resolved our attraction to each other, but maybe we really haven't. Sometimes he sparkles again for a moment, but it doesn't stay long. Of course, his whole life up the creek is in question now because of the Explorers.

From my journal:

...I explained that the State of Alaska asserts a right-of-way up the creek under federal Revised Statute 2477, which essentially takes jurisdiction over travel to the mines away from the Park Service. The State also asserts ownership of the road to Darwin from Bettles under provisions of the State-hood Act. Of course, the State will do nothing to limit prospecting or mining, particularly in a National Park it would prefer did not exist.

Regardless of these State claims, under the provisions of the Alaska National Interest Lands Conservation Act (ANILCA), which set up the park, all inholders (including the Explorers) are guaranteed reasonable access to their private property.

Furthermore, the Park Service believes that under the provisions of ANILCA, it can do nothing to regulate activities on private lands within Park boundaries. The mining claims and the lot the Explorers say they own next to the creek are private lands.

Despite these limitations, I believe the Park Service could be much more assertive, using its remaining authority under the Mining in the Parks Act to require detailed plans of operation from the Explorers in advance, and its general mandate to protect Park resources as the basis for prohibiting damaging activities. Under the anti-environment Neanderthal administration of President Reagan and Interior Secretary Watt, however, the Park Service staff is demoralized and their hands are tied.

Therefore, if anything's going to be done, I've got to do it.

From Mike's journal:

I felt the strength in each of us. More, I felt the power of our bond, outgrowth of our mutual experience of Winter and our attachment to this land, and of the work and hardships we have shared together. I felt this bond growing even now, as we, each such an individual, came together to encounter a common difficulty. It is a bond without words, a cause without ideology, a trust born of necessity, a community of anarchists. We simply do what we need to do, and out of that comes love.

Love is our sustenance. Can it solve problems? It is supposed to. I seem to remember that once upon a time I had no problems. But now the Explorers are a problem. My relationship with Terri is unresolved, thus a problem. The issue of establishing a monastic foundation here is a problem. I have slid back in my spiritual progress.

I remember winter with nostalgia. I tell myself to live in the present moment within this field of love. But then I am dependent upon it, and when I feel this dependence, love weakens and can no longer support me. A contradiction.

Jot's response to our situation is to move forward.

Contradiction. We talked about mining. Les reminded us that we live in a town built by miners. We use their roads and trails, live in their abandoned buildings. The Explorers are really doing nothing different than was done before.

Les has worked as a cook for prospecting crews, and he grew up in mining country, in Colorado. He likes being with geologists. He says miners are fine folks. But the Explorers are not miners. They are not even real prospectors—there's no evidence they've found any ore, Jot says, and yet here they are putting in roads and bridges. That's to impress investors, I guess. That makes them promoters, not developers.

Jot questioned: But what if the Explorers were real miners and fine folks? How much difference would it make? They would still have to come in here with heavy equipment, bridge the river, build a road up the creek, construct housing. Their attitude would be different. But still, what we came here for would be gone. Not forever, but for our time.

I wonder. What does a life work of cutting the earth with a bulldozer blade and blasting the mountain with dynamite do to a person's spirit?

Jot told us that he was going up the creek for a while. If he wasn't back in two weeks, we should come looking for him. He went over the top, because with the rain the creek was now too high to ford, and he didn't want to deal with Les's half-canoes.

I did not see him when he got back a week later. Terri said he stopped in briefly at the lodge, then hired Sam Ross to fly him out immediately to Bettles and Fairbanks.

ELDORADO EXPLORATIONS UNLIMITED
Memorandum

June 13, 1982

TO: F. Carleton Manley, President
FROM: Ed Butler, Site Development Director

I am dragging those girders for the bridges across the creek and here comes a helicopter but it is not ours. This is Park Service who land just about on top of me and say we gotta stop because of the curlews.

They are not even down here. Park Service says they are up on the Butte. I am not driving over no curlews and to tell you the truth I do not really care if I do but this Park Service says not to.

You know we gotta blast a little up there to make the platforms for the drill rig. But it is a big mountain as you know and I am sure there is lots of room for us and the curlews both. This I explained very reasonable to that Park Service but they do not listen.

Eggs is the problem. They say the little birdies got nests up there and they don't sleep good or something with us around. Eggs I care not much about but this Park Service does.

I guess if they was ordinary curlews this would be OK. But these is *bristle thighed* curlews. They don't want us messing around with the *bristle thighed* curlews.

This Chief Park Ranger, Bill he calls himself, is a big guy and I decide guys with badges I do not like but I will not mess with him. He says cease and desist and I will not pay any attention but he tells me consequences.

There are consequences. This he says.

Boss, what should we do about the *bristle thighed* curlews? Fried with a side of omelet sounds good to me but I am not so sure because there is contempt of court or something and since I do not like jail we are shut down.

—Butler

Manley wrote to Ed Butler on the same day, June 13:

...You may hear that we are being sued by the environmentalists. The suit is simple harassment. You are to proceed with operations unless otherwise instructed by me personally. I attach a letter from counsel for your information....

From Manley's lawyer's letter:

...The suit was filed on 6/12 by The Trans-Pacific Coalition for the Protection of the Bristle-Thighed Curlew (TPC/PBTC). Membership of the TPC/PBTC includes the Sierra Club, the Friends of the Earth, the Audubon Society, The International Society of South Pacific Island Ecologists, the Wilderness Society, the Northern Alaska Environmental Center, the Northern Alaska Native Association, and the Petaluma (California) Garden Club. I have been able to obtain no additional information regarding this organization....Sources in Alaska report that Rockefeller money is behind the suit....

Listed defendants include the Secretary of the Interior, the Director of the National Park Service, the Superintendent of Dagheeloyee National Park and Preserve, and Eldorado Explorations Unlimited....Plaintiffs assert defendants have failed to comply with provisions of the Mining in the Parks Act, National Parks Organic Act, the Alaska National Interest Lands Conservation Act and the Endangered Species Act....

How had the suit come about? I had gone up the creek just to poke around, to see what I could find, to look for a way to get leverage on the Explorers; and also I simply needed to get away into the mountains....

From my field notebook, before my trip to Fairbanks:

5 June 1982

Location: Alpine zone on Eldorado Butte, 1300 meters elevation.

...Snow is melting rapidly, with bare patches of ground on south facing slopes, particularly in the lee of large, dark rocks. I am sitting on such a rock now, with the forest spread velvet below and the white expanse of the Dagheeloyee volcanic cone rising in the East. Air temperature is 3 degrees C, but I feel the the sun overhead burning my face.... I am glassing the rim of this alpine bowl to identify several birds I have noticed fluttering in the distance....

I presumed they would be ptarmigan. But they are large, brown shore-birds, at least a half dozen of them. They look like the whimbrels *(Numenius phaeopus)* I have seen on migration in the San Joaquin Valley. But I can hear the call, a slurred "chi-u-it," more like a black-bellied plover, and also a whistle, "whee-wheeo." Not a godwit; the bills are decurved. The distinguishing mark is the tawny, unbarred rump—they're not whimbrels, they're bristle-thighed curlews *(Numenius tahitiensis)*!

BRISTLE-THIGHED CURLEW

My hunch is they are going to nest here. The habitat is right. This is a real find: The only other recorded breeding ground for this mysterious rare bird is in the Andreafsky Highlands of the Yukon-Kuskokwim Delta. They make an 8000 km non-stop flight over water from their wintering grounds in the mid-Pacific to get to Alaska.

Endangered Species Act, for sure. That's the main handle. And of course the Explorers' plan of operations doesn't mention impact on curlews—that's Mining in the Parks Act. And there must be more. NPS will have to send an ornithologist out here. The study will take years. I doubt we could get an injunction in time for this summer, but a suit might prompt the NPS to quick administrative action. That's what we need.

And that's what we got. While I was still in Fairbanks, Mike wrote in his journal about the helicopter making several trips, taking out the Explorers' work crew. Butler was indeed shutting down, leaving only himself in town to watch over the camp and equipment. With the helicopter gone, town was quieter again, although he kept the straight-pipe generator going around the clock. I don't know how he could sleep with it running next to his trailer. Maybe he didn't. Mike's journal says Butler was more than usually irritable those next few days, until he talked with Jasper....

Yes, Jasper, who had finagled a ride in on the helicopter when it was shuttling out the Explorers' workmen. Mike wrote:

...He arrived in fine spirits, high-stepping out of the chopper as if he owned it. I think the pilot thought he did. He has a great tan. "Hawaii," he says, at his "con-do-minium." He says he's "making preparations for going up the creek" to "his claims."

He moved into the hardware store again with me. I found out when I returned from a walk, discovering he had moved my bedroll and things out of the bright corner room upstairs and taken it over for himself. While he ate the dinner I cooked, I firmly informed him I wanted that room back.

I gather that Butler was ticked off at Manley. From what Les heard him say, apparently Manley ordered him to continue operations in the face of a possible jail sentence. Butler refused. Back in Wenatchee, Butler had had enough of jail. I never did get all the facts, but later in the summer, he talked about how he once picked up a rap that properly belonged to Manley, who got off scott-free. How much truth there was to this story I don't know.

I do know that a few days after Jasper arrived, he and Ed were drinking together in the bar. Sara overheard it all:

June 19, 1982

Dear Diary,

I never cease to be amazed at grownups, even though I am almost one myself already. There I was in plain sight, sitting on the bar reading. And who should come in? Well, who do you think would come into the bar before lunch? Of course it was Jasper and old Grimy-Slimy, whom I now call G.S. for short. Come on mom! Toss old G.S. out on his ear!

But no, he soft-talks old mom. She lets him stay, but makes him pay cash up-front. We need the money, I guess. He buys a couple of beers for himself and for old Jasper, who should not be drinking at all and especially before lunch. You know that his liver is not as healthy as it was formerly. He suffers from Delirium Tremens. That means he sees things that are not there. Mrs. Henry explained that to me.

Well, now they do not see something that is there, namely me, even though I am in plain sight on top of the bar. (They are sitting at a table.)

They talk and they drink, and I pretend to read. Jasper tells many interesting stories about his business ventures, which all three of us certainly know are not true. G.S., however, listens as if he believes them. This is consistent with his slimy character. He thinks he is buttering up Jasper. However, Jasper is crazy, but he is no dope. That's what Mrs. Henry says.

Let me tell you what is really happening: G.S. knows that Jasper has found valuable minerals. He also knows that the Explorers haven't been able to find them yet. He wants Jasper to tell him where they are. Also, you should remember that G.S. is mad at Carl Manley and that G.S. is a very greedy and unscrupulous person.

For a long time, Jasper will not talk about what is in the mines. G.S. tries to get him to, but he won't. He talks about land investments and condominiums instead. He is doing this in order to build up the suspense. Then he buys another beer from Kitty and has G.S. pay for it. Old G.S. is getting red under his collar. He is not widely known as a patient person.

I can tell that old G.S. is about to give up and leave, because he pushes his chair away from the table, leans it back on two legs, and wiggles his big, fat bottom. Normally, I would tell him to stop, because I don't want his fat, slobby self to break our valuable, historic chair. But this time, I stay quiet, because I want to see what Jasper will do.

Jasper starts to talk about the mines. He describes his extensive explorations. He explains that there is no ore left in the Syndicate tunnels. They mined it all out before they left. But just beyond the end of the deepest tunnel there is a natural chamber. Jasper had to move big rocks to get to it.

Then Jasper explains that this chamber was not part of the Syndicate claims. It was just outside their property. Jasper did not include it in the claims he sold to Manley. Jasper staked the claim to the chamber himself. He still owns it.

Old G.S. is sitting right up to the table now. Jasper calls for Kitty to bring him another beer and waits for G.S. to pay for it.

The chamber is in solid chalcocite (which, as you know, is the most valuable kind of copper ore). The chalcocite is filled with veins of silver and gold. Jasper takes a piece of rock out of his jacket. It is grey with white lines in it.

Did you know that old G.S. has very weird glands? It is amazing to see the little round beads of sweat form on his neck when he holds the rock.

Jasper says that he is engaged in several significant business enterprises which occupy all of his attention these days. These are very successful. However, just now he has a problem of "cash-flow." (That means he doesn't have any money.) Unfortunately, therefore, he has to sacrifice his mining claims for a small price. Of course, he'd have to get paid for them right away.

I begin to smell old G.S.'s body odor. Pee-Youuu! Yuck. He is kneading the side of our chair with his fingers.

Jasper says he has to go out to Bettles tomorrow to make a phone call. This is to finalize a deal to sell the claims to a large corporation in Los Angeles, California.

Old G.S. reaches for his wallet, which is in the right rear pocket of pants that are too tight for him. The wallet is slimy, too. It is quite thick. He must be uncomfortable when he sits on it. Well, it is not so thick anymore, so maybe he is is more comfortable now. I hope not.

Old G.S. counts out hundred-dollar bills onto our table with his stubby, red, fat hands. One, two, three, four, five, six, seven, eight, nine, and so on. Lots. Boy, that could pay for the whole summer's groceries and a new bike for me. I outgrew my old bike. We can't afford a new one. Old G.S. is trying to look *so* cool.

Jasper picks up the money and counts it twice. His fingers are not very steady. This is money old G.S. got working for the Explorers last summer. Ha! It really belongs to us. They owe it to us. I think about telling them that, but I don't, because I want to see what is going to happen.

Jasper says this is a good down payment. Old G.S. says there is more after he sees the chamber himself. Then Jasper pulls a couple of pieces of wrinkled paper out of his shirt pocket. One of them is a map. He shows it for a second to old G.S., whose little, beady, red eyes are suddenly open very wide. Quickly, Jasper puts that piece of paper back into his pocket. He says the other piece of paper is a contract. Impolitely, old G.S. grabs the piece of paper. Did you know that old G.S. moves his lips when he reads? He must not have paid attention in school. Probably, he played hooky.

Old G.S. scowls. He tells Jasper that this contract is unreasonable. Jasper looks absent-minded, as if he is watching a spider crawl up the wall. He talks some more about having to go out to make the phone call. Did you know that scowling improves old G.S.'s appearance? Then old G.S. asks Jasper if he has a pen. Jasper gets one from his pocket amazingly fast. They both write on the contract. Then Jasper gives old G.S. the map.

Old G.S. doesn't say anything. He gets up and walks out.

Then Jasper asks me to get him another beer. He pays me for it himself.

June 20, 1982

Dear Diary,

Let me tell you, Diary, Kitty is totally unenlightened. Well, she has a few days off coming, and mom says we can't tell her what to do. However, you can imagine that I tried. This was when she was packing up the food. Clearly, she had already decided to do it. Dumb, dumb, dumb, I think, but she is a grown-up and, as mom says, she has to lead her own life.

Let me tell you a secret. Ever since the helicopter left, Kitty has been hanging out with old G.S. again. When I asked her why she was doing this dumb thing of hanging out with his dumb, big, fat, self, she said he is a lonely person who needs company. I admit I have never thought of old G.S. that way.

So this morning there was Kitty throwing cans of beans into dad's big old backpack. She was packing for a hike up the creek. With Guess Who. I suggested she could take food that didn't weigh so much. I mentioned that old Guess Who had a cat load of supplies up there already. He asked her to pack for the trip. Fortunately, she had me there to help her decide what to take, such as peanut butter sandwiches for lunch and sleeping bags.

Nonetheless, dad's big old backpack was crammed full of stuff when they left, for example her make-up. You can easily sprain your ankle up the creek. It is not a good idea to go there in high-heeled shoes, or even in black silk slippers. Fortunately, Kitty and I have the same size feet. She was willing to wear my hiking boots, because they matched her dress.

Let me tell you, they looked weird when they walked out of town. Old G.S. carried a teeny-tiny rucksack on his big, fat back and a giant, long rifle. The top of Kitty's big packframe kept bumping into her hairdo and messing it up. The floppy brim of her pink hat bounced up and down when she walked. The two sleeping bags were not tied very well to the bottom of the packframe. Kitty used string, because we could not find my father's straps. I hope the sleeping bags don't fall off into the creek. Well, I hope hers doesn't.

From a letter of Terri's:

June 23, 1982

...I was out hanging up laundry when they came back. I didn't expect them so soon. They must have gotten into trouble, crossing the creek maybe. Ed was carrying Kitty piggyback. She'd lost her boots and pack and her pink floppy hat, and her dress was torn and muddy. At first I thought they were all right, just exhausted, like they hadn't slept at all last night.

They came to the front of the lodge and he put her down. They just stood there. That's when I realized maybe they weren't OK. Kitty's eyes were wide as saucers. She didn't blink. She just stood still and stared. Her mouth was frozen into an open circle. Butler mumbled but I couldn't understand him. Kitty hasn't said a word yet.

I led them inside and sat them down and asked Sara to get them hot soup. I had to put the spoon in Kitty's hand, but then she ate by herself, slowly and silently. Butler slurped up three bowls, mumbling.

Butler seemed to be able to take care of himself, so I gave him a room and let him know he could use the shower. Then I took Kitty to her room and stripped off her torn clothing. Her feet were bruised and had raw, open blisters, but otherwise she was physically OK. She let me give her a bath, but she didn't do anything for herself. Afterward, she slept fifteen hours straight. I was getting worried, but she got up by herself and dressed and came out into the kitchen.

She helped make breakfast, so I guess she is improving. But she still doesn't say anything, and she moves so slowly, staring off into space.

Butler is eating with us. I can understand what he says now, but he won't discuss what happened to them....

By the time Kitty and Butler got back to town, Jasper had disappeared. Mike didn't even see him go. One tourist had been camped at the end of the road across the river, and we presumed Jasper hitched a ride out with him.

The next day, Terri wrote:

...Ed Butler asked if he can stay at the lodge. He said he has quit the Explorers. He said he will pay cash in advance. Then he took a rock out of his pocket and gave it to me. It looks like a gold nugget, but it couldn't be, because it is so large. He said it is gold, and I don't know whether to believe him. Something makes me want to trust him. He seems different now, none of that blustering. If it is gold, I don't know how I can take it from him. It would be worth twenty or thirty thousand dollars. He wanted me to have it. He seems to want to be rid of it.

He spent the afternoon fixing the carburetor on our truck. He got it tuned up just right. I don't understand what happened to him and Kitty. I'll let him stay at the lodge for now, as long as he behaves himself.

I wonder if what happened to them has anything to do with the earthquake we had while they were gone? We got a strong jolt, more than the one we had last summer. This one cracked one of our big windows. But I can't see how it would have affected them along the creek, except maybe to scare them for a moment.

From the Fairbanks Daily News-Miner, *June 21, 1982, page 1:*

An earthquake measuring 6.9 on the Richter scale shook buildings in northern Alaska this morning, the most severe tremor in recent years. No damage was reported. The quake was centered near Dagheeloyee Peak, two hundred miles east of Kotzebue. Seismologists at the University of Alaska expressed concern that the event may signal renewed volcanic activity in the mountain, which has been venting steam intermittently. Scientists say the ice-clad peak has not erupted in nearly two thousand years....

From Mike's journal:

June 25, 1982

I woke up at midnight feeling like I had eaten something indigestible. I had to walk it off. The long shadow of Dagheeloyee Peak lay over Darwin; overhead, the clear sky gave a color-saturated full light, emphasizing the green of early summer leaves, the chestnut brown of unpainted, tilting wooden buildings, and the blue flowers blooming amidst fresh grass in the edge of the gravel streets. No one was about. The birds had briefly stopped their singing. Only the creek roared in the background.

A thin plate of ice covered a pothole in the street out front. I went back upstairs to get my jacket.

I remembered I had been dreaming, a dream of tunnels and chambers and lizards, and a bear I had followed, or who followed me, of a search for Jesus, for a peace I could not find, of an eternal wandering. I felt like something uncomfortable was curled up inside me. This was not a new dream.* It was an old one, a repetition, feeling stale, as if I needed to make movement but could not. I needed space, wide open space, so I walked slowly out of town toward the glacier, listening to my footsteps.

I went out to where the path leaves the woods and drops down to the open gravel before the glacier. Yellow rays fanned from a sun hidden behind the volcanic peak. A cloud of steam drifted from its summit, flawing the robin's egg dome of the sky. I wandered across the dry floodplain channels, climbing a bare hill of rocks near the base of the ice face, and stood there, listening to muddy meltwater streams drip into the pond below. The amphitheater of the surrounding peaks felt vast; me a single, heavy speck in its midst.

I prayed for simplicity, for the ability to take everything as it comes. I prayed for peace in this place, for resolution of the difficulties which confront us. Then I felt I did not want even to pray, at least that way. I stood there forming no words, feeling the presence of the ice and the mountains and the sky, and that was better prayer.

---

* *See Mike's journal entry of August 8, 1981.*   —*JBS*

I sensed someone behind me and turned around. But there was no one. Then in the distance I saw a moving figure. I did not want to be interrupted, not here, not now. I sat down to blend in with the rocks, pulled my grey wool cap over my chilled ears, and waited motionless, wanting to become a part of the hill.

The figure, tiny against the rocky plain, walked toward me. I tried to look like a boulder.

It moved along with grace, without hurry. It was Terri. I wanted her to come. She was the only one I would want to be here. She climbed the hill, not seeing me. She stood at the top, looking at the ice. Huddled between boulders, I looked at her.

Here was my friend. I knew she understood. She knew about winter. I understood the look in her face as she stood there, the longing, the searching.

She spoke. She spoke to Ted. She said, my husband, where are you. She said, I want to be with you my beloved. And then she said no words that I could hear, and tears came down my cheeks.

Where are you, my beloved, I thought, and I felt like a little lost boy.

I felt the pain inside me. My body heaved to flush it out. The contractions came in waves through my chest and belly. She heard me and saw. At first she startled, surprised. Then she saw the tears, and for a long moment we stared into each other's eyes. She came over and kneeled in front of me, where I sat against the boulder, and held my hands, and I saw the calm in her face. It was a calm as vast and as still as the mountains behind us, a calm I could fall into and be lost forever. And she said, "breathe," and I let go of my held breath and followed the slow, firm rhythm of her breathing. Then the pain was still in me, but it was no longer pain.

We breathed together, and then we stood and walked so very slowly together back toward town, holding hands. The sun burst out from the side of the great mountain. In the woods, we sat on the earth absorbing the new warmth. A bird began to sing. I fell asleep with my head on Terri's shoulder. I think she slept too.

June 25, late evening

After dinner I walked over toward the lodge and sat on the back of the Model A Ford flatbed, watching the swallows swoop and sail after mosquitos in the open air above the street.

Finally, Terri came out. She looked at the swallows, too. Then I hopped off the truck and we walked out the trail toward the creek. I felt like holding her hand and so, once we were out of town, I talked instead:

Me: How are Ed and Kitty doing?

Terri: Kitty still isn't speaking. This morning she went out and picked flowers, set water glasses of lupines and chiming bells all over the lodge. Dozens of them.

She did the laundry and the dishes, then just sat and looked out the window.

Ed, well Ed keeps out of my way and makes himself useful. He talks alright now, but only to say whatever practical things are necessary to get by. His bill is paid up in cash, and today he fixed the leaky pipes in the shower and replaced the washers in the drippy faucets. Sara complains that he still doesn't use the shower. But I think that if he just fixes it, that's a big step....

Me: Yesterday evening Ed walked into the hardware store. I was just finishing my spaghetti. He sat down at the table and looked at me. My mouth was full of noodles. I offered him the platter. But he shook his head, no.

He said he needed a priest. So I said, OK. Then he fidgeted and mumbled and looked away. I ate another bite of spaghetti.

Then he asked me about dinosaurs. Are they all really dead? Do I believe in devils? I said "I guess so," and "I don't know." Then he mumbled some more under his breath and looked away again, as if he were looking at something that wasn't there.

I poured him some tea, but he didn't touch it. He sat while I cleared the table. Then he excused himself and walked out.

Terri: Les says the nugget is real gold....

I offered Terri my bottle of bug dope, but she declined. I rubbed more over my face, neck and socks.

I felt I wanted to say something or do something more, but I did not. And then we saw a cow moose break out of the woods across the creek and walk with ungainly grace toward the water. A calf followed on stilt legs. The cow plunged into the main channel and crossed without pause. The calf hesitated, then followed. I held my breath as the standing waves surged over the little head bobbing downstream. But the baby emerged, right in front of us, and ran up to its mother. Then she noticed us, and trotted off upstream with powerful, high steps, the little one scurrying close behind.

I felt like I did in junior high school on my first date. Here was Terri and I didn't know what to say. Of course, since junior high school I had been ordained a priest.

"Terri," I said, "those are really moose, aren't they."

Good start.

"Yes," she said.

She had picked a handful of dandelions and was weaving them into a headband, like I had seen Sara do.

"And you are really a priest," she said.

Uh oh. Right to the point.

"I know this is pretty bad to say," I said. "But I'm wondering if being a priest is real at all. Oh, I believe the right way and all, you know.

"I say Mass and follow the ritual every day, and I like to. But, you know, I admit I've changed it here and there to fit my situation. Well...so much that I don't think the Church would approve.

"I have fond memories, I love my brothers in the monastery. They're nice people, but they are so far away. And I'd have so little to say to them now, or them to me. Kitty is the only Catholic I've seen in months, and she hardly counts. It's you who understands me, who I can talk to. You, and well, Les, and Sam too. The people who know winter here, the people we've gone through things with together. Jot, too. Maybe even sullen old George, I don't know.

"Maybe I should quit the priest business. You know, hang it up and move in with you and help run the lodge. I like kids. We could have some more. It'd be good for Sara."

"And how would you feel if you did that?" she said.

"Awful," I said.

The breeze dropped and squadrons of mosquitos appeared out of the grass. One had bitten my lip while I was talking, and now the lip swelled painfully. We walked swiftly back to town, outpacing the bugs. I put my arm around Terri. She stopped, gave me a hug, and took my hand.

June 26, 1982

First I heard uneasy buzzing. As I rose from unconsciousness, I recognized the attempts of a yellowjacket wasp to free itself from entrapment between the shade and the cracked windowpane. I opened my eyes. Faintly swaying in a light breeze, the tattered green shade tossed a few sunbeams through the dusty air of my darkened bedroom. The yellowjacket settled on the windowsill, exploring the glass with its antennae for a way out.

I lay in my sleeping bag. I was still filled with the dream image of a woman's face. It was Terri. I looked into her face, and we were sitting by the creek with the sun shining and the flowers blooming. Her eyes were wide and gentle. They invited, and I moved toward them to come in. She was Eve and she was mother of all the children in the world, and I was a child, and she held me. She sat on the roots of a tree, garlanding flowers, and she offered me succulent fruit which I nuzzled with my lips. She was Mary, holding the Christchild, nursing with sweet milk from her lush breast. And I stared up lovingly into her eyes that reflected the blue sky and the puffy white clouds and the grass and the soil. In her eyes I saw the breeze-tossed tree branches flutter with new leaves and the waters of the creek sparkle over its rocky bed.

I saw myself in her eyes, walking along the creek through woods spiced with early summer, until I came to where I could go no further. I sat by the edge of the water, resting against a fallen log, watching the willow branches sway, and stared up at the bluff on the opposite shore, a steep, watercut bluff made of dark rock veined serpentine. The clouds cast moving shadows on the bluff face and the veins moved before me, coiling and slithering through the rock in a sensuous dance paced to the movement of the wind and the flow of the creek below. I looked to the creek, and the waters stood still while the rocks flowed upstream.

Dizzy, I sat up in my bed, clutching the cotton mat for support. The wasp buzzed again, knocking against the glass. I went to the window to let it out. When I pulled back the shade, I was momentarily blinded by the sun. I slid the window up and the wasp sailed out. No one was on the street below. The town was quiet. It must still be night.

I dressed, went downstairs and walked out the door.

I wandered out along the path up the creek. When I got to one-mile, I stopped and chanted the night office, but it did not mean very much. In the forest a bird was singing the most exquisitely intricate and wistful song. Instead of returning to town, I continued out the trail. I did not want to go back.

I walked to two-mile, where the trail crosses the creek, but I could not cross. With the warm weather, the creek was near flood with snow and ice melt, turbid with silt. Les's ferry-canoe was on the other side and tangled in the ropes. Ed and Kitty must have used it and left it there, inaccessible and unusable. I stood looking at the creek pouring around the bend, descending from that place I could not see and could not go. Moose and bear tracks marked the soft places along the shore.

A seep of clear water flowed out of the bank at the edge of the woods. I kneeled down to drink from a shallow pool. The water was cold and sweet. Circular waves expanded across its surface from my lips, pulsing my reflected face. I drank slowly, looking into my eyes. In them I saw the sky and the clouds, and the bluff across the way mottled with moving shadows. I pulled back, and single drips from my chin splashed into the pool. The image of the bluff filled the pool, the dark bluff penetrated with white sinuous veins, and it danced in the resonating circles.

This was my true prayer. I felt the presence of Christ there in the water. I heard Him speaking to me in the lapping of the waves at the edge of the pool.

I reached in to embrace Him, but I muddied the pool, and all I came up with was dark sand.

July 3, 1982

Today is rainy and cold after weeks of sunshine. Jot flew in on the mail-plane. He looks tired. After dinner, Sam, Les, Jot and I sat around at the lodge with Terri. Jot told us about his trip.

He said at first it went very well. After they landed in Fairbanks, Sam drove him right to the environmental center. Jot was on the phone all day and most of the night, talking with people he knows in various organizations, explaining our situation to them and getting their support. They re ferred him to others. He called as far away as Guam and Japan, because the rare bird that nests up the creek winters in the Pacific. By morning he had created a new organization—"The Trans-Pacific Coalition for the Protection of the Bristle-Thighed Curlew," with officers and everything.

After a couple hours sleep on the couch, he sat down at the typewriter and wrote a two page summary of a scientific study which describes how the Explorers threaten the existence of the rare species, and how this threat is a major issue for the National Park.

Meanwhile, an ornithologist friend of his at Colorado State University spent the day writing the study which Jot was summarizing. He sent it up by express mail.

Jot also produced a press release expressing the outrage of the Trans-Pacific Coalition, explaining that it was considering filing suit because the National Park Service had violated several major laws. It referred to the study of the distinguished ornithologist.

Jot said that when he wrote these things, he hadn't yet gotten the members of his new Coalition to approve the lawsuit, but he was working on it. He said he was on the phone quite a bit, even while he was writing. He also had to line up funding, from various environmental law foundations I guess.

He also did not know *for sure* that the curlews nest here. He had just seen them up on the Butte, and it was alpine habitat, which they like. But they hadn't actually nested yet, and maybe they wouldn't. This was a point that could be dealt with later.

Before lunch, he borrowed the environmental center director's car and made a quick side trip to the printer to pick up the Trans-Pacific Coalition letterhead he had ordered. The letterhead listed many impressive names on the board of directors and executive committee. Returning, between bites of a Big Mac he retyped final versions of his memo and press release on letterhead and xeroxed off a couple dozen copies of each.

He had an appointment with the superintendent of the national park at 2 pm. The environmental center director and the environmental defense fund lawyer in Fairbanks went with him. The way Jot put it, they had the appointment and Jot was along as a technical advisor.

Jot's plan for the meeting was for them to impress upon the Park Service that a national and international constituency had developed for preservation of the curlew, and that the agency was in the midst of a controversy of major proportions which might generate considerable publicity. They even knew that a lawsuit was in the works, but it probably could be avoided if the Park Service exercised its administrative authority under the law to shut down the Explorers pending full environmental impact studies.

Actually, the lawsuit was a bluff. Nobody wanted a lawsuit. They are expensive and a lot of work, and they take too long. Of course, the Park Service wouldn't want a lawsuit, either.

The superintendent was sympathetic but non-committal. Lengthy studies would be needed before the agency could take action. Research budget priorities must be adhered to, and so forth. The director and his staff were very concerned about the curlew. They would do what they could.

Jot's perception was that the NPS needed a push. He filed the lawsuit.

We already knew what happened the next day. The Park Service decided to close down the Explorers.

Manley countersued. The cases were complex. Jot had to write the legal briefs. The vice-president of the environmental center took him in. Jot didn't get much sleep on her family room couch.

Then Manley went to Washington, where he spoke to the senior Alaska senator and then to an Assistant Secretary of the Interior. After that, orders came down to Fairbanks: The Park Service interpreted the law so that the Explorers could operate during the period the environmental studies were conducted.

The studies could take years. There was no money for the studies.

So Jot tried to get a temporary injunction. However, the judge is a Reagan appointee with a conservative view of the role of law. Also, Jot could no longer ignore the fact that no one really knows if the curlews nest up on the Butte.

So now the Explorers can start up again. We should expect them soon.

Jot needs to prove that the curlews nest up the creek and that the Explorers are bothering them. If he can do that, he thinks he can get an injunction.

From Terri's letters:

July 5, 1982

Quiet Fourth of July this year. Very few people around. Jordan's out again. Les's brother Tim is still in Oregon, seems like he's moved there for good....Still no sign of the Explorers. Maybe Jot was wrong about them coming back. A few tourists found their way into town, a family from Maine and a retired couple from New Jersey, so we had some lodge business.

Ed Butler made us an outdoor grill. He cut an oil barrel in half lengthwise, mounted it on rebar legs, and found an old grate to put on top. He works fast, did it in one afternoon. So we cooked hotdogs. Mike and Sara organized games, a potato-sack race and an egg-catching contest. They even got George to play. Jot, too, but that's not so surprising anymore.

It was all nice and OK, but I felt an emptiness in it. Maybe the weather was part of it, warm, humid and overcast.

Ed is getting restless, but he hasn't left. He and Kitty spend a lot of time sitting together in the bar. Ed drinks some beer, but he doesn't get drunk, and he's not an alcoholic. Maybe it's Kitty that is holding him here. Or maybe he doesn't have another place to go to, or doesn't like what he'd have to face back in Wenatchee. Yesterday he did say it was time for him to go out and get a job. Kitty does need him. He is the one who seems to be able to communicate with her, even though she still doesn't talk. I've overheard her hum quietly to herself, but that's all. Otherwise she seems to be OK, just subdued. When I asked her about what happened, she turns away. I've learned not to ask. Ed won't talk about it either, just mumbles and pretends to be gruff and changes the subject....

July 8, 1982

...Jot was in a dilemma. He said he needs to watch the curlew nests around the clock to see what they are doing, what they eat, and so forth. He needs to start right away, so he doesn't miss any more of the nesting season. And he has to carry quite a bit up there to the top of the Butte, cameras and scientific equipment and such. Also he has to finish that study for the Park Service, the one that pays his way to come up here, the one I never could really understand. So he needs help.

I suggested Ed. Jot's got enough money from the Park Service contract to pay him. Ed's a hard worker, he's strong and can carry a lot, and he knows his way around up the creek already. Jot said no to me, he couldn't do it, just couldn't trust Ed under the circumstances, and also Ed wouldn't get the job done. Les and I talked, and Les had been thinking the same thing. So Les took Jot aside, too. Afterward, Jot said he'd give Ed a try.

Sam's out flying fish at Bristol Bay, so they had to walk up.

...A bear's been scattering garbage at the dump. Sam says he's seen one near his place a couple of times. Just a little one, he says, but they can be a nuisance....

———————

Ed and I had to make two trips to get the gear up the creek. It took us awhile to untangle Les's ferry ropes and get the canoe halves where we needed them. But at least Ed and Kitty hadn't left the boats in the middle of the current. Ed kept a fire going, while I worked in the icewater. It rained most of the time, on and off.

When we got to the Syndicate town, we still had a long climb to the tundra on the butte above. I remember Ed sweated profusely, and I was concerned he would have a heart attack. But he carried heavy loads and did not complain much.

Previously, I would have found Ed's presence intolerable. But this time I was so intent on my task that I didn't mind. In fact, we got along quite well. If he had an opinion about my project, he didn't say.

The curlews were indeed breeding: We found dozens of nests. I made the necessary measurements and took photographs, and set Ed to the tedious task of observing the movements of the adult and juvenile birds, physically demanding but simple work. He had to record data at four-hour intervals around the clock. Of course, it never got dark. But the blowing rain almost never stopped.

I can still see him sitting on the wet ground in his billowing yellow raincoat and rainpants, binoculars hanging from his neck, holding the pencil with thick, red fingers as he wrote in a waterproof notebook puddled with drops streaming off the brim of his hood, while long-billed shorebirds bobbed around on skinny legs, whistling "chi-u-it, whee-wheeea." Sometimes the rain became wet snow, and then the ground turned white. He spent his off hours lying in Ted Charles' two-person mountaineers' tent, which he filled by himself. He kept good records on "his little birdies," and he never missed an observation.

But he refused to go anywhere near the mine entrances, even though I found several curlew nests there.

He stayed and I hiked back to Darwin, to continue the regular work I had to do on my park planning contract.

At the Syndicate town, the Explorers' bulldozer was just as Ed had left it, ready to go, next to the pre-fab building parts, portable drill rig, and other supplies. Neither of us touched any of it.

The day after I got back down the creek, the helicopter returned to Darwin, ferrying in the Explorers' new crew, under the command of Dr. Perry W. Huntingford. —JBS

From Mike's journal:

July 19

...The Explorers flew in today under a leaden sky. The weight we have felt suspended over us has fallen. I actually sense an easing of tension in all of us, and a closeness between Jot, Terri, Les, Sara, Kitty and myself as we await whatever happens. I see Sara losing some of her child's freshness, revealing a depth not unlike her mother's, less calm but with a potent un-settled fertility. I see it in the movement of her eyes when she holds her arms around Kitty, as they sit silently together on the lodge couch, watching the falling rain.

I suppose in the outside world, Kitty would be diagnosed schizophrenic and taken away from us, doctors attempting to penetrate whatever mystery she holds within. But here it is not that way. We keep her in our circle, feed her with our love, and she shares the unspeakable with us. Outside, that is not allowed.

Why do we resist the Explorers? Maybe it is because their coming makes inevitable our assimilation into a society where the unspeakable is denied, repressed, forced underground.

That is why monasteries have walls. They are not to keep the monks in.

The long, tortuous dirt road from Bettles. The unbridged Loohana River. These are our walls. And especially the jagged ridges and dangerous waters of the Dagheeloyee Creek valley, guardians of the inner sanctum, of the altar of the mystery of the holy sacrament....

July 21

...The Explorers are grounded, the creek valley closed off by impene-trable clouds and fog. I hear their generator and sometimes see the work-men wandering about town. But Perry must have instructed them not to speak with us, and they stay out of the lodge. He, however, is under no such restriction. Terri hasn't thrown him out, yet. (And he buys only a cup of tea, getting free hot refills until his teabag barely stains the water)... I am so immersed in my own regimen that I am not at the lodge much....

July 23

...Perry talks about a huge grizzly hanging out right around town. Only the Explorers have seen it. But a bear did tip over a trash can behind the lodge last night. Perry goes around now accompanied by a workman with a rifle, bear protection.

July 25

I was reading Krishnamurti this morning, when I heard half a dozen shots fired out in the direction of the Explorers' trailers. Later at the lodge Sara told me the Explorers had shot a bear. She'd seen it lying by the road.

We put on our raincoats and walked out to look at it. So this was the huge bear. It was a grizzly alright, with tan fur tipped silver and a high forehead.

But it was not much more than a cub. They'd pulled out the claws and canine teeth, leaving the rest of the little body sprawled in the dirt.

Terri says they can sell the claws and teeth to people who think they have magical powers.

Sara and I went and got shovels. We dug a shallow hole in a nearby poplar grove overlooking the creek and rolled little bear into it and covered him up. We spoke to his bear soul, reminding him that someday we would all be joined together again. We went back to the lodge, scraped the mud from our boots, and sat next to the fire, drinking tea and saying very little. When Perry came to the door, Terri told him the lodge was closed.

Les says it was necessary to shoot the bear. Once they get used to people, they hang around and cause damage. A domestic bear is a dangerous bear.

July 27

...I went to the grave to meditate and pray, but I could smell the rotting stink from the road. Something dug up the bear and ate at the decaying body. I guess it was another bear....

Toward the end of July, the clouds lifted, although the overcast remained. I hiked up the creek to check on Ed, who mumbled and cursed when I saw him, but his notes looked complete and he wanted to stay. His tent sagged under six or eight centimeters of wet snow. I resupplied him with Kitty's fresh baked cookies as well as fuel for his campstove and other necessities.

While I was up there, we heard the helicopter down below ferrying the Explorers in to begin operations. Ed told me that soon they'd be up here drilling for ore samples. Where the slope was steep, they would blast a platform first. The baby curlews were growing, just about to leave their nests.

I took his field observations, exchanging them for a new notebook, and hustled back to Darwin to see if I could find a ride out to Fairbanks to get our injunction.

On the way down the slope, I passed Kitty hiking up. She'd hitched a ride on the helicopter and was coming to join Ed.

I took the route over the top back to Darwin, so the canoes would be left on the correct shore in case Ed and Kitty needed them to get out in an emergency. When I crossed it, the Dagheeloyee Glacier sat grey under clouds. Biting flies followed me up the mountain slope all the way to the pass. Hiking from Ed's camp to Darwin in one day, I arrived at the lodge worn out, needing sleep, needing to get to Fairbanks quickly, and not knowing how I would get there. I dropped my pack in the corner and let Terri bring me camomile tea, while I sank into a chair, this time not minding the springs poking into my back. I tried to focus my mind: When I got to Fairbanks, I had to convince the judge to give us the injunction.

I bought dinner at the lodge that evening, a huge plate of steaming spaghetti with tomato sauce and orange delicious mushrooms Sara had gathered that afternoon. It was a good year for mushrooms. Terri added the remnants of last fall's canned moose, just for me.

The helicopter, roaring in overhead, barely kept me from falling asleep over my tea. Les came for pie and coffee. Then Mike arrived and sat by Terri. Sara had transformed a corner of the main room into her artist's studio and was painting in tempera on large sheets of paper. It was no longer children's play. I still remember the smell of the paint. I remember the pounding of rain on the tin lodge roof. I thought of Kitty and Ed Butler curled together in the little tent up there in the storm, emerging every four hours to watch curlews.

Terri offered me the keys to her truck on the other side of the river. It's a long trip, hundreds of miles on potholed roads. I asked Mike for a prayer, since I didn't know how to use the mechanic's tools I'd have with me.

We spoke philosophically about the Explorers. What if the Explorers actually opened a mine? Terri thought she would stay. There would be lots of business, and she could do some beautiful things with the lodge. And there would be other kids for Sara. Les said real miners, if they came, probably would be good folks for neighbors up the creek. And maybe he would go to Los Angeles for a while, where he knew a group of artists and musicians.

I don't remember Mike saying anything.

Then the bells hanging from the doorknob clanged and Perry W. Huntingford's oxfords tracked in mud all the way to the dining room. Not needing psychological help just then, I went out to my tent to get some sleep. —JBS

From Mike's journal:

...Perry hung his umbrella on the hatrack and combed his grey beard in front of the mirror. Then he sat down next to Jot without paying any attention to him, staring lustfully at Terri. Jot left. I wanted to hold Terri's hand. She went to fill Perry's order for pie smothered in whipped cream.

Without our asking, he informed us that operations were going exceedingly well and the new cat operator was soon to begin road construction up the creek. Our horizons were to be enlarged. He asked where Kitty was. We told him she was out.

I could see Sara in the other room. She'd put down the paints and was working in charcoal. She was sketching a ludicrous caricature of Perry. He didn't notice....

I must put in the following piece by George Johnston, although I myself would rather not re-read it. We suspected nothing. —*JBS*

July 23, 1982, 3:34:46 a.m.

The damn rain. Darwin is a hellish place. They are ruining it with bull-dozers, scraping up the dirt and killing the flowers. They are all part of the situation. They think they are each different, the lady and the priest and the professor and the miners and so on. That is only how it appears to them. I have an overview perspective which enables me to see that they are all parts of a single whole. I can see the true nature of the complex enterprise in which they are engaged, even though they themselves cannot. I therefore have a responsibility to act, which I shall fulfill.

In order to resolve the matter, the entire must be dealt with. This task can be accomplished by interfering with any subset of the parts. The components of the system are interrelated and mutually interdependent.

The plan has the advantage of consisting of simple actions, each of which impacts multiply on more than one element. For example, shooting the people negates directly their future destructive activity, while at the same time enabling the hijack of the mailplane and, therefore, the subsequent sabotage of the pipeline. Furthermore, once the sabotage is completed, my return to Darwin and suicide among the bodies disguises my participation in the event—a perfect cover, because the murderer will remain unknown forever and it will be impossible to suspect my involvement in the demolition one hundred fifty miles away.

The plan follows a set of systemic ecological principles. It is environmentally sound in multiple aspects.

The precise schedule is being adhered to. This is further evidence of the integrity of the plan.

I will rip their bellies out with submachine gun bullets.

Early the next morning, I trammed across the river and drove off for Fairbanks in Terri's truck, creeping through the puddles. About twenty-five kilometers out of Darwin, beavers had plugged a culvert, backing water up over the road. I used the shovel and axe to clear it out. For hours I saw no other traffic and settled into a steady, twenty-kilometers-per-hour routine. I began to relax. Then suddenly on a flat, straight stretch of road the engine just quit. I couldn't get it restarted. There I sat. I remembered the nearest cabin was thirty-five kilometers back. It was raining again.

Less than two minutes later, a semi-truck approached at high speed. It rumbled to a stop in front of me. It had to. My pickup was blocking the road. I looked up past a hectometer of dirty chrome into the cab overhead. The driver got out. So did I. He could have played defensive lineman for the Chicago Bears.

He extended a meaty hand and said his name was Jeff. Jeff's smile showed a big gap between his top front teeth. He had me turn on the ignition while he worked with a screwdriver in my engine. My coil was shorting out, whatever that meant. He dried it with a rag and Terri's truck started right up.

I thanked him and asked him what he was hauling, way out here in nowhere. He said was bringing in a railroad flatcar. The miners were going to make a bridge of them in the fall, when the water level dropped so they could work in the Loohana River.

I pulled off into the bushes so he could squeeze by. I didn't see another vehicle for hours, until I was almost to Bettles.   —JBS

In town I had no time for anything but lawyer's work. I wrote my next journal entry on the way back to Darwin:

9 August 1982

...Why wouldn't the judge understand? Is my case really inadequate, *prima facia*? The defendants are right: The curlews are probably done nesting by now, soon leaving for the year (unless the Explorers have already driven them off). No need, of course, for an injunction now. So the Explorers can build their road and establish themselves, and then we can talk about it again. We can talk about it all winter.

Who cares about curlews anyway. Not me. Curlews are bullshit. All the law can deal with is bullshit. No, it can't even take care of curlews. It's not even good for bullshit.

Years of training, law school and graduate school, and can I convey what matters to the court, or to anybody back there in the city? No. Only the creek can convey it, and the mountains and the glaciers and the forest and the animals. Only directly, and they back there don't listen or see, so they don't understand, and they don't care, and they lock themselves into a sterile prison, unaware that anything else exists. Nothing is real for them but the prison. It takes all their energy to maintain the illusion of its existence. Anyone who breaks out of it is a threat and must be annihilated. That's why they can't give me the injunction.

I was one of them, too, until I saw through the walls and got another perspective. After that experience, a man can never be the same again. It gives me a responsibility to act. But how to make them understand? I can't. I've tried. I don't know how. But I have to. I have to keep trying....

I pulled myself across the tram and walked into town. The scene from the tram was as I had known it: mountain peaks disappearing into overcast; the great, icy Loohana amphitheater silent except for the roar of the river on its boulder bed. Town was the same, leaves fluttering on poplar trees growing up against the walls of the buildings, empty gravel streets, the slow chug of the lodge generator muffled in its unpainted shed. Les was under the lodge Ford Model A, surrounded by wrenches and a pan of dirty oil. I went on to my campsite and pitched my tent. Whatever it was I cared about, it was still here. I could not believe that anything had changed, or ever could change.

But that evening, the helicopter shuttled into town four times.

I checked at the lodge. Ed and Kitty had not yet returned. So the next morning, I set out up the creek to make sure they were OK. I walked up the valley, instead of over the top, because I had a masochistic desire to see the cat at work, to feel the pain and get it over with.   —*JBS*

12 August 1982
Location: On the road at the terminus
of the Dagheeloyee Glacier.

The bulldozer, cutting through the forest, piled the trees into crude berms. Resin drips from torn boughs still green with living needles. The road is a soft mush of silt and gravel, mixed with broken wild roses and mosses.

Gouge marks show where the cat winched trees out of the woods for the bridge. Where Les's ferry used to be, the creek is spanned with un-peeled trunks suspended between rough log cribbing. I found the canoe itself nearby, run over by the cat and smashed against a boulder. The anchor tree for Les's upper rope is pushed over; the rope severed, its ends dangling loose in the brown current.

From the bridge, the road cuts through the bank and continues up a massive ramp and through the tunnel. Some material for the ramp came from a gravel pit dug into the floodplain below the glacier face. The cat pulled the rest down from the hillside above, tearing off the soapberry, juniper, bearberry and willow, along with the soil. The Explorers' crew is pushing on downstream. Yesterday, they were working at six-mile.

Kitty and Ed are resting down by the creek. It's a slog through the mud on the road. We'll be lucky to make it to Darwin by dark.

I got to the Syndicate town yesterday afternoon after a hard, depressing walk up the desecrated valley. Fortunately, Kitty had their laundry hanging out, so I found them before I started the hike up the butte to their high camp. She and Ed were living in one of the abandoned Syndicate buildings.*

The curlews left, Ed said, so he and Kitty had come down. He didn't know whether the birds successfully fledged young. Just when the juveniles were leaving the nest, the helicopter began repeated landings, carrying in the drill rig and equipment, and the Explorers started blasting and running gasoline engines. Ed said the birds flew around a lot then and soon just disappeared.

The curlews don't matter anymore, anyway.

...So what is left here for me? Not too much. I am tired of slogging through mud on an ugly road. But my job now is chronicler, to tell the world what happened here. I will devote the rest of the summer to taking pictures, writing, recording events....

---

* *I didn't put this sort of thing in my notes back then, but I do remember that the laundry was unmistakably theirs—cavernous wool pants with suspenders, plaid shirts, a couple of slinky black dresses, at least a half-dozen lacy bras, and purple tights, all hanging from a piece of telephone wire stretched between two buildings.*

Looking back, I remember how established they were in that abandoned house. The windows were cracked, the water-stained wallpaper was peeled, and the floor sagged so much the door didn't close completely, but they'd collected items from around the town—furniture (a couch and chairs, fancy dining room table, dresser with mirror, big brass double bed), a complete set of dishes and silverware, even a framed painting of a four-masted schooner on the wall. It felt like a family home. During my wanderings about the valley in later years, I stayed there several times.   —JBS

I brought Ed and Kitty down to town, then walked back up the creek myself, camping by the road, watching the Explorers work. They paid no attention to me.

The Explorers spanned the creek at two mile with another crude log bridge and bulldozed on in to Darwin. Then they took the cat all the way back to the Syndicate town, patching the places that had already begun to erode and slide. They stole planks off the Syndicate buildings and decked their bridges with them. Reading back over my field notes, I realize now that I never could have written the emotional, convincing articles I had planned. I was being emptied out, my foundations undercut.

I tried to formulate precisely why I came to the valley originally and what was now lost. I could not. I knew I had forgotten something, but what was it?

Meanwhile, Kitty and Ed were back at the lodge. I set Ed to finishing the measurements I needed for the Park Service contract, getting the dimensions of each of the buildings in Darwin, street widths, and so forth. One day after work, he went to Mike's.   —JBS

―――――――――

From Mike's journal:

August 17

I was sitting on the bench in the yard, whittling on the crucifix, digesting dinner, and enjoying the gold evening sunlight. Carving the cross part is easy, but getting His body to feel right is not. I feel close to His suffering as I carve. It is different than prayer in words. Now is the fruiting season. I nibbled raspberries I picked by the outhouse. Their red juice dripped from my fingers. I touched the crucifix and He bled.

Ed came by. He had on a clean shirt, and the fringe of hair on his head was still slicked down from taking a shower at the lodge. He stood about ten feet away, his baseball cap in his hands, looking at me. I invited him to sit down on the bench. He sat fidgeting with his cap, looking into my eyes uncomfortably. I tried to keep whittling, but could not.

He took a deep breath and held it. Then he started, "What do you think about dreams?

"Like, I mean, do you believe dreams mean anything? Well, like for example, lets just say that a guy had this dream. I mean, like what would you think? Is this guy OK? Like, is he crazy or anything? I mean, it's just a dream, isn't it. For example, what if a guy came to you and said...

"Well, I'm not saying this is a dream. But of course that is what you would think it is. Wouldn't you. Regular people like you and me, that's what we'd do. Or maybe we'd say this guy is a pretty good story teller. We wouldn't take him serious, or anything. We'd say he's OK, he just can't tell the truth. But let's say this guy ain't no liar. Then what?..."

His face was too close to mine. I wiggled on the bench.

"Suppose the guy said he was in this mine tunnel, you know, up there at the mines, just looking around and, you know, not hurting nobody. Them mines are interesting, full of old stuff and geology and like that. There's lots of reasons a guy goes in there that's not trying to steal ore or make trouble or anything. Just minding his own business and he brings a dame with him. You know, she wanted to come. It was her idea to come along, really.

"He was just curious. You know, the Syndicate quit because they found... Well, lets just say they found more ore. Lots of it. But they never got it out. Instead, they just up and quit. Why would they do this? So a reasonable guy, he would wonder why, wouldn't he? And he'd want to go in there and take a look. Just curious, you'd want to take a look. And I'd got the map. I had it in my pocket."

I raised my eyebrows. Ed winced.

"Well, here I am telling the story. Just like the guy would tell it, so you can tell me what you think."

I said, "OK." Ed stopped, took a deep breath, and then relaxed, as if he'd plunged in and there was no turning back. He leaned against the gray hardware store wall and looked away toward the sun, which was lowering toward Mount Chalcocite. Now the words spilled out without restraint. I watched him for a minute, then relaxed, too, letting the sun warm my eyelids, letting him tell his story in the gentle evening—not even any mosquitos—like a dream.

"So he's got the map to the mother lode. It's a long way for a dame to walk and she gets tired and so we go slow. We do OK and don't step in no grizzlies."

"Grizzlies?" I said.

"You know, them's the shafts between mine levels. You dump the ore down them. A guy don't want to fall in no grizzlies.

"We go all the way to number 1 sublevel, which is miles at least, and this is the stope the Syndicate was working when they quit and it takes so long to get there we camp on the way. You know, this is not where Schultz said to look, so I wasn't there before with the Explorers.

"At first I see nothing so I think this is a dead end. Looks like the Syndicate went farther maybe but they had a cave-in here and did not re-open. Then I look again and I see this is no cave-in. They dynamited the drift on purpose. This here is all limestone and no sign of ore. Then we find some gloves and other stuff. I figure Russell must have left them. When I look there I think maybe the drift is not so blocked. I can move some rocks so we can get through.

"We crawl on hands and knees and this is hard on the dame whose gotta leave her stuff behind because her pack gets hung up on the rocks. You know how they are. Does not want to leave her make up and such but she does. I carry the dynamite. We each got a headlamp of course. I tell you this because later it figures in.

"After a while we get past the cave-in and the drift it angles down and curves this way and that. Why does the miners curve the drift I think, and then I see those rock icicles on the walls and I figure no miners made this drift.

"A drift. I suppose you don't know what that is, either, Father. So let me tell you. A drift, that's a tunnel they make following the ore." °

"Rock icicles," I said. "Sounds like a natural cave. Stalactites I think they call them."

"Yea, those. Rock icicles, and some of 'em growing upside down.

"So we are in where Russell was talking about. So far so good. We walk not very far and we are in this big room. This is as big as the Kingdome in Seattle.

"You ever watch the Seahawks play in the Kingdome, Father? No? You oughtta some time. Well, this place is as big as the Kingdome. That's where they play.

"I shine my light around and Russell is right. It is all made of chalcocite and it has quartz veins." Ed paused. "Quartz veins, you know, that's what's got the gold in it, like on the piece Russell had. On the floor there is this creek and it flows over these big nuggets. I pick one up and I think ah ha! native copper. Even copper will be a fortune. But this is gold. I am thinking Russell is not too smart to sell me the map. But then when I am looking at the nugget I trip over something.

"A rock I figure. So I shine the light on it. It is green and long with hard plates. I shine the light along it to see where it goes. Something big is there. You know, in caves sometimes the rocks look like wings and things and it does on this.

"The front end has got a head. So it is no rock. It is a dead snake or something instead. But it is bigger than a house so maybe it is one of them dead dinosaurs? I give it a kick. The eye opens so then I think something is fishy. Maybe it is time we oughtta leave.

"At this time the dame is taking off her boots. She does not see then that she sits on the tail. Her feet is what she is concerned with since being a dame they got blisters.

"So when the tail, all of a sudden it goes across the room, she yells loud and now the thing is awake. The dame got us in hot water for sure.

° *They were probably actually in a "crosscut," running at right angles to the vein, rather than in a drift.*   —*JBS*

"Now we gotta go. The eyes got green lights. These is like searchlights. It has got wings like a B-52. Also a red tongue."

I looked at Ed. He stared wide-eyed at the sun and kept talking.

"At first I can't find the doorway. But the dame gets to it and I am holding onto her hand to protect her so out we go the both of us. She can't run fast. She has left the boots behind, so all we got with us is the lights and I still got the dynamite.

"It is good we got out of there, because now the thing belches fire and we would be toasted.

"We duck into a side passage. The thing goes running by. The dame has got to rest. In a minute the thing comes back. But again it does not see us so it goes back into its room.

"Now I think again about the mineral riches and I got a plan. We take a look around and there is lots of side passages and tunnels. The plan is the dame will go back into the room. She needs to get her boots anyway. The thing will go after the dame. She will let it chase her down one of these side tunnels that makes a loop back to the main one. Meanwhile, I will have placed the dynamite. The dame goes past the dynamite. But when the thing is in position I push the plunger and bango, no more thing. It takes awhile to explain this to the dame.

"It works perfect. We get set up and in goes the dame and pretty soon out they come. The dame even carries the boots. This I see because them big green eyes light up the tunnels. I am in one of them passageways off to one side away from the tunnel with the dynamite. The dame runs by. Then here comes the thing. Whammo. Surely I got the timing just right.

"Now this I do not understand. The thing is blown to smithereens for sure. Out I come. I will cut a souvenir with my knife. Maybe one of them green plates. I shine my lamp around.

"All of a sudden there is this blast of fire. The thing still got its toaster working. In fact there is the whole thing and mad now but good. All lit up purple and green. You know, like them Christmas lights at the mall. Man does it belch flames and the air stinks pretty bad. These great big claws it's got, they pound the floor and the tunnel shakes. I am lucky no falling rocks hit me. I decide to go out of there and pretty soon I pass the dame and there we are with the thing right behind.

"It lets out another blast of the toaster and this is a close one. I see another side passage and so we duck in and the thing goes by. Then it is dark because our lights are blown out or anyway they do not work and the thing is gone which was lighting up the tunnel. The dame has dropped her boots. I decide we should be quiet for a while. At first we hear the thing running around and blasting flames somewhere but then we hear nothing. I decide we should go back to Darwin. We walk slowly because I do not want us falling in no grizzly and the dame got no boots.

"Now I cannot tell you how far we go. There are lots of tunnels. How do you know which one? I gotta feel my way along careful. After a while it gets pretty tight going, and I gotta stoop not to bang my head. I think I do not know if we ever will get out of this place but the slope is upward and maybe we will get to the surface yet.

"So far we come to no timbers so I figure this is not a mining tunnel but one of them cave tunnels instead. But then there is this wooden door overhead. So maybe we have found a raise and I hope a manway with a ladder to climb out on.

"I push on the door and it opens up.

"At first I see nothing because I have been in the dark tunnels, and then all of a sudden there is so much light it hurts. So first I think, uh oh, here is old searchlight eyes and he has got us now, but no. My head is sticking up through the door and in a minute I see something. In front of my face is peanut butter and a dozen eggs.

"This is a cabin it looks like. What is a cabin doing under the ground I think, and then I see daylight in the windows. Well, we are out of those tunnels, I figure. That is the main thing. Let me tell you, by now this whole business is getting to me.

"I see dirt on the floor and stove legs. I am still standing in the hole reconnoitering the situation. This is one of them old log cabins. This one got red shag carpets."

"Les's house..." I said. °

"Then I look some more and I see two feet over there and so I look up and there is Les Brown sitting in a beat-up easy chair. So I say Les Brown, what the *fuck* is going on.

"Oops. Pardon me, Father.

"The guy he looks at me and takes another drink outa his coffee cup. There he sits so calm and easy, just like he was expecting visitors. However, you think a guy is going to answer questions to visitors, but not mine. The guy just looks at me and I think maybe there is something wrong with him. Maybe he is crazy or something. So I yell at him a little louder, Les Brown what the...heck...is going on here.

"To Kitty I am about to say lets get up outa the damn tunnel and get outa here and to hell with Les Brown anyway, at least we are out safe. But then I notice something is lying on the floor on the other side of the stove. Holy shit. It is one of them things. This is a baby one about the size of a pony, but it got all the parts including the toaster. Once more I tell him, Les Brown, what the shit is going on here, and then the thing stands up and looks at me, so I decide we better skedaddle. By the time I am down through the trap door, the thing is after me doing the blast furnace number and I barely get the door shut behind me. I got to get the dame to safety. So down the tunnel we hustle.

"Like I said before, I dunno how far we go in there. Dark, no food, cold. The dame got no shoes, so pretty soon I am carrying her. Sometimes we take a rest. Even sleep maybe. I dunno.

"So what happens? There is a light at the end of the tunnel, and so we go there. At first I do not want to go out because of the things. So the dame checks out the scene, and when she comes back she says OK, no things. So I pick up the dame again and out we go.

° *Butler apparently opened Les's root cellar door from underneath and stuck his head up into the kitchen. Les usually kept items such as peanut butter jars and egg cartons under the counter next to the trap door. Of course, Mike would have recognized the scene.* —JBS

"I figure out where we are, but it takes awhile. We are out by the glacier somewhere. I can tell by the mountains where Darwin is.* So now we just gotta walk. So after a while we come to the tram and we are back to Darwin."

Ed was done. We were facing each other now on the bench. The sun had set below the ridge, and I shivered. Ed looked at me with intense hope. What would I say? Sweat beads stood out on his forehead.

"Let's go in," I said. "I need to put on a jacket."

We moved into the front room of the hardware store, which still held the day's warmth. I made tea for myself and instant coffee for Ed. He seemed exhausted and very sober.

"I didn't mean to say all this, Father. You gotta understand. I mean, just because a guy has a dream like this, it doesn't mean he's crazy like old Jasper or like that. Right?"

"I guess so," I said. "We all have our dreams."

"Yea, that's what it is. Just a dream." Ed seemed more comfortable now, a weight off his shoulders. I didn't interfere. He drank his coffee and didn't say anything. I sipped my tea. The berry-stained, unfinished crucifix lay on the table.

He was done talking about his dream. But we sat up late, and when it got dark I lit a lamp. He spoke for the first time about his wife and kids in eastern Washington, two daughters, aged eight and two, not a fulfilling marriage. Tried college, one semester. Got thrown out, for something that was really Manley's fault. He asked me about a priest's life. I told him about the monastery, getting permission to come here; the celibacy, you get used to it. He seemed at ease by the time he left.

---

* *That is, he could orient himself in relation to Dagheeloyee Peak, Malachite Ridge, and Mt. Ezra Darwin. From what I can gather, they must have come out one of the cave entrances at the base of Malachite Ridge along the fosse of Great Lateral Moraine of the Loohana Glacier—possibly the same one to which I had followed the bear the previous summer after my descent from the pass. It is a long, difficult walk from there to Darwin, much of it over sharp rocks and steep moraine. Butler would have had to carry shoeless Kitty the whole way, except perhaps the first part in the fosse, which traverses soft sand. (Remember that a fosse is long narrow valley—a moat—between a glacier and the base of a ridge.)* —JBS

From Sara's diary:

...Mrs. Henry says Old G.S. saw it sort of right.

Actually, she says, the dragon is sleeping. It dreams the world. Everything, such as the glacier and the mountains and us, is just the dream of the dragon. When the dragon wakes up, the world will end. It is best, she says, not to disturb the dragon. The bears and the ravens work for the dragon. Mrs. Henry says they are its emissaries. That means they tell it what is going on and do things for it that it can't do for itself....

From Mike's journal:

August 20

...Sara has been doing quite a bit of painting and sketching. Les gives her suggestions occasionally, but mostly she works on her own. That's how Les learned, just practice.

This afternoon I put on my raincoat and went over to the lodge. Kitty was there in the main room folding laundry, while Sara drew. Sara worked a long time, trying to get the perspective right in a picture of the laundry basket. Sometimes Sara or I said something, not much.

Sara made a few sketches, was dissatisfied, erased lines, tried more. Finally, Kitty laid down the sheet she had been folding for ten minutes and slowly walked over to the easel. She held Sara by the forearm, watching the paper as if there was something in it she could not quite see. She took the pencil gently from Sara's hand.

She sketched the laundry basket with a few quick strokes. The perspective was perfect. A smile drifted across her face, the first emotion I had seen since she hiked off up the creek carrying that big pack for Ed.

Sara clipped a fresh piece of paper to the easel. Kitty looked at the pencil, fondling it with both hands. She stepped over to Sara's paints, touched each of the jars, and ran her palm over the upturned brushes. Sara sat on the arm of my chair and we watched.

First Kitty drew faces, an old man's face, a child, several women. Then she drew the bodies, ethereal and winged. The forms emerged from the blank white surface, minimally sketched with pencil.

But suddenly the door slammed and Perry Huntingford strode in, demanding his afternoon tea. She turned away to serve him. "Drawing," he said. "I studied the theory of art in graduate school. Art is a culturally therapeutic activity. You are to be commended, my dear." He did not look at what she had done.

Sara left the easel as it was. We both walked out and went about our business.

August 21

Sara came over to the hardware store this morning to get me. Kitty was still sleeping and it was almost noon. Apparently, she had gotten up in the night and gone to work at the easel, because her drawing was much more complete. We went over to the lodge to look. The angels had the most amazing depth and grace. I wanted to enter into the picture and fly with them. She had sketched in a background that looked like waterfalls and icicles....

August 22

I dreamed last night of Kitty's angels. They held me and comforted me, and I became one of them, rising beyond the blue sky.

I awoke at first light to another cloudy morning and walked out to smell the misty air. The poplar leaves hung limp; gray is spreading over them. Is it mold? I heard the sound of an ax at the lodge: Terri was up early. I walked by and saw her in the woodshed. I helped her stack the wood she had split. Then we walked hand in hand out to the glacier.

We climbed a hill some distance from the ice. Young willows grew between the rocks, their leaves mottled yellow and brown with the coming change of season. I lay on my back, feeling mist fall on my face from the expanse of overcast sky.

Little plants covered the ground next to us, their dried flower stalks poking up between low-growing leaves. Dryas, Terri said they are called, named after the dryads, nymphs of the forest. She lifted one gently. I saw that the separateness of the plants was actually an illusion. It was one big plant, with many flowers, growing like a mat over the ground, its parts connected underneath the leaves by tough, woody stems. An unkempt burst of white strands made a head of hair atop each flower stalk. "Little Einsteins," Terri called them.

She picked one and held it while she talked: Mrs. Henry, Sara's imaginary friend, is a dryas plant growing down by the river. Sara went out to the river yesterday. When she returned, she told Terri that Mrs. Henry had explained what Kitty is drawing. It is what she saw in the mines with Ed....

August 27

...Yesterday I walked out the Explorers' road to two mile. The clear-water seep flows in a ditch; its pool is gone. Les's ferry is ripped out. The tree Terri and I rested against is pushed into a brush pile. The creek is bridged. I can cross easily to the other side, but now I have no reason to go.

I looked across to the bluff. Hard as I tried, I saw only veins of dull white rock in the gray shale.

Who knows what will happen, Les says. We cannot know. Perhaps the Explorers will leave this fall and never return. But I have to write to the abbot and say that this is not a place for hermits, not now. I will have to leave, go back. I don't want to.

At Matins in my hardware store bedroom, I kneel before my hand-carved crucifix, watch it by the yellow light of a single candle, and the sad face of Christ stares into my own, and I reach out for Him.

From one of Terri's letters:

September 5, 1982

...The Explorers have finished building their road up the creek. Now they are building a bridge across the Loohana River. It is made out of railroad flatcars. They are building it fast, but I wonder how long it will last in the summer floods....

Les, who has coffee with the workers (regardless of what Perry says), found out they are all done for the year up the creek. They plan to finish up the bridge quick and be out by mid-September. That is when the investors come, they say. I don't know anything more about it. Carl Manley certainly hasn't contacted me, and they aren't staying at the lodge....

So another winter will come, and it will be quiet again, with time to compose ourselves for whatever life will bring....

...Mike was sitting in front of the stove here yesterday afternoon. It was a sunny day but he was inside. Sara came marching through the living room beating a coffee can drum with a stick and chanting, "Mike the monk is in a funk." He chased her out of the house, pretending to smile, but right afterward he came back in and sat down again, caught up in himself. I want to help, but I'm not sure yet what I can do.

From Mike's journal:

September 7, 1982

I was sitting at the table yesterday evening, dawdling with the chess set I found out back. It had been sunny, but I'd gone into the dark, chilly storeroom, poking around in sixty years of rummage. The chess set was under an ore sack filled with kidney beans. Except for some water stains and the tooth marks in one corner, the board was OK. Almost all the pieces were there. I had to whittle a new black knight. I tried to darken it with my pen, but the ink didn't stick very well to the green wood. It looks sort of scribbled on.

There I was, still fiddling with the knight after dinner, when I saw George walk by. I wandered out and asked him in for tea. I was surprised when he said yes. We played a couple of games of chess. I hadn't played since junior high school, when I was runner-up in the junior division once. George wasn't any better. We were a good pair. But he really wanted to win, and I couldn't match his concentration.

My mind wandered off, to Ed Butler's tale. I asked George what he knew about his namesake, St. George. I had taken George's knight, the new one, so I was working on it some more while he concentrated, trying to blacken it with my pen again.

He didn't know much about St. George, so I told him about how he was able to do everything he tried, converted the heathen, brought the dead to life, saved the lady, put the lady's girdle around the dragon's neck and led it into town with everybody cheering, and so on.

George listened intently. I guess I needed a listener. So then I went on about how I wasn't as successful as St. George, maybe having to go back to the monastery, not wanting to, and all that. I mentioned the passage from John 12 that I've been praying over lately, "unless the grain of wheat dies, it remains itself alone." It's hard to talk about these things with Les or Terri. They are too upbeat, not so moody. I didn't expect it would be easier with George. He said he understood and wanted to help. Maybe we have more in common than I thought.

September 15, 1982

...Why are we all on edge? It's not just me. I sense a great emptiness, a hollow waiting. Maybe it is the season. The little birds are gone. The leaves are off the trees. There should be an excitement to this season, though— the anticipation of snow. But I don't feel that, and I don't think the others do, either. It's like before a thunderstorm in Rochester. The air feels confining. Of course, it is the Explorers. They opened their bridge across the Loohana day before yesterday, a string of flatcars on log pilings.

I thought I knew the sound of each vehicle in town—the lodge Model A, Sam's flatbed, Les's jeep, even Jasper's pickup, which he got running once, with Les's help. But yesterday morning I woke to the sound of a big engine, purring. Motors here don't purr. They belch and chug and knock.

I looked out the window, down to the street. It was a bright blue new Chevrolet Suburban station wagon, four-wheel drive, a bit muddy around the fenders, windshield wipers sweeping off the rain without leaving streaks on the glass. It drove on to the Explorers' trailer camp and parked.

A hired man drove it in from Fairbanks. Later in the day, he chauffeured Perry back and forth to the lodge for his tea. I was there with Terri. The blue Suburban parked out front filled the lodge window. Perry was nervous and excited because Carl Manley was coming with the investors to inspect "the mine." Perry talked non-stop about benefits to the community. It didn't seem to bother him when Terri and I went back into the kitchen to get away. He kept talking to his driver.

Later, another strange vehicle drove in over the bridge, a dark red pickup, battered but roadworthy, with rifles mounted in the back of the cab. It drove around town five or six times without stopping. Two guys with dull, tired eyes finally got out at the lodge and had a couple of beers. They said they were looking for the land they'd bought. They think it is across the street from the lodge. They are going to put in a gas station. When they left, Sara noticed her bike was missing. She'd outgrown it, anyway.

This morning about 10 a.m., a twin-engined plane roared over town and landed. I was out getting water at the brook. Perry and his driver went by in the Suburban on their way to the airstrip. It was Manley and the investors, but they didn't stop in town or talk to us. I saw them drive out to the river to look at the bridge. Then they came back through town and drove away up the creek.

I think the investors flew back to their hotel in Fairbanks in time for dinner.

So now the Explorers can be done for the season. Perry came into the lodge for tea this evening. He says they are pulling out tomorrow.

How about me? Is it time for me to pull out, too? Once snow closes the road, there will be another quiet winter here. Should I stay for it? But to what end? There can be no future here for a hermit. And there's nothing I can do about that, is there?

What about my responsibility to my friends here? Worldly entanglements, that's what I've got. OK, I've got to get free, so I can do what a monk has to do. That means going back to the monastery. I guess.

As Sara would say: Yuk.

September 16, 1982

...I dreamed I was lost on a dark ocean in a storm, tossing in a rowboat without oars. I got seasick and vomited over the side. I think I woke up then, and the hardware store was swaying back and forth, creaking and popping, and I could hear timbers snap. But it didn't fall.

One of the front windows in the lodge is cracked right down the middle today. Terri put duct tape over the crack. Of course, there's no way to replace a window that size. It came in on the railroad sixty-five years ago.

Well, now you could drive a new one in over the bridge, if you had enough money.

Les says the '64 earthquake was worse. There was another big, two story building in town then, sort of like the hardware store. It fell down. Afterward, he and Jasper cut it up for firewood.

September 17, 1982

...A wealthy couple from Hanover, Germany, drove in today in a Winnebago. Tried to. There aren't any guardrails on the Explorers' bridge and the flatcars aren't much wider than a Winnebago. Fortunately, they didn't fall off into the river. Unfortunately, somehow they got it crosswise with the wheels hanging off on both sides. Fortunately, that will block the bridge for awhile. Unfortunately, the Winnebago is rented by the day from an agency in Anchorage....

September 18, 1982

...The European tourists hired Sam to fly them out to Fairbanks. I don't know what will happen to the Winnebago....

September 19, 1982

Scrap the monk business, marry Terri, move to Rochester, and open a bookstore. Or raise goldfish. I've always liked goldfish. They seem so serene and carefree. Goldfish. Rochester really isn't such a bad city. I don't know if I could take the winters, though. Maybe Phoenix. But I don't know anybody in Phoenix. Maybe Terri does....

September 20, 1982

I went to sleep having overeaten my dinner of oatmeal. Why do I cook oatmeal. I don't have the initiative left for anything else. I sat all evening in the hardware store, eating one serving, then another. With peanut butter and raisins. I think it was too much peanut butter that did me in. First I fell asleep in my chair in the kitchen. The fire went out, the room got cold, and

I woke up in the dark. I stumbled up the stairs to bed without brushing my teeth. So they felt fuzzy and uncomfortable.

Once I got to bed, I couldn't sleep. I tossed and turned until I got tangled in my sleeping bag. By then I was asleep but I got so cramped from being tangled up that I woke. Then I needed to pee but I didn't bother to go downstairs and out the door. I peed out the window.

I got back into bed and tried to think about goldfish swimming peace-fully in a deep, still pool. Finally, I felt myself drifting off to sleep. I was a goldfish in a pond full of goldfish and Jesus was feeding us fishfood, a mixture of grain flakes and dried insect parts, which he sprinkled onto the water. I looked up through the water into his kind face, watching its shape wiggle and pulsate as the gently-tossed fishfood made little waves on the water's surface. I felt a little seasick. I worried about sharks.

Then I heard Terri's whistle down on the street outside my window. I thought, I don't want to dream about women. Let me dream about goldfish. I don't need any more troubles.

I heard soft footsteps slowing climbing the rickety hardware store stairs. The building swayed in rhythm. I swam to the very bottom of my pool and hid among the weeds, pulling the sleeping bag over my head.

The door scraped against the floor when Terri came into the room. The upstairs floor had been sagging, so Les put in a post to hold it up. Now it bulges up against the door.

I could feel her standing over my bed. In the bottom of the sleeping bag, I was a fish caught in a net. I squirmed. I felt her looking at me in the dark.

I tried to go to sleep. This is a dream, I thought. I am at the monastery in Rochester, and this whole business is a bad dream. Pretty soon I'm going to make my trip to Alaska and find my hermitage and God and so forth, and everything's going to be great.

I pretended to snore. I lay very still so she wouldn't notice me.

OK, I'm asleep, I said to myself. In the morning, I'll wake up and she won't have come and everything will be normal.

I felt her eyes on my body. Right through the sleeping bag and the Duofold navy-blue long underwear.

I'll wait it out, I thought. I thought maybe I had. Anyway, nothing happened, who knows for how long. I got a cramp in my leg muscles, lying there squished into the bottom of the sleeping bag. It was stuffy in there. I hadn't washed my feet in a couple of days. Maybe longer.

Gradually, I unwound myself. Like a tortoise coming out of its shell. All clear?

Slowly, I advanced my head out the top of the bag. Dark. Cool, fresh air. The creek quietly roaring in the distance. I blinked, and a blur condensed into two parallel lines, faint light slipping past the sides of the window shade, greenish light, maybe auroral light.

I felt eyes behind me. I ducked back into my shell. I knew they focused on me. I could not escape.

This was all a dream anyway, so it didn't matter. I could surrender. So I dreamed I had a white flag on a stick, and I stuck it out and waved it.

A shark came by and ate it. It was a huge great white shark, effortlessly undulating, and it ate it and kept going, vanishing into the murk.

I hid among the weeds at the bottom of my bowl.

I was a sea turtle, a leatherback gliding between corals. I knew the shark was out there, but I thought with my reptilian brain and so was not concerned.

I was a reptile, waiting deep under the surface. I knew I could wait forever.

My leg muscle cramped up again. It must have awakened me, because I smelled my feet again. I couldn't breathe. I had to get out of there. No, I couldn't wait forever. I was not that type of creature.

I felt her eyes and rolled over to face them, tangling myself further in the sleeping bag. I felt a moment of panic. I had to get out of there.

But where could I go? Her eyes blocked the door.

I untangled my arms and legs. The bedsprings squeaked. Slowly, I pushed my head out. Surely, I must be awake now. It was still dark.

She was kneeling by the bed, looking down at me. I made out the silhouette of long, soft hair. I felt the warmth of her breath, catlike, not a shark. I saw her eyes looking at me, reflecting green auroral light.

What to do? I tried the alternatives. Terri, I thought, we'll get married and fix up the lodge and have a bunch more kids and it'll be great....I stared into those eyes and I knew. That would not do.

OK, I give up. I'll go back to the monastery in Rochester. I know my limits. I gave it my best and now it's over....

I stared into those eyes and I knew. That would not do.

I could not escape. She kept looking. I felt love that would not let me go. I had to rise to meet it. I was a trout, rising to a fly. I had no way of knowing if it was a natural fly, or a fisherman's fly with a hook in it. Hungry trout rise to flies. They have to.

So I dreamed of rising with my mouth, my eyes locked on hers, then my mouth on hers. I would move from cold into warmth, touching deep into soft muscles, feel the emergence of flowers, relaxation and sleep.

I stared into those eyes and I knew. That would not do.

So I reached out to embrace her, my strength meeting hers. We would roll over creekbed rocks and mate in foaming brown icewater.

She matched my embrace and we held tight. But her eyes stayed open, locked on mine.

Yes. No. This was closer to the answer. Closer. What lay beyond? I locked my eyes into hers and trusted what I saw. And then I could let go.

Now the earth moved, undulating. The old hardware store picked up the rhythm, tossing and groaning. But again it did not fail. I gave myself up to the motion.

Afterward, in the calm, I pushed down the sleeping bag and stepped into the room, feeling my chest expand against my longjohn tops. I pulled the bottom of the shade and it snapped upward, hitting the roller at the top of the window and spinning around twice before stopping. I felt cold blowing in through the crack in the window. I saw a sky filled with auroral green, red and violet. I was alone.

But I knew I was not alone. I felt Jesus there with me, right there in my own body.

I dressed and clomped down the stairs to the street. The town slept, while dawn blued the East. The aurora faded, and the stars of the Great Bear pointed toward Polaris in the North.

I walked out the Explorers' road to Two-Mile.

I gathered sticks and pulled dry branches from a bulldozed spruce, making a great heap in the center of the road. A boy scout uses one match. I used ten and didn't care. Flames leapt into the sky. I threw on whole logs. Across the creek, the dragon in the bluff twisted and turned in a shower of sparks. I stripped off my clothes and threw them into the blaze. Sweat kept the sparks from igniting the hairs on my chest. I ran to the creek and threw myself in, letting it rage over my head and freeze my buttocks.

I flipped over and lay spreadeagled to the sky in the icewater, letting the current pull me downstream over the rounded rocks. Jagged ridgetops surrounded me. If I relaxed now, the creek would pulp me against the rocks. But I did not let go. I stood up with the current pressing against my knees and waded to shore. As I climbed back onto the road, I tripped and fell into the bulldozed dirt. I wallowed in it, making mud with my body. I opened my mouth and took in a wad of the Explorers' dirt. Jesus was there in the dirt. I ate him. I spit out the stones and swallowed the rest. I ran back to the fire and jumped up and down around it, yelling, while the mud dried in my hair and on my face.

It was daylight now and anybody could come by and see, but I didn't care. I was in my place and I wasn't going to leave. I'm staying.

I ran laughing back to town and into the hardware store, washed up and put on clothes. Now I'm ready to meet the mail plane.

I, Jotham Shechter, will tell the rest of the story myself, although it will not be easy. I am no longer in the habit of using words to the extent that I did before. And there are events I do not enjoy remembering. But to confront the truth I must recall everything.

The Explorers drove away in their blue Suburban on September 16. Terri, intent on completing her fall Fairbanks supply trip before the first snow fell on the road, was closing up the lodge and preparing for winter.

Les decided to go up to his place. Now he could drive almost all the way on the Explorers' road. Sara had never been up the creek—the journey had been too difficult before. Les invited her, Terri said OK, and Les and Sara went up on the 17th. They intended to be there a few days, "probably coming down for mail," Terri wrote in a letter to her sister.

I was going out on the mail plane. I had a meeting scheduled with the park superintendent in Fairbanks, then responsibilities in Berkeley starting the following Monday.

One last trip up the creek. Probably, I would never return to Darwin. My field work for the Park Service was finished, and given the bridge, road and mine, I had no desire to come back. One final trip, to try to remember what had been and to reflect on how to give meaning to what had taken place. I left early in the morning, walking the Explorers' dirt road, climbing the flights of stairs through the mill building at the Syndicate town, emerging from the top of the sloping structure to hike the trail up to the high meadows of Eldorado Butte.

Les and Sara passed me in the old grey jeep just after I had walked through the tunnel at the Dagheeloyee Glacier. I remember that they stopped, and we shared some smoked salmon Les had gotten from Sam. Les offered me a piece to take with me. But I declined, concerned that the smell would bring bears to my camp.

It was late in the season and the previous winter's snow was gone from the alpine meadows. Up there it had recently snowed again a couple of times, I knew, but the new snow had melted, and the high country was dry. Searching, I found water flowing in a ravine eroded into the limestone ridge that rises above the meadows to the summit of Eldorado

Butte. I camped in the bottom of the ravine at the highest level spot, just below the cliffs.

The Dagheeloyees spread out before me: Dagheeloyee Peak white, then pink with evening, far overhead; ridges, becoming blue with distance, extending to the horizon. The further summits looked not so high. I concluded that was an illusion, caused by the curvature of the earth. Below, the forest lay in shadow. Ice was building on the edge of the little creek by the time I brushed my teeth. I lay in my sleeping bag with the tent door open—the bugs were frozen—watching the stars emerge. A procession of white dots appeared over the far edge of the meadow below, wild mountain sheep grazing.

The next two days I did nothing. During the chill of morning and evening, I wandered the meadows, following sheep trails to high overlooks. During the day, I pressed against south-facing rocks, feeling the warmth of the sun. No wind blew. No cloud marred the sky, just the steam plume always rising from the volcano. I heard no airplane. From my campsite, I could see no human sign, except the rusted ore-tram cables running down the mountain from the mines. They blended with the now brown and flowerless meadows. The road below, the bridge over the Loohana River, the blue Suburban station wagon—they were all an impossibility. Berkeley, too. Even Les and Sara down in the valley, and Terri and the others in Darwin. A ground squirrel stole the burner plate off my gasoline camp stove. So I cooked on a fire of willow twigs I gathered from the bushes that survived in the shelter of the ravine.

One day, two days. It could have been a hundred.

For the first time, I did not write in my journal.

But then tomorrow I had to hike back to Darwin, to catch the mail plane the next day.

I woke in the morning, dressed, and stuffed my sleeping bag before I looked out of the tent.

The bear was rooting with its forepaws in the meadow at the entrance to my ravine. It was a grizzly, with shimmering golden fur across the nape of the neck. I could hear it snuffling like a pig as it pushed its snout into a bank laced with squirrel holes. Like a dog intent on a buried bone, it paid no attention to me. I would have to walk around it to get down to the trail.

Bears come up to the high meadows in fall to fatten for winter on roots and tubers, taking squirrels opportunistically.

One eye on the bear, I pulled on my boots and crawled out of the tent. I took down the tent and packed up as quietly as I could, making no sudden movement. Not wanting to release any attractive odor, I put away my food bag without eating.

Shovelsfull of dirt flew as the bear dug in pursuit of a squirrel.

I could wait, hoping it would finish and leave without noticing me. But if it did find me up here, I would be trapped against the cliffs with the bear below. Or I could take advantage of its distraction and sneak around behind it now, down and away. I needed to get back to Darwin to make the mail plane tomorrow.

Quietly, slowly, I edged down along the side of the ravine, keeping as far as possible from the bear. Perhaps it would not scent me in the still air. The gurgle of the stream at the bottom of the ravine might cover up any sound. The bear was still preoccupied with its squirrel. It paused a moment and sniffed the ground, deciding what direction to dig.

> Dirty dishes lay piled on the counter in George Johnston's cabin in Darwin. They were still dirty when the police subsequently found them. The tattered green window shades were drawn down. He sat at the table, practicing the motions for firing the mail-order submachine gun.

> > "At 11:00 a.m. on September 21, 1982, I will kill everyone in Darwin, Alaska. I will emplace myself behind the berm at the airstrip and shoot them as they come to get their mail. I will then hijack the mail plane to Dietrich Camp. There I will blow up the trans-Alaska oil pipeline.

*Then I will return to Darwin and I will shoot myself. My
father will never know that I am the one that did it.*

*"The dirty, foul oil pouring out over the beautiful, pure,
clean tundra. White swans besmurched by black filthy
oil. I will save them.*

*"They in Darwin deserve it. They live in a National
Park, my God. They cut the trees. They shoot and eat the
animals. They must be stopped."*

*The sun broke out over Malachite Ridge as I was almost even with the
bear. Just then the bear turned and stared into my face. Almost blinded
by the sunlight, at first I could hardly see it. The bear rose on hind legs
and peered, sniffing. I froze.*

*The bear dropped to all fours and turned its head toward the squirrel
holes. I took a step down hill, which had to be toward the bear.*

Immediately, the bear swayed around to face me.

*I knew I should not look into the bear's eyes. Direct eye contact is
instinctively an act of aggression. But I could not help it. For a split
second I looked into them. The eyes were black and empty. I felt dizzy,
as if I were going to fall in.*

*I stepped backward, up against the rock. regaining my balance. The
bear's lowered head pendulumed slowly. It advanced with its forefeet,
hind legs remaining in place. It made more of a bark than a growl. I retreated uphill, my back to the cliff, as fast as I could without panicking.*

*I made it back up to my campsite. By then, the bear was inspecting
its diggings, chewing on a tuber. All I could do was wait.*

*The bear was digging again, piling rocks on the sides of its deepening
hole. With both paws it lifted a boulder onto the pile and meticulously
adjusted it to balance. I took a step forward. It aimed its snout my way
and leaned in my direction. I retreated and sat against the cliff, trying to
keep warm in the sun.*

Suddenly dirt flew. The bear stripped off sod—no flowers would bloom there next year. It hurled slabs of rock into the ravine. Then it lunged, jarring the earth with its weight. A squirrel dashed out. The bear pounced like a fat cat. It missed. It tried again. After the third pounce, the bear sat in the bottom of the ravine, chewing the squirrel, whose tail hung out the side of its mouth.

I was able to get a drink from the creek, but dared not open my food bag to eat.

All day I waited. The bear slept next to its diggings. I tried once to sneak by. But as I approached, it woke, sniffed in my direction, made motions to rise, and I went back. I tried to climb out of the ravine, but the cliffs were steep and the rocks unstable, and I could find no way.

Bears are protective of their food source. It was reasonable that it would guard its territory.

I was hungry. Finally, I opened my bag and ate dry granola.

I was up for tenure that year. The dean and the department chairman, already skeptical of my Alaska research, would not accept this excuse for missing the committee meeting in Berkeley on Monday.

The sun set behind the edge of the ravine. I put on my parka. I thought about setting up the tent, but when I made too much motion, the bear peered my way and I dared not. Water splashing onto the rocks along the creek began to freeze. Slowly, I took out my sleeping bag and pulled it up over my feet. The stars emerged, one by one, as the valley disappeared in a pool of black. No sheep came over the ridge. Perhaps they sensed the presence of the bear. I watched the arc of the new moon move to the horizon and set. I thought I heard the bear pawing again at the hillside below.

Eventually I fell asleep. I heard heavy breathing beside me, then felt a crushing weight on my chest. I dared not move. There was a foul damp smell and a massive shadow. Then the ground itself heaved from below, and I heard the sound of boulders rolling down the sides of the ravine. As the earth swayed, the weight lifted off my sleeping bag and vanished into the night. When finally all was still, I lay motionless, terrified, staring upward into a green and violet auroral sky.

At dawn, the bear was grazing on the hillside just below me. It was gradually working its way in my direction, scraping up Hedysarum roots, turning over chunks of sod and pawing them apart. My teeth chattered with cold. I had a headache from hunger and lack of sleep.

George Johnston set his alarm for 6 a.m. He ate two fried eggs with crackers, because he did not know how to bake bread. We know these details from his interview with the state psychiatrist. His backpack was filled with the dynamite, wire, blasting caps, bandoleers of ammunition, and other paraphernalia. He slung the submachine gun over his shoulder, hiding it under his coat in case anyone should see him prematurely.

He walked the mile of road to the the airstrip, through the bare woods in heatless autumn sunlight. He passed Sam's parked plane and walked along the gravel runway to the mail shack, alone, the scraping of his shoes raising dust.

He emplaced himself behind a gravel berm at the edge of the woods near the shack, where he had a clear field of fire and could see, but not be seen.

Gradually, the bear worked its way up the ravine. Why did it graze here, on isolated sod patches among the rocks, instead of on the meadow below? It made no sense.

I had to get away from it. The only way I could go was up, but yesterday I had come to a dead end against the cliffs. Perhaps I could climb the rocks where the bear would not follow and wait for it to leave. I *couldn't take my awkward packframe. So I put a few things in my day-pack, left the rest, and crawled away, trying not to attract the bear.*

Poking its nose into holes and overturning rocks here and there, the bear moseyed up the ravine, while I searched the cliffs for some escape, anyplace to hide. I shivered in the shade of the rocks, watching its golden fur glisten in the sunlight at the campsite below, where it discovered my backpack. It tossed the pack playfully in the air and shredded it with a swipe of its right paw. While it scattered my tent poles and spare socks, I desperately explored the cliff.

The earthquake the night before had released a rockfall: What had been a sheer face yesterday was now a sort of staircase with rubble at the bottom. The steps were steep and far apart, and probably not stable. Maybe I could get up, stretching and clinging; almost certainly I could not get down again. But maybe they led to a way out of the ravine or over the top of the ridge. I had no choice.

> *Les and Sara finished a sourdough pancake breakfast, washed the dishes, and closed up the house in preparation for driving down the creek to Darwin for the arrival of the mail. The jeep would not start. It was not the plugs. It was not the coil or the alternator. Something was wrong with the carburetor. They opened up the house again, disarming the solar-electric cattle fence Les had installed to keep away the bears and taking off the chicken-wire window covers. Soon pieces of the carburetor covered the dining table, while Les explained to Sara how it was supposed to work.*

The bear was exploring the rubble pile below, when I found the ledge. The ledge wound along the cliff face, just wide enough. I had to be careful not to slip on mountain goat scat. From the ledge the bear was out of sight, but I could hear it rolling rocks down into the gully.

For a long time I followed the upward slope, back into the recesses of the crenelated limestone mountaintop. At one place the ledge had been swept away by an avalanche. I thought I was blocked, and my knees shook at the prospect of returning down the narrow path. But I managed to scramble across the loose rock and pick up the ledge again.

The ledge ended abruptly. Unstable, impassible, vertical black-stained yellow limestone extended endlessly, hopelessly, in every direction. Was I imagining I heard the bear following me? It could not be the wind. There was no wind.

But when I stopped, I was cold. It seemed like the sun never reached back in here. Crevices in the rock were already slick with winter ice. I saw the autumn sunlight warming the valley forest below and longed for the secure comfort of Darwin so far away.

I could not go on. I could not stay. I had to turn back.

I had not gone back a hundred meters when I saw a niche in the rock wall that I had not noticed on my way up. It looked like a flat place behind a bulge in the face, where I could sit down and eat and rest and figure out what to do. I had to climb to get there and I almost slipped. My hands were wet with tension. I stumbled forward onto the flat surface, rolled over and lay on my back, finally able to let myself be paralyzed with exhaustion and fear.

> *Mike walked out of the hardware store and on up the street in the morning sunshine toward the airstrip. Terri was in front of the lodge, starting the Model A. She was driving to pick up groceries she expected in the mail. So Mike hopped in and they went to meet the mail plane together.*

I lay panting, my eyes stinging with sweat, expecting to feel the penetrating chill of the rock against my back. Gradually, I realized I did not. Instead, a warm breeze blew over my face. As I relaxed, I sat up. The air came from the direction of the cliff. I turned around to see a hole, a tunnel or cave entrance, at the rear of my little platform. Stale air came out of it.

I went and looked in. I could almost stand up in it without stooping. It was a round hole, perhaps an air shaft connecting to the mine tunnels. Maybe I could go in and find my way to one of the mine entrances, and to safety.

I would go in until I used up the batteries in my flashlight, knowing that I could find my way back using the spare set I had with me in the daypack.

At first it looked promising. The tunnel sloped downward, with ribbed walls just wider than my outstretched hands. If it were in fact man-made, possibly it would be my salvation. The light at the entrance became a small circle behind and above. The tunnel angled right, and the light disappeared.

Then I found something even more encouraging. My flashlight played on something black ahead: charcoal, the remains of a fire. Someone had been here before me. Then I wondered, why would the miners build a fire in here? I had seen no timbering, no other signs of their activity. I had figured this was just an airshaft.

I bent over the ashes, poked into them with my fingers, idling a moment. The warm, stale wind still blew over my back, out of the depths. I had begun to sweat under the arms.

The flashlight found a white rock next to the fire. I picked it up. It fit exactly in the palm of my hand, a stone tool, carefully chipped on one edge. The Koyukon Indians must have been here. This was their fire. So this is not a mining tunnel. Now my palms sweated, too. Later, when I knew more about stone tools, I realized that what I had found could not be Koyukon. It was older than that.

Not much beyond, the tunnel pinched off. It looked like a dead end. The warm air hissed up out of a hole between the rocks on the floor. I stood despondent. It was too far, too hard, too dangerous to go back—the tunnel, the ledge, the ravine—and what about the bear? I turned off the flashlight to save the batteries, found a slab to sit on, and thought.

The sound of the rushing air was not a hiss, but more a distant, echoing roar, speaking of other, inaccessible passageways. It frightened me. I thought I heard the bear. Of course it had not followed me into the tunnel, had it? I thought I felt the mountain shaking, like reverberating footsteps. It could not be.

I had to escape. I turned on the flashlight, shined it around on the rocks, turned it off again.

I realize now it was not just fear of the bear. The vent into the earth pulled my attention like some long-neglected memory, not quite forgotten. I shined my light into it: It was round and ribbed, bigger than I thought, descending and curving out of sight. Maybe I should go on. Until this set of batteries wore out. I knew I could get back on the spare set. The bear could not get its shoulders through the hole. I would be safe

The bear was an excuse. I wanted to go down the hole. The bear was coming for me. I heard the pounding of its clawed paws. I had to find sanctuary.

> *Lying behind the berm, George Johnston observed Terri and Mike sitting together in the cab of the Model A flatbed, which ground slowly along the airstrip toward the mail shack. When they were within range, he fired the submachine gun. The first burst wounded them both. Terri, driving, jammed the accelerator to the floor to get away. The truck roared across the airstrip and, out of control, crashed into an aspen at the edge of the woods.*

George Johnston fired a second burst, which missed. They were too far away. Mike reached over and unlatched the door. "Run," he said and shoved Terri out the door. She scrambled into the brush as another burst of gunfire sprayed across the airstrip.

George Johnston walked toward them. First he looked toward Terri. Mike yelled, "Here, over here. Here I am," waving his arms out the window of the truck. George Johnston's attention was diverted. He went over to the truck and killed Mike. The delay allowed Terri to crawl off into the woods and curl down into a depression behind a clump of alders.

George Johnston walked into the woods to find Terri. She listened to his footsteps in the dry leaves, stalking her.

I stared into the blackness of the hole. The air pouring out felt hotter, or was it only my tension as salt water stung my eyes, tears or sweat. I felt the pounding, the bear, or the cave shaking, or just my heart.

No, I could not go on. I had to go back. I lacked the courage. Rationally, I knew the bear could not be there. I stood to go back. Irrationally afraid of something behind me in the dark, I turned and played the flashlight one last time around the end of the tunnel.

The woman lay reclining above the hole, legs outspread, with pendulous breasts and fecund hips. The bas-relief sculpture was almost effaced by weathering, but once I noticed her, I could not take my eyes off her. I leaned back against the far side of the tunnel. She invited me to enter. This was not Koyukon art. Could it be a miner's work? It must be. It couldn't be. Slowly, I advanced.

I found I could almost crawl down the passageway. But immediately, I had to back up to be able to take off my jacket, which was too warm now anyway and took up too much space in the passage. I strapped it to my pack, and started again, pushing the pack in front of me.

The passage turned and twisted, but the direction was always down. I felt a quiver. It was not me; it was the earth moving. I gripped the sides and fought back a panic scream. All was still again. I moved on, faster.

George Johnston clumped around looking for her here and there. He did not know how to see things in the forest. Then he cursed, realizing others might be coming. He had to be in position. She waited while he crossed back to the mail shack and emplaced himself behind the berm. Feverish and weak, she walked through the woods along the length of the airstrip, almost a mile, and down into town without coming into his sight.

At the lodge, she found Kitty and Ed. They could not bring themselves to believe her story, but in fact she was shot in the head, losing blood. Ed went immediately to get Sam, to fly her to the hospital. Sam drove over in his truck. When he saw her, he did not think she would live. They drove up to the airstrip. Ed brought his 30-.06 rifle.

While Sam stood on his stepladder, pouring gasoline from five-gallon cans into the plane's wing tanks, Ed,

rifle ready, walked up along the edge of the strip toward
the mail shack to investigate. Met by a burst of gunfire,
he fired back and retreated.

He told Kitty and Sam it was true, it was really true.

The passageway opened into a room. I stood up, legs quivering. I could hear the hush of moving air, definitely warmer now. I shined the flashlight around the walls. The beam was still bright. The room was about fifteen meters in diameter, roughly circular, and the ceiling higher than I could reach.

In the center, facing me on a pedestal of stone slabs, was the skull of a bear. I froze my beam on it. The eye sockets stared back at me. I turned off the flashlight and screamed.

Ed stood guard, watching down the airstrip, while Sam
and Kitty loaded Terri into the airplane. Sam started the
engine. There was still room in the plane. Ed told Kitty
to get in. He would stay and warn the others, Les, Sara
and Jot, who would be coming to meet the mail plane.
Kitty refused to leave him. They would do it together.
They stood back as Sam revved the engine.

They had forgotten about the back trail, a path used
sometimes for getting firewood, that went through the
woods, parallel to the airstrip.

They did not know that George Johnston had left his
emplacement and was circling around on the trail to get
the plane before it took off. He was too late for that. Sam
had safely cleared the trees at the far end of the strip
when George Johnston emerged from the woods behind

Kitty and Ed. They were watching the plane disappear down the valley, keeping an eye on the mail shack. He killed them both.

I turned on the light again and advanced toward the bear. The skull was huge, with massive lower jaws and canine teeth. I concluded later that it probably was a gigantic extinct Pleistocene Arctodus. °

I searched toward the source of the wind. It moaned out of a shaft descending at the rear of the room, behind the bear. At first I thought it was too steep, and I had had enough. But then I saw steps chipped into the rock. I followed them down, perhaps ten meters or more. They led to another passageway. The entrance was framed by an arch of two tusks, some sort of elephant tusks, mastodon or mammoth. Now I was simply going on. It involved no decision.

This passageway was narrower than the first, the wind warmer. My shoulders hardly fit; my belt buckle caught. I backed up and removed my clothes, tying them to the pack. I pushed both my pack and my boots ahead of me as I inched along.

The limestone had been smoothed by the flow of water, a former subterranean channel. And by the passage of many bodies?

The passageway was endless. I lay exhausted, turned off the light to save the batteries, fell asleep. My watch, banged repeatedly against rock, no longer worked. I crawled and rested and went on.

° *This bear would have been contemporaneous with the archaic* Homo sapiens *of Mousterian culture, who worshiped the similarly gigantic cave bear in Eurasia c. 100,000–40,000 B.C. Either the later paleolithic peoples left the skull untouched or—more likely—reused the skull, left by the cave's previous human inhabitants, for their own purposes.*   —JBS

No one could have ever come here before me. This was a dead end, a death trap. I panicked in a claustrophobic seizure. It would take forever to back out. I screamed again. This time my scream echoed back at me, screams compounded on screams. I screamed again and again, until the echoing returns merged into a single hum, and I lay outstretched, eyes closed, beyond panic. The hum reverberated, picking up a beat which matched the pumping of my heart.

I do not know why it took me so long to realize that a narrow passageway could not make this sound. I had come almost to its end. The hum was the resonance of a giant stone chamber.

I entered between the jagged teeth of stalactites and stalagmites. My flashlight beam could not find the distant cavern walls. My boots, hanging tied from my pack, accidently swung against a limestone pillar. It resounded like a gong. I took five slow, deep breaths, while the chamber vibrated in sympathy. Then there was silence and, when I turned off the light, a velvet darkness. But I heard a drip of water, the splash of each drop distinct and alone. The warm, stale wind, still coming from someplace ahead, blew lightly over my sweaty body.

I turned on the light again and wandered out across the stone floor. I played the light around me, on curtains and icicles of limestone which rimmed the chamber, and then on the domed ceiling above.

It was a vast procession: animals and people—an elk with ornate antlers; woolly mammoths with curved tusks; men with erect phalluses, some carrying spears; moose; round women with big breasts and full wombs; caribou and bison—covering the ceiling, in ocher and black, running and prancing. I remembered ancient cave paintings from my childhood reading. But not like this: they looked down at me life-sized, alive. I turned off the light and they vanished. There was only the distant drip of water, and the warm, stale wind. I stood still, listening, ready to cringe, expecting to hear that someone was in there with me, a heavy browed ancient ready to crack my skull with a thighbone. I darted the beam of the flashlight around me, expecting to see human skeletons on the floor.

But no, I was alone. Whoever made these incredible paintings was gone, leaving no other trace, and I was utterly alone. I looked up again at the figures, and they looked down at me. I half wanted to be terrorized by footsteps in the darkness, the presence of others, not to confront this place alone. I listened for them, but they were not there.

There was only the sound of my own footsteps as I walked forward.

Now, finally, the flashlight beam paled, and I realized I had to change batteries and make my way back to the surface. I felt let down. I did not want to go back. I got out the spare batteries. I sat down to do the job, taking apart the flashlight in the dark.

But the spring that holds in the batteries popped out onto the floor. I lit a match to find it. I thought I saw it before the match went out, but I was not sure. Again I felt my hands wet with tension. I sat a moment to calm myself. I had only a small box of matches with me. I could not afford to make any more mistakes.

Then I realized I could see. The blackness was no longer complete. I made out the forms of stalactites and stalagmites. I turned around. Faint light was coming from behind a limestone curtain against the chamber wall. I watched, who knows how long, as the light gradually increased. I stood and looked upward as the panoramic ceiling glowed, illuminated by this source. Was I dizzy from standing with my head thrown back? The procession seemed to rotate; the chamber itself seemed to be unsteady, my footing insecure.

I turned again in the direction of the light. Fully illuminated, deeply engraved into the wall, painted with the richest oranges and yellows and browns, a lifesize dancing bear looked out over the procession and over me. My eyes locking on his, I advanced toward the light.

He danced over a broad tunnel entrance, from which came light and the warm, steady wind. I stared up at him and then out to the multitudes on the ceiling.

I felt the chamber sway and shake, or was it only my exhausted legs, or something in the air that drugged me. The chamber was spinning, and I gripped a limestone column and clung. The painted figures blended, slithering and sliding over one another. They assembled into a coiling tangle, a giant dragon with the bear as its head. Then I steadied myself, and they were the animals, the people, and the bear again. The brightness increased, faster now, and the paintings faded in intense light.

I felt myself bathed in warm light and air, tingling my skin and easing my aching muscles. I walked as if floating, toward the tunnel. The fear, which possessed me since I first discovered the grizzly in the ravine, melted away.

I turned and, for the first time, looked directly at the source of the light.

Les and Sara heard the explosion as they were driving down Dagheeloyee Creek. As they watched, steam and ash rumbled from the summit of the volcano, sooting the white cone, darkening the sky to the stratosphere. Lightning, flashing through brown rain, highlighted swaying trees as Les drove the jeep as fast as he could toward Darwin. He was thinking about Iceberg Lake.

Heat rising from the interior was partially melting the Dagheeloyee and Loohana Glaciers from below. The volume of water descending under Dagheeloyee Glacier floated it off its bed, releasing the ice-dammed lake and sending a surge of water down the creek. It was like pulling the plug on a giant bathtub.

The wall of water tore out the Explorers' road. Reaching Darwin, it undercut the Explorers' trailers, tossing them with the current into the Loohana River. There they hit the bridge of flatcars, already loosened by floodwaters, demolished it, and sent the pieces downstream, to be buried in rolling gravel and boulders.

My next memory is of violent shaking and roaring.

I looked, and then, I presume, there was the eruption. But I think something happened inbetween. My memory of it is blank. Did I forget something? Instead of memories, what is there is a stillness, an empty space filled with no memories. I cannot help, even now, dwelling on that still, empty space.

And then I remember crawling in darkness through a long and narrow passageway, which finally widened so I could stand.

Finally, I saw daylight and emerged from a cave entrance into the Loohana Glacier fosse, a few miles from Darwin.

It was late night, and cold, by the time I staggered into town, naked, feet bruised. I saw but one light, at Les's; the rest of the town was entirely dark. He took me in, cared for me tenderly, and explained what had happened. He and Sara had driven into town just before the flood; they found the police helicopter parked in the street in front of the lodge.

Les told me: Sam had warned off the mail plane by radio and notified the authorities in Bettles. George Johnston waited at the mail shack for some hours. The mail plane never landed; when no one else came, he walked down to the river, crossed the tram, and started down the road in his truck. Then the helicopter arrived. He surrendered without resisting arrest. Terri was in the hospital in Fairbanks; we had no word yet on her condition. Sara had gone out to her with the troopers.

I myself could say nothing. Eventually, of course, Les heard it all, all I could remember.

By morning the volcano settled down, and the eruption and earthquakes ceased. The thin layer of ash covering Darwin washed away in the next rains.

I rested at Les's, regaining strength and healing my feet. The first snow had fallen and melted when we went up the creek to his place together. As freeze-up came and the nights lengthened, Les helped me repair the old log house across Dagheeloyee Creek, using materials abandoned by the Explorers. And I stayed at that house many years.

Terri recovered slowly, incompletely. Her vision was affected. Her sister let us know, and Sara did, too, before Terri herself could write. They came back, even to run the lodge a few summers, but she and Sara spent most of the year Outside, with her sister. I would go to the lodge when Terri was there, and she would be working hard in a practical, straightforward way. Sometimes we would sit together, not talking. I watched Sara grow into a woman and find her place in the world. I do not see her often now, but our bond is deep.

The Explorers never reappeared.

George Johnston was sentenced to life imprisonment without parole. As far as I know, he is still living in the Anchorage penitentiary.

Les and I shared winters up the creek. Then he moved to Los Angeles and enjoyed the friendship of artists and musicians there. And I lived on up the creek by myself. Les, by then advanced in age, eventually returned. One winter day he ventured out down the creek alone, and I never found trace of him again.

Still I stayed on, until the time came for being elsewhere, and I moved to San Francisco, taught in a community college, lived here at the Zen Center.

And so the story is over. Finally, I have told it whole, all at once, as best I can, as it needs to be told.

And it is finished.

And now what shall I do? Shall I go back again to that place, so powerful in memory, so charged with experience? Shall I return now, before I am too feeble to haul firewood logs, fix machinery, and meet the necessities of life in those mountains?

I go to the office towers of downtown San Francisco. I enter the vast commercial complex of the Embarcadero Center. I cross the lobby and walk into the elevator and press the button, down. All others exit at their proper floors and I am left alone. The elevator descends to the basement and to the subbasement, where the machinery that operates the complex is located.

At the lowest level, the door slides open and I get out. I enter a passageway between giant machinery, gears and belts. The machinery is old, rusted, and still. As I walk, I notice that it is dusted with snow.

At the end of the corridor I come to a door. I open the door and walk out onto the snow. I see the trail in the moonlight. It leads down alongside the mill building and through the streets of the Syndicate town, and up along the frozen creek to a squat log cabin, hung with icicles, perched on a bluff overlooking the valley. There is a lamp in the window of Les's cabin. He opens the door for me and I walk in. Terri and Mike are sitting around the big black stove. Les pours me a cup of bitterly strong coffee, and they welcome me.